THE EXPLOSION WAS ENORMOUS.

Alex had never felt anything like it. The very air had been turned into a giant fist, a boxing glove that pounded into him—hot and violent—and for a moment he thought he must have broken a dozen bones. He couldn't hear. He couldn't see. The inside of his head was boiling. Perhaps he was unconscious for a few seconds, but the next thing he knew, he was lying on the ground with his face pressed into a clump of wild grass and sand in his hair and eyes. His shirt was torn and there was a throbbing in his ears, but otherwise he seemed to be unhurt. How close had the missile fallen? Where had it come from? Even as Alex asked himself these two questions, a third, more unpleasant one entered his mind. Were there going to be any more?

There was no time to work out what was going on. Alex spat out sand and dragged himself to his knees. At the same time, something burst out in the sky: a white flame that hung there, suspended high above the trees. Alex had tensed himself, expecting another blast, but he quickly recognized it for what it was: a battle flare light, a lump of burning phosphorus, designed to illuminate the area for miles around. He was still kneeling. Almost too late, he realized that he had turned himself into a target, a black cutout against the brilliant, artificial glare. . . .

D0052898

BOOKS BY ANTHONY HOROWITZ

The Complete Horowitz Horror
The Devil and His Boy
Granny

THE ALEX RIDER ADVENTURES
Stormbreaker
Point Blank
Skeleton Key
Eagle Strike
Scorpia
Ark Angel
Snakehead

THE DIAMOND BROTHERS MYSTERIES
Public Enemy Number Two
The Falcon's Malteser
Three of Diamonds
South by Southeast
The Greek Who Stole Christmas

SNAKEHEAD

AN ALEX RIDER ADVENTURE

ANTHONY HOROWITZ

speak

An Imprint of Penguin Group (USA) Inc.

SPEAK

Published by the Penguin Group

Penguin Group (USA) Inc., 345 Hudson Street, New York, New York 10014, U.S.A.
Penguin Group (Canada), 90 Eglinton Avenue East, Suite 700, Toronto, Ontario, Canada M4P 2Y3
(a division of Pearson Penguin Canada Inc.)
Penguin Books Ltd, 80 Strand, London WC2R 0RL, England
Penguin Ireland, 25 St Stephen's Green, Dublin 2, Ireland (a division of Penguin Books Ltd)
Penguin Group (Australia), 250 Camberwell Road, Camberwell, Victoria 3124, Australia
(a division of Pearson Australia Group Pty Ltd)
Penguin Books India Pvt Ltd, 11 Community Centre, Panchsheel Park, New Delhi - 110 017, India
Penguin Group (NZ), 67 Apollo Drive, Rosedale, North Shore 0632, New Zealand
(a division of Pearson New Zealand Ltd)
Penguin Books (South Africa) (Pty) Ltd, 24 Sturdee Avenue,
Rosebank, Johannesburg 2196, South Africa

Registered Offices: Penguin Books Ltd, 80 Strand, London WC2R 0RL, England

Published in Great Britain by Walker Books Ltd, London

First published in the United States of America by Philomel Books,
a division of Penguin Young Readers Group, 2007
Published by Speak, an imprint of Penguin Group (USA) Inc., 2008

3 5 7 9 10 8 6 4 2

Copyright © Anthony Horowitz, 2007

All rights reserved

THE LIBRARY OF CONGRESS HAS CATALOGED THE PHILOMEL EDITION AS FOLLOWS:
Horowitz, Anthony. Date.
Snakehead / Anthony Horowitz—1st American ed.   p.   cm.
Summary: While working with the Australian Secret Service on a dangerous mission,
teenaged spy Alex Rider uncovers information about his parents.
[1. Spies—Fiction. 2. Orphans—Fiction. 3. Adventure and adventurers—Fiction.] I. Title.
PZ7.H7875Sn2007   [Fic]—dc22   2007020505

Speak ISBN 978-0-14-241212-1
Printed in the United States of America

Except in the United States of America, this book is sold subject to the condition that
it shall not, by way of trade or otherwise, be lent, re-sold, hired out, or otherwise
circulated without the publisher's prior consent in any form of binding or cover
other than that in which it is published and without a similar condition
including this condition being imposed on the subsequent purchaser.

The publisher does not have any control over and does not assume
any responsibility for author or third-party Web sites or their content.

To B&CD.

CONTENTS

SNAKEHEAD

1

DOWN TO EARTH

SPLASHDOWN.

Alex Rider would never forget the moment of impact, the first shock as the parachute opened and the second—more jolting still—as the module that had carried him back from outer space crashed into the sea. Was it his imagination, or was there steam rising up all around him? Maybe it was sea spray. It didn't matter. He was back. That was all he cared about. He had made it. He was still alive.

He was still lying on his back, crammed into the tiny space with his knees tucked into his chest. Half closing his eyes, Alex experienced a moment of extraordinary stillness. He was completely still. His fists were clenched. He wasn't breathing. Was it really true? Already he found it impossible to believe that the events that had led to his journey into outer space had really taken place. He tried to imagine himself hurtling around the earth at seventeen and a half thousand miles an hour. It couldn't have happened. It had surely all been part of some incredible dream.

Slowly he forced himself to unwind. He lifted an arm. It rose normally. He could feel the muscle connecting. Just minutes before he had been in zero gravity. But as he rested, trying to collect his thoughts, he realized that once again his body belonged to him.

Alex wasn't sure how long he was left on his own, floating on the water somewhere . . . it could have been anywhere in the world. But when things happened, they did so very quickly. First there was the hammering of helicopter blades. Then the whoop of some sort of siren. He could see very little out the window—just the rise and fall of the ocean—but suddenly a man was there, a scuba diver, a palm slamming against the glass. A few seconds later, the capsule was opened from outside. Fresh air came rushing in, and to Alex it smelled delicious. At the same time, a man loomed over him, his body wrapped in neoprene, his eyes behind a mask.

"Are you okay?"

Alex could hardly make out the words, there was so much noise outside. Did the diver have an American accent? "I'm fine," he managed to shout back. But it wasn't true. He was beginning to feel sick. There was a shooting pain behind his eyes.

"Don't worry! We'll soon have you out of there . . ."

It took them a while. Alex had only been in space a short time, but he'd never had any physical training for it, and now his muscles were turning against him, reluctant to start pulling their own weight. He had to be manhandled out of the capsule, into the blinding sun of a Pacific afternoon. Everything was chaotic. There was a helicopter overhead, the blades beating at the ocean, forming patterns that rippled and vibrated. Alex turned his head and saw—impossibly—an aircraft carrier, as big as a mountain, looming out of the water less than a quarter of a mile away. It was flying the Stars and Stripes. So he had been right about the diver. He must have landed somewhere off the coast of America.

There were two more divers in the water, bobbing up and down next to the capsule, and Alex could see a third man leaning out of the helicopter directly above him. He knew what was going to happen, and he didn't resist. First a loop of cable was passed around his chest and connected. He felt it tighten under his arms. And then he was rising into the air, still in his space suit, dangling like a silver puppet as he was winched up.

And already they knew. He had glimpsed it in the eyes of the diver who had spoken to him. The disbelief. These men—the helicopter, the aircraft carrier—had been rushed out to rendezvous with a module that had just reentered the earth's atmosphere. And inside, they had found a boy. A fourteen-year-old had just plummeted a hundred miles from outer space. These men would be sworn to secrecy, of course. MI6 would see to that. They would never talk about what had happened. Nor would they forget it.

There was a medical officer waiting for him on board the USS *Kitty Hawk*—which was the name of the ship that had been diverted to pick him up. His name was Josh Cook, and he was forty years old, black with wire-frame glasses and a pleasant, soft-spoken manner. He helped Alex out of the space suit and stayed in the room when Alex finally did throw up. It turned out that he'd dealt with astronauts before.

"They're all sick when they come down," he explained. "It goes with the territory. Or maybe I should say terra firma. That's Latin for 'down to earth.' You'll be fine by the morning."

"Where am I?" Alex asked.

"You're about ninety miles off the coast of Australia. We were on a training exercise when we got a red alert that you were on your way down."

"So what happens now?"

"Now you have a shower and get some sleep. You're in luck. We've got a mattress made out of memory foam. It was actually developed by NASA. It'll give your muscles a chance to get used to being back in full gravity."

Alex had been given a private cabin in the medical department of the *Kitty Hawk*—in fact, a fully equipped "hospital at sea" with sixty-five beds, an operating room, a pharmacy, and everything else that 5,500 sailors might need. It wasn't huge, but he suspected that nobody else on the *Kitty Hawk* would have this much space. Cook went over to the corner and pulled back a plastic curtain to reveal a shower cubicle.

"You may find it difficult to walk," he explained. "You're going to be unsteady on your feet for at least twenty-four hours. If you like, I can wait in the room until you've showered."

"I'll be okay," Alex said.

"All right." Cook smiled and opened the main door. But before he left, he looked back at Alex. "You know— every man and woman on this ship is talking about you," he said. "There are a whole pile of questions I'd like to ask you, but I'm under strict orders from the captain to keep my mouth shut. Even so, I want you to know that I've been at sea for a long, long time and I've never encountered anything like this. A kid in outer space!" He nodded one last time. "I hope you have a good rest. There's a call button beside the bed if there's anything you need."

Cook left.

It took Alex ten minutes to get into the shower. He had completely lost his sense of balance, and the roll of the ship didn't help. He turned the temperature up as high as he could bear and stood under the steaming water, enjoying the rush of it over his shoulders and through his hair. Then he dried himself and got into bed. The memory foam was only a couple of inches thick, but it seemed to mold itself to the shape of his body exactly. He fell almost instantly into a deep but troubled sleep.

He didn't dream about the Ark Angel space station or his knife fight with Kaspar, the bald ecoterrorist who had been determined to kill him even though it was clear that all was lost. Nor did he dream about Nikolei Drevin, the billionaire who had been behind it all.

But it did seem to him that, sometime in the middle of the night, he heard the whisper of voices that he didn't recognize but that, somehow, he still knew. Old friends. Or old enemies. It didn't matter which because he couldn't make out what they were saying, and anyway, a moment later they were swept away down the dark river of his sleep.

Perhaps it was a premonition.

Because three weeks before, seven men had met in a room in London to discuss an operation that would make them many millions of dollars and would change the shape of the world. And although Alex had never met any of them, he certainly knew them.

Scorpia was back again.

2

"DEATH IS NOT THE END"

IT WAS THE SORT of building you could walk past without noticing: three stories high, painted white with ivy, perfectly trimmed, climbing up to the roof. It stood about halfway down Sloane Street in Belgravia, just around the corner from Harrods, surrounded by some of the most expensive real estate in London. On one side there was a jewelry shop and on the other an Italian fashion boutique—but the customers who came here would no longer be needing either. A single step led up to a door painted black, and there was a window that contained an urn, a vase of fresh flowers, and nothing else. The name of the place was written in discreet gold letters. It read: Reed and Kelly, Funeral Directors. And beneath that, a brief motto: Death is not the End.

At ten thirty on a bright October morning, exactly three weeks before Alex landed in the Pacific Ocean, a black Lexus LS 430 four-door sedan drew up outside the front door. The car had been chosen carefully. It was a luxury model, but there was nothing too special about it, nothing to attract the eye. The arrival had also been exactly timed. In the past fifteen minutes, three other vehicles and a taxi had briefly pulled up and their passengers, either singly or in pairs, had exited, crossed the pavement, and entered the parlor. If anyone had been watching, they would have assumed that a large family had gathered to make the final arrangements for someone who had recently departed.

The last person to arrive was a powerfully built man with massive shoulders and a shaved head. There was something quite brutal about his face: the small, squashed-up nose, thick lips, and muddy brown eyes. But his clothes were immaculate. He wore a tailored silk shirt, a dark suit, and a cashmere coat, hanging loose. There was a large platinum ring on his fourth finger. He had been smoking a cigar, but as he stepped from the car, he dropped it and ground it out with a brilliantly polished shoe. Without looking left or right, he crossed the pavement and entered the building. An old-fashioned bell on a spring jangled as the door opened and closed.

He found himself in a wood-paneled reception room where an elderly, gray-haired man, also wearing a suit, sat with his hands folded behind a narrow desk. He looked at the new arrival with a mixture of sympathy and politeness.

"Good morning," he said. "How can we be of service?"

"I have come about a death," the visitor replied.

"Someone close to you?"

"My brother. But I hadn't seen him for some years."

"You have my condolences."

The same words had been spoken seven times that

morning. If even one syllable had been changed, the bald man would have turned around and left. But he knew now that the building was secure. He hadn't been followed. The meeting that had been arranged just twenty-four hours earlier could go ahead.

The older man leaned forward and pressed a button concealed underneath the desk. At once, a section of the wooden paneling clicked open to reveal a staircase, leading up to the second floor.

Reed and Kelly was a real business. There once had been a Jonathan Reed and a Sebastian Kelly, and for more than fifty years they had arranged funerals and cremations until, at last, the time had come to arrange their own. After that, the undertaker's had been purchased by a perfectly legitimate company and registered in Zurich, and it had continued to provide a first-class service for anyone who lived—or rather, *had* lived—in the area. But that was no longer the only purpose of the building in Sloane Street. It had also become the London headquarters of the international criminal organization that went by the name of Scorpia.

The name stood for "sabotage, corruption, intelligence, and assassination," which were its four main activities. The organization had been formed some thirty years before in Paris, its members being spies from different intelligence networks around the world who had decided to go into business for themselves. There had been twelve of them at first. Then one had died of illness and two had been killed in the field. The other nine had congratulated themselves on surviving so long with so few casualties.

But quite recently, things had taken a turn for the worse. The oldest member of the organization had made the foolish and inexplicable decision to retire, which had, of course, led to his being murdered immediately. Soon afterward, his successor, a woman called Julia Rothman, had also been killed. That had been at the end of an operation—Invisible Sword—that had gone catastrophically wrong. In many ways this was the lowest point in Scorpia's history, and there were many who thought that the organization would never recover. After all, the agent who had beaten them, destroyed the operation, and caused the death of Mrs. Rothman had been fourteen years old.

However, Scorpia had not given in. They had taken swift revenge on the boy and gone straight back to work. Invisible Sword was just one of many projects needing their attention, for they were in constant demand from governments, terrorist groups, big business . . . in fact, anyone who could pay. And now they were active once again. They had come to this address in London to discuss a relatively small assignment but one that would net them ten million dollars, to be paid in uncut diamonds . . . easier to carry and harder to trace than banknotes.

The stairs led to a short corridor on the first floor with a single door at the end. One television camera had watched the bald man on his way up. A second followed him as he stepped onto a strange metal platform in front of the door and looked into a glass panel set in the wall. Behind the glass, there was a biometric scanner that took an instant image of the unique pattern of blood vessels on the retina behind his eye and matched them against a computer at the reception desk below. If an enemy agent had tried to gain access to the room, he would have triggered a ten-thousand-volt electric charge through the metal floor plate, incinerating him instantly. But this was no enemy. The man's name was Zeljan Kurst, and he had been with Scorpia almost from the beginning. The door slid open, and he went in.

He found himself in a long, narrow room with three windows covered by blinds and plain, white walls with no decoration of any kind. There was a glass table surrounded by leather chairs and no sign of any pens, paper, or printed documents. Nothing was ever written down at these meetings. Nor was anything recorded. Six men were waiting for him as he took his place at the head of the table. Following the disaster of Invisible Sword, now just the seven of them were left.

"Good morning, gentlemen," Kurst began. He spoke with a strange, mid-European accent. The last word had sounded like "chintlemen." All the men at the table were equal partners, but he was currently the acting head. A new chief executive was chosen as fresh projects arrived.

Nobody replied. These people were not friends. They had nothing to say to each other outside the work at hand.

"We have been given a most interesting and challenging assignment," Kurst went on. "I need hardly remind you that our reputation was quite seriously damaged earlier this year. In addition to providing us with a much-needed financial injection following the heavy losses we sustained on 'Invisible Sword,' this new project will put us back on the map. Our task is this. We are to assassinate eight extremely wealthy and influential people exactly one month from now. They will all be in one place at one time, which provides us with the ideal opportunity. It has been left to us to decide on the method."

Zeljan Kurst had been the head of the police force in Yugoslavia during the 1980s and had been famous for his love of classical music—particularly Mozart—and extreme violence. It was said that he would interrogate prisoners with either an opera or a symphony playing in the background and that those who survived the ordeal would never be able to listen to that piece of music again. But he had seen the breakup of his country on the horizon and had decided to quit before he was out of a job. And so he had changed sides. He had no family, no friends, and nowhere he could call home. He needed work, and he knew that Scorpia would pay him extremely well.

His eyes flickered around the table, waiting for a response. "You will have read in the newspapers," he continued, "that the G8 summit is taking place in Rome this November. This is a meeting of the eight most powerful heads of government, and as usual they will talk a great deal, have their photographs taken, consume a lot of expensive food and wine . . . and do absolutely nothing. They are of no interest to us. They are, in effect, irrelevant.

"However, at the same time, another meeting will be taking place on the other side of the world. It has been arranged in direct competition with the G8 summit, and you might say that the timing is something of a publicity stunt. Nonetheless, it has already attracted much more attention than G8. Indeed, the politicians have almost been forgotten. Instead, the eyes of the world are on Reef Island, just off the coast of northwest Australia in the Timor Sea.

"The press have given this alternative summit a name: Reef Encounter. A group of eight people will be coming together, and their names will be known to you. One of them is a pop singer named Rob Goldman. He has apparently raised millions for charity with concerts all over the world. One is a billionaire, among the top-ten richest men on the planet. He created a huge property empire, but he is now giving his fortune away to developing countries. There is an ex-president of the United States. A famous Hollywood actress—Eve Taylor. She actually owns the island. And so on." Kurst didn't even try to keep the contempt out of his voice. "They are amateurs, do-gooders . . . but they are also powerful and popular, which makes them dangerous.

"Their aim, as they put it, is 'to make poverty history.' In order to achieve this, they have made certain demands, including the cancellation of world debt. They want millions of dollars to be sent to Africa to fight AIDS and malaria. They have called for an end to war in the Middle East. It will come as no surprise to those of us in this room that there are many governments and business interests who do not agree with these aims. After all, it is not possible to give to the poor without taking from the rich, and anyway, poverty has its uses. It keeps people in their place. It also helps to hold prices down.

"A representative of one of the governments has been in contact with us. He has decided that the Reef Encounter should end the moment it begins—certainly before any of these meddlers begin to address the television cameras of the world—and that is our assignment. Disrupting the conference is not enough. All eight of them are to be killed. The fact that they will all be in one place at one time makes it easier for us. Not one of them must leave Reef Island alive."

One of the other men leaned forward. His name was Levi Kroll. He was an Israeli and about fifty years old. Very little of his face could be seen. Most of it was covered by a beard, and there was a patch covering the eye that he had once, by accident, shot out. "It is a simple matter," he rasped. "I could go out this afternoon and hire an Apache helicopter gunship. Let us say two thousand rounds of 30-millimeter cannon fire and a few Hellfire air-to-ground laser-guided missiles and this conference would no longer exist."

"Unfortunately, it isn't quite as straightforward as that," Kurst replied. "As I said in my opening remarks, this is a particularly challenging assignment. Why? Because our client does not wish the Reef Island eight to become martyrs. If they were seen to be assassinated, it would only add weight to their cause. And so he has specified that the deaths must seem accidental. In fact, this is critical. There cannot be even the tiniest amount of doubt or suspicion."

There was a soft murmur around the table as the other members of Scorpia took this new information on board. To kill one person in a way that would arouse no suspicion was simple. But to do the same for eight people on a remote island that would doubtless have a tight security system . . . that was quite another matter.

"There are certain chemical nerve agents . . . ," someone muttered. He was French, exquisitely dressed with a black silk handkerchief poking out of his top pocket. His voice was matter-of-fact.

"How about R-5?" Mr. Mikato suggested. He was a Japanese man with a diamond set in his tooth and—it was rumored—Yakuza tattoos all over his body. "It's the virus that we supplied to Herod Sayle. Perhaps we could feed it into the island's water supply . . ."

"Gentlemen, both of these methods would be effective but still might show up in the subsequent investigation."

Kurst shook his head. "What we require is a natural disaster, but one that we control. We need to eliminate the entire island with everybody on it, but in such a way that no questions will ever be asked."

He paused, then turned to the man sitting at the end of the table opposite him. "Major Yu?" he asked. "Have you given the matter your consideration?"

"Absolutely . . ."

Major Winston Yu was at least sixty years old, and although he still had a full head of hair, it had turned completely white. The hair looked artificial, cut in the style of a schoolboy with a straight line above the eyes and the whole thing perched on top of a head that was yellow and waxy and that had shrunk like an overripe fruit. He was the least impressive person in the room, with circular glasses, thin lips, and hands that would have been small on a child. Everything about him was somehow delicate. He had been sitting very still at the table as if he was afraid he might break. An ornamental walking stick with a silver scorpion entwined around the handle rested against his chair. He wore a white suit and pale gray gloves.

"I have taken a very careful look at this operation," he continued. He had a perfect English accent. "And I am happy to report that although on the face of it this seems to be a rather difficult business, we have been blessed with three very fortunate circumstances. First, this island, Reef Island, is in exactly the right place. Second, December 2, just a few weeks from now, will be exactly the right time. And third, the weapon that we require just happens to be here in England, in fact, less than thirty miles from where we are sitting now."

"And what weapon is that?" the Frenchman demanded.

"It's a bomb. But a very special bomb . . . a prototype. As far as I know, there is only one in existence. The British have given it a code name. They call it Royal Blue."

"Major Yu is absolutely right," Kurst cut in. "Royal Blue is currently in a highly secret weapons facility just outside London. That is why I chose to hold the meeting here today. The building has been under surveillance for the past month, and a team is already waiting on standby. By this evening, the bomb will be in our possession. After that, Major Yu, I am placing this operation in your hands."

Major Yu nodded slowly.

"With respect, Mr. Kurst," It was Levi Kroll speaking. His voice was ugly, and there was very little respect in it. "I was under the impression that *I* would be in command of the next operation."

"I am afraid you will have to wait, Mr. Kroll. As soon as Royal Blue is in our hands, it will be flown to Jakarta and then carried by sea to its final destination. This is a region of the world where you have no working experience. For Major Yu, however, it is another matter. Over the past seven years he has been active in Bangkok,

Jakarta, Bali, and Lombok. He also has a base in northern Australia. He has constructed and now controls a huge criminal network that goes by the name of *shetou*— or, in English, snakehead. They will smuggle the weapon for us. The snakehead is a formidable organization, and in this instance it is best suited to our needs."

The Israeli nodded briefly. "You are right. I apologize for my interruption."

"I accept your apology," Kurst replied, although he hadn't. It occurred to him that one day Levi Kroll might have to go. The man spoke too often without thinking first.

There was little left to be said. Winston Yu took off his glasses and polished them, using his gloved fingers. His eyes were a strange, almost metallic gray with lids that folded in on themselves. "I will contact my people in Bangkok and warn them the machine is on its way. I already have some thoughts as to its location with regard to Reef Island. And as to this conference with its high ideals, you need have no worries. I am very happy to assure you . . . it will never take place."

At six o'clock in the evening, two days later, a blue Renault Megane turned off the M11 highway, taking an exit marked Service Vehicles Only. There are many such turnings on the British highway system. Thousands of vehicles roar past them every hour, and the drivers never glance at them twice. And indeed, the great majority of them are completely innocent, leading to service areas or to police traffic control centers. But the highway system has its secrets too. As the Renault made its way slowly forward and came to a shuddering halt in front of what looked like a single-story office compound, it was tracked by three television cameras, and the security men inside went onto immediate alert.

The building was in fact a laboratory and weapons research center, belonging to the Ministry of Defense. Very few people knew of its existence, and even fewer were allowed in or out. The car that had just arrived was unauthorized and the two security men—both of them recruited from the special forces—should have immediately raised the alarm. That was the protocol.

But the Renault Megane is one of the most innocent and ordinary of family cars, and this one had clearly been involved in a bad accident. The windshield had shattered. The hood was crumpled, and steam was rising from the grille. A man wearing a green anorak and a cap was in the driving seat. There was a woman next to him with blood pouring down the side of her face. Worse than that, there were two small children in the backseat, and although the image on the television screen was a little fuzzy, they seemed to be in a bad way. Neither of them was moving. The woman managed to get out of the car—but then she collapsed. Her husband sat where he was as if dazed.

The two security men ran out to them. It was human nature. Here was a young family that needed help, and anyway, it wasn't that much of a security risk. The front door of the building swung shut behind them and would need a seven-digit code to open again. Both men carried radio transmitters and nine-millimeter Browning automatic pistols underneath their jackets. The Browning is an old weapon, but it's a very reliable one, making it a favorite with the special forces.

The woman was still lying on the ground. The man who had been driving managed to open the door as the two men arrived.

"What happened?" one of them asked.

It was only now, when it was too late, that they began to realize that none of this added up. A car that had crashed on the highway would have simply pulled onto the hard shoulder—if it had been able to drive at all. And how come it was only this one car, with these four people, that had been involved? Where were the other drivers? Where were the police? But any last doubt was removed when the two security men reached the car. The two children in the backseat were dummies. With their cheap wigs and plastic smiles they were like something out of a nightmare.

The woman on the ground twisted around, a machine pistol appearing in her hand. She shot the first of the security guards in the chest. The second was moving quickly, reaching for his own weapon, taking up a combat stance. He never had a chance. The driver had been balancing a silenced micro-Uzi submachine gun on his lap. He tilted it and pulled the trigger. The gun barely whispered as it fired twenty rounds in less than a second. The guard was flung away.

The couple were already up and running toward the building. They couldn't get in yet, but they didn't need to. They made their way toward the back, where a silver box, about two yards square, had been attached to the brickwork. The man carried a tool kit that he had brought from the car. The woman stopped briefly and fired three times, taking out all the cameras. At the same time, an ambulance appeared, driving up from the highway. It drew in behind the parked car.

The next phase of the mission took very little time. The facility was equipped with a standard CBR air filtration system—the letters stood for "chemical, biological, and radioactive." It was designed to counter an enemy attack, but in fact the exact opposite was about to happen as the enemy turned the system against itself. The man took a miniaturized oxyacetylene torch out of his toolbox and used it to burn out the screws. This allowed him to unfasten a metal panel, revealing a complicated tangle of pipes and wires. From somewhere inside his anorak, he produced a gas mask, which he strapped over his face. He reached back into his toolbox and took out a metal vial, a few inches long, with a nozzle and a spike. The man knew exactly what he was doing. Using the heel of his hand, he jammed the spike into one of the pipes. Finally, he turned the nozzle.

The hiss was almost inaudible as a stream of potassium cyanide mixed with the air circulating inside the building. Meanwhile, four men dressed as paramedics but all wearing gas masks had approached the front door. One of them pressed a magnetized box, no bigger than a cigarette pack, against the lock. He stepped back. There was an explosion. The door swung open.

It was early evening, and only half a dozen people had still been working inside the facility. Most of them were technicians. One was an armed security guard. He had been trying to make a telephone call when the gas had hit him. He was lying on the floor, a look of surprise on his face. The receiver was still in his hand.

Through the entrance hall, down a corridor, and through a door marked RESTRICTED AREA . . . the four paramedics knew exactly where they were going. The bomb was in front of them. It looked remarkably old-fashioned, like something out of World War II—a huge metal cylinder, silver in color, flat at one end, pointed at the other. Only a data screen, built into the side, and a series of digital controls brought it back into the twenty-first century. It was strapped down to a power-assisted cart, and the whole thing would fit inside the ambulance with just inches to spare. But that, of course, was why the ambulance had been chosen.

They guided it back down the corridor and out through the front door. The ambulance was equipped with a ramp, and it rolled smoothly into the back, allowing room for the driver and one passenger in the front. The other three men and the woman climbed into the car. The dummies of the children were left behind. The entire operation had taken eight and a half minutes. Thirty seconds less than planned.

An hour later, by the time the alarm had been raised in London and other parts of the country, everyone involved had disappeared. They had discarded the wigs, contact lenses, and facial padding that had completely changed their appearance. The two vehicles had been incinerated.

And the weapon known as Royal Blue had already begun its journey east.

3

VISA PROBLEMS

"ALEX RIDER."

The blind man spoke the two words as if they had only just occurred to him. He let them roll over his tongue, tasting them like a fine wine. He was sitting in a soft leather armchair, the sort of furniture that would have been normal in an executive office but that was surprising in a plane, twenty-five thousand feet above Adelaide. The plane was a Gulfstream V executive jet that had been specially adapted for its current use, equipped with a kitchen and bathroom, a satellite link for worldwide communications, a forty-inch plasma TV connected to three twenty-four-hour news services, and a bank of computers. There was even a basket for Garth, the blind man's guide dog.

The man's name was Ethan Brooke, and he was the chief executive of the Covert Action Division of ASIS— the Australian Secret Intelligence Service. His department was inevitably known as CAD, but only by the people who worked in it. Very few other people even knew it existed.

Brooke was a large man, in his mid-fifties, with sand-colored hair and ruddy, weather-beaten cheeks that

suggested years spent outdoors. He had indeed been a
soldier, a lieutenant colonel with the commandos, until a
land mine in East Timor had sent him first into the
hospital for three months and then into a new career in
intelligence. He wore Armani sunglasses, tinted silver,
rather than the traditional black glasses of a blind man,
and his clothes were casual: jeans, a jacket, and an open-
neck shirt. A senior minister in the Australian defense
department had once complained about the way he
dressed. That same minister was now carrying luggage in
a three-star Sydney hotel.

He was not alone. Sitting opposite him was a second
man, almost half his age, slim, with short, fair hair. He
was wearing a suit. Marc Damon had applied to join Australian intelligence the day after he had left the university.
He had done this by breaking into the main offices of
ASIS in Canberra and leaving his application on Brooke's
desk. The two of them had now worked together for
six years.

It was Damon who had produced the file—marked
TOP SECRET: CAD EYES ONLY—that lay on the table
between them. Although its contents had been translated
into Braille, Brooke no longer had any need to refer to
them. He had read the pages once and had instantly
memorized their contents. He now knew everything he
needed about the boy called Alex Rider. The only part
that was missing from his consciousness was a true pic-

ture of the fourteen-year-old. There was a photograph attached to the cover, but as always he had been forced to rely on the official report:

Physical description/attributes

Subject is five feet, seven inches tall, still short for his age, but this adds to his operational value. Weight: 140 pounds. Hair color: fair. Eyes: brown. His physical condition is excellent but may have been compromised by his recent injury (see Scorpia file). The boy is known to be fluent in two languages—French and Spanish—and is also proficient in German. He has practiced karate since the age of eight and has reached first *kyu* grade (black belt). Weapons training: none. Progress at school has been slow, with negative feedback from many of his teachers. Spring and summer reports from Brookland School are attached. However, it must be remembered that he has been absent from class for much of the past nine months.

Psychological profile

AR was recruited by the Special Operations Division of MI6 in March of this year, age fourteen years and one month. His father was John Rider—alias Hunter—who was killed in action. His mother died at the same time, and he was brought up by his uncle, Ian Rider, also an active agent with MI6.

It seems certain that the boy was physically and mentally prepared for intelligence work from the earliest age.

Quite apart from the languages and martial arts, Ian Rider equipped him with many skills, including fencing, mountain climbing, white-water rafting, and scuba diving.

And yet, despite his obvious aptitude for intelligence work (see below), AR has shown little enthusiasm for it. Like most teenagers, he is not a patriot and has no interest in politics. MI6 (SO) found it necessary to coerce him to work for them on at least two occasions.

He is popular at school . . . when he is there. Hobbies: soccer (Chelsea supporter), tennis, music, movies. Evident interest in girls—see separate file on Sabina Pleasure + report by CIA operative Tamara Knight. Lives with American housekeeper, Jack Starbright (note: despite first name she is a female). No ambitions to follow his father or uncle into intelligence.

Past assignments—active service

The British secret service refuses to admit that it has ever employed a juvenile, and so it has been difficult to draw together any concrete evidence of his record as an agent in the field. We believe, however, that he has worked for them on four occasions. He has also been loaned to the United States, where he has been employed by the CIA with equal success at least twice.

United Kingdom: See Herod Sayle: Sayle Enterprises, Cornwall. Dr. Marius Grief: Point Blanc Academy, France. Damian Cray: Cray Software Technology, Amsterdam. Julia Rothman: Scorpia executive. Operation Invisible Sword.

United States: FILES CLOSED. Possible link with General Alexei Sarov—Skeleton Key. Nikolei Drevin—Flamingo Bay (termination of Ark Angel project).

Although it has so far proved impossible to confirm details, it appears that in the space of one year, AR has been involved in six major assignments, succeeding against impossible odds. He has survived assassination attempts by both Scorpia and the Chinese triads.

Current status: available.

Footnote: In 2006, the FBI attempted to recruit a teenage agent to combat drug syndicates operating out of Miami. The boy was killed almost immediately. The experiment has not been repeated.

Secret service files are the same the world over. They are written by people who live in a very black-and-white world and who, by and large, have no time for creative imagination . . . certainly not if it gets in the way of the facts. The various pages on Alex Rider had given Brooke a vague impression of the boy. They had certainly been enough to set his mind working. But he suspected that they left out as much as they revealed.

"He's in Australia," he muttered.

"Yes, sir." Damon nodded. "He sort of dropped in on us from outer space."

Brooke smiled. "You know, if anyone else told me that, I'd swear they were yanking my chain. He really went into space?"

"He was pulled out of the sea a hundred miles off the west coast. He was sitting in the reentry module of a Soyuz-Fregat. Of course, the Americans aren't telling us anything. But it's probably no coincidence that according to NIWO, the Ark Angel space station blew up at around the same time."

NIWO is the National Intelligence Watch Office. It employs around 2,000 people who keep up a constant surveillance on everything happening in the world . . . and outside it.

"That was Drevin's big idea," Brooke muttered. "A space hotel."

"Yes, sir."

"I always had a feeling he was up to no good."

There was a moment of turbulence and the plane dipped down. The dog, in its basket, whined. It never had cared much for flying. But then they steadied and continued in their arc over the clouds, heading northeast to Sydney.

"You think we can use him?" Brooke demanded.

"Alex Rider doesn't like being used," Damon replied. "And from what I've read, there's no way he's going to volunteer. But it did occur to me that if we could find some sort of leverage, he would be perfect for what we need. Put a kid into the pipeline and nobody's going to suspect a thing. It's exactly the same reason the Americans sent him to Skeleton Key—and it worked for them."

"Where is he now?"

"They flew him over to Perth, sir. A bit of a hike, but they wanted him somewhere safe and they settled on SAS HQ at Swanbourne. He's going to need a couple of days to wind down."

Brooke fell silent. With his eyes permanently covered, it was always difficult to work out what he was thinking—but Damon knew that he would be turning over all the possibilities, that he would come very quickly to a decision and stick by it. Maybe there was no way that ASIS could persuade this English kid to work for them. But if there was a single weakness, anything they could use to their advantage, Brooke would find it.

A moment later he nodded. "We could connect him with Ash," he said.

And there it was. Simple but brilliant.

"Ash is in Singapore," Damon said.

"Operational?"

"A routine assignment."

"As of now he's reassigned. We'll put the two of them together and send them in. They'll make a perfect team."

Damon couldn't help smiling. Alex Rider would work with the agent they all called Ash. But there was just one problem. "You think Ash will work with a teenager?" he asked.

"He will if this kid's as good as everyone says he is."

"He'll need proof of that."

This time it was Brooke's turn to smile. "Leave that to me."

• • •

The SAS compound at Swanbourne is a few miles north of Perth and has the appearance of a low-rise vacation village, although perhaps one with more security than most. It stretches out next to the white sand and blue water of the Indian Ocean, sheltered from public view by a series of sand dunes. The buildings are clean, modern, and unremarkable. But for the rise and fall of the barrier at the main gate, the military vehicles passing in and out, and the occasional sighting of men in khaki and black berets, it would be hard to believe that this is the HQ of Australia's toughest and most elite fighting force.

Alex Rider stood at the window of his room looking out over the main square with the indoor shooting range on one side and the gymnasium and fitness center on the other. He wanted to go home and wondered how long they were going to keep him here. Certainly, his stay on the *Kitty Hawk* had been short enough. He had barely had time to eat breakfast before he had been bundled onto a Hawkeye jet, an oxygen mask strapped over his face, and then blasted off back into the sky. Nobody had even told him where they were taking him, but he had seen the name written in large letters on the airport terminal. Perth. There had been a jeep parked on the runway, and the next thing he knew, he was bouncing through the very ordinary-looking suburb of Swanbourne. The jeep drove into the SAS compound and stopped. A single soldier was waiting for him, his face set, his mouth a straight line that gave nothing away. Alex was shown into a comfortable room with a bed, a TV, and a view of the sand dunes. The door was closed, but it wasn't locked.

And here he was now. At the end of a journey that had been literally out of this world. He wondered what would happen next.

There was a knock on the door. Alex opened it. A second soldier in green-and-ocher battle fatigues stood in front of him.

"Mr. Rider?"

"I'm Alex."

"Colonel Abbott sends his compliments. He'd like to speak to you."

Alex followed the soldier across the compound. For the moment there was nobody else around. The sun was beating down on the empty parade ground. It was almost midday, and the Australian summer was already making itself felt. They reached a bungalow, standing on its own near the edge of the complex. The soldier knocked and, without waiting for an answer, opened the door for Alex to go in.

A thin, businesslike man in his forties was sitting behind a desk, also wearing battle fatigues. He had been writing a report, but he stood up as Alex came in.

"So you're Alex Rider!" The Australian accent came almost as a surprise. With his short, dark hair and craggy features, Abbott could have been mistaken for an Englishman. He reached out and shook Alex's hand firmly.

"I'm Mike Abbott, and I'm really pleased to meet you, Alex. I've heard a lot about you." Alex looked surprised, and Abbott laughed. "Six months ago, there was a rumor that the Brits were using a teenage agent. Of course, nobody believed it. But it seems they've been keeping you busy, and after you took out Damian Cray . . . well, I'm afraid you can't blow up Air Force One in the middle of London without someone hearing about it. But don't worry! You're among friends."

Abbott gestured toward a chair and Alex sat down. "It's very kind of you, Colonel," he said. "But I really want to get back home."

Abbott returned to his own chair. "I can understand that, Alex. And I really want to send you on your way. We just need to fix a couple of things."

"What things?"

"Well, you landed in Australia without a visa." Abbott held up two hands before Alex could interrupt. "I know that sounds ridiculous, but it has to be sorted out. As soon as I've got the green light, I'll book you on the first plane back to London."

"There's someone I want to call. . . ."

"I suppose you're thinking about Jack Starbright. Your housekeeper." Abbott smiled, and Alex wondered how he knew about her. "You're too late, Alex. She's been kept fully informed, and she's already on her way. Her flight left Heathrow about an hour ago, but it'll take her another twenty-five hours to arrive. The two of you will meet up in Sydney. In the meantime, you're my guest here at Swanbourne, and I want you to enjoy yourself. We're right on the beach, and right now it's the start of the Australian summer. So relax. I'll let you know as soon as there's any news about the visa."

Alex wanted to argue but decided against it. The Colonel seemed friendly enough, but there was something about him that made Alex think twice before speaking. You don't rise up the ranks of the SAS unless you're exceptionally tough—and there was certainly steel behind that smile.

"Anything else you want to know?"

"No thanks, Colonel."

The two of them shook hands. "I've asked some of the boys to look after you," Abbott said. "They've been looking forward to meeting you. Just let me know if anyone gives you a hard time."

When Alex had been training with the SAS in the Brecon Beacons in Wales, a hard time is exactly what he had been given. But from the moment he left the bungalow, he saw that things were going to be different here. There were half a dozen young soldiers waiting for him on the other side, and they all seemed to be easygoing and eager to introduce themselves. Maybe his reputation had gone ahead of him, but he could see right away that the Australian special forces were going to be the complete opposite of their British counterparts.

"It's great to meet you, Alex." The man who was

speaking was about nineteen and incredibly fit, with a green T-shirt stretched tight over finely chiseled pectorals and arms that filled his sleeves. "I'm Scooter. This is Texas, X-Ray, and Sparks." At first Alex thought they were using code names. But he quickly realized that they were actually just nicknames. All the other men were in their early twenties and equally fit. "We're just heading for lunch," Scooter went on. "You want to join us?"

"Thanks." Alex hadn't been given any breakfast, and his stomach was still empty from the day before.

They moved off as a pack. Nobody had even commented on his age. There was clearly no secret who he was. Alex began to feel a little more relaxed. Maybe a day or two here wouldn't be so bad.

From inside the office, Colonel Mike Abbott watched them go. He had an uneasy feeling in his stomach. He was married with three children, and the oldest was only a few years younger than the boy he had just met. He had been impressed. After all he had been through, Alex had a sort of inner calm. Abbott didn't doubt that he could look after himself.

But even so . . .

He glanced again at the orders that he had received just a few hours ago. It was madness. What was being suggested was simply out of the question. Except that there was no question about it. He had been told exactly what he had to do.

And what if Alex was crippled? What if he was killed?

Not his problem.

The thought didn't comfort him one bit. In twenty years, Mike Abbott had never questioned his commanding officers, but it was with a sense of anger and disbelief that he picked up the telephone and began to issue the instructions for the night ahead.

4

NO PICNIC

ALEX WAS WORN OUT after all his traveling, and that afternoon he went back to his room and slept. When he was woken up—by the sound of knocking—the day was already drawing to a close. He went over to the door and opened it. The young soldier who had introduced himself as Scooter was standing there. Sparks was with him, holding a cooler.

"How are you doing?" Scooter asked. "We wondered if you'd like to come with us."

"Where are you going?" Alex asked.

"A picnic on the beach. We'll set up a barbecue. Maybe swim." Scooter gestured at the compound behind him. There was nobody in sight. "There's a big exercise tonight, but we aren't part of it, and the colonel thought you might like to see a bit of the ocean before you leave."

The last three words caught Alex's attention. "Am I leaving?"

"Tomorrow morning. That's what I've heard. So how about it?"

"Sure . . ." Alex had nothing else to do that evening. He didn't particularly want to watch TV on his own.

"Great. We'll pick you up in ten minutes."

The two men walked off, and it was only much later,

when he was ten thousand miles away, that Alex would re-member the moment and the way they had glanced at each other as if there was something that bothered them. But if he noticed it at the time, he didn't register it.

He went back into the room and pulled on his sneak-ers. The SAS had provided him with some fresh clothes, and he took a combat jacket out of the wardrobe. Scooter had talked about swimming, but the sun was getting lower and Alex had already felt a cool breeze rolling in. He thought for a moment, then took a towel and a spare pair of boxers, which would have to do instead of swimming trunks. Just as he was about to leave, he hesitated. Was this a good idea, heading off down the coast with a group of strangers, some of them as much as ten years older than he was? Suddenly he felt very alone and a long, long way from home. But Jack was on her way. Scooter had told him that he would be leaving the next day. He shook himself out of his mood and left the room, closing the door behind him.

Almost at once, a jeep drew up with Sparks driving and Scooter in the passenger seat. Texas and X-Ray were in the back with bags and coolers, blankets, and a guitar piled up around them. They had left a narrow space for Alex. As he climbed in, he noticed that Texas was balanc-ing an automatic pistol on his lap, testing the mechanism.

"You ever fired one of these?" Texas asked.

Alex shook his head.

"Well, now's your chance. When we get out there, I'll set up a few targets. See how you do."

Once again, Alex couldn't shake off a vague feeling that something was wrong, but then Sparks turned on the radio and with a blast of music from some Australian band he had never heard of, they set off. It was going to be a beautiful evening. There were a few streaks of red in the sky but no clouds, and the sun—close to the horizon—was throwing long, stretched-out shadows across the ground. Scooter was slumped in his seat with one foot resting on the dashboard. X-Ray had his hand up, the wind streaming through his fingers. By the time they had passed through the barrier and hit the main road, Alex had relaxed. He only had one evening in Australia. He might as well enjoy it.

They followed the coast for about ten miles, then turned inland. Why had they come so far? Alex couldn't shake off a sense of unease. After all, the compound at Swanbourne had been right on the beach to begin with.

They had already passed a number of suburban houses and shopping malls, but they soon left those behind, and by the time they had joined a four-lane highway, they were driving through open countryside. None of them spoke. It was impossible in the open-top jeep with the wind rushing past. The music pounded out, but any words were snatched away and lost. After about twenty minutes, Scooter turned around and shouted, "You okay?" Alex nodded. But secretly he was wondering how far they intended to travel and when they would arrive.

The journey took over an hour. They came off the highway and took a road that cut through a wooded area. Then they turned onto a track, and suddenly they were bumping over a rough, uneven surface with eucalyptus and pine trees pressing in on both sides. X-Ray had taken out a map. He leaned forward and tapped Sparks on the shoulder.

"Is this the right way?" he shouted.

"Sure!" Sparks shouted back without looking behind him.

"I think we've come too far!"

"Forget it, X-Ray. This is the right way . . ."

There was a barrier ahead of them, similar to the one at Swanbourne except that it was old and rusted. There was a sign next to it.

MILITARY ZONE
ABSOLUTELY NO ADMITTANCE.
TRESPASSERS WILL BE PLACED UNDER ARREST
AND MAY BE IMPRISONED.

Scooter slowed down and, without opening the door, Sparks leapt out of the jeep.

"Where are we?" Alex asked.

"You'll see," Scooter replied. "We come to a load of places around here. You'll like it."

"We've come too far," X-Ray insisted. "We should have turned off a mile back."

Sparks had opened the barrier—it obviously hadn't been locked—and the jeep rolled forward. As it passed him, he leapt back into the passenger seat, and at once Scooter stepped on the accelerator and they shot forward, bumping over roots and potholes.

It had become very dark. The last of the daylight had slipped away without Alex noticing, and suddenly the trees seemed very close, threatening to block the way ahead. The surface was getting worse and worse. Alex had to cling onto the side as he was thrown around, the coolers lifting themselves into the air and hanging there before crashing down again. Leaves and branches flickered briefly, a thousand black shadows caught in the headlights, before they whipped into the windshield and disappeared behind. The track didn't seem to be going anywhere and Alex was having to fight back a sense of unease, wishing he hadn't come, when suddenly they burst through a clump of foliage and came to a shuddering halt with soft sand underneath the wheels. They had arrived.

Scooter turned off the engine, and at once the gentler sounds of the evening surrounded them. Alex could hear the whisper of the breeze and the rhythmic breaking of the waves. They had come to a beautiful place: a private beach that curved around in the shape of a crescent with perfect white sand next to a black-and-silver sea. There was a full moon and a fantastic cluster of stars that seemed to go on forever, stretching to the very ends of the Southern Hemisphere.

"Everybody out!" Scooter shouted. He kicked the door open and tumbled out onto the beach. "X-Ray . . . get me a Coke. Texas, it's your turn to cook."

"I always cook!" Texas complained.

"Why do you think we invite you?"

X-Ray turned to Alex. "You thirsty?"

Alex nodded, and X-ray threw him a can of Coke.

Meanwhile, Texas had begun to unload the jeep. Alex saw that the SAS men had brought sausages, burgers, steaks, and chops . . . enough meat to feed a small army. But apart from a greasy, blackened steel grill, there was no sign of the promised barbecue. Scooter must have read his mind. "We're going to build a bonfire, Alex," he said. "You can help collect wood."

Sparks had taken the guitar out of the back. He rested it on his knee and strummed a few chords. The music sounded tiny, lost in the emptiness of the night.

"Okay. Here's the plan," Scooter said. It seemed that he was the natural leader even if all four men were the same age and rank. "Alex and I will fetch firewood. Texas can start setting things up. Sparks—you keep playing." He took out a flashlight and threw it to Alex. "If you get lost, just listen for the music," he said. "It'll guide you back to the beach."

"Right." Alex wasn't sure he would be able to hear the

guitar once he was in the woods, but Scooter seemed to know what he was doing.

"Let's go," Scooter said.

He also had a flashlight and flicked it on. The beam was powerful. Even with the moonlight, it leapt ahead, cutting a path through the shadows. Alex did the same. The two of them moved away from the jeep, heading back up the track that had brought them here. The evening was warmer than Alex had expected. The breeze couldn't penetrate the trees. Everything was very still.

"You all right?" Scooter asked.

Alex nodded.

"We'll build a fire, get things cooking . . . then we can have a swim."

"Right."

They were still walking. It seemed to Alex that they had left the beach a long way behind them. He could still hear the music—but it was so distant that the notes seemed to have broken up and he couldn't make out any tune.

"See if you can find any dead wood. It burns better."

Alex trained his flashlight on the forest floor. There were broken branches everywhere, and he wondered why they had come so far to collect them. But there was no point arguing. He reached down and gathered a few pieces, then a few more. It didn't take him long to build up a pile . . . any more and it would be too heavy to carry.

Clutching the wood to his chest, he straightened up and looked around for Scooter.

That was when he realized that he was on his own.

"Scooter?" He called out the name. There was no reply. Nor was there any sign of the SAS man's flashlight. Alex wasn't worried. It was likely that Scooter had already collected his first bundle and was making his way back to the beach. Alex listened for the sound of the guitar. But it had stopped.

Now he felt the first prickle of doubt. He had been so busy collecting the branches, he had lost his sense of direction. He was in the middle of the woods, surrounded on all sides. Which way was the beach?

Ahead of him, he saw a blink of white. A flashlight. Scooter was there after all. Alex called out his name a second time, but there was no reply. It didn't matter. He had definitely seen the light and, as if to reassure him, it flashed again. He headed toward it anxiously.

It was only when he had taken twenty or thirty paces that he realized that he was nowhere near the beach, that he had in fact been drawn even farther into the woods. It was almost as if it had been done on purpose. He was the moth, and they had shown him the candle. But just then the light vanished. Even the moon was invisible. Annoyed with himself, Alex dropped the wood. He could always pick more up later. All he wanted to do right now was to find his way back.

Ten more steps and abruptly the trees fell away. But he

wasn't at the beach. Alex's flashlight showed him a wide, barren clearing with little hillocks of sand and grass. The wood circled all around him. There was no sign at all of Scooter or the second, flickering flashlight that had brought him here.

Now what? Was Scooter playing a prank on him?

Alex decided to go back the way he had come. He might be able to pick up his own footprints. The pile of wood that he had dropped couldn't be too far away. He was about to turn when something—some animal instinct—made him hesitate. About two seconds later, the whole world stopped.

He knew it was going to happen before it actually did. Alex had been in danger so many times that he had developed a sense, a sort of telepathy, that forewarned him. Animals have it—the awareness that makes their hackles rise and sends them running before there is any obvious reason. Alex was already throwing himself to the ground even before the missile fell out of the sky, smashing the trees into matchsticks, scooping up a ton of earth and throwing it into the sky, shattering the silence of the night and turning darkness into brilliant, blinding day.

The explosion was enormous. Alex had never felt anything like it. The very air had been turned into a giant fist, a boxing glove that pounded into him—hot and violent— and for a moment he thought he must have broken a dozen bones. He couldn't hear. He couldn't see. The inside of his head was boiling. Perhaps he was unconscious for a few seconds, but the next thing he knew, he was lying on the ground with his face pressed into a clump of wild grass and sand in his hair and eyes. His shirt was torn and there was a throbbing in his ears, but otherwise he seemed to be unhurt. How close had the missile fallen? Where had it come from? Even as Alex asked himself these two questions, a third, more unpleasant one entered his mind. Were there going to be any more?

There was no time to work out what was going on. Alex spat out sand and dragged himself to his knees. At the same time, something burst out in the sky: a white flame that hung there, suspended high above the trees. Alex had tensed himself, expecting another blast, but he quickly recognized it for what it was: a battle flare light, a lump of burning phosphorus, designed to illuminate the area for miles around. He was still kneeling. Almost too late, he realized that he had turned himself into a target, a black cutout against the brilliant, artificial glare. He threw himself forward onto his stomach one second before a cascade of machine-gun bullets came fanning out of nowhere, pulverizing branches and ripping up the leaves. There was a second explosion, smaller than the first, this one starting at ground level and sending a column of flame shooting up. Alex covered his head with his hands. Earth and sand splattered all around him.

He was in a war zone. It was beyond anything he had ever experienced. But common sense told him that no war had broken out in Western Australia. This was a training exercise and somehow—insanely—he had stumbled into the heart of it.

He heard the blast of a whistle and two more explosions followed. The ground underneath him trembled, and suddenly he found that he could no longer breathe. The air around him had been sucked away by the force of the blasts. More machine-gun fire. The entire area was being strafed. Alex glanced up, but even with the battle flares he knew there was no chance he would see anyone. Whoever was firing could be half a mile away. And if he stood up and tried to make himself seen, he would be cut in half before anyone realized their mistake.

And what about Scooter? What about X-Ray and the others? Had they brought him here on purpose? Alex couldn't believe that. What motive could they have to want him dead? Briefly, he remembered what X-Ray had said in the jeep. *"We've come too far. We should have turned off a mile back."* And when they'd picked him up at the base, Scooter had said there was a big training exercise on that night. That was why they'd been free for a picnic on the beach. Some picnic! As impossible as it seemed, the four SAS men must have driven to the very edge of the war zone. Alex had managed to wander away from the beach when he was collecting wood and had chosen the worst-possible direction. This was the result— a mixture of bad luck and stupidity. But the two of them were going to get him blown apart.

A rhythmic pounding had begun, perhaps a mile away,

a mortar bombarding a target that had to be somewhere close by. As each shell detonated, Alex felt a stabbing pain behind the eyes. The power of the weapons was immense. If this was just a training exercise, he wondered what it must be like to get caught up in a real war.

It was time to go. With the mortars still firing, Alex scrabbled to his feet and began to move, not sure which way he should go, knowing only that he couldn't remain here. There was the scream of something falling through and a great *whumph* as it struck the ground somewhere over to Alex's left. That told him all he needed to know. He headed off to the right.

A crackle of machine-gun fire. Alex thought he heard someone shout, but when he looked around, there was no one there. That was the most unnerving thing, to be in the middle of a battle with not a single one of the combatants actually visible. A tree had caught fire. The entire trunk was wrapped in flames, and there were black-and-crimson shadows leaping all over the ground ahead. Just beyond, Alex caught sight of a wire fence. It wasn't much to aim for, but at least it was man-made. Maybe it defined the perimeter of the war zone and he would be safer on the other side. Alex broke into a run. He could taste blood in his mouth and realized he must have bitten his tongue when the first bomb went off. He felt bruised all over. Vaguely, he wondered if he might be hurt more than he actually knew.

He reached the fence—it was made of barbed wire

and carried another sign: DANGER, KEEP OUT. Alex almost smiled. What danger could there possibly be on the other side that was worse than this? As if to answer the question, there were three more explosions no more than a hundred yards behind him. Something hot struck Alex on the back of the neck. Without hesitating, he rolled under the fence, then got up and continued running across the ground on the other side.

He was in a field. There was still no sign of the ocean. He was surrounded by trees on all four sides. He slowed down and tried to take his bearings. His neck hurt. He had been burned by the little fragment of whatever it was that had hit him. He wondered if Scooter and the others were looking for him. He would certainly have a few things to say to them . . . if he ever got out of here alive.

He continued forward. His foot came down on something small and metallic. He heard—and felt—it click underneath his sole. He stopped. And at the same time, a voice came out of the darkness just behind him.

"Don't move. Don't even move a step . . ."

Out of the corner of his eye, he saw a figure roll underneath the fence. At first he thought it must be Scooter—but he hadn't recognized the voice, and a few seconds later he saw that it was an older man with black, curly hair and the beginnings of a rough beard, dressed in full military gear and carrying an assault rifle. The bombs and the shelling seemed to have faded into the distance. They must have been redirected at a target farther away.

The man loomed up next to him, looking at him with unbelieving eyes. "Who the hell are you?" he asked. "How did you get here?"

"What am I standing on?" Alex demanded. Part of him knew the answer. He hadn't dared look down.

"The field is mined," the man replied briefly. He knelt down. Alex felt the man's hand press gently against his sneaker. Then the man straightened up. His eyes were dark brown and bleak. "You're standing on a mine," he said.

Alex was almost tempted to laugh. A sense of disbelief shivered through him and he swayed a little, as if he were about to faint.

"Stay exactly as you are!" the man shouted. "Stand up straight. Don't move from side to side. If you release the pressure, you're going to kill both of us."

"Who are you?" Alex exclaimed. "What's going on here? Why is there a mine?"

"Didn't you see the sign?"

"It just said danger—keep out."

"What more did you need?" The man shook his head. "You shouldn't be anywhere near here. How did you get here? What are you doing out here in the middle of the night?"

"I was brought here." Alex could feel a cold numbness creeping through his leg. It got worse, the more he thought about what lay beneath his foot. "Can you help me?" he asked.

"Stay still." The man knelt down a second time. He had produced a flashlight. He shone it on the ground. It seemed to take an age, but then he spoke again. "It's a butterfly," he said, and there was no emotion in his voice at all. "They call it that because of its shape. It's a Soviet PFM-1, pressure-sensitive blast mine. You're standing on enough high explosive to take your leg off."

"What's it doing here?" Alex cried. He had to fight the instinct to lift his foot off the deadly thing. His entire body was screaming at him to run away.

"They train us!" the man rasped. "They use these things in Iraq and Indonesia. We have to know how to deal with them. How else are they going to do it?"

"But in the middle of a field . . . ?"

"You shouldn't be here! Who brought you here?" The man straightened up. He was standing very close to Alex, the brown eyes boring into him. "I can't neutralize it," he muttered. "Even if I had the training, I couldn't risk it in the dark."

"So what do we do now?"

"I'm going to have to get help."

"Do you have a radio?"

"If I had a radio, I'd have already used it." The man laid a hand briefly on Alex's shoulder. "There's something else you need to know," he said. He was speaking softly. His mouth was next to Alex's ear. "These things have a delay mechanism . . . a separate fuse that you'll have activated when you stepped on it."

"You mean—it's going to blow up anyway?"

"In fifteen minutes."

"How long will it take you to find someone?"

"I'll move as quickly as I can. If you hear a click—you'll feel it under your foot—throw yourself flat onto the ground. It's your only hope. Good luck . . ."

"Wait . . . ," Alex began.

But the man had already gone. Alex hadn't even asked him his name.

Alex stood there. He had lost any sense of feeling in his leg, but his shoulder was burning and he was beginning to shiver violently as the shock set in. He forced himself to bring his body back under control, afraid that the slightest movement could bring a hideous end to this ordeal. He could imagine the sudden flash, the pain, his leg separated from his body. And the worst of it was that there was nothing he could do. His foot was glued to the device that was ticking away, even now, beneath him. He looked around. Although he hadn't noticed it before, the mine had been placed on the top of a ridge, the ground sloping away steeply to a ditch at the bottom. Alex tried to work out the distances. If he threw himself sideways, could he reach the ditch before the mine exploded? And if the force of the blast was above him, would he escape the worst of it?

The bombing had stopped. Suddenly everything was very still. Once again Alex experienced the sense of being completely alone, standing like a scarecrow in the middle of an empty field. He wanted to call out but was afraid to, in case he accidentally shifted his body weight. How long had it been since the man had left? Five minutes? Ten? And how accurate was the timer anyway? The mine could go off at any time.

So did he wait? Or did he take his life into his own hands? Alex made his decision.

He took a deep breath, tensing his body, trying to think of the muscles in his legs as coiled springs that could launch him to safety. His right foot was resting on the mine. The left foot was on flat ground. That was the one that would have to do most of the work. *Do it!* Alex had to force himself, knowing that he might be making the worst mistake of his life, that seconds from now he could be crippled, in agony.

He jumped.

At the very last moment he changed his mind but continued anyway, launching himself down the slope with all his strength. He thought he felt the mine shudder very slightly as his foot left it. But it hadn't exploded, at least not in the half second that he had left the ground. Automatically, he crossed his arms in front of his face, to protect himself from the fall—or from the blast. The slope was rushing past him, a dark streak at the corner of his vision. Then he hit the ditch. Water, cold and muddy, splattered into his face. His shoulder hit something hard. Behind him, there was an explosion. The mine. Clumps of earth and torn grass rained down on him. Then nothing.

His face was underwater. He pulled his head back, spitting mud. A plume of smoke rose into the night sky. The fuse must have given him three seconds before it detonated the mine. He had taken those three seconds and they had saved him.

He got unsteadily to his feet. Water was dripping out of his hair and down his face. His heart was pounding. He felt drained, exhausted. Briefly he lost his balance, put a hand out to steady himself, and winced as he caught it on the barbed wire fence. But at least he had found his way out of here. He rolled back underneath and tried to work out which way to go. Seconds later, the question was answered for him. He heard the sound of an engine, saw two beams of light cutting through the trees. His name was being called out. He hurried forward and found a track.

The four SAS men were in the jeep. This time X-Ray was driving. They were rolling slowly through the wood, searching for him. Alex saw that they had left the coolers behind. But Sparks had remembered his guitar.

"Alex!" X-Ray slammed on the brakes and at the same time Scooter leapt out of the passenger seat. He looked genuinely concerned, his face white in the glare of the headlights. "Are you okay? Jesus! We completely screwed up. We've got to get out of here. We shouldn't be anywhere near."

"I told you . . . ," X-Ray began.

"Not now!" Scooter snapped. He grabbed hold of

Alex. "As soon as the bombs went off, I knew what had happened. I looked for you, but we must have got separated. You look terrible, mate. Are you hurt?"

"No." Alex didn't trust himself to say any more.

"Get in. We'll get you home. I don't know what to say to you. We're complete idiots. We could have gotten you killed."

This time Alex took the front seat. Scooter climbed in the back with the others, and they set off back down the track and out toward the main road. Alex still wasn't sure what had just happened—how the SAS men had managed to get themselves into this mess. Nor did he care. He allowed the noise of the engine and the cool night air to drift away, and seconds later he was sound asleep.

5

ON THE ROCKS

TWO DAYS LATER, ALEX had put his experiences at Swanbourne behind him. He was sitting outside a café in Sydney, the opera house on one side, the great stretch of the Harbour Bridge on the other. It was the world's favorite postcard view, and he had seen it many times. But now he was actually in it, eating vanilla-and-strawberry ice cream and watching as the Manly ferry came grinding into the dock, scattering the smaller craft all around it. The sun was beating down and the sky was a dazzling blue. It was hard to believe that he was really here.

And he wasn't alone. Jack had joined him the day before, bleary-eyed with jet lag but awake and bursting with excitement the moment she saw him. It had taken her twenty-six hours to get here, and Alex knew she would have been worrying all the way. Jack was meant to look after him. She hated it when he was away—and this time he had never been farther. From the very start she had made it clear that all she wanted was to get him onto a plane and take him back to London. Yes, it was cold and drizzling there. The English winter had already arrived. Yes, they both deserved a vacation. But it was time to go home.

Jack was also eating ice cream, and although she was

twenty-eight, she suddenly looked younger with her untidy red hair, her lopsided smile, and her brightly colored kangaroo T-shirt. More a big sister than a housekeeper. And above all a friend.

"I don't know why it's taking so long," she was saying. "It's ridiculous. By the time you get back, you'll have missed half the semester."

"They said they'd have it this afternoon."

"They should have had it two days ago."

They were talking about Alex's visa. That morning, Jack had taken a call at the hotel where they were both staying. They had been given an address, a government office in Macquarie Street, just past the old parliament building. The visa would be ready at four o'clock. Alex could pick it up then.

"Could we stay here a couple more days?" Alex asked.

Jack looked at him curiously. "Don't you want to go home?" she asked.

"Yes." Alex paused. "I suppose so. But at the same time . . . I'm not quite sure I'm ready to go back to school. I've been thinking about it. I'm sort of worried I'm not going to be able to fit in."

"Of course you'll fit in, Alex. You've got lots of friends. They've all been missing you. Once you're back, you'll forget any of this stuff ever happened."

But Alex wasn't so sure. He and Jack had talked about it the evening before. After all he had been through, how could he go back to geography lessons and school lunches and being told off for running too fast down the corridor? The day MI6 had recruited him, they had built a wall between him and his past life, and he wondered if there was now any way back.

"I've hardly been to school this year," he muttered. "I'm way behind."

"Maybe we can get Mr. Grey to come over this Christmas break," Jack suggested. Mr. Grey was the teacher who had given Alex extra tutoring during the summer. "You got along well with him, and he'd soon help you catch up."

"I don't know, Jack . . ." Alex looked at the ice cream, melting on his spoon. He wished he could explain how he felt. He didn't want to work for MI6 again. He was sure of that. But at the same time . . .

"It's three thirty," Jack said. "We ought to be on our way."

They got up and made their way along the side of the opera house and up into the botanical gardens—the incredible park that seemed to contain the city rather than the other way around. Looking back at the harbor, the bustle of life below, and the gleaming skyscrapers stretched out behind, Alex wondered how the Australians had managed to get it all so right. It was impossible not to love Sydney, and despite what Jack had said, he knew he wasn't ready to leave.

Together, the two of them made their way up past the

gallery of New South Wales and into Macquarie Street, where the parliament building stood, two stories high, an elegant construction of pink and white that somehow reminded Alex of the ice cream he had just eaten. The address they had been given was just beyond, a modern glass block that was presumably filled with minor government offices. The receptionist already had visitor passes waiting for them and directed them to the fourth floor and a room at the end of a corridor.

"I don't know why they couldn't have just put you on a plane and sent you out of here," Jack grumbled as they left the elevator. "It seems a lot of fuss about nothing."

There was a door ahead of them. They walked through without knocking and stopped dead in their tracks. There had obviously been some sort of mistake. Wherever they were, this certainly wasn't a visa office.

Two men were talking to each other in what looked like a library, with antique furniture and a Persian rug on a highly polished wooden floor—Alex's immediate impression was that the room didn't belong to the building it was in. A golden Labrador lay curled up on a cushion in front of a fireplace. One of the men was behind a desk. He was the older of the two, wearing a shirt and jacket and no tie. His eyes were concealed behind designer sunglasses. The other man was standing by the window with his arms folded. He was in his late twenties, thin and fairhaired, dressed in an expensive suit.

"Oh . . . I'm sorry," Jack began.

"Not at all, Miss Starbright," the man behind the desk replied. "Please come in."

"We're looking for the visa office," Jack said.

"Sit down. I take it Alex is with you? The question may seem odd, but I'm blind."

"I'm here," Alex said.

"Who are you?" Jack asked. She and Alex had moved farther into the room. The younger man came over and closed the door behind them.

"My name is Ethan Brooke. My colleague here is Marc Damon. Thank you very much for coming in, Miss Starbright. Do you mind if I call you Jack? Please—take a seat."

There were two leather chairs in front of the desk. Feeling increasingly uncomfortable, Jack sat down. The man called Damon walked across and took a third seat at the side. Next to the fireplace, the dog's tail thumped twice against the wooden floor.

"I know you're in a hurry to get back to London," Brooke began. "But let me explain why the two of you are here. The fact of the matter is, we need a little help."

"You want our help?" Jack looked around her. Suddenly it all made sense. "You want Alex." She spoke the words heavily. She knew now who the men were, or at least what they represented. She had met their type before.

"We'd like to make Alex a proposition," Brooke agreed.

"Forget it. He's not interested."

"Won't you at least listen to what we have to say?" Brooke spread his hands. He looked completely reasonable. He could have been a bank manager advising them on their mortgage or a family lawyer about to read a will.

"We want the visa."

"You'll have it. As soon as I'm done."

Alex had said nothing. Jack looked at him, then turned to Brooke and Damon with anger in her eyes. "Why can't you people leave him alone?" she demanded.

"Because he's special. In fact, I'd say he's unique. And right now we need him, just for a week or two. But I promise you, Jack. If he's not interested, he can walk out of here. We can have him on a plane tonight. Just give me a minute to explain."

"Who are you?" Alex asked.

Brooke glanced at Damon. "We work for ASIS," the younger man replied. "The Australian Secret Intelligence Service."

"Special Operations?"

"Covert Action. The two are more or less the same. You could say that we're the rough equivalent of the outfit that Alan Blunt runs in London."

"I've read your file, Alex," Brooke added. "I have to say, I'm impressed."

"What do you want me for?" Alex demanded.

"I'll tell you."

Brooke folded his hands, and to Alex it seemed some-how inevitable, unsurprising, even. It had happened to him six times before. Why not again?

"Have you ever heard the term *snakehead*?" Brooke began. There was silence, so he went on. "All right, let me start by saying that the snakehead groups are without doubt the biggest and most dangerous criminal organiza-tions in the world. Compared to them, the mafia and the triads are amateurs. They have more influence—and they're doing more damage—even than Al Qaeda, but they're not interested in religion. They have no beliefs. All they want is money. That's the bottom line. They're gangsters, but on a huge scale.

"Have you ever bought an illegal DVD? The chances are that it was manufactured and distributed by a snake-head. And the profits they'll have made out of it will have gone straight into one of their other concerns, which you may not find so amusing. Maybe it's drugs or slaves or body parts. You need a new kidney or a heart? The snake-heads operate the biggest market in illegal organs, and they're not fussy about where they get them or even if the donors are deceased. And then there are weapons. In this century alone, there have been at least fifty wars around the world that have used weapons supplied by the snake-heads . . . shoulder-launched missiles, AK-47s, that sort of thing. Where do you think the terrorists go if they want a bomb or a gun or something nasty and biological that comes in a test tube? Think of it as an international supermarket, Alex. But everything it sells is bad.

"What else can you buy? You name it! Paintings stolen from museums. Diamonds mined illegally using slave labor. Ancient artifacts plundered from Iraq. Elephant's tusks or tiger skin rugs. A few years ago a hundred kids died on the island of Haiti because someone had sold them cough medicine that happened to contain antifreeze. That was a snakehead—and I don't think they offered anyone their money back.

"But the biggest moneymaker for the snakeheads is people smuggling. You probably have no idea how many people there are being smuggled from one country to another all around the world. These are some of the poorest families in the world, desperate to build themselves a new life in the West. Some of them are fleeing hopelessness and starvation. Others are threatened in their own countries with prison and torture." Brooke paused and looked directly at Alex, fixing him with his sightless eyes. "Half of them are under the age of eighteen," he said. "About five percent of them are younger than you—and they're traveling on their own. The lucky ones get picked up by the authorities. What happens to the rest of them . . . you don't want to know.

"Illegal immigration is a huge problem for Australia, and the people smugglers just make it worse. The immigrants want to break in, and the smugglers sell them tickets. Many of them start in Iraq and Afghanistan. They come in boats from Bali, Flores, Lombok, and Jakarta. What's sad is that my country used to welcome immigrants. We were all of us once immigrants ourselves. All of that's changed now—and I have to say, the way we treat these people leaves a lot to be desired. But what can we do? The answer is, we have to stop them from coming. And one of the main ways to do that is to take on the snakeheads face-to-face.

"There's one snakehead in particular. It operates throughout Indonesia, and it's more powerful and more dangerous than any of them. As it happens, we know the name of the man in charge. A certain Major Yu. But that's all we've managed to find out. We don't know what he looks like or where he lives. Twice now, we've tried to infiltrate the organization. We put agents inside, pretending to be customers."

"What happened to them?" Jack asked.

"They both died." It was Damon who had answered the question.

"And so now I suppose you're thinking about sending Alex."

"We have no idea how our agents were uncovered," Brooke went on. It was as if Jack hadn't spoken. "Somehow this man—Yu—seems to know everything we're doing. Either that, or he's very careful. The trouble is, these gangs operate under a system known as *guanxi*. Basically, it means that everyone knows everyone. They're like a family. And the fact is, a single agent, coming in from outside and operating on his own, is too obvious. We need to get inside the snakehead in a way that is completely original and also above suspicion."

"A man and a boy," Damon said.

"We have an agent in Bangkok now. We've set him up as a refugee from Afghanistan planning to be smuggled into Australia. He'll meet with the snakehead and gather names, faces, phone numbers, addresses . . . anything he can. But he won't be on his own. He'll be traveling with his son."

"We'll fly you to Bangkok," Damon continued, speaking directly to Alex. "You'll join our agent there, and the two of you will be passed down the pipeline back here. And here's the deal. As soon as you're back on Australian soil, we'll send you first class direct to England. You won't have to do anything, Alex. But you'll provide perfect cover for our man. He'll get the information we need, and maybe we'll be able to break up Yu's network once and for all."

"Why Bangkok?" There were a hundred questions Alex could have asked. This was the first one that came to his mind.

"Bangkok is a major center for the sale of false documents," Damon replied. "In fact, we'd very much like to know who supplies Yu's people with fake passports, export certificates, and the rest of it. And now we have a chance. Our agent was told to wait there until he was contacted. He'll be given the papers he needs, and then he'll continue the journey south."

There was a brief silence.

Then Jack Starbright shook her head. "All right," she said. "We've listened to your proposition, Mr. Brooke. Now you can listen to my answer. It's NO! Forget it! You said it yourself. These people are dangerous. Two of your spies have already been killed. There's no way I'm going to allow Alex into that."

Alex glanced briefly at Jack. She hadn't given him a chance to speak, and he understood why. She had been afraid of what he might say.

Brooke seemed to have picked up on that too. "I'd have thought after all Alex has been through, he could have made up his own mind," he said.

"He can make up his own mind. And I'm telling you what he's going to say. The answer's no!"

"There is one thing we haven't mentioned." Brooke rested his hands on his desk. His face gave nothing away, but Damon knew what was about to come. His boss was the poker player, preparing to show his hand. "I didn't tell you the name of our agent in Bangkok."

"And who is that?" Jack asked.

"You know him, I think. His name is Ash."

Jack sat back, unable to keep the shock out of her eyes. "Ash?" she faltered.

"That's right."

Alex had seen the effect the name had had on her. "Who's Ash?" he demanded.

"You don't know him?" Brooke was enjoying himself now, though of all the people in the room, only Damon could see it. He turned to Jack. "Maybe you'd like to explain."

"Ash was someone who knew your dad," Jack muttered.

"He was rather more than that," Brooke corrected her. "Ash was John Rider's closest friend. He was the best man at your parents' wedding. He's also your godfather, Alex."

"My . . . ?" Alex couldn't believe what he'd just heard. He hadn't even known he had a godfather.

"For what it's worth, he was also the last person to see your parents alive," Brooke went on. "He was actually with them the morning they died. He was at the airport when they got on the plane for the south of France."

The plane had never arrived. There had been a bomb on board, placed there as an act of revenge by the criminal organization known as Scorpia. That much Alex knew.

"Did you meet him?" Alex gazed at Jack. He was feeling completely disoriented, as if the ground had just been stolen from under his feet. She looked exactly the same.

"I met him a few times," Jack replied. "It was just after I started working for your uncle. He used to come around and visit. You were the one he wanted to see. I knew he was your godfather."

"How come you've never mentioned him to me?"

"He disappeared. You must have been about four years old. He told me he was emigrating, and I never saw him again."

"Ash was an agent with MI6," Brooke explained. "That was how he and your father met. They worked together as a team. Your dad even saved his life once—in Malta. You can ask him about that . . . if you meet. I think the two of you would have a lot to talk about."

"How can you do this?" Jack whispered. She was looking at Brooke with utter contempt.

"Ash left MI6 and emigrated here," Brooke continued. "He came with great references, so we were happy to take him on at ASIS. He's been with us ever since. Right now he's in Bangkok, undercover—like I said. But there's nobody better placed to pretend to be your father, Alex. I mean, he's almost that already. He'll look after you. And I think you'll find him interesting. What do you say?"

Alex said nothing. He had already made up his mind, but somehow he knew that Brooke wouldn't need to be told. He had figured that out for himself.

"I need time," he said at length.

"Sure. Why don't you and Jack go and talk about it?" Brooke nodded, and Damon produced a white card. He must have had it ready in his pocket from the very start. "Here's a number where you can reach me. We'll need to fly you into Bangkok tomorrow. So maybe you could call me sometime tonight?"

. . .

"I know what you're thinking, but you can't possibly go," Jack said. "It's wrong."

Alex and Jack had wandered over to The Rocks, the little cluster of shops and cafés that nestled on the very edge of the harbor, right underneath the bridge. Jack had brought them here on purpose. She wanted to mingle with the crowds somewhere bright and ordinary, a world apart from the hidden truths and half-lies of the Australian secret service.

"I think I have to," Alex replied.

And it was true. Only an hour ago, he had been promising himself that he would never work for MI6 again. But this was different—and not just because it was the Australians that were asking him this time. It was Ash. Ash made all the difference, even though the two of them had never met and it was a name he had only just heard for the first time.

"Ash can tell me who I am," he said.

"Don't you know who you are?" Jack asked.

"Not really, Jack. I thought I knew. When Ian was alive, everything seemed so simple. But then when I found out the truth about him, it all went wrong. All my life he was training me to be something I never wanted. But maybe he was right. Maybe it was what I was always meant to be."

"You think Ash can tell you?"

"I don't know." Alex squinted at Jack. The sunlight was streaming over her shoulders. "When did you meet him?" he asked.

"It was about a month after I started working for your uncle," she said. "At the time, it was just meant to be a vacation job, to support myself while I was doing my studies. I didn't know anything about spies, and I certainly didn't know I'd be sticking with you forever!" She sighed. "You were about seven years old. Do you really not remember him?"

Alex shook his head.

"He was in London for a few weeks, staying in a hotel. But he came over to the house two or three times. Now I come to think of it, he never did talk to you very much. Maybe he felt awkward with kids. But I got to know him a bit."

"What was he like?"

Jack thought back. "I liked him," she admitted. "In fact, if you want the truth, I even went out with him a couple of times although he was quite a lot older than me. He was very good-looking. And there was something dangerous about him. He told me he was a deep-sea diver. He was fun to have around."

"Is Ash his real name?"

"It's what he calls himself. ASH are his initials—but he never told me what they stood for."

"And he's really my godfather?"

Jack nodded. "I've seen photos of him at your christening. And Ian knew him. The two of them were friends. I never knew what he was doing in London, but he was eager to check up on you. He wanted to be sure you were okay."

Alex drew a deep breath. "You don't know what it's like, not having parents," he began. "It never used to bother me because I was so small when they died and I had Uncle Ian. But now I wonder about them. And it sometimes feels like there's a hole in my life, a sort of emptiness. I look back, but there's nothing there. Maybe if I spend some time with this man—even if I do have to dress up like an Afghan refugee—maybe it'll fill something in for me."

"But Alex . . ." Jack looked at him, and he could see she was afraid. "You heard what that man said. This could be terribly dangerous. You've been lucky so far, but your luck can't last forever. These people—the snakehead—they sound horrible. You shouldn't get involved."

"I have to, Jack. Ash worked with my dad. He was with him the day he died. I didn't know he existed until today, but now I've got to meet him." Alex forced a smile to his lips. "My dad was a spy. My uncle was a spy. And now it turns out I've got a godfather who's a spy. You have to admit, it certainly runs in the family."

Jack rested her hands on Alex's shoulders. Behind them, the sun was already setting, reflecting bloodred in the water. The shops were beginning to empty. The bridge hung over them, casting a dark shadow.

"Is there anything I can say to stop you?" she asked.

"Yes." Alex looked her straight in the eyes. "But please don't."

"All right." She nodded. "But I'll be worried sick about you. You know that. Just make sure you look after yourself. And tell Ash from me that I want you home by Christmas. And maybe this time, just for once, he'll remember to send a card."

Quickly, she turned around and continued walking. Alex waited a minute, then followed. Bangkok. The snakehead. Another mission. The truth was that Alex had always suspected it might happen—but even he hadn't thought it would come so soon.

6

CITY OF ANGELS?

TWENTY-FOUR HOURS LATER, Alex touched down at Suvarnabhumi International Airport in Bangkok. Even the name warned him that he had arrived at the gateway to a world that would be completely alien to him. For all his travels, he had never been to the East, and yet now, following the thirteen-hour flight from Sydney, he was on his own. Jack had wanted to travel with him but he had decided against it. He'd found it easier to say good-bye to her at the hotel. He knew that he needed time to prepare himself for what might lie ahead.

He had met once more with Brooke and Damon the night before. There hadn't been much more to say. Alex was booked into a room at the Peninsula Hotel in Bangkok. A driver would meet him at the airport and take him there. Ash would meet him as soon as he arrived.

"You realize we'll have to disguise you," Brooke said. "You don't look anything like an Afghan."

"And I don't speak their language," Alex added.

"That's not a problem. You're a child and a refugee. No one will be expecting you to say anything."

The flight had seemed endless. ASIS had booked him in business class, but in a way that made him feel all the more alienated and alone. He watched a movie, ate a meal, and rested. But nobody spoke to him. He was in a strange metal bubble, surrounded by strangers, being carried once again toward danger and possible death. Alex looked out the window at the gray-pink light glowing at the edge of the world and wondered. Was he making a mistake? He could get another plane at Bangkok and be back in London in twelve hours. But he had made his decision. This wasn't about ASIS or the snakehead.

"He was the last person to see your parents alive."

Alex remembered what Brooke had told him. He was about to meet his father's best friend. His godfather. This wasn't just a flight from one country to another. It was a journey into his own past.

The 747 rumbled into its gate. The Fasten Your Seat Belt signs blinked off and the passengers stood up as one, scrabbling for the overhead bins. Alex had one small suitcase and quickly passed through immigration and customs and out into the hot, sticky air of the arrivals area. Suddenly he found himself in a crowd of shouting, gesticulating people.

"Taxi! Taxi!"

"You want hotel?"

It felt strange emerging from business class into this. He was suddenly back in the noise and chaos of the real world. Down to earth in more senses than one.

And then he saw his name, being held on a placard by a Thai man—black-haired, short, casually dressed like almost everyone around him. Alex went over to him.

"Are you Alex? Mr. Ash send me to collect you. I hope you had a good flight. The car is outside . . ."

It was as they made their way out of the airport that Alex noticed the man with the poppy in his buttonhole. It was the poppy that first drew his attention. Of course, it was November. Remembrance Sunday, when the whole of England wore poppies and held two minutes' silence for those killed in wars, would be taking place in England sometime around now. It was just strange to see any sign of it out here.

The man was wearing jeans and a leather jacket. He was European, in his twenties, with dark hair cut short and watchful eyes. He had very square features with high cheekbones and narrow lips. The man had stopped dead in his tracks and seemed to be staring at something on the other side of the arrivals area. It took Alex a moment to realize that the man's attention was actually fixed on him. Did the two of them know each other from somewhere? He was just asking himself the question when a crowd of people moved between the two of them, making for the exit. When the floor cleared again, the man had gone.

He must have imagined it. Alex was tired after the long flight. Maybe the man had simply been one of the other passengers on the plane. He followed the driver to the parking garage, and a few minutes later they were on the wide, three-lane highway that led into Bangkok—or, as the Thai people called it, *Krung Thep.* City of Angels.

Sitting in the back of the air-conditioned sedan, gazing out the window, Alex wondered quite how it had gotten that name. He certainly wasn't impressed by his first sight of the city, a sprawl of ugly, old-fashioned skyscrapers, blocks of apartments that were like discarded boxes piled up on top of each other, electricity and satellite towers. They stopped at a toll booth where a woman sat in a cramped cubicle, her face hidden behind the white mask that protected her from the traffic fumes. Then they were off again. Next to the road, Alex saw a huge portrait of a man: black hair, glasses, open-neck shirt. It was painted on the entire side of a building, twenty stories high, covering both the brickwork and the windows.

"That's our king," the driver explained.

Alex looked again at the figure. What would it be like, he wondered, to work at a desk inside that office? To pound away at a computer for eight or nine hours a day but to look out at Bangkok through the eyes of a king.

They left the highway, driving down a ramp into a dense, chaotic world of shrubs and food stalls, traffic jams and policemen at every intersection, their whistles screaming like dying birds. Alex saw *tuk-tuks*—motorized rickshaws—bicycles and buses that looked as if they had been welded together from a dozen different models. He felt a hollow feeling in his stomach. What was he letting himself into? How was he going to adapt to a country that was, in every last detail, so different from his own?

Then the car turned a corner. They had entered the

driveway of the Peninsula Hotel and Alex learned something else about Bangkok. It was actually two cities: one very poor and one very rich, living side by side and yet with a great gulf between. His journey had brought him from one to the other. Now he was driving through a beautifully tended tropical garden. As they drew up at the front door, half a dozen Thai men in perfect white uniforms hurried forward to help—one to take the luggage, one to help Alex out, two more bowing to welcome him, two holding open the hotel doors.

The cold embrace of the hotel air-conditioning reached out to welcome him. Alex crossed a wide marble floor toward the reception area with piano music tinkling somewhere in the background. He was handed a garland of flowers by a smiling receptionist. Nobody seemed to have noticed that he was only fourteen. He was a guest. That was all that mattered. His key was already waiting for him. He was shown into an elevator—itself the size of a small room. The doors slid shut. Only the pressure in his ears told him that they had begun the journey up.

His room was on the nineteenth floor.

Ten minutes later, he stood in front of a floor-to-ceiling window, looking at the view. His suitcase was on his bed. He had been shown the luxury bathroom, the wide-screen TV, the well-stocked fridge, and the complimentary basket of exotic fruit. Alex tried to shrug off the heavy fingers of jet lag. He knew he had little enough time to prepare himself for what lay ahead.

The city was spread out on the other side of a wide brown river that curved and twisted as far as he could see. Skyscrapers stood in the far distance. Nearer by, there were hotels, temples, palaces with perfect lawns, and— standing side by side with them—shacks and slum houses and warehouses so dilapidated they looked as if they might fall over at any time. All manner of boats were making their way up and down the murky water. Some were modern, carrying coal and iron. Some were ferries with strange, curving roofs, like floating pagodas. The nimblest were elongated, long and wafer thin with the driver leaning wearily over the tiller at the very back. The sun was setting. The sky was huge and gray. It was like looking at a television screen with the color turned off.

The telephone rang. Alex went over and picked it up.

"Hello? Is that Alex?" It was a man's voice. He could make out a slight Australian accent.

"Yes," Alex replied.

"You arrived okay then?"

"Yes, thanks."

"I'm in the reception area. You feel like a bit of dinner?"

Alex wasn't hungry, but that didn't matter. Even though the man hadn't introduced himself, he knew who he was talking to. "I'll come right down," he said.

He hadn't had time to shower or change after the flight. It would just have to wait. Alex left the room and took the elevator back down. It stopped twice on the way, letting people in on the ninth and seventh floors. Alex stood silently in the corner. He was suddenly nervous, although he wasn't quite sure why. Finally, they arrived. The elevator doors opened.

Ash was standing in the reception area, dressed in a blue linen jacket, a white shirt, and jeans. There were plenty of other people around, but Alex recognized him instantly, and somehow he wasn't even surprised.

They had met before. Ash was the soldier in Swanbourne, the man who had told him he was standing on a grenade.

"It was all a setup, wasn't it?" Alex said. "The training exercise. The minefield. All of it."

"Yeah." Ash nodded. "I expect that must make you pretty annoyed."

"You could say that," Alex growled.

There was an eating area just outside the hotel, softly lit, with the river in front of them and a long, narrow swimming pool to one side. The two of them were sitting at a table, facing each other. Ash had a Singha beer. He had ordered Alex a fruit cocktail: orange, pineapple, and guava blended with crushed ice. It was almost dark now, but Alex could still feel the heat of the evening pressing down on him. He realized it was going to take time to get used to the climate in Bangkok. The air was like syrup.

He looked again at his godfather, the man who had played such a major part in his early life. Ash was leaning back with his legs stretched out, untroubled by the trick that had been played at the beach near Swanbourne. Out of uniform, with his shirt open and a silver chain glinting around his neck, he looked nothing at all like a soldier or a spy. He was more like a movie star with his long, black hair, rough beard, and suntanned skin. Physically, he was slim—*wiry* was the word that sprang to Alex's mind. Fast-moving rather than particularly strong. He had brown eyes that were very dark, and Alex guessed he could easily play the part of an Afghan. He certainly didn't look European.

There was something else about him that Alex found harder to place. A certain guarded quality in the eyes, a sense of tension. He might look relaxed, but he never would be. He had been touched by something at some time, and it would never let him go.

"So why did you do it?" Alex asked.

"It was a test, Alex. Why do you think?" Ash had a soft, lilting voice. The eight years he had spent in Australia had given him an accent, but Alex could hear the English there too. "ASIS wasn't going to use a fourteen-year-old boy—not even you. Not unless they were damn sure that you weren't going to panic at the first sign of danger."

"I didn't panic with Drevin. Or with Scorpia . . ."

"The snakeheads are different. You have no idea what sort of people we're up against. Didn't they tell you? They've already killed two agents. The first one came back minus his head. They sent the second one back in an envelope. They'd had him cremated to save us the trouble." Ash drank his beer and signaled to the waiter for another. "I had to see for myself that you were up to the job," he went on. "We set up a situation that would have terrorized any normal kid. Then we watched how you dealt with it."

"I could have been killed." Alex remembered how the first bomb had blown him off his feet.

"You weren't in any real danger. All the missiles were launched with pinpoint accuracy. We knew exactly where you were all the time."

"How?"

Ash smiled. "There was a beacon inside the heel of one of your sneakers. Colonel Abbott arranged that while you were asleep. It sent out a signal to the nearest inch."

"What about the mine?"

"It had less explosive in it than you probably thought. And it was activated by remote control. I set it off a couple of seconds after you made that dive. You did pretty well, by the way."

"You were watching me all the time."

"Just put it behind you, Alex. It was a test. You passed. That's all that matters."

The waiter arrived with the second beer. Ash lit a

cigarette—Alex was surprised to see that he smoked—
and blew smoke out into the warm evening air.

"I can't believe we're finally meeting," he said. He examined Alex closely. "You look a hell of a lot like your dad."

"You were close to him."

"Yeah. We were close."

"And my mother."

"I don't want to talk about them, Alex." Ash shifted
uncomfortably, then reached out and drank some of his
beer. "Do you mind? It was all a long time ago. My life's
moved on since then."

"It's the only reason I'm here," Alex said.

There was a long silence. Then Ash smiled briefly.
"How's that housekeeper of yours?" he asked. "Jack
What's-her-name. Is she still with you?"

"Yes. She said hello."

"She was an attractive girl. I liked her. I'm glad she
stuck by you."

"You didn't."

"Well . . . I moved on." Ash paused. Then suddenly he
leaned forward. His face was utterly serious and Alex saw
that this was a tough, cold-hearted man and that he was
going to have to watch himself when they were together.

"All right. This is how we're going to play it," he
began. "You're in this smart luxury hotel because I wanted
to ease you in. But tomorrow that all comes to an end.
We're going to have breakfast, and then we're going up to

your room and you're going to become an Afghan boy, a refugee. We're going to change the way you look, the way you walk, and even the way you smell. And then we're going out there . . ." He pointed across the river. "You enjoy your bed tonight, Alex, because where you sleep tomorrow night is going to be very different. And trust me. You're not going to like it."

He lifted the cigarette and inhaled. Gray smoke curled out of the corner of his mouth.

"We should make contact with the snakehead in the next forty-eight hours," he went on. "I'll explain all that tomorrow. But this is what you've got to understand. You do nothing and you say nothing unless I tell you. You play dumb. And if I think the situation is getting out of hand, if I think you're in danger, you'll clear out. With no argument. Do you understand?"

"Yes." Alex was taken aback. This wasn't what he had expected. It wasn't what he'd flown six thousand miles to hear.

Ash softened. "But I'll make you this promise. We're going to be spending a lot of time together, and when I feel I know you better, when the time is right, I'll tell you everything you want to know. About your father. About what happened in Malta. About your mother and about you. The only thing I'll never talk to you about is the way they died. I was there and I saw it and I don't want to remember it. Is that okay with you?"

Alex nodded.

"Right. Then let's get some food in us. I forgot to mention . . . the stuff you're going to eat from now on may not be to your taste either. And you can tell me a bit about yourself. I'd like to know what school you go to and if you have a girlfriend and things like that. Let's enjoy the evening. There may not be a lot of fun ahead."

Ash picked up his menu, and Alex did the same. But before he could read it, a movement caught his eye. It was just chance, really. The hotel had a private ferry that ran between the two banks of the river—a wide, spacious boat with antique chairs placed at intervals on a polished wooden floor. It had just arrived, and it was the roar of the engine going into reverse that had made Alex look up.

A man was just climbing aboard. Alex thought he recognized him and his suspicion was confirmed when the man turned around and looked purposefully in his direction. The poppy had gone, but it was the man from the airport. He was sure of it. A coincidence? The man hurried on board, disappearing underneath the canopy as if anxious to get out of sight, and Alex knew that there was no chance about it. The man had spotted him in the arrivals area and followed him here.

Alex wondered if he should mention it to Ash. Almost at once he decided against it. It was impossible for the snakehead to know that he was here, and if he made a fuss, if Ash decided he had been compromised, he might be sent home before the mission had even begun. No.

Much better to keep quiet. But if he saw the man a third time, then he would speak out.

So Alex said nothing. He didn't even watch as the ferry began its crossing back to the other side. Nor did he hear the click of the camera with its special night scope and long-distance lens trained on him as his picture was taken again and again in the dwindling light.

7

FATHER AND SON

THE NEXT MORNING, ALEX ate the best breakfast of his life. He had a feeling he was going to need it. The hotel offered a hot-and-cold buffet that included just about every cuisine—French, English, Thai, Vietnamese—with dishes ranging from eggs and bacon to stir-fried noodles. Ash joined him but spoke little. He seemed to be deep in thought, and Alex wondered if he wasn't already having reservations about what lay ahead.

"You've had enough?" he asked as Alex finished his second croissant.

Alex nodded.

"Then let's go up to your room. Mrs. Webber will be here soon. We'll wait for her there."

Alex had no idea who Mrs. Webber was, and it didn't seem that Ash wanted to tell him. The two of them went back up to the nineteenth floor. Ash hung the Do Not Disturb sign on the door and pointed Alex to a seat next to a window. He sat down opposite.

"Okay," he began. "Let me tell you how this works. Two weeks ago, working with the Pakistani authorities, ASIS managed to pick up a father and a son heading into India on their way here. We interrogated them and discovered they'd paid the snakehead four thousand American dollars to get them into Australia. The father's name is Karim. The son is Abdul. Get used to the names, Alex, because from now on that's you and me. Karim and Abdul Hassan. The two of them were given an address in Bangkok. They were told to wait there until they were contacted by a man called Sukit."

"Who's he?"

"It took us a while to find out. But it turns out we're talking about a Mr. Anan Sukit. He works for Major Yu. One of his lieutenants, you might say. Very high up. Very dangerous. It means we're one step down the pipeline, Alex. We're on our way."

"So we wait for him to get in touch."

"Exactly."

"What about the real Adbul?" Alex asked. He wondered how he could pretend to be someone he had never even met.

"You don't need to know much about him or his father," Ash replied. "The two of them are Hazaras—a minority group in Afghanistan. The Hazaras have been persecuted for centuries. They get the worst education and the poorest jobs—in fact, most people think of them as hardly better than animals. *Kofr*—that's the word they use for them. It means 'infidel,' and in Afghanistan it's the worst four-letter word you can use about anyone."

"So where did they get their money?" Alex asked.

"They had a business in the city of Mazar that they managed to sell just before it was taken from them. They hid out in the Hindu Kush until they made contact with a local agent for the snakehead, paid the money, and began their journey south."

"I don't suppose I look anything like an Afghan," Alex said. "What do these Hazara people look like?"

"Most of them are Asiatic . . . Mongul or Chinese. But not all of them. In fact, a lot of them managed to survive in Afghanistan precisely because they didn't look too Eastern. Anyway, you don't need to worry. Mrs. Webber will take care of that."

"How about language?"

"You won't talk. Ever. You're going to pretend to be a simpleton. Just stare into the corner and keep your mouth shut. Try and look scared . . . as if I'm about to beat you. Maybe I will from time to time. Just to make us look authentic."

Alex wasn't sure if Ash was being serious or not.

"I speak Dari," Ash went on. "That's the language of the majority in Afghanistan and it's the language the snakehead will use. I speak a few words of Hazaragi too—but we shouldn't need them. Just remember. Never open your mouth. If you do, you'll kill us both."

Ash stood up. While he had been talking, he had been grim—almost hostile. But now he turned to Alex with something close to desperation in his dark brown eyes. "Alex . . ." He paused, scratching at his beard. "Are you sure you want to do this? ASIS has got nothing to do with you. People smuggling and all the rest of it . . . you should be at school. Why don't you just go home?"

"It's a little late now," Alex said. "I agreed. And I want you to tell me about my dad."

"Is that the main reason you agreed to this?"

"It's the only reason."

"I don't think I could forgive myself if anything happened to you. I'd be dead if it wasn't for your father. That's the truth of it." Ash looked away, as if trying to avoid the memory. "One day I'll tell you about it . . . Malta, and what happened after Yassen Gregorovich had finished with me. But I'll tell you this right now. John wouldn't thank me for getting you into trouble. In fact, he'd probably chew my head off. So if you'll take my advice, you'll call Brooke. Tell him you've changed your mind. And get out now."

"I'm staying," Alex said. "But thanks anyway."

In fact, what Ash had just said—the mention of Yassen Gregorovich—had made Alex determined to learn more. Suddenly things were beginning to come together.

Alex knew that his father, John Rider, had pretended to be an enemy agent, working for Scorpia. When MI6 wanted him back, they had arranged for him to be "captured." That had been in Malta. But it had all been a setup. And Yassen Gregorovich had been there. Yassen was an international assassin, and Alex had met him fourteen years later—first when he was working for Herod

Sayle, a second time inside the evil empire of Damian Cray. Yassen was dead now, but it seemed that he was still destined to be part of Alex's life. Ash had met him in Malta. And whatever had happened on that island was part of the story that Alex wanted to know.

"You're sure?" Ash asked him one last time.

"I'm sure," Alex said.

"Very well." Ash nodded gravely. "Then I'd better teach you this. *Ba'ad az ar tariki, roshani ast.* It's an old Afghan proverb, and there may come a time when you need to remember it. 'After every darkness there is light.' I hope it will be true for you."

There was a knock at the door.

Ash went over and opened it and a short, rather dumpy woman walked in, carrying a suitcase. She could have been a retired principal or perhaps a very old-fashioned schoolteacher. She was wearing a two-piece olive green suit and heavy stockings that only emphasized the fact that she had very shapeless legs. Her hair hung loose, with no apparent color or style. Her face could have been made of putty. She wore no makeup. There was a single brooch—a silver daisy—pinned to her lapel.

"How are you doing, Ash?" She smiled as she came in and that, along with her broad Australian accent, seemed to bring her to life.

"Good to see you, Cloudy," Ash replied. He closed the door. "This is Mrs. Webber, Alex," he explained. "She

works for ASIS—a specialist in disguise. Her name is
Chlöe, but we call her Cloudy. We think it suits her better. Cloudy Webber—meet Alex Rider."

The woman stumped over to Alex and examined him.
"Hmmm . . . ," she muttered disapprovingly. "Mr. Brooke
must need his head examined if he thinks we're going to
get away with this one. But I'll see what I can do." She
heaved the suitcase onto the bed. "Let's have all those
clothes off you, boy. Socks, boxers, the lot. The first thing
we're going to start with is your skin."

"Wait a minute . . . ," Alex began.

"For heaven's sake!" the woman exploded. "You think
I'm going to see anything I haven't seen before?" She
turned to Ash, who was watching from the other side of
the room. "And it's the same for you, Ash. I don't know
what you're grinning about. You may look a bit more like
an Afghan than him, but I'm going to have all your
clothes too."

She unzipped the suitcase and took out half a dozen
plastic bottles filled with various dark liquids. Next came
a hairbrush, a vanity bag, and several tubes that might
have contained toothpaste. The rest of the bag was packed
with clothes that looked—and smelled—as if they had
come out of a trash can.

"The clothes are all from the thrift store," she explained. "Donated in England and picked up in the
market in Mazar-i-Sharif. I'll give you two sets each,

which is all you'll need . . . you'll wear them day and night. Ash—go and run a bath." She unscrewed one of the bottles. The smell—seaweed and mineral spirits—reached Alex even on the other side of the room. "Cold water!" she added sharply.

In the end, she let Alex take a bath on his own. She had mixed two bottles of brown dye with half a bath of cold water. Alex was instructed to lie in it for ten minutes, submerging both his face and his hair. He was shivering by the time he was allowed out and he didn't dare look in the mirror as he dried himself—but he noticed that the hotel towels now looked as if they'd been dragged through a sewer. He pulled on a pair of ragged, shapeless boxers and came out.

"That's better," Mrs. Webber muttered. She noticed the scar just above his heart. It was where Alex had been shot and nearly killed by a sniper following his first encounter with Scorpia. "That might be useful too," she added. "A lot of Afghan boys have bullet wounds. Together, the two of you make quite a pair."

Alex didn't know what she meant. He glanced at Ash—and then he understood. Ash was just pulling on a shapeless, short-sleeved shirt, and for a moment his chest and stomach were exposed. He too had a scar—but it was much worse than Alex's, a distinct line of white, dead skin that snaked across his belly and down below the waistline of his trousers. Ash turned away, buttoning up the shirt, but he was too late. Alex had seen the terrible injury. It was a stab wound. He was sure of that. He wondered who had been holding the knife.

"Come and sit down, Alex," Mrs. Webber said. She had produced a tarp, which she had spread underneath a chair. "Let me deal with your hair."

Alex did as he was told, and for next few minutes he heard only the click of scissors and watched as uneven clumps of his hair tumbled to the ground. From the way she worked, he doubted that Mrs. Webber had received her training in a London salon. A sheep-shearing farm was more likely. When she had finished cutting, she opened one of the tubes and smeared a thick, greasy ointment over his head. Finally, she stepped back.

"He looks great," Ash said.

"The teeth still need work. They'd give him away in a minute."

There was another tube of paste for his teeth. She rubbed it in, using her own finger. Then she produced two small plastic caps. They were both the size of a tooth, but one was gray and one was black.

"I'm going to glue these in," Mrs. Webber warned him.

Alex opened his mouth and allowed her to fix the fake teeth into place. He grimaced. His mouth no longer felt like his own.

"You'll notice them for a day or two, but then you'll

forget them," she said. She stepped back. "There! I'm all done. Why don't you get dressed and take a look at yourself?"

"Cloudy, you're damn good," Ash muttered.

Alex pulled on a faded red T-shirt and a pair of jeans—both of them dirty and full of holes. Then he went back into the bathroom and stood in front of the full-length mirror. He gasped. The boy he was looking at certainly wasn't him. He was olive-skinned, with hair that was short, dark brown, and matted in thick strands. Somehow the clothes made him look thinner than he really was. He opened his mouth and saw that two of his teeth seemed to have rotted and the rest were ugly and discolored.

Mrs. Webber came in behind him. "You won't need to worry about the skin color for two weeks," she said. "Not unless you bathe . . . and I don't think you'll be doing that. You'll have to check on the hair and teeth every five or six days. I'll make sure Ash has plenty of supplies."

"It's amazing," Ash muttered. He was standing at the door.

"I've got some sneakers for you," Mrs. Webber added. "You won't need socks. I doubt a refugee boy would wear socks."

She went back into the hotel room and produced a pair of sneakers that were stained and torn. Alex slipped them on.

"They're too small," he said.

Mrs. Webber frowned. "I can cut a hole for your toes."

"No. I can't wear them."

She scowled at him, but even she could see that the sneakers were far too small. "All right." She nodded. "You can hang on to your own. Just give me a minute."

She dug back into the suitcase and produced a razor, some old paint, and another bottle of some sort of chemical. Two minutes later, Alex's own sneakers looked like they'd been thrown away ten years before. As he slipped them on, she set to work on Ash. He too had completely changed. He didn't need to dye his skin, and his beard would have suited a Hazara tribesman. But his hair had to be hacked around, and he needed a completely new set of clothes. It was strange, but by the time she had finished, Alex and Ash really could have been father and son. Poverty had brought them closer together.

Mrs. Webber packed again, taking all the clothes that Alex and Ash had been wearing with her. Finally, she zipped her bag shut and straightened up. She jabbed a finger in Ash's direction.

"You look after Alex," she commanded. "I've already had words with Mr. Brooke. Sending a boy this age into the field, I don't think it's right. Just you make sure he comes back in one piece."

"I'll look after him," Ash promised.

"You'd better. Take care, Alex!"

And with that, she was gone.

Ash turned to Alex. "How are you feeling?"

"Grimy."

"It's going to get worse. This grime is fake. Just wait till the real dirt gets stuck to you. Are you ready? It's time we left."

Alex moved toward the door.

"We'll take the service elevator," Ash said. "And we'll find the back way out. If anyone sees us looking like this in the Peninsula Hotel, we're going to get arrested."

The driver who had met Alex at the airport was waiting for them outside the hotel, and he took them over the river and then upstream toward Chinatown. Alex felt the air-conditioning blowing cold against his skin and knew that it was a luxury he wasn't going to enjoy again for a while. The car dropped them off at a corner, and at once the heat, the grime, and the noise of the city hit him. He was sweating before the door was even closed. Ash dragged a small battered case out of the trunk and that was it. Suddenly they were on their own.

Bangkok's Chinatown was like nowhere Alex had ever been before. When he looked up, it seemed to have no sky—all the light had been blocked out by billboards, banners, electric cables, and neon signs. Tom Yum Kung Restaurant. Thai Massage. Seng Hong Dental Clinic (Great Smile Start Here). The sidewalks were equally cluttered, every inch of them taken up by stalls spilling food and cheap clothes and electronics into the street. There were people everywhere, hundreds of them, weaving their way between the traffic, which seemed frozen in an endless, diesel-infested jam.

"This way," Ash muttered, keeping his voice low. From now on, whenever he spoke in English, he would make sure he wasn't overheard.

They pushed their way into the chaos, and in the next few minutes Alex passed vegetables that he had never seen before and meats he hoped he would never see again: hearts and lungs bubbling in green soup and brown intestines spilling out of their cauldrons as if trying to escape. Every scent on the planet seemed to be mixed together. Meat and fish and garbage and sweat—every step brought another smell.

They walked for about ten minutes until at last they came to an opening between a restaurant—with a few plastic tables and a single glass counter displaying plastic replicas of the food it served—and a paint factory. Here at last was an escape from the main road. A soiled, narrow alleyway led down between the backs of two blocks of apartments—the apartments piled up on one another as if thrown there at random. There was a miniature altar at the entrance, the incense adding another smell to Alex's collection. Farther down, a couple of cars had been parked next to a dozen crates of empty Pepsi bottles, a pile of old gas canisters, a row of tables and chairs. A Chinese woman was sitting cross-legged in the gutter, fixing ribbons to baskets of exotic fruit. Alex remembered the complimentary fruit basket that had been waiting for him in his hotel. Maybe this was where it had come from.

"This is it," Ash said.

It was the address that Karim Hassan and his son had been given by the snakehead. This was where they were expected to stay.

All the apartments opened directly onto the alley, so that Alex could see straight in. There were no doors or curtains. In one front room, a Chinese man sat smoking at a table, dressed in shorts and glasses, his huge stomach bulging over his knees. In another, a whole family was eating lunch, crouching on the floor with chopsticks. They came to a room that looked derelict—but it was occupied. An old woman was standing beside a stove. Ash signaled to Alex to wait, then went over and spoke to her, relying on sign language as much as words and waving a sheet of paper under her face.

She understood and pointed to a staircase at the back. Ash grunted something in Dari and, pretending to understand, Alex hurried forward.

The stairs were made of cement, with pools of murky water on at least half of them. Alex followed Ash to the third floor and a single door with no handle. Ash pushed it open. On the other side there was a bare room with a metal bed, a spare mattress on the floor, a sink, a toilet, and a grimy window. There was no carpet and no light. As Alex walked in, the biggest cockroach he had ever seen climbed over the side of the bed and scuttled across the wall.

"This is it?" Alex muttered.

"This is it," Ash said.

Outside, in the alleyway, the man who had followed them all the way from the hotel made a note of the building. Then he took out a cell phone and dialed a number. At the same time, he walked quietly away, and by the time he had been connected, he had disappeared into the crowd.

8

FIRST CONTACT

"SUPPOSE THEY DON'T come . . . ," Alex said.

"They'll come."

"How much longer do you think we're going to have to wait?"

They had been living in Chinatown for three days, and Alex was feeling hot, frustrated . . . and bored. Ash wouldn't let him have a newspaper or a book in English. There was always the chance that he might be caught reading it by someone entering the room. Nor was he able to see very much of Bangkok. There was no way of knowing when the snakehead might show up, and they couldn't risk being out.

But Alex had been allowed to spend a couple of hours each morning wandering on his own through the streets. It amused him that nobody treated him like a tourist—indeed, tourists stepped aside to avoid him. Mrs. Webber had done her job well. He looked like a street urchin from somewhere far away, and after more than sixty hours without a shower or a bath, without even changing his clothes, he imagined he could be smelled long before he could be seen.

Slowly he managed to come to grips with the city, the way the shops and the houses, the sidewalks and the streets all tumbled into one another, the clammy heat, the never-ending noise and movement. There seemed to be a surprise around every corner. A cripple with withered legs, scuttling past on his hands like a giant spider. A temple sprouting out of nowhere like an exotic flower. Bald monks in their bright orange robes, moving in a crowd.

He also learned a little more about Ash.

Ash slept badly. He had given Alex the bed and taken the mattress for himself, but sometimes in the night he would begin muttering and then jerk awake. Then he would clasp his hand to his stomach and Alex knew that he was remembering the time he had been stabbed and that it was hurting him even now.

"Why did you become a spy?" Alex asked one morning.

"It seemed like a good idea at the time," Ash growled. He hated being asked questions and seldom gave straightforward answers. But that morning he was in a better mood. "I was approached while I was in the army."

"By Alan Blunt?"

"No. He was there when I joined—but he wasn't in the top spot. I was recruited the year after your dad. I'll tell you why he joined, if you like."

"Why?"

"He was a patriot." Ash grimaced. "He really thought he had a duty to serve his queen and country."

"Don't you?"

"I did . . . once."

"So what happened? What made you change your mind?"

"It was a long time ago." Ash had a way of cutting off a conversation if he didn't want to say more. Alex had come to learn that when that happened, there was no point in trying to go on. Ash could wrap silence around him like a coat. It was infuriating, but Alex knew he would just have to wait. Ash would talk in his own time.

And then, on the fourth day, the snakehead came.

Alex had just gotten back with food from the local market when he heard the stamp of feet on the concrete steps. Ash threw him a look of warning and swung himself off the bed just as the door crashed open and one of the ugliest men Alex had ever seen walked into the room.

He was short, even for a Thai, wearing a suit that looked as if it had shrunk in the wash to fit him. He was bald and unshaven, so that both the top and bottom of his head were covered in a thin black stubble. On the other hand, he didn't seem to have any eyebrows—as if his skin were too thick and pockmarked to grow through. His mouth was impossibly wide, like an open wound, with as many gaps as teeth. Worst of all, he had no ears. Alex could see the discolored lumps of flesh that remained. The rest had at some time been cut off.

This had to be Mr. Anan Sukit. There was a second Thai man with him, dressed in a white T-shirt and jeans, carrying a camera—a clunky wooden box that could have come out of an antique shop. A third man followed. He looked similar to Ash—presumably an Afghan brought along to translate.

Alex quickly sat down in the corner. He glanced at the three men but tried not to show too much interest, as if he didn't want to be noticed himself.

Sukit snapped a few words at the translator, who then spoke to Ash. Ash replied in Dari, and a three-way conversation began. As it continued, Alex noticed Sukit examining him. The snakehead boss had tiny pupils that moved ceaselessly, traveling left and right across his eyes. At the same time, the cameraman had started his work. Alex sat still as several shots were taken of him. Then it was Ash's turn. He had already explained to Alex what sort of papers would be prepared. Passports, possibly with visas for Indonesia. A police arrest form for Ash. A hospital report showing that he had been injured during questioning. Perhaps an old membership card for the Communist Party. All these things would help him get refugee status once he arrived in Australia.

The photographer finished, but the discussion went on. Alex became aware that something was wrong. Sukit nodded in his direction a couple of times. He seemed to be making some sort of demand. Ash was arguing. He looked unhappy. Alex heard his name—Abdul—mentioned several times.

Then suddenly Anan Sukit walked over to him. He was sweating, and his skin smelled of garlic. Without warning, he reached down and dragged Alex to his feet.

Ash stood up and shouted something. Alex couldn't understand a word that was being said, but he did what Ash had told him and stared with unfocused eyes as if he was a simpleton. Sukit slapped him, twice, on each side of his face. Alex cried out. It wasn't just the pain. It was the casual violence, the shock of what had just happened. Ash let loose a torrent of words. He seemed to be pleading. Sukit spoke one last time. Ash nodded. Whatever had been demanded, he'd agreed. The three men turned and left the room.

Alex waited until he was sure they had gone. His cheeks were stinging. "I take it that was Anan Sukit?" he muttered.

"That was him."

"What happened to his ears?"

"A gang fight. It happened five years ago. Maybe I should have mentioned it to you before. Someone cut them off."

"He's lucky he doesn't need glasses." Alex rubbed the side of his face with a grimy hand. "So what was all that about?" he asked.

"I don't know. I don't understand . . ." Ash was deep in thought. "They're getting the papers for us. They'll be ready this evening."

"That's good. But why did he hit me?"

"He made a demand. I refused. So he got angry— and he took it out on you. I'm sorry, Alex." Ash ran a hand through his long dark hair. He looked shaken by what had just taken place. "I didn't want him to hurt you, but there was nothing I could do."

"What did he want?"

Ash sighed. "Sukit insisted that you collect the papers. Not me. He just wants you."

"Why?"

"He didn't say. He just told me they'd pick you up at Patpong at seven o'clock this evening. You've got to be there on your own. If you're not there, we can forget it. The deal's off."

Ash fell silent. He had lost control of the situation, and he knew it. Alex wasn't sure how to respond. His first encounter with the snakehead had been short and unpleasant. The question was—what did they want with him? Had they seen through his disguise? If he turned up at this place—Patpong—they could bundle him into a car and he might never be seen again.

"If they wanted to kill you, they could have done it here and now," Ash said. It was as if he'd read Alex's thoughts. "They could have killed both of us."

"Do you think I should go?"

"I can't make that decision, Alex. It's up to you."

But if he wasn't there, there would be no forged papers, no way for Ash to find out where they were being manufactured. Nor would the two of them be able to continue down the pipeline. The mission would be over before it had even begun. And Alex would have learned nothing from Ash—about his father, about Malta, about Yassen Gregorovich.

It was a risk. But it was one worth taking.

"I'll do it," Alex said.

Patpong showed Alex another side of Bangkok—and not one that he wanted to see. It was a tangle of bars and strip clubs where backpackers and businessmen gathered to drink the night away. Through the doorways he glimpsed half-naked dancers writhing in time to western pop music. Fat men in floral shirts strolled past with Thai girlfriends. The neon lights flickered and the music pounded out and the air was thick with the smell of alcohol and cheap perfume. It was the last place on earth that a fourteen-year-old English boy would want to find himself, and Alex was feeling distinctly uncomfortable, standing at the entrance to the main square. But he'd only been there a few minutes when a beat-up black Citroën pulled over with two men inside. He recognized one of them. The man in the passenger seat had been carrying the camera and had taken the pictures of him and Ash.

So this was it. He had come to Thailand to investigate the snakehead and now he was delivering himself to them with no weapons, no gadgets—nothing to help him if things went wrong. Were they simply going to hand over the papers as promised? Somehow he doubted it. But it was too late for second thoughts. He climbed into the back of the car. The seat was plastic—and it was torn. A pair of furry dice swung beneath the driver's mirror.

Nobody spoke to him, but then, of course, they didn't know his language. Ash had warned him not to say anything, no matter what happened. One word of English would mean an immediate death sentence for both of them. He would pretend that he was simple, that he understood nothing at all. If things got out of hand, he would try to break away.

The Citroën joined in the sluggish flow of traffic, and suddenly they were surrounded by cars, trucks, buses, and *tuk-tuks*—the three-wheeled taxis that were actually nothing more than motorcycles with a makeshift cabin built on the back. As always, everyone was hooting at everyone. The heat of the evening only intensified the noise and the smell of exhaust fumes that hung thick in the air.

They drove for about thirty minutes. It had grown dark, and Alex had no idea in which direction they were heading. He tried to pick out a few landmarks—a neon sign, a skyscraper with a strange gold dome on the roof, a hotel. Part of his job was to find out as much about the snakehead as he could, and the following day he might have to show Ash exactly where he'd been taken. The car turned off the main road, and suddenly they were traveling down a narrow alleyway between two high walls. Alex was liking this less and less. He had the feeling that he was delivering himself into some sort of trap. Sukit had said he would hand over the papers, but Alex didn't believe him. There had to be another reason for all this.

And then they broke out and he saw the river in front of him, the water black and empty but for a single rice barge making its way home. In the far distance, a tower block that he recognized caught his eye. It was the Peninsula Hotel, where he had spent his first night. It was less than half a mile upstream, but it might as well have belonged to a different world. The car slowed down. They had come right to the river's edge. The driver turned off the engine. They got out.

The smell of sewage. That was what hit him first: thick, sweet, and heavy. The surface of the water was completely covered with a layer of rotting vegetables and garbage that rocked back and forth with the current like a living carpet. One of the men pushed him, hard, in the small of his back, and he made his way over to a broken-down jetty where a boat was waiting to ferry them across, another hard-faced Thai man at the rudder. Alex climbed in. The other men followed.

They set off. The moon had risen, and out in the open, everything was suddenly bright. Ahead of him, Alex could see their destination. There was a long, three-story building with a green-painted sign advertising it to any passing river traffic. Chada Trading Agency & Consultant. Alex didn't like the look of it one bit.

The building was on the very edge of the river, half falling into it, propped up on a series of concrete posts that held it about two yards above the water. It was made of wood and corrugated iron: a slanting, leaning assembly of roofs, verandas, balconies, and walkways that could have been hammered together by a child. It seemed to have no windows and few doors. As they drew closer, Alex heard a sound: a low shouting that suddenly rose up like a crowd at a soccer match. It was coming from inside.

The boat drew in. A ladder led up to a landing platform, and once again Alex felt a fist jabbing into his lower back. It seemed to be the only way these people knew how to communicate. He got unsteadily to his feet and grabbed the ladder. As he did so, he heard something splash in the water and saw a streak of movement out of the corner of his eye. Some sort of creatures were living in the dark space underneath the building. There was another roar from inside and the chime of a bell. How had he gotten himself into this? Alex gritted his teeth and climbed up.

Now he found himself in a narrow corridor that sloped down with doorways facing each other on opposite sides. Naked bulbs hung at intervals, throwing out a damp yellow light. The whole place smelled of the river. Halfway down, they stopped at one of the doors, which was thrown open to reveal a room that was like a cell, a couple of yards square with a tiny barred window, a bench, and a table. There was a pair of bright red shorts lying on the bench. Cameraman—Alex didn't know his name, and that was how he thought of him—picked up the shorts and spat out a sentence in Thai. This time the meaning was clear.

The door slammed shut. There was another roar from somewhere nearby, the sound echoing outward. Alex picked up the shorts. They were made of silk, recently laundered, but there were still dark spots embedded in the material. Old bloodstains. Alex clamped down the rising sense of fear. He looked at the window, but there was no way he was going to be able to climb out. He had no doubt the Thai men were standing guard on the other side of the door. He heard the whine of a mosquito and slapped it against the side of his head. He began to undress.

Ten minutes later, they led him back down the corridor and along to a flight of steps that seemed to have collapsed in on itself like a house of cards. Alex was now wearing the shorts and nothing else. They started high on his body, above the waist, and came down to his knees. They were the sort of thing worn for a boxing or wrestling match. Which of them was it going to be? he wondered. Or was he being led toward something worse than either?

He heard music playing. The crackle of a loudspeaker and a stream of words, amplified, all in Thai. Laughter. The soft babble of many people talking. At last he emerged into a scene that was like nothing he had ever experienced before—and something he would never forget.

It was an arena, circular in shape with dozens of narrow pillars holding up the ceiling, a raised boxing ring in the middle and wooden seating slanting up around the sides. It was lit by neon strips that dangled on chains, and there were twenty or thirty fans turning slowly, trying to redistribute the hot, sticky air. Thai music was blaring out of speakers, and, bizarrely, there were old television sets facing outward, each one showing a different program.

The ring itself was surrounded by a wire fence that had been built either to keep the players in or the audience out. There must have been about four hundred Thais in the room, chattering excitedly among themselves as they swapped bright yellow slips of paper. Alex had read somewhere that betting was illegal in Thailand, but he recognized at once what was going on here. He had arrived just at the end of a fight. A young man was being dragged feetfirst across the ring, his arms splayed out, his shoulders painting a red streak along the canvas as he was carried away. And the members of the audience who had bet on his opponent were collecting their winnings.

Alex was at the very back of the auditorium. As he arrived, another man—dressed like him in shorts—was led down to the ring, his entire body taut with fear. Seeing him, the audience laughed and applauded. More yellow betting slips changed hands. Someone put a hand on Alex's shoulder and pushed him down onto a plastic seat. There was a crack in the floor, and he caught a glimpse of silver, the river water lapping at the concrete posts underneath. He was sweating, and the mosquitoes had picked up his scent. He could hear them right inside his ear. His skin crawled as he was bitten again and again.

The new challenger had passed through the audience and reached the wire fence. Someone had placed a laurel of flowers around his neck. He looked as if he was about to be sacrificed. It occurred to Alex that in a sense he was. Two burly Thai men led him through a door in the fence and helped him climb into the ring. They forced him to bow to the audience. Then, in the far corner, the champion appeared.

He wasn't big—very few people in this country were—but he emanated power and speed. Alex could see every single muscle on his body. They were locked together like metal plates, and he didn't have a single spare ounce of fat. His hair, very black, was cut short. His eyes were black too. He had a boy's face, completely smooth, but Alex guessed he was in his mid-twenties. His name—Sunthorn—was written in white letters on his shorts. He bowed to the audience and danced on his feet, raising his fists to acknowledge their applause.

The other man awaited his fate. The flower garland had been removed, and the Thai men had left the ring. The music stopped. A bell rang.

At once, Alex understood what he was seeing. He had been expecting the worst, and this was it. *Muay Thai,* also known as the science of eight limbs, one of the most aggressive and dangerous martial arts in the world. Alex had learned karate, but he knew that it was a world apart from *muay Thai,* which permitted strikes by the fists, elbows, knees, and feet with no fewer than twenty-four targets— from the top of the head to the rear calf—on your opponent. And this was a dirty, illegal version. Neither of the fighters had hand wraps, shin pads, or abdomen protectors. The fight would continue until one of them was carried out unconscious . . . or worse.

Alex watched the first round with a mixture of fascination and horror, knowing that he was going to be next. The fight had begun with both men weaving around each other, weighing up each other's weaknesses. Sunthorn had struck out a few times, first with a right-side elbow attack, then twisting his body around in a fast knee strike. But the challenger was faster than he looked, dodging both blows and even trying a counterkick, slicing his left foot into the air and missing Sunthorn's neck by inches, a move that got a roar of excitement from the crowd.

But then, at the end of the first round, he made his fatal mistake. He had allowed his guard to drop, as if waiting for the bell. Suddenly Sunthorn lashed out, a rear leg push kick that slammed into the other man's chest, winding him and almost throwing him off his feet. It was only the chime of the bell a second later that saved him. He staggered into the corner, where someone forced a bottle of water into his mouth and wiped down his face. But he was barely conscious. The next round wouldn't last long.

In the brief interval, more music blasted out of the speakers. The televisions flickered back on. Yellow slips were exchanged, and Alex noticed people gesticulating wildly, angrily tapping their watches. He was feeling sick. He realized now that the audience wasn't betting on who was going to win the fight. With Sunthorn in the ring, there could be no doubt of that. They were betting on how long a fighter could last against him.

The bell rang for the next round, and as expected, it was all over very quickly. The challenger moved forward as if he knew he was walking to his execution. Sunthorn examined him with a cruel smile, then finished the fight in the most vicious way he could: a kick to the stomach followed by a second, much-harder kick straight into the face. A great flower of blood erupted into the ring. The audience howled. The challenger crashed down on his back and lay still. Sunthorn danced around him, waving his fists in triumph. The seconds climbed into the ring to clear away the mess.

And now it was Alex's turn.

He was suddenly aware of a man leaning over him—a weird, stretched-out face like a reflection in a fairground mirror. It was Anan Sukit. The snakehead lieutenant spoke to him first in Thai, then in another language, perhaps Dari. Once again, Alex smelled the stale scent of garlic. Sukit paused. Alex stared straight ahead, as if he hadn't even heard what had just been said. Sukit leaned forward. He said something in bad French. Then he repeated it in English.

"You fight, or we kill you."

Alex had to force himself to pretend that he hadn't understood. The man couldn't possibly have known who he was or where he came from. He was simply saying the same thing in as many languages as possible. And finally he used the most effective language of all, grabbing Alex by the hair and pulling him out of his seat and then propelling him down the aisle toward the ring.

As he walked down between the audience, Alex felt himself being examined and evaluated on every side. Once again the yellow markers were being handed out, and he could imagine the bets being placed. Fifteen seconds . . . twenty seconds . . . it was obvious that this foreign boy wouldn't last long. His heart was pounding—he could actually see the movement in his naked chest. Why had he been chosen for this? Why not Ash? He could only assume that these people got a sick satisfaction out of a change of pace. During the course of the evening, they had seen a number of men beaten up. Now they were going to watch the same thing happen to a teenager.

He passed through the opening in the fence. The two seconds were waiting for him, grinning and offering to help him up into the ring. One of them was carrying a garland of flowers to put around his neck. Alex had already made up his mind about that. As their hands reached toward him, he struck out at them, drawing laughter and jeers from the crowd. But he wasn't going to be touched by them, nor was he going to parade in their flowers. He pulled himself into the ring just as two cleaners climbed out, lowering themselves between the ropes. They took with them the bloody rags that they had just used to clean the canvas floor.

Sunthorn was waiting in the opposite corner.

It was only now that he was closer that Alex could see the arrogance and the cruelty of the man he was about to face. Sunthorn had probably been training all his life and knew that this next fight was going to be over as soon as it began. But he didn't care. Presumably he was being paid and would cheerfully maim Alex for life, provided he got his check. Already he was smiling, showing cracked lips and uneven teeth. His nose had been broken at some time, and it had set badly. He might have the body of a world-class athlete, but he had the face of a freak.

A plastic bottle of water was forced between Alex's lips, and he drank. It was horribly warm in the stadium, and that would only sap his strength. He wondered how Sunthorn had managed to continue for so long. Perhaps he was given some sort of drug. The military music was blasting all around him. The fans were turning. Alex clung to the rope, trying to work out some sort of strategy. Would it be easier just to take a dive the moment the fight began? If he allowed himself to be knocked out in the opening seconds, at least it would all be over. But there was a risk in that too. It would all depend on how hard Sunthorn hit him. He didn't want to wake up with a broken neck.

The music stopped. The bell rang. The spectators fell silent. It was too late to work out any plan. The first round had begun.

Alex took a couple of steps forward. He could feel the eyes of the crowd boring into him, waiting for him to go down. In front of him, Sunthorn looked completely relaxed. He had taken up the standard stance, with his body weight poised on his front foot—the basic defense in almost every martial art—but he barely looked interested. It occurred to Alex that if he had any chance at all in this fight, it would be in the opening seconds. Nobody in the arena could possibly know that he was a first-grade *dan*—with a black belt in karate. The fight was completely unfair. Sunthorn had the advantages of size, weight, and experience. But Alex had the advantage of surprise.

He decided to use it. He continued forward and, at the last second, when he knew he was close enough, he suddenly twisted around and lashed out with all his strength. He had used the back kick, one of the most powerful blows in karate, and if he had made contact, he would have taken his opponent out then and there. But to his dismay, his foot hit only empty air. Sunthorn had reacted with fantastic speed, springing back and twisting so that the kick missed his abdomen by an inch. The audience gasped, then chattered with new excitement. Alex tried to follow through with a front jab, but this time Sunthorn was ready. He blocked the attack with his own right arm, then followed through with a counterkick that slammed into Alex's side, propelling him back against the ropes. Alex was bruised and winded. Red spots danced in front of his eyes. If Sunthorn hit him a second time, it would be over. Alex rested with the ropes against his shoulder and waited for the end.

It didn't come. Sunthorn was smiling again, enjoying himself. The foreign boy hadn't been the easy kill that everyone expected, and he knew he could enjoy himself here. The audience wanted blood, but they wanted drama too. He could play with the boy for a while, weaken him before the final blow that would put him into the hospital. He reached out with his hand, bending his fingers as if to say, "Come on!" The crowd roared its approval. Even the gamblers who had already lost and were tearing up their yellow slips wanted to see more.

Alex drew a deep breath and straightened up. There was a red mark where Sunthorn's foot had caught him, just above the waist. The man had a sole that could have been made of the toughest leather and leg muscles like steel rods. How could Ash have got him into this? But Alex knew it wasn't his godfather's fault. He should have listened to Jack when he was in Sydney. Right now he could have been safely back at school.

For the next couple of minutes, the two of them circled

each other, throwing a few feints, but neither of them landing a real punch. Alex tried to keep his distance while he recovered his breath. How long did each round last? He had seen that there were intervals, and he desperately needed a few seconds on his own, unthreatened: time to think. The sweat was dripping off him. He wiped his eyes, and that was when Sunthorn attacked him, a whirl of jabbing elbows, knees, and fists, any one of which could have knocked Alex down.

In the next thirty seconds, Alex used every defense technique he had ever been taught, but he knew that in truth, he was simply relying on his instincts, dodging and weaving as the arena seemed to spin around him, the audience shouting, the fans turning, and the sluggish heat weighing down on him from all sides. A right hook caught him on the side of the face and his whole head jerked around, a spasm of pain traveling down his neck and spine. Sunthorn followed through with a side knee to the ribs. Alex doubled up, unable to help himself. He hit the canvas just as the bell rang for the end of the first round.

There was applause and cheering. The music blared out. Sunthorn leapt back, grinning and waving his hands, enjoying the fight. Alex felt he had no strength left. He was aware of the two men acting as his seconds, shouting at him, gesticulating for him to return to his corner. Somehow he forced himself to his feet. His nose was bleeding. He could taste the blood as it trickled into his mouth.

He wasn't going to last another round: that much was obvious. All the odds were against him. But he had come to a decision. Sunthorn was older, taller, heavier, and more experienced than he was, and there was only one way Alex was going to beat him.

He was just going to have to cheat.

9

ONCE BITTEN . . .

ONE OF THE MEN who had been chosen to look after Alex while he was fighting wiped away the blood with a wet sponge. The other helped him drink. Alex felt the cold water trickle down the sides of his face and over his shoulders. Both the men were grinning at him, muttering words of encouragement as if he could understand a single word they were saying. They had probably done exactly the same during the previous fight—and Alex had seen the result. Well, he wasn't going to let that happen to him. These people were in for a surprise.

He felt the water bottle being forced one last time between his lips and sucked in as much as he could. A moment later, a bell rang and the bottle was whisked away. The interval music stopped. There were shouts from different parts of the audience. Glancing to one side, Alex saw Anan Sukit striding forward to take a place in the front row. He probably wanted a closer view of the final knockout.

Alex moved forward cautiously, his fists raised, his weight evenly distributed on the balls of his feet. Sunthorn was waiting for him. That was good. The one thing that Alex had most feared was a fast, direct attack. That wouldn't leave him time for what he had in mind. But

Alex had shown his true colors in the first round. Sunthorn knew that he had trained in at least one martial art, and he was planning his moves carefully. Alex had come close to knocking him out. Sunthorn wasn't going to give him a second chance.

In the end, he went for a straight clinch . . . a wrestling grip that in *muay Thai* is also known as the standard tie-up. Suddenly they were face-to-face, their feet almost touching. Sunthorn had locked his hands behind Alex's head and he was sneering, utterly confident. With his extra height, he had the complete advantage. He could throw Alex off balance or finish him with an explosive strike from his knee. The audience saw that the last seconds of the fight had arrived and roared their approval.

It was exactly what Alex wanted. It was exactly what he had been inviting. Before Sunthorn could make his move, he acted. What nobody knew—not Sunthorn, nor the seconds nor the audience—was that Alex's mouth was still full of water and had been since the round began. Now he spat it out, straight into Sunthorn's face.

Sunthorn reacted instinctively, jerking his head back in surprise and loosening his grip. For a second he was blinded. Alex acted instantly, striking out with a savage uppercut that sent his fist crashing into the man's jaw. But that wasn't enough. He wouldn't get a second chance and had to finish this now. Alex swung around, putting all his strength into a single powerhouse kick, his bare foot landing square in the man's solar plexus.

Even Sunthorn's advanced muscle structure wasn't up to such a blow. Alex heard the breath explode out of his lips. All the color left his face. For a moment, he stood there, his hands hanging limply beneath him. The crowd had fallen silent—as if in shock. Then Sunthorn collapsed onto his knees and finally slammed facedown, unconscious, onto the floor.

The entire arena erupted with cries of anger and outrage. The audience had seen what had happened—and they couldn't believe it. The foreign boy had been brought here to entertain them, but he had cheated them instead. They had lost money. And their champion—Sunthorn—had been humiliated.

It was only now, hearing the shouting all around him, that Alex realized that he had put himself in fresh danger. If he had played his part as expected, he might have been carried out on his back and with a broken nose . . . or worse. But presumably there would have been a consolation prize. He would have been driven home with the false documents that Ash had sent him here to collect. There was no longer any of that. He had offended the snakehead, taken out their prize fighter. Somehow he doubted that they were going to thank him and give him a gold cup.

He stepped over the unconscious body and made as if to climb out of the ring. But he saw at once that he was right. Anan Sukit was back on his feet, his face dark with fury, his eyes ablaze. He had pulled a gun out of an inside pocket of his suit. Unbelieving, Alex watched as he brought it around and aimed. Sukit was going to shoot him, right there, in front of all these people . . . a punishment for the trick that had just been played. And there was nothing Alex could do, nowhere to hide. He watched as the cold eye of the muzzle focused on his chest.

Then all the lights went out.

The darkness was absolute. It seemed to fold in from all sides, like a collapsing box. Sukit had chosen that moment to fire. Alex saw two bursts of orange flame and heard the shots. But he was already moving. The bullets had been aimed at his head, but he had dropped down onto the canvas and was rolling away, searching for the ropes on the other side of the ring. He found them. Reaching up with one hand, he swung himself through, then down into the ringside area below.

The spectators had reacted to the blackout with silence, but the sound of the two shots had provoked instant panic. They were suddenly blind, and someone had a gun! Alex heard screams, the clatter of seats being pushed to the ground. Someone ran into Alex, then tumbled back. There were more cries of protest. Alex crouched where he was, waiting for his eyes to get used to the dark.

At least that happened quickly. As Alex had approached the arena from the river, he had seen how dilapidated it was—and although there were no windows, the roof and the walls were full of cracks. The moon was still shining and the light was spilling in everywhere . . . not enough to make out faces, but Alex was in no mood to make new friends. All he wanted was the way out and he could see it, straight in front of him, up a flight of concrete steps.

He got to his feet and ran forward—crashing into the wire fence that surrounded the ring. Where was the opening? Desperately he felt his way along, using his palms against the wire. Somehow he found the gap and stumbled through, forcing himself on toward the sloped seating that climbed steeply up to the door where he'd come in. There was a third shot and a man standing next to him twisted around and fell. Sukit had spotted him, which was hardly surprising. Alex's bare shoulders and light-colored shorts would make him a target even in the dark. He scrambled forward, fighting his way through the crowd. His skin was slippery, covered in sweat, and at least that made it difficult for anyone to grab hold of him. A Thai man stepped in front of him, muttering something in his own language. Alex raised a hand, driving the heel straight into the man's face. The man grunted and fell backward. The knife he had been holding clattered to the floor. So now Alex understood the rules. He was to be captured and killed. That seemed to be the price of winning the fight.

Alex was unarmed. He was half naked. And members of the snakehead were all around him. He knew that only speed and the darkness were on his side. He had to find his way out of this building in the next few minutes. And that meant retrieving his own clothes. He reached the door—and it was at that moment that the lights flashed back on.

Sukit saw him at once. He pointed with a single, stubby finger and shouted. Alex saw half a dozen young men running toward him—all of them black-haired, dressed in black shirts. They were coming at him from both sides. Sukit fired. The bullet hit a pillar and ricocheted into one of the television sets. The glass shattered and there was a crackle of electricity. Alex saw a tongue of flame and wondered if the whole place might catch fire. That would help him. But the walls were too damp. The river was everywhere, even in the air he was breathing. He hurled himself through the doorway and down the wooden staircase on the other side, almost losing his balance on the crazy fairground steps. A splinter buried itself in his toe. Alex ignored the pain. He was back in the corridor. Which way had they led him? Left or right? He had less than a second to make a decision and the wrong choice might kill him.

He went right. That way, the corridor sloped upward, and he remembered that coming in, he had gone down. Behind him, he heard a burst of gunfire . . . not one gun but several. That was strange. He was out of sight now, so who were they firing at? The dull yellow lightbulbs flickered overhead. It seemed that war had broken out in the arena. Was it possible . . . ? Alex wondered if Ash could have somehow followed him here. Certainly there seemed to be someone on his side.

He found the room where he had undressed and ran in, swinging the door shut behind him. His clothes were where he'd left them, and gratefully he pulled them on. At least he looked normal again—and he needed the sneakers if he was going to run over any more wooden floors. When he was dressed, he went back to the door and slowly opened it. Sweat trickled down the side of his face. His hair was drenched. But there didn't seem to be anyone outside.

The end of the corridor and the exit to the jetty were about twenty yards away. But as he made his way toward the open air, Alex heard the roar of an engine, and knew that a boat had just pulled in. He guessed what was going to happen next. Luckily, he was outside one of the other rooms. He threw himself inside just as the main door crashed open and the new arrivals began to make their way down the corridor. There were two of them. They were both carrying old-fashioned, Russian-made RPK-74 light machine guns. The barrels had been modified to make them shorter. As Alex crouched in the shadows, he heard them move toward him. They were searching the changing rooms, one by one. In less than a minute they would be here.

Alex looked around him. This room was almost identical to the one he had left, with no cupboards, nowhere to hide, and a single window, securely barred. But there was one difference. Part of the floor had rotted away. He could just make out the water, churning underneath. Could he fit through? There was a crash as the door of the room next to his was thrown open. He heard one of the men call out in Thai. They would be here in the next few seconds. Alex didn't like to think what he might be letting himself into. The water was a long way down, and the current might suck him beneath the surface. But if he stayed here, he would die for certain. He went over to the hole, took a deep breath, and dropped through it.

He fell into darkness and just had time to put a hand over his nose before he hit the river. The water was warm and sluggish, covered by a layer of filth and rotting vegetation. The stink was almost unendurable. It was like plunging into the oldest, dirtiest bath in the world. As Alex broke back through the surface, he could feel the liquid, like oil, running down his cheeks and over his lips. Some sort of slime was clinging to his face. He tore it off, forcing himself not to swallow.

He was out of the arena, but he still hadn't escaped. He could hear voices above him and in the distance. It was almost impossible to see anything. He was underneath the building, treading water, surrounded by the concrete pillars that held the place up. In the distance, he could just make out the shape of the boat that must have brought the two men with machine guns. It was moored next to the jetty, its engine still running. There was the stamp of footsteps, and he looked up as two flickering shadows passed above his head. They belonged to men running along the veranda outside the arena. Sukit must have given the order to surround the place. His men would be searching it inch by inch.

And then something climbed onto his shoulder.

It was only now that he remembered the movement he had seen when he had arrived: something living in the water and the shadows beneath the building. Alex reached out and grabbed one of the pillars, steadying himself. Then, very slowly, he turned his head.

It was a river rat, heavy and bloated, at least fifteen inches long, with vicious white teeth and eyes the color of blood. Its tail, curling around behind Alex's neck, added another ten inches to its length, and it was clinging to his shirt with feverish little claws, scrabbling at the material. And it wasn't alone. As Alex froze, in utter horror, two more rats appeared, then a third. Soon the water was swarming with them. Another one climbed onto the side of his face, scratching the skin as it pulled itself on top of his head. Alex wanted to scream—but it was the one thing he couldn't do. There were armed men standing above him, only a few yards away. If he so much as splashed too loud, it would all be over.

Were the rats going to bite him? That was the terrible thought. Would they try to eat him alive? He felt something nudge his shirt. One of the creatures had dived underwater and was trying to burrow its way inside. He could feel its nose and claws, burrowing against the soft flesh of his stomach. With a feeling of nausea, he reached down and gently pushed it away. If he was too rough, the rat would bite him, and once the others got a scent of his blood . . .

He stopped himself. Better not even to imagine.

His only hope was to do nothing. Let the rats decide that he was just another bit of pollution that had been dumped in the river. I'm not edible. You wouldn't like me. He tried to send his thoughts out to the pack. The rat that had climbed onto his head was now nestling in his hair. Alex winced as it pulled out a few strands and began to chew on them, checking out the taste. The first rat, the one that had started this all, was still on his shoulder. Without moving, Alex looked down and saw a pointed nose twitching right beside his jugular. Behind it, he could make out two black eyes, gleaming with excitement, fascinated by the rapid pulsing—in exact time with Alex's heart. All it had to do was bite through the flesh, find the vein. Alex was certain it was about to strike.

That was when the explosion occurred, a fireball that erupted in the very center of the building. At once, all the rats took flight, leaping off him and disappearing behind the columns. What in the world was going on? Had he perhaps wandered into some war between two rival snakeheads? That didn't matter now. Alex had to move before the rats came back. He launched himself away from the column and swam through the muck, trying to keep his face out of the water.

The arena was on fire. He heard voices yelling and saw the flicker of red in the water. A piece of blazing wood tumbled out of nowhere and fell, hissing and spitting, into the river. Alex glanced upward. The building had been rickety to begin with. He didn't want it collapsing now—not when he was underneath. The jetty was straight ahead of him. Even if there were men standing guard, Alex doubted he would be noticed. With all that was going on inside the building, nobody would be looking down into the water. Anyway, he didn't care anymore. He'd had enough of this. It was time to go.

He reached the side of the boat, a sheer metal wall rising up into fresh air and freedom. There was a net hanging over the side, and Alex grabbed it gratefully. Somehow he found the last reserve of strength he needed to climb up. The boat was one of the old river ferries— with a red roof to show that it crossed continually from one side to the other. There was one man on board— presumably the driver—a Thai wearing jeans and a jacket but no shirt. He was leaning against the side, watching the fire with a look of astonishment.

The wooden building was crackling loudly. Flames had caught hold of the roof and the back wall. They were leaping up into the night sky. The wood was splintering, pieces of it splashing down. Alex didn't even try to keep quiet. He hauled himself over the side rail on the other side of the ferry, behind the driver. The man didn't turn around. Alex ran across the deck, then grabbed him by his collar and belt. He was lucky. The man weighed very little. Alex heaved him up over the rail and into the river. Then, still dripping wet, with the water running into his eyes, he went over to the controls and slammed the throttle as far as it would go.

This was going to be his way out of here. Once he was downriver, nobody would be able to find him. The engines roared and the propellers thrashed at the water, turning it white. The boat surged forward. Alex grinned. But a second later, he was almost thrown off his feet as the boat seemed to slam into a brick wall. Still gripping the steering wheel, he turned around and saw to his dismay that the boat had been moored to one of the columns supporting the arena. The propellers were churning up the water. If the rats were anywhere near, they would have been chopped to pieces. But the boat wasn't going anywhere. A length of rope, almost as thick as Alex's arm, stretched between the stern and the column.

And he didn't have time to untie it. Alex lowered the throttle, afraid that the engines would explode, and the rope sagged. Then somebody shouted something and with a heavy heart he saw Anan Sukit appear on the walkway outside the arena, anger stretching his mouth even farther across his hideous face. He had seen Alex. He still had his gun. Once again he took aim. He was about ten yards away, but he had a clear shot.

Alex did the only thing he could. Once again he

slammed down the throttle, and from that moment it seemed to him that everything happened at once.

There were three shots. But Alex hadn't been hit. And it wasn't Sukit who had fired. The snakehead lieutenant seemed to throw his own gun into the river as if he no longer had any use for it. Then he followed it in, pitching headfirst into the water. He had been shot from behind, the bullets hitting him between the shoulders. Alex thought he saw a shadowy figure standing in a doorway, but before he could make out who it was, the boat surged forward. And this time it took the column with it, ripping it out from beneath the burning building.

Alex felt himself propelled into the middle of the river, moving incredibly fast. He risked a last look back and saw the arena, consumed by fire, sparks dancing above it. In the distance, he could hear fire engines. But they weren't going to be needed. It seemed that he had torn out a vital part of the structure. Even as he watched, the entire building slumped to its knees, as if in surrender, then slid off the bank and into the river. All of it went. The water rushed in through the rotting wood, eager at last to reclaim it. Alex heard screams coming from inside. Another burst of gunfire. And then the Chada Trading Agency had gone as if it had never existed. Only the green sign floated on the surface, surrounded by other pieces of splintered wood and debris. The flames sat briefly on the river before extinguishing themselves. Dozens of dark figures thrashed and shouted in the water, trying to reach dry land.

Alex dragged at the steering wheel and brought the ferry under control. It was incredible, but he really was the only person on board. So which way now? North would take him to familiar territory. He could see the Peninsula Hotel in the far distance. He wondered what he must look like. Bruised, scratched, soaked, in rags—he didn't think they'd be too happy to let him check in.

And anyway, there was still Ash, presumably waiting for him in Chinatown. Alex steered the ferry toward the next public jetty. It seemed they would have to do without the forged papers. He just hoped Ash wouldn't mind.

So far, he had to admit, things hadn't quite gone as planned.

10

WAT HO

MAJOR WINSTON YU SELECTED an egg-and-cress sandwich and held it delicately between his gloved fingers. He was at the Ritz Hotel in London, which—even if they did allow too many tourists into the main rooms—was still his favorite hotel in the world. And tea was definitely his favorite meal. He loved the little sandwiches, cut in perfect triangles, with a scone served with jam and cream to follow. It was all so very English. Even the bone-china teapot and cup had been made by Wedgwood, the Staffordshire family established in 1759.

He sipped his tea and dabbed his lips with a napkin. The news from Bangkok, he had to admit, was not good. But he wasn't going to let that spoil his tea. His mother had always told him that every cloud has a silver lining, and he was looking for one now. It was true that it wouldn't be easy to replace Anan Sukit. On the other hand, every organization—even a snakehead—needs a change of personnel from time to time. It keeps people on their toes. There were plenty of young lieutenants who deserved promotion. Yu would make a choice in due course.

Much less welcome was the man sitting opposite him. It was very rare for two members of Scorpia to be seen together in public, but Zeljan Kurst had telephoned him and insisted on a meeting. Major Yu had suggested the Ritz, but now he felt it had been a mistake. The big Yugoslavian, with his bald head and wrestler's shoulders, couldn't have looked more out of place. And he was drinking mineral water! Who drank mineral water at four o'clock in the afternoon?

"Why didn't you report to us about the boy?" Kurst asked.

"I didn't think it was relevant," Yu replied.

"Not relevant?"

"This is my operation. I have everything under control."

"That's not what I've heard."

It didn't surprise Yu that the executive board had learned about the destruction of the Chada Trading Agency and the death of Sukit. They were always watching each other's backs, doubtless working out where to place the knives. It was sad that criminals weren't the same anymore. No one trusted anyone.

"We're still not sure what happened last night," Yu said. It might be teatime in England but it was midnight in Bangkok. "It's not even clear the boy was responsible."

"This is Alex Rider," Kurst snapped. "We underestimated him once before and it was an expensive mistake. Why haven't you killed him already?"

"For obvious reasons." Yu's hand hovered over another sandwich, but he changed his mind. He had rather lost his appetite. "I was aware of Alex Rider's presence in Bangkok the moment he arrived," he continued. "I knew they were coming—a boy and a man—even before they left."

"Who told you?"

"That's my secret, and I intend to keep it that way. I could have arranged to have had the Rider child gunned down at Suvarnabhumi airport. It would have been simple. But that would have told ASIS that I was aware of their plans. They already suspect I have inside information. This would have confirmed it."

"So what do you intend to do?"

"I want to play with him. The fight at the arena was just the beginning, and there's no real harm done. The place was falling down anyway. But if you ask me, the situation is quite amusing. Here's the famous Alex Rider, dressed up as an Afghan refugee. He thinks he's so clever. But I have him in the palm of my hand and I can crush him at any time."

"That was what Julia Rothman thought."

"He's a child, Mr. Kurst. A very clever child, but a child all the same. I think you're overreacting."

Something deadly flickered in Kurst's eyes, and Yu made a mental note not to eat anything more. He wouldn't put it past Scorpia to slip a radioactive pellet into an egg-and-cress sandwich. They had done it before.

"We will be monitoring the situation," Kurst said at

length. "And I'm warning you, Major Yu, if we feel that things are getting out of hand, you will be replaced."

He got up and left.

Yu stayed where he was, thinking about what had just been said. He suspected that Levi Kroll was behind this. The Israeli had been maneuvering to take over control of Scorpia ever since Max Grendel had retired. He had also volunteered for the Reef Island business. He would be itching to move in if Yu failed.

He was not going to fail. Royal Blue had been thoroughly tested by Yu's operatives in Bangkok. The detonation system had been adapted. And in just two days' time it would set off on the next leg of its journey. All according to plan. But at the same time, Yu had decided to take out a little insurance. He and he alone would set off the bomb. He was the one who would take the credit for the worldwide devastation that would follow.

But how to stop Kroll from seizing control?

It was very simple. A little technological tinkering and nobody would be able to replace him. Yu smiled to himself and called for the bill.

"I should never have let you go," Ash exclaimed. "I can't believe I let them do that to you."

It was one o'clock in the morning in Bangkok, and Alex and Ash were back in their room on the third floor.

Alex had abandoned the ferry downriver on the other

side of an ugly modern bridge. From there, he'd had to
find his way across the city on foot, dripping wet, without
money and relying only on his sense of direction. He had
stopped twice to ask for directions from a monk and from
a stall holder closing up for the night. They spoke little
English but were able to understand enough to point him
in the right direction. Even so, it had been well after midnight by the time he had reached Chinatown. Ash had
been pacing the room like a lion in a cage, sick with
worry, and had grabbed hold of Alex when he finally arrived. He had listened to the story with disbelief.

"I shouldn't have let you go," he said again.

"You couldn't have known."

"I've heard about these fights. The snakeheads use
them all the time. Anyone who crosses them can end up
in the ring. People get crippled . . . or killed."

"I was lucky."

"You were smart, Alex." Ash looked at him approv-
ingly, as if seeing him in a completely different light. "You
say someone was there shooting. They attacked the building. Did you see who they were?"

"I got a glimpse of someone. But I'm sorry, Ash. It was
dark and it was all happening too quickly."

"Were they Thai or European?"

"I didn't see."

Alex was sitting on the bed, wrapped in a blanket. Ash
had put his clothes out to dry—not that there was much

chance of that. The night itself was damp, on the edge of a tropical storm. He had also brought Alex a bowl of chicken broth from the restaurant at the end of the alleyway. Alex needed it. He hadn't eaten since late that afternoon. He was starving and exhausted.

Ash examined him. "I remember the first time I met your father," he said suddenly. The change of subject took Alex by surprise. "I'd been sent out on a routine operation . . . in Prague. I was just backup. He was in charge . . . for the first time, I think. He was only a couple of years older than me." He took out a cigarette and rolled it between his fingers. "Anyway, everything that could go wrong did go wrong. A building blown to smithereens. Three ex-KGB agents dead in the street. The Czech police crawling all over us. And he was just like you are now."

"What do you mean?"

"I mean you take after him," Ash explained. "John always had the luck of the devil. He'd walk into trouble and somehow he'd get out of it in one piece. And then he'd sit there—the same as you—as if nothing had happened. Untouched by it."

"His luck ran out in the end," Alex said.

"Everyone's luck runs out in the end," Ash replied, and turned away, a haunted look in his eyes.

They didn't talk much more after that. Alex finished his soup and fell asleep almost immediately. The last thing he remembered was Ash, hunched over a cigarette, the red tip winking at him in the darkness as if sharing a secret.

Despite everything, Alex woke early the next morning. There were a couple of fat cockroaches crawling up the wall right next to him, but by now he had gotten used to them. They didn't bite or sting. They were just ugly. He ignored them and got out of bed. Ash had already been out, taking Alex's wet clothes to a laundry to be spun dry. He got dressed quickly, and the two of them went out for a bowl of *jok*—the rice porridge that many of the stalls served for breakfast.

They ate in silence, squatting on two wooden crates at the edge of the road with the traffic rumbling past. It had rained in the night, and there were huge puddles everywhere that somehow slowed the city down even more. Once again, Ash had slept badly and there were dark rings under his eyes. His wound was hurting him. He did his best not to show it, but Alex noticed him wince as he sat down, and he looked more ragged and drawn out than ever.

"I'm going to have to cross the river," he said at last.

"The Chada Trading Agency?" Alex shrugged. "You won't find very much of it left."

"I was thinking the same thing about our assignment." Ash threw down his spoon. "I'm not blaming you for what happened last night," he said. "But it may well be that our friends in the snakehead have no further interest in smuggling us into Australia. One of their main lieutenants is probably dead. And it has to be said, you took out a large chunk of their operation."

"I didn't set fire to the arena!" Alex protested.

"No. But you pulled it into the river."

"That put the fire out."

Ash half smiled. "Fair point. But I need to find out how things stand."

"Can I come?"

"Absolutely not, Alex. I think that's a bad idea. You go back to the room . . . and watch out for yourself. It's always possible that they'll send someone around to settle the score. I'll be back as soon as I can."

He walked off. Alex thought back over what he'd just said. Was Ash angry with him? It was difficult to read his moods . . . as if a life in the secret service had put any display of emotion under wraps. But Alex could see that things hadn't quite gone as expected. His job was to infiltrate the snakehead, not start a war with it. And the fake papers that were so important to Ash might well be sitting on the bottom of the river—and the rest of the Chada Trading Agency with them.

Alex got to his feet and began to walk slowly along the street, barely glancing at the brightly colored silks that every shop in this area seemed to sell. Thai main streets certainly weren't like English ones. In England, things were spread out. Here, you'd get whole clusters of shops all selling the same thing: whole streets of silk, whole streets of ceramics. He wondered how people chose where to go.

He wished Ash had taken him along. The truth was that he didn't want to spend any more time on his own and he'd had enough of Bangkok. As for his hopes that meeting Ash would tell him anything about himself, so far all he had been given were a few glimpses of the past. He was beginning to wonder if his godfather would ever open up enough to say anything meaningful at all.

He had just reached the top of the alleyway when he realized he was being followed.

Ash had warned him to keep his eyes open—and perhaps it was thanks to him that Alex spotted the man on the other side of the road, half hidden behind a vegetable stall. He didn't need to look twice. The man had changed his clothes. Gone were the red poppy and the leather jacket. But Alex was absolutely certain. This was the same square, hard-edged face that he had already seen at the airport and then again outside the Peninsula Hotel. Now he was here. He must have been trailing Alex for days.

The man had dressed himself up as a tourist, complete with camera and baseball cap, but his attention was fixed on the building where Alex and Ash were staying. Perhaps he was waiting for them to come out. Once again, Alex got the feeling that he knew the man from somewhere. But where? In which country? Could this be one of his old enemies catching up with him? He examined the cold blue eyes beneath the fringe of dark hair. A soldier? Alex was just about to make a connection when the man turned and began to walk away. He must have decided that there was no one at home. Alex made an instant decision. To hell with what Ash had told him. He was going to follow.

The man had set off down Yaowarak Road, one of the busiest streets in Chinatown, with huge signs carrying Chinese hieroglyphics high into the air. Alex was confident he wouldn't be seen. As ever, the pavement was cluttered with stalls, and if the man glanced back, Alex could find somewhere to hide in an instant. The real danger was that Alex could lose him. Despite the early hour, the crowds were already out—they formed a constantly shifting barrier between the two of them—and the man could disappear all too easily into a dozen entranceways. There were shops selling gold and spices. Cafés and restaurants. Arcades and tiny alleyways. The trick was to stay close enough not to lose him but far enough away not to be seen.

But the man didn't suspect anything. His pace hadn't changed. He took a right turn, then a left, and suddenly they were out of Chinatown and heading into the Old City, the very heart of Bangkok, where every street seemed to contain a temple or a shrine. The pavements were emptier here, and Alex had to be more careful, dropping farther back and hovering close to doorways or parked cars in case he had to duck out of sight.

They had been walking for about ten minutes when

the man turned off, passing through the entrance to a large temple complex. The gateway itself was decorated with silver and mother-of-pearl and opened into a courtyard filled with shrines and statues: a fantastic, richly decorated world where myth and religion collided in a cloud of incense and a blaze of gold and brilliantly colored mosaic.

The Thai word for a Buddhist monastery or temple is *wat*. There are thirty thousand of them scattered across the country, hundreds in Bangkok alone. There was a sign outside this one, giving its name in Thai and—helpfully—in English. It was called Wat Ho.

Alex only had a few moments to take in his surroundings: the ornamental ponds and *bodhi* trees that grow in every *wat* because they once gave shelter to the Buddha. He glanced at the golden figures—half woman, half lion—that guarded the main temple, the delicate slanting roofs, and the *mondops* . . . incredible, intricate towers with hundreds of tiny figures that must have taken years to carve by hand. A group of monks walked past him. Everywhere there were people kneeling in prayer. He had never been anywhere so peaceful.

The man he was following had disappeared behind a bell tower. Alex was suddenly afraid that he was going to lose him, at the same time wondering what it was that had brought him here. Could he have been mistaken? Could the man be a tourist after all? He hurried around the corner and stopped. The man had gone. In front of him, a crowd of Thais were kneeling at a shrine. A couple of backpackers were having their photograph taken in front of one of the terraces. Alex was angry with himself. He had been too slow. The entire journey had been a waste of time.

He took a step forward and froze as a shadow fell across him and a hand pressed something hard into his back.

"Don't turn around," a voice commanded, speaking in English.

Alex stood where he was, a sick feeling in his stomach. This was exactly what Ash had warned him against. The snakehead had sent someone after him, and he had allowed himself to be led straight into a trap. But why here—in a Thai temple? And how did the man know he spoke English?

"Walk across the courtyard. There's a red door on the other side of the shrine. Do you see it?"

Alex nodded. The man had a Liverpool accent. It sounded completely weird in the context of a Bangkok temple.

"Don't turn around. Don't try anything. We're going through the door. I'll give you more instructions on the other side."

Another jab with the gun. Alex didn't need any more prompting. He walked away from the bell tower, skirting the Thai people lost in their prayers. Briefly, he considered starting a fight, out here, while there were still witnesses. But it would do him no good. The man could shoot him in the back and disappear before anyone knew what had happened. The moment would come . . . but not yet.

The red door was set in the wall of a cloister—somewhere for the monks to walk in silent contemplation. It was surrounded by images of the *Ramakien,* the great story of gods and demons known to every child in Thailand. Gods or demons? He had little doubt to which one of them the man belonged.

As he approached, the door clicked open automatically. There had to be a surveillance camera somewhere, but, looking around, Alex couldn't see it. There was a modern corridor on the other side, with bare brick walls slanting down toward a second door. This one opened too. All the sounds of the temple had faded away behind him. He felt as if he was being swallowed up.

Alex wasn't going to let that happen. He timed his move very carefully. The second doorway was narrow, leading into a square-shaped hall that could have been the reception area of a lawyer's office or a stylish private bank. The walls were covered in wooden panels. There was an antique table with a lamp, a fan turning overhead. And more bizarre than anything, on the opposite wall, a picture of the queen of England.

As Alex made his way in, he hesitated, allowing the

man to catch up. Then suddenly he punched backward with his elbow, bringing his fist swinging around in the same motion.

It was a move he had been taught when he was training with the SAS in the Brecon Beacons in Wales. The elbow jab winds your man. The fist carries the gun aside, giving you time to spin around and kick out with all your strength. Never try it in the open because you'll end up getting shot. It only works in a confined space.

But not this time. The man seemed to have been expecting the maneuver. He had simply stepped aside the moment Alex began his move. Alex's first strike didn't make contact with anything, and before he could even begin to turn, he felt the cold farewell of the gun pressed against the side of his head.

"Nice try, Cub," the man said. "But much too slow."

And that was when Alex knew. "Fox!" he exclaimed.

The gun didn't matter anymore. Alex turned to stand face-to-face with the man—who was now grinning at him like an old friend. Which, in a sense, he was. The two of them had actually met in the Brecon Beacons. There had been four men in the unit to which Alex had been assigned: Wolf, Eagle, Snake, and Fox. None of them had been allowed to use their real names. While he was with them, Alex was Cub. And now that he thought about it, there had been one with a Liverpool accent. It seemed incredible that the two of them should have met up again in Bangkok, but there could be no doubt about it. Fox was standing in front of him now.

"You were at the airport," Alex said. "I saw you, wearing a poppy."

"Yes. I should have taken that off. But I'd just flown in from London myself."

"And you were at the Peninsula Hotel."

Fox nodded. "I couldn't believe it was you when I first saw you, so I followed you to be sure. I've been keeping an eye on you ever since, Alex. Lucky for you . . ."

"Last night . . ." Alex's head swam. "Was that you at the arena? You set the place on fire!"

"I followed you over to Patpong, and I was there when those men picked you up. Then I followed them down to the Chada Trading Agency. It wasn't easy, I can tell you. And it took me ages to weasel my way in. When I arrived, you were already in the ring. I thought you were going to get beaten to a pulp. But I'd seen where the main fuses were, so I sneaked back and turned out all the lights. Then I came looking for you. Things got a bit dicey when the lights came back on and I had to shoot a few of the opposition and throw a couple of grenades. The last time I saw you, you were in a ferry, trying to get away. It might have helped if you'd untied it first."

"You shot Anan Sukit."

"Was that his name? Well, he was trying to shoot you. It was the very least I could do."

"So what is this place?" Alex looked around. "What are you doing in Bangkok? And what's your real name? You can't go on expecting me to call you Fox."

"My real name's Ben Daniels. You're Alex Rider. Of course, I know that now."

"You've left the SAS?"

"I got assigned to MI6 Special Operations. And since you ask, that's where you are now. This is what you might call the Bangkok office of the Royal and General Bank."

The words were hardly out of his mouth when a door opened on the other side of the hallway and a woman walked into the room. Alex caught it at once . . . the faint smell of peppermint.

"Alex Rider!" Mrs. Jones exclaimed. "I have to say, you're the last person I expected to see. Come into my office immediately. I want to know—why aren't you at school?"

11

ARMED AND DANGEROUS

THE LAST TIME ALEX had seen Mrs. Jones, she had been visiting him in a North London hospital. Then she had seemed unsure of herself, regretful, blaming herself for the security lapse that had left Alex close to death on the pavement outside the MI6 offices on Liverpool Street. She had also been at her most human.

Now she was much more like the woman he had first met, dressed severely in a slate-colored jacket and dress with a single necklace that could have been silver or steel. Her hair was tied back, and her face—with those night black eyes—was utterly serious. Mrs. Jones was not exactly attractive, but neither did she try to be. In a way, her looks exactly suited her work as head of MI6, Special Operations, one of the most secretive departments of the British secret service. They gave nothing away.

Once again she was sucking a peppermint. Alex wondered if she had given up smoking at some time. Or was the habit also related to her job? When Mrs. Jones spoke, people had a tendency to die. It wouldn't surprise him if she felt the need to sweeten her breath.

The two of them were sitting in an office on the first floor of the building that stood directly behind Wat Ho. It was a very ordinary room with a wooden table and three leather chairs. Two large square windows looked out over the temple courtyard. Alex knew that all this could be deceptive. The glass was probably bulletproof. There would be hidden cameras and microphones. How many agents were there, mingling among the orange-robed monks? When it came to MI6, nothing was ever quite what it seemed.

Ben Daniels, the man he had known as Fox, was also there. He was younger than Alex had first thought—no more than twenty-two or twenty-three, laid back and thoughtful. He was sitting next to Alex. The two of them were opposite Mrs. Jones, who had taken her place behind the table.

Alex had told her his story, from the time he had splashed down off the Australian coast to his recruitment by ASIS, his meeting with Ash in Bangkok, and his first encounter with the snakehead. He noticed that she had reacted sharply at the mention of Ash. But then, of course, she must have known him. She had been there when his father went undercover, working for Scorpia. She might even have been involved in the operation in Malta that had brought him safely home.

"Well, Ethan Brooke certainly has nerve," she remarked when he had finished. "Recruiting you without so much as a by-your-leave! He could have talked to us first."

"I don't work for you," Alex said.

"I know you don't, Alex. But that's not the point. At the very least you're a British citizen, and if a foreign gov-

ernment is going to use you, they might as well ask." She
softened slightly. "For that matter, whatever prompted
you to go back into the field? I thought you'd had enough
of all this."

"I wanted to meet Ash," Alex said. Another thought
occurred to him. "Why did you never tell me about him?"
he asked.

"Why should I have?" Mrs. Jones replied. "I haven't
seen him for almost ten years."

"But he worked for you."

"He worked for Special Operations at the same time
as me. In fact, I had very little to do with him. I met him
once or twice. That's all."

"Do you know what happened in Malta?"

Mrs. Jones shook her head. "You'd have to ask Alan
Blunt," she said. "That was his operation. You know it
was all a setup. John Rider—your father—was pretending to work for Scorpia, and we had to get him back. We
set up a fake ambush in a place called Mdina, but it all
went wrong. Ash was nearly killed, and shortly after that
he left the service. That's all I can tell you."

"Where is Mr. Blunt?"

"He's in London."

"So why are you here?"

Mrs. Jones looked at Alex curiously. "You've
changed," she said. "You've grown up a lot. I suppose
we're to thank for that. You know, Alex, we weren't going
to use you again. I'd agreed with Alan—after what hap-

pened with Scorpia, that was going to be the end of it. But the next thing I knew, you're in America, up to your neck in it with the CIA. I ought to congratulate you, by the way. That business with the Ark Angel space station was quite remarkable."

"Thank you."

"And now ASIS! You certainly get around." Mrs. Jones reached forward and flipped open a file lying on the table in front of her. "It's strange that we should have run into you this way," she went on. "But it may be less of a coincidence than you think. Major Yu. Does that name mean anything to you?"

"He's in charge of the snakehead." Ethan Brooke had told Alex the name when he was in Sydney.

"Well, to answer your question, I'm here because we're investigating him. That's why Daniels is here too." Mrs. Jones tapped the file with her index finger. "How much did ASIS tell you about Major Wu?"

Alex shrugged. He felt uncomfortable suddenly, caught in the middle of two rival intelligence agencies. "Not very much," he admitted. "They don't seem to know a lot about him. That's part of my job . . ."

"Well, maybe I can help you." Mrs. Jones paused. "We've been interested in Major Winston Yu for some time, although we haven't managed to find out too much about him ourselves. We know he had a Chinese mother. His father is unknown. He was brought up in poverty in Hong Kong—his mother worked at a hotel—but cut forward eight years and you find him being privately educated in England. He went to Harrow School, for heaven's sake! How his mother managed to afford the fees is another question.

"He was an average student. We have copies of his reports. On the other hand, he seems to have fit in quite well, which is surprising, considering his race and background. There was a question mark over a rather nasty incident that took place in his first term—a couple of boys killed in a car accident—but nothing was ever proved. He was also very good at sports, a triple house blood, whatever that means.

"He left with reasonable grades and studied politics at London University, got a degree. After that, he went into the army. Trained at Sandhurst and did much better there. He seems to have taken to army life and was at the top of his class with the highest score in military, practical, and academic studies, for which he received highest honors. He joined one of our country's most distinguished regiments—the Household Cavalry—and served in the Falklands and the first Gulf War.

"Unfortunately, he developed a bone condition that brought an end to his army career. But he was snapped up by intelligence, and for a time he worked for MI6—not Special Operations. He was fairly low-level, gathering and processing information . . . that sort of thing. Well, eventually he'd had enough of it because one day he disappeared. We know he was active in Thailand and Australia, but there's no record of his activities, and it was only recently that we were able to identify him as the leader of one of the most powerful snakeheads in the region."

Mrs. Jones paused. When she looked up again, her eyes were bleak. "This may put you off, Alex. It may even persuade you to go home—and believe me, I wouldn't blame you. According to our sources, Major Yu may have contacts with Scorpia. It's even possible that he's on the executive board."

Scorpia. Alex had hoped he would never hear that name again. And Mrs. Jones was right. If Ethan Brooke had given him that information, he might have thought twice about the whole thing. He wondered if the head of ASIS had known. Almost certainly. But he'd needed Alex, so he'd decided to keep it under his hat.

"You still haven't told me why you're interested in him," Alex said.

"That's top secret." Mrs. Jones gestured with one hand. "But I'll tell you anyway. Apart from anything else, it may well be that you're in a position to help us— assuming that's something you'd even consider. Anyway, I'll explain and you can make up your own mind . . .

"Have you ever heard of the Daisy Cutter?"

Alex thought for a moment. "It's a bomb," he said. He remembered talking about it once at school, during history. "The Americans used it in Vietnam."

"They've also used it in Afghanistan," Mrs. Jones said.

"The Daisy Cutter, also known as BLU-82B or the Blue Boy, is the largest conventional bomb in existence. It's the size of a car . . . and I mean a Lincoln. Each bomb contains twelve-and-a-half-thousand pounds of ammonium nitrate, aluminum powder, and polystyrene, and it's powerful enough to destroy an entire building, easily. In fact, it'll probably take out a whole block."

"The Americans used it because it's terrifying," Daniels muttered. He was speaking for the first time. "It may not compare to a nuclear bomb, but there's nothing on the earth like it. The shock wave that it releases is unbelievable. You have no idea how much damage it can do."

"They used it in Vietnam to clear landing sites for helicopters," Mrs. Jones went on. "Drop one on the jungle and you'd have no jungle for half a mile around. They called it the Daisy Cutter because that was the pattern the explosion made. It was used in Afghanistan to scare the Taliban . . . to show them what they were up against."

"What's this got to do with Major Yu?" Alex asked. He was also wondering, with a sense of growing unease, what it might have to do with him.

"For the last few years, the British government has been developing a second generation of Daisy Cutters," Mrs. Jones explained. "They've managed to create a similar type of bomb except that it's a little smaller and it's more powerful, with an even greater shock wave. They gave it a code name, Royal Blue, and they'd built a prototype at a secret laboratory just outside London." She took out a peppermint and twisted off the wrapper with a single movement of her thumb and forefinger. "Three weeks ago the prototype was stolen. Eight of our people were killed. Three of them were security guards. The rest were technicians. It was a very professional operation: perfectly timed, ruthlessly executed." She slid the peppermint between her lips.

"And you think Major Yu . . . ?"

"These things aren't easy to transport, Alex. They need to be transported in a Hercules C-130 transport plane. We lost sight of the bomb, but two days later a C-130 took off with a flight plan that brought it to Bangkok via Albania and Tajikistan. We were able to identify the pilot . . . his name was Feng. He in turn had been employed by a criminal based here in Bangkok . . . a man called Anan Sukit . . ."

". . . and he works for the snakehead!" Alex finished the sentence.

"He *worked* for the snakehead," Mrs. Jones remarked sourly. "Until Daniels put three bullets into him."

It was all beginning to make sense. MI6 Special Operations were chasing a missing bomb that had led them to the snakehead. Alex was investigating the snakehead and that had led him to MI6. It was as if they had met in the middle.

"We were planning to put Daniels into the snakehead," Mrs. Jones continued. "We'd arranged a cover story for him. He was a rich European who'd flown out from London, hoping to put together a big drug deal. Of course, everything changed the moment he spotted you. As soon as we realized you were here, we decided to keep an eye on you and find out what you were up to. I have to say, we were very surprised when you changed your appearance." She ran an eye over Alex. "If we hadn't seen you at the airport, we wouldn't have recognized you."

"I like the teeth," Daniels muttered.

"So what now?" Alex asked. "You said you wanted me to help you."

"You and Ash have already penetrated the snakehead. You've also shaken things up a bit—no surprises there. Maybe you can find Royal Blue for us."

"It shouldn't be too hard to spot," Daniels said. "It's bloody huge. And if it goes bang, you'll hear it ten miles away."

Alex considered. Getting involved with MI6 again was the last thing he wanted, but in a way, what Mrs. Jones had told him had changed nothing. He was still working for ASIS. And if he did come across a bomb the size of a family car, there would be no harm in reporting it.

"What do they want it for?" he asked.

"That's what worries us most," Mrs. Jones replied. "We've got no idea. Obviously they must be planning something big—but not that big. A nuclear bomb would have been about one thousand times more powerful."

"So they're not out to destroy a whole city," Daniels added.

"But if this is a Scorpia operation, you can be pretty sure it's serious and large scale. These people aren't bank robbers . . . you know that better than anyone. I have to admit, we're in the dark. Anything you can find out will be helpful to us."

Once again, Alex fell silent. But he had made up his mind. "I'll have to tell Ash," he said.

Mrs. Jones nodded. "I don't see any harm in that. And in return, we can help you. You and Daniels already know each other. There's no point in trying to put him in undercover now. But he can continue to watch over you."

Ben smiled. "I'd be happy to do that," he said.

"We can give you something to contact him anytime. Has ASIS provided you with any equipment?"

Alex shook his head.

Mrs. Jones sighed. "That's the trouble with the Australians. They always rush into everything without a second thought. Well, we can give you what you need."

"Gadgets?" Alex's eyes lit up.

"You've got an old friend here. I think you ought to meet."

Smithers was down the corridor in a room that was a cross between a library, an office, and a workshop. He was sitting at a desk, surrounded by bits of machinery—like a destructive child on Christmas Day. There was a half-dismantled alarm clock, a laptop computer with its insides spilling out, a video camera divided into about

fifty different pieces, and a whole tangle of wires and circuits. Smithers himself was wearing sandals, baggy
shorts, and a bright yellow, short-sleeved shirt. Alex wondered how he could possibly carry so much weight around
in this heat. But he looked perfectly composed, sitting
with his great stomach stretching out toward his knees
and two very plump pink legs tucked away below. He was
fanning himself with a Chinese fan decorated with two in-
terweaving dragons.

"Alex? Is that you?" he exclaimed as Alex came into
the room. "My dear boy! You don't look like yourself at
all. Don't tell me! You must have spent some time with
Cloudy Webber."

"Do you know her?" Alex asked.

"We're old friends. The last time we met was at a party
in Athens. We were both in disguise, as it happened, and
we chatted for half an hour before we recognized each
other." He smiled. "But I can't believe you're back again.
So much has happened since I last saw you. That was
in America. Did my Stingo mosquito lotion come in
useful?"

Now it was Alex's turn to smile. The liquid that
Smithers had invented attracted insects instead of re-
pelling them and it had been very useful indeed, helping
to get him past a checkpoint on Flamingo Bay. "It was
great, thanks," he said. "What are you doing here?"

"Mrs. Jones asked me to think up a few gadgets for
our agents out here in the East," Smithers replied. He

lifted the fan. "This is one of them. It's very simple, but I rather like it. You see, it looks like an ordinary fan, but actually there are very thin plates of galvanized steel hidden under the silk. And when you bring them together . . ." He folded the fan, then brought it smashing down onto the desk. The wood shattered. ". . . it becomes a useful weapon. I call it . . ."

". . . the fan club?" Alex suggested.

Smithers laughed. "You're getting used to my little ways," he said. "Anyway, I've had all sorts of ideas since I came to Bangkok." He rifled around the surface of the desk and finally found a packet with a dozen sticks of incense. "Everyone burns incense out here," he explained. "It comes in jasmine and musk and it's rather lovely—but my incense has no smell at all."

"So what's the point?"

"After thirty seconds it will cause a whole room full of people to throw up. It's quite the most disgusting gadget I've ever invented, and I have to say we had no fun at all testing it. But it's still quite useful, I think."

He unfolded a sheaf of drawings. "I'm also working on one of these local taxis. They call them *tuk-tuks,* but this one has got a missile launcher built into the front headlight and a machine gun directly controlled by the handlebars, so I suppose you could say it's an attack *tuk.*"

"What's this?" Alex asked. He had reached out and picked up a small bronze Buddha sitting in the lotus position. With its round stomach and bald head, it reminded him a little of Smithers.

"Oh—do be careful with that!" Smithers exclaimed. "That's my Buddha hand grenade. Twist the head twice and throw it and anyone within ten yards can say their prayers."

He took it back and placed it carefully in a drawer.

"Mrs. Jones said you're taking on the snakeheads," he continued, and suddenly he was serious. "You be careful, Alex. I know you've done tremendously well in the past, but these people are seriously nasty."

"I know." Alex thought back to his first meeting with Anan Sukit and the fight in the riverside arena. He didn't need to be told.

"There are all sorts of things I'd love to equip you with," Smithers said. "But as I understand it, you're working undercover as an Afghan refugee. Which means that you won't be carrying very much. Is that right?"

Alex nodded. He was disappointed. Smithers had once given him a Game Boy jammed with special devices, and he would have felt more confident having something like that with him now.

Smithers reached forward and opened an old cigar box. The first thing he took out was a watch, a cheap fairground thing on a plastic strap. He handed it to Alex.

Alex looked at the time. According to the watch, it was six thirty. He shook it. "The watch doesn't work," he said.

"We have to think about the psychology," Smithers explained. "A poor Afghan refugee wouldn't own many possessions, but he would be very proud of the few he did have . . . even a broken watch. But this watch will work when it matters. There's a powerful transmitter and a battery inside. If you get in trouble, set the hands to eleven o'clock and it will send out a signal that will repeat every ten minutes for twenty-four hours. We'll be able to pick you up anywhere on the globe."

Smithers rummaged around in the box again and took out three coins. Alex recognized them. They were Thai currency—one baht, five baht, and ten baht, worth about fifty cents between them. "I don't think anyone would worry about a few local coins," he said, "but these are rather fun. They're actually miniature explosives. Let me show you how you detonate them."

He produced a half-empty packet of chewing gum. At least, that was what it looked like. But then he turned it around in his pudgy fingers and slid open a secret panel. There were three tiny switches on the other side, marked with the figures 1, 5, and 10. "This is how it works," he explained. "The coins are magnetic. You have to stick them to a metal surface to activate them. That'll stop you from accidentally blowing them up in your pocket. Then you flick the appropriate switch . . . just make sure you get the right value. The coins will blow open a lock or even smash a hole in a wall. Think of them as miniature land mines. And do try not to spend them!"

"Thanks, Mr. Smithers."

"And finally, I've got something that might come in very useful if you find yourself off the beaten track." Smithers pulled open a drawer in the desk and took out an old belt with a heavy silver buckle. "You can slip it into your jeans. There's a particularly sharp knife hidden inside the buckle. It's actually made out of toughened plastic, and it's rather cunningly designed so it won't show up on x-ray machines if you go through an airport. And if you slice open the belt, you'll find matches, medicine, water-purifying tablets, and knockout pills that are guaranteed to work on eleven different varieties of snake. I developed it for use in the jungle, and although you're not heading that way, you never know." He handed it across. "It's a shame, really. I'd love to give you the pants that go with it. The legs are highly flammable."

"Exploding jeans?" Alex asked.

"Flares," Smithers replied. He reached out and shook Alex's hand. "Good luck, my boy. And one last word of advice." He leaned forward as if afraid of being overheard. "I wouldn't trust these Australians if I were you. I mean, they're not a bad lot. But they are a bit rough, if you know what I mean. They don't play by the rules. Just keep your wits about you." He tapped the side of his nose. "And call for help the moment you need us. That Ben Daniels is a good guy. He won't let you down."

Alex gathered up his few weapons and left the room. As he left, he heard Smithers humming behind him. The song was that old Australian favorite, "Waltzing Matilda." Alex wondered what Smithers had meant by his warning. Did he really know something that Alex didn't, or was he just being mischievous?

Ben Daniels was waiting on the other side.

"Are you ready, Cub?" he asked.

"Armed and dangerous," Alex replied.

The two of them left together.

12

THE SILENT STREETS

ASH WAS ALREADY IN the room when Alex got back. At first he was angry.

"Where the hell have you been, Alex?" he growled. "I was worried about you. I told you to wait for me here." Then his eyes narrowed. He glanced down at Alex's waist. "That's a nice belt. Where did you get it?"

Alex was impressed. His godfather had spent half his life as a spy, and of course he had been trained to notice every detail. Despite everything that had happened in the last twenty-four hours, Ash had immediately picked up on this one tiny change in Alex's appearance.

"It was given to me," Alex said.

"Who by?"

"I met some old friends . . ."

Quickly Alex described what had happened: how he had seen Ben Daniels in the crowd, followed him to Wat Ho, and found himself in the MI6 stronghold. Mrs. Jones had given him permission to tell Ash about Royal Blue, and he mentioned the possible link between Major Yu and Scorpia. Ash's eyes grew dark when he heard the name.

"Nobody told me they were involved," he muttered. "I don't like this, Alex. And nor will Ethan Brooke. You and

I are meant to be gathering information. Nothing more, nothing less. Now it's getting messy."

"That's not my fault, Ash."

"Maybe I should go to this temple, have a word with Mrs. Jones." Ash thought for a moment, then shook his head. "No. There's no point in arguing with her. Go on . . ."

Alex went on with his story. It seemed that he was now working not for one but two secret services. He supposed Ash had a point. The mission had certainly been bent out of shape, and suddenly there was a ticking bomb at the heart of it. Why did Scorpia need Royal Blue? If Scorpia was involved, it was bound to be something big—and they wouldn't care how many people died. But why this bomb? Why not any other?

Alex tried to put it out of his head. He finished by describing how once again Smithers had equipped him.

"So Smithers is still with MI6!" Ash smiled briefly. "He's quite a character. And he supplied the belt? What does it do . . . besides keep your pants up?"

"I haven't had a chance to examine it yet," Alex admitted. "But there's a knife in the buckle. And there's stuff hidden inside. Some sort of jungle survival kit."

"Who said you were heading into the jungle?"

Alex shrugged.

Ash shook his head. "I'm not sure you should keep it," he said.

"Why not?"

"Because it may not fit in with your cover. It didn't come from Afghanistan like everything else you're wearing. If we get into any more trouble, it could be noticed."

"Forget it, Ash. I'm keeping it. But if you like, I'll make sure it's out of sight." Alex untucked his shirt and let it hang over the belt.

"What about the watch? Did Smithers give you that too?"

"Yes." Alex wasn't surprised that Ash had also noticed the watch. He held out his wrist. "In case you're wondering, the hands don't move. It's got a transmitter in it. I can call MI6."

"Why would you want to do that?"

"I might need help."

"If you need help, you can call me."

"I don't have your number, Ash."

Ash scowled. "I'm not sure ASIS would be too happy about any of this."

Alex held his ground. "I'm not sure I'd be too happy if I ended up dead," he said.

Ash could see that Alex was in no mood for an argument. "All right," he said. "Maybe it's for the best. I won't have to worry about you so much if I know you've got backup. But don't call MI6 without telling me—okay? Promise me that. I don't work for them anymore and when all is said and done, I've got my reputation to consider."

Alex nodded. He had decided not to mention the three

exploding coins and the detonators concealed in the chewing gum packet. Ash might try to take those too. He changed the subject. "How did you make out?" he asked. "Did you go to the river?"

Ash lit a cigarette. It still surprised Alex that a man who looked after himself so carefully in every other respect chose to smoke. "It's all good news," he said. "I found the arena where you were taken—or what was left of it—and spoke to a guy called Shaw. You may remember him. He was the one who took the photographs. Richard Shaw. Or Rick to his friends."

"What was he doing there?"

"There were dozens of them, salvaging what they could out of the wreckage. Papers, computer disks . . . that sort of thing. Our late friend, Mr. Sukit, had his offices there, and there was plenty of stuff they wouldn't want the police to find."

"What did Shaw say?"

"I got him to take me to Sukit's deputy. Another charming guy. Looked like he'd been in a street fight . . . face all over the place. He obviously had a lot on his mind but I persuaded him to send us on the next step of our journey. After all, we'd paid the money. And you'd done what they wanted. You'd taken part in their fight . . . even if you had humiliated their champion."

"What about the fire and all the rest of it?"

"Nothing to do with you. They think the Chada Trading Agency was hit by a rival gang. The long and the short of it is that they're happy to get us out of the way. We leave for Jakarta tonight."

"Jakarta?"

"We're moving farther down the pipeline, Alex. They're smuggling us into Australia via Indonesia. I don't know how—but it'll almost certainly involve some sort of ship. Jakarta's only about forty-eight hours by sea from Darwin. Maybe it'll be a fishing boat. Maybe something bigger. We'll find out soon enough."

"How do we get to Jakarta?"

"We fly just like anyone else." Ash produced a folder containing two airplane tickets, passports, visas, and a letter of credit written on fancy paper with the name Unwin Toys printed across the top. "We're being met at Jakarta International Airport," he went on. "I'm now a sales manager for Unwin Toys. Flying in to look at their new range and bringing my son with me."

"Unwin Toys . . . I've heard of them."

The name had seemed familiar the moment he saw it. Now Alex remembered. He had had seen their products all over London, often on market stalls or bargain basements on Oxford Street. They specialized in radio-controlled cars, building kits, and water pistols—always made out of colored plastic, manufactured in the Far East and guaranteed to fall apart a few days after they were opened. Unwin Toys wasn't a great name, but it was a well-known one and he found it hard to believe that it could be tied in with the snakehead.

It was as if Ash knew what was in his mind. "Think about it, Alex," he said. "A big company like Unwin Toys would be a perfect cover for a smuggling operation. They're moving goods all over the world and the fact that they're for little kids . . . it's the last place you'd think of looking."

Alex nodded. He could imagine it. A crate full of plastic trucks, each one loaded with a stash of heroin or cocaine. Water pistols that were actually the real thing. Teddy bears with God knows what inside. All sorts of unpleasant secrets could hide behind such an innocent facade.

"We're making real progress," Ash said. "But we still have to be careful. The more we know, the more dangerous we become to the snakehead." He thought for a moment. "What you said just now, about calling me. You're right. I want you to remember a telephone number. Write it on your hand."

"What telephone number?"

"If anything happens, if we get separated, call the number before you contact anyone else. It's my cell phone. But the number's special, Alex. It was given to me by ASIS. You can call from anywhere in the world and you'll be put through instantly. It will cost you nothing. The numbers will override any security system in any telephone network so you can reach me anytime, anywhere. What do you say?"

Alex nodded. "Fine."

Ash gave him the number. There were ten digits, but otherwise it was like no cell number Alex had ever heard before. He wrote them on the back of his hand. The numbers would soon fade, but by then he would have memorized them.

"What now?" he asked.

"We rest. Then we get a taxi to the airport. It's going to be a long night."

Alex realized the moment had come. They might not be able to speak to each other in Jakarta or on the way to Australia—certainly not in English—and very soon after that, the whole business would be over. Once they had arrived on the northern coast, Alex wouldn't be needed anymore.

"All right, Ash," he said. "You promised you'd tell me about my mom and dad. You were the best man at their wedding, and they made you my godfather. And you were there when they died. I want to know all about them because for me, it's like they didn't exist. I want to know where I came from . . . that's all . . . and what they thought about me." He paused. "And I want to know what happened on Malta. You said that Yassen Gregorovich was there. Was he the one who gave you that scar on your stomach? How did that happen? Was my dad to blame?"

There was a long silence. Then Ash nodded slowly. He stubbed out his cigarette.

"All right," he said. "On the plane."

They were thirty thousand feet above the Gulf of Thailand, heading south on the short flight to Jakarta. The plane was only half full. Alex and Ash had a whole row to themselves, right at the back. Ash had smartened himself up a little with a white shirt and a cheap tie. He was, after all, meant to be a sales manager. But Alex hadn't changed. He was grubby and a little ragged, still wearing the clothes he had been given in Bangkok. Perhaps that was why the two of them had been seated on their own. In front of them, the other passengers were dozing in the strange half-light of the cabin. Outside, the sun had set. The plane hung in the darkness.

Ash hadn't spoken while they took off and climbed into the sky. He had accepted two miniature whisky bottles from the stewardess, but he was still sitting in silence, his dark eyes blacker than ever, fixed on the ice in his glass as it slowly melted. He looked even more bummed out than usual. Alex had noticed him swallow two pills with his drink. It had taken him a while to realize that Ash was in constant pain. He was beginning to wonder if his godfather really was going to tell him what he wanted to know.

And then, without warning, Ash began to speak.

"I met your dad on my first assignment for Special

Operations. He'd only joined a year before me, but he was completely different. Everyone knew John Rider. Top of his class. Golden boy. On the fast track to the top." There was no rancor in Ash's voice. There was no emotion at all. "He couldn't have been more than twenty-four. Recruited out of the parachute force. Before that he'd been at Oxford University. A first class degree in politics and economics. And—oh yes—did I mention that he was also a brilliant athlete? Rowed for Oxford—and won. A good tennis player too. And now he was in Prague, in charge of his first operation, and I was a nobody sent along to learn the ropes.

"Well, as it turned out, the whole thing was a shambles. It wasn't John's fault. Sometimes it just happens that way. But afterward, at the debriefing, I met him properly for the first time and you know what I liked most about him? It was how calm he was. Three agents had died . . . not ours, thank God. The Czech police were going crazy. And the Museum of East European Folk Art and Antiquities had burned down. Actually, it wasn't really a museum, but that's another story. And as I say, your dad was more or less the same age as me and he wasn't even worried. He didn't shout at anyone. He never lost his temper. He just got on with it.

"After that, we became friends. I'm not sure how it happened. We lived near each other—he had an apartment in an old warehouse in Blackfriars, set back from the river. We started playing squash together. In the end we must have played about a hundred games, and you know what? I won at least a couple of them. Sometimes we met for a drink. He liked Black Velvet. Champagne and Guinness. He was away a lot, of course, and he wasn't allowed to tell me what he'd been doing. Even though we were in the same service, I didn't have clearance. But you heard things . . . and I looked in on him a couple of times when he was in the hospital. That was how I met your mother."

"She was a nurse."

"That's right. Helen Beckett. That was her maiden name. She was very attractive. Same color hair as you. And maybe the same eyes. I actually asked her out, if you want to know. She turned me down very sweetly. It turned out that she actually knew your dad from Oxford. They'd met a couple of times when she was studying medicine."

"Did she know what my dad did?"

"I don't know what he told her, but she probably had a pretty good idea. When you're treating someone with two broken ribs and a bullet wound, you don't imagine they fell over playing golf. But it didn't bother her. She looked after him. They started seeing each other. The next thing I knew, she had moved in with him and we weren't playing squash quite so often."

"Did you ever get married, Ash?" Alex asked.

Ash shook his head. "Never met the right girl . . . although I had fun with quite a few of the wrong ones. I'm actually quite glad, Alex. I'll tell you why.

"You can't afford to get scared in our business. Fear's the one thing that will kill you faster than anything, and although it's true to say that all agents are fearless, generally what that means is that they're not afraid for themselves. All that changes when you get married, and it's even worse when you have kids. Alan Blunt didn't want your dad to marry. He knew that in the end, he'd be losing his best man."

"He knew my mother?"

"He had her investigated." Alex looked shocked, and Ash smiled. "It was standard procedure. He had to be sure she wasn't a security risk."

So somewhere inside MI6 Special Operations there was a file on his mother. Alex made a mental note of it. Maybe one day it would be something he would dig up.

"I was quite surprised when John asked me to be his best man," Ash went on. "I mean, he was such a hotshot and nobody had even noticed I existed. But he didn't really have much choice. His brother, Ian, was away on an assignment . . . and there's something else you might as well know. Spies are pretty solitary. It goes with the territory, and I was the closest thing he had to a best friend. John was still seeing one or two people from the university—he'd told them he was working for an insurance company—but friendship doesn't really work when you have to lie all the time."

Alex knew that was true. It was the same for him at school. Everyone at Brookland believed he had been struck down by a series of illnesses in the past ten months. He'd been back at school a bit, and he'd even joined a school trip to Venice. But he'd felt like an outsider. Somehow his friends knew that something wasn't adding up and the knowledge made them less good friends than they had once been.

"Did he have any other family?" he asked.

"Apart from his brother?" Ash shook his head. "There was no family that I knew of. The wedding was at a registry office in London. There were only half a dozen people there."

Alex felt a twinge of sadness. He would have liked his mother to have had a white wedding in a country church with a big party in a tent and speeches and dancing and too much to drink. After all, he already knew, her happiness wasn't going to last long. But he understood that he was getting a glimpse of a secret agent's life. Friendless, secretive, and a little empty. The plane trembled briefly in the air, and farther down the aisle, one of the call lights blinked on. Outside the window, the sky was very black.

"Tell me more about my mother," Alex said.

"I can't, Alex," Ash replied. He twisted in his seat, and Alex noticed a flicker of pain in his eyes. The pills hadn't kicked in yet. "I mean, she liked to read. She went to the movies a lot—she preferred foreign films if she had a choice. She never bought expensive clothes, but she still looked good." Ash sighed. "I didn't know her that well. And she didn't really trust me, if you want the truth.

Maybe she blamed me. I was part of the world that put John in danger. She loved your dad. She hated what he did. And she was smart enough to know that she couldn't talk him out of it."

Ash opened the second miniature and poured the contents into his plastic glass.

"Helen found out she was expecting you at around the same time that John was sent out on his toughest assignment," Ash continued. "The two things couldn't have happened at a worse time. But a new organization had come to the attention of MI6. I don't need to tell you its name. I guess you know more about Scorpia than I do. Anyway, there it was: an international network of ex-spies and intelligence officers. People who'd gone into business for themselves.

"At first, they were useful. You have to remember that MI6 actually welcomed them when they first arrived. If you wanted information about what the CIA was up to or how the Iranians were getting on with their nuclear program, Scorpia would sell it to you. If you wanted to do something outside the law with no way of having it traced back to you, there they were. That was the whole point about them. They were loyal to no one. They were only interested in money. And they were very good at their job. Until you came along, Alex, they had never really failed.

"But MI6 got worried about them. They could see that Scorpia was getting out of control . . . particularly when a couple of their own agents got murdered in Madrid. All around the world, intelligence agencies were regulated, which is to say they played by the rules . . . at least, to a certain extent. But not Scorpia. They were growing bigger and more powerful, and at the same time they were becoming more ruthless. They didn't care how many people they killed so long as they got their check.

"So Alan Blunt—who'd just become the director of MI6 Special Operations—decided to put your father into Scorpia. The idea was to put him inside the organization . . . to get them to recruit him. Once he was there, he'd find out everything he could about them. Who was on the executive board? Who was paying them? Who were their connections within the intelligence agencies? That sort of thing. But to do that, MI6 had to put your dad into deep cover. That meant faking everything about him."

"I know about this," Alex interrupted. "They pretended he'd been in jail."

"They actually sent him to jail for a time. They had to be thorough. There were newspaper stories about him. Everyone turned against him. It looked like he lost all his money and he had to sell the apartment. He and Helen moved to some dump in Bermondsey. By then she was three months pregnant. It was very hard on her."

"But she must have known the truth."

"I can't tell you that. Maybe your dad told her. Maybe he didn't."

Alex couldn't believe that. Somehow he was sure his mother must have known.

"Either way, the setup worked," Ash continued. "He was recruited into Scorpia. They sent him to their training facility on the island of Malagosto, just a couple of miles from Venice."

The name made Alex shiver. He had been sent there himself when Scorpia had tried to recruit him.

"As far as Scorpia was concerned, John Rider was a gift," Ash said. "He was a brilliant operator. He had a track record inside British intelligence. And he was desperate. He was also a very good-looking man, by the way. One of the senior executives at Scorpia took a fancy to him."

"Julia Rothman." Alex had met her too. She had talked about his father over dinner in Positano.

"The very same. She quickly saw John's potential, and soon he was a senior training officer with special responsibility for some of Scorpia's younger recruits. And she gave him a code name. He was called Hunter."

"How do you know all this?" Alex asked.

"That's a good question." Ash smiled. "Because, finally, someone had noticed I existed. Alan Blunt sent me out to shadow John in the field. I was his backup. My job was to stay close but not too close . . . to be there if he needed to make contact. And that's how I came to be there when it all ended."

"In Malta."

"Yeah. In Malta."

"What happened?"

"Your dad was coming in. He'd had enough of Scorpia *and* MI6. You were on your way into the world. John just wanted a normal life—and anyway, he'd achieved what he'd set out to do. Thanks to him, we knew the entire structure of command within Scorpia. We had the names of most of their agents. We knew who was paying them and how much.

"The job now was to bring him home without arousing suspicion. Julia Rothman would kill him if she found out he was a spy. The plan was to get him back to England and then let him disappear. A new home. A new identity. The whole works . . . he'd start a new life in France with your mom. I should have mentioned that he spoke fluent French, by the way. If things had gone the way they'd planned, you'd be speaking French now. You'd be in a lycée in Marseilles or somewhere and you wouldn't know anything about all this.

"Well, it was right at this time that Scorpia provided the opportunity to get John out. There was a man called Caxero. He was a petty criminal. A drug dealer, a money launderer . . . that sort of thing. But he must have rubbed someone the wrong way because someone had paid Scorpia to hit him. Your dad was sent to do the job.

"Caxero lived in Mdina in the middle of Malta. It's an old citadel, completely surrounded by walls. In fact *ma-dina* is an Arabic word meaning exactly that . . . 'walled city.' Caxero's hometown had another name too. It was so quiet and full of shadows, even in the winter, that the locals called it the silent city. And MI6 realized it was the perfect place for the ambush that would bring John home.

"Your dad wasn't sent there alone. He was accompanied by a young assassin, one of the best who ever came out of Malagosto. I understand you met him. His name was Yassen Gregorovich."

Alex shivered again. He couldn't help himself. They were certainly digging deep into his past tonight.

He had met Yassen on his first mission and remembered the slim, fair-haired Russian with the ice-cold eyes. Yassen could have killed Alex then but had chosen not to. And then they had met a second time in the south of France. It had been Yassen who had led him into the nightmare world of Damian Cray. Alex thought back to the last moments they had been together. Once again Yassen had refused to kill him, and this time it had cost him his own life.

"What can you tell me about Yassen?" he asked.

"An interesting young man," Ash replied—but there was a sudden coldness in his voice. "He was born in a place called Estrov. You won't have heard of it but it was certainly of interest to us. The Russians had a secret facility there . . . bio-chemical warfare, but one day the whole place blew up. Hundreds of people were killed—and Yassen's father was one of them. His mother died six months later.

"The Russians tried to hush the whole thing up. They didn't want to admit anything had happened, and even now, we don't know the whole truth. But one thing was certain. By the end of the year, Yassen was totally alone. He was just fourteen years old, Alex. The same age as you are now."

"How did Scorpia find him?"

"He found them. He crossed the whole of Russia on his own, with no money and no food. He worked in Moscow for a while, living on the street and running errands for the local Mafiya. We still don't know how he managed to find his way to Scorpia, but the next thing we know, he turns up in Malagosto. Curiously, your dad was in charge of his training for a time. He told me the boy was a natural. It's funny, isn't it. In a way, you and Yassen had a lot in common." Ash turned to Alex, and he seemed suddenly ghostlike in the artificial light of the plane. A strange look came into his eyes. "John had a soft spot for Yassen," he said. "He really liked him. What do you make of that? The spy and the assassin. A bit of an odd couple, I'd say . . ."

And more than ten years later, Yassen had sacrificed himself for Alex, repaying the debt of an old friendship. But Alex didn't tell Ash that. For some reason, he wanted to keep it to himself.

"This was the deal," Ash said. Suddenly he sounded tired, like he wanted to get this over with. "Caxero was a man of habit—and that's dangerous if you're in crime.

He liked to have a black coffee and a cognac every night at a little café in the square opposite St. Paul's Cathedral in Mdina. That was where they were going to kill him. John let me know when the hit was arranged. It was going to be at eleven o'clock at night on November 11. All the elevens. We'd be there waiting. We'd let them take Caxero—he was a nasty piece of work and we might as well let Scorpia get him out of the way—and then we'd move in and grab John. But we'd let Yassen escape. He'd report back to Scorpia. He'd tell them that their man had been captured.

"It had to look good. I was in charge of the operation. This was the first time I was given command. I had nine men, and even though John was our target, we were all carrying real ammunition—not blanks. Yassen might have been able to tell the difference. He was that smart. We were all wearing concealed body armor. John wouldn't be aiming at us when we moved in, but Yassen would. And we already knew he was a crack shot.

"I'd put a couple of my people in place that morning. The cathedral had these two towers—one on either side—and I put one in each. I remember it also had two clocks. One of them was five minutes slow. I thought it was strange, the two faces showing different times. Anyway, the men in the towers had night vision glasses and radios. They could see the whole town from up there. They'd make sure that nothing went wrong."

Ash paused.

"Everything went wrong, Alex. Everything."

"Tell me."

Ash sipped his whisky. All the ice had melted.

"We arrived at Mdina just after ten thirty. It was a beautiful night. This was November, and all the tourists had gone. There was a sliver of a crescent moon and a sky full of stars. As we came in through the south gate, it was like stepping back a thousand years in time. The roads in Mdina are narrow and the walls are high. And all the bricks are different shapes and sizes. You can almost imagine them being put in place one by one.

"The whole place felt deserted. The shutters were closed on the houses, and the only light seemed to come from the wrought-iron lamps hanging over the corners. As we made our way up the Triq Villgaignon—that was the name of the main street—a horse-drawn carriage crossed in front of us. They use them to ferry tourists, but this one was on its way home. I can still hear the echo of the horse's hooves and the rattle of the wheels on the cobbles.

"I got a whisper in my earpiece from the lookout in the tower. Caxero was in his usual place, drinking his coffee and smoking a cigar. No sign of anyone else. It was a quarter to eleven.

"We crept forward . . . past an old chapel on one side of the road, a crumbling palazzo on the other. All the shops and restaurants were closed—some for the whole winter. I had seven men with me. We were all dressed in black. We'd spent half the day studying the map of Mdina, and I signaled them to spread out. We were going to surround the square, ready to move in.

"Ten to eleven. I could see the time on the cathedral clock. And there was Caxero. He was a short, round man in a suit. He had a fancy mustache, and he was holding his coffee cup with his little finger pointing into the air. There were a couple of cars parked in the square next to some cannons and a waiter standing in the door of the café. Otherwise, nothing.

"But then, suddenly, they were there . . . John Rider and Yassen Gregorovich—or Hunter and Cossack. Those were the names they used. They were five minutes early . . . that was what I thought. That was my first mistake."

"The clocks . . ."

"The cathedral clocks. Yes. One was right and one was wrong and in all the tension I'd been looking at the one that was five minutes slow. As for Yassen, it was like some trick in a movie. One minute he wasn't there, the next he was, with John next to him. It was a ninja technique—how to move and to stay invisible—and the irony was it was probably your dad who'd taught him.

"I don't think Caxero saw them coming. They walked straight up to him and he was still holding that coffee cup in that stupid way. He looked up just as a complete stranger shot him in the heart. Yassen didn't do it quickly. I remember thinking that I'd never seen anyone so relaxed.

"I was worried that my men wouldn't be in place yet, that not all the exits from the square would be covered. But in a way that didn't matter. Don't forget. We wanted Yassen to escape. That was part of the plan.

"I stepped out of my hiding place.

"Yassen saw me and all hell broke loose.

"Yassen fired at me. Two of his bullets missed, but I felt the third slam into my chest. It was like being hit by a sledgehammer, and if I hadn't been wearing an armor-plated vest, I'd have been killed. As it was, I was blown off my feet. I went smashing down into the cobbles, almost dislocating my shoulder. But I didn't hang around, Alex. I got straight back up again. That was my second mistake. I'll come to that later.

"Anyway, suddenly everyone was firing at once. The waiter turned around and dived for cover. About half a second later, the plate-glass window of the café shattered. It came down like a shower of ice. The men high up in the cathedral were using rifles. The others were entering the square from different sides. Your dad and Yassen had separated—as I knew they would. It was standard procedure. Staying together would have just made it easier for us to catch both of them. For a moment, I thought everything was going to work out all right after all.

"It didn't.

"Three of my men grabbed hold of John. They'd cornered him, and it really would look as if there had been nothing he could have done. They made him throw down his weapon and lie flat on his face. That left three others to go after Yassen. Of course, they'd let him get away. But it would still be close. That was the plan.

"Only Yassen Gregorovich had plans of his own. He was halfway across the square, making for one of the side streets. But then suddenly he stopped, turned around, and fired three times. The gun had a silencer. It hardly made any sound. And this time he wasn't aiming for the chest. His bullets hit one of my men between the eyes, one in the side of the neck, and one in the throat. Two of them died instantly. The third went down and didn't move.

"There was still one agent left. His name was Travis, and I'd chosen him personally. He was on the far side of the square, and I saw him hesitate. He didn't know what to do. After all, I'd given him orders not to shoot Yassen. Well, he should have disobeyed me. The situation was out of control. Enough people had already died that night. He should have got the hell out of there—but he didn't. He just stood there and Yassen gunned him down too. A bullet in the leg to bring him down and then another in the head to finish him off. The whole square was littered with bodies. And this whole thing was meant to be bloodless!"

Ash fell silent.

Alex noticed he had finished his whisky. "Do you want another drink, Ash?" he asked.

Ash shook his head. Then he went on.

"Yassen had gone. We had John. So in a way, we'd succeeded. Maybe I should have left it at that. But I couldn't. This was my first solo operation, and Yassen Gregorovich had wiped out almost half my task force. I went after him.

"I don't know what I was thinking. Part of me knew that I couldn't kill him. But I couldn't just let him go. I pulled off my body armor. It had a quick release and I couldn't run with it on. Then I started across the square and toward the northern wall. I heard someone shout after me—it might even have been John. But I didn't care. I turned a corner. I remember the pink stone and a balcony like something in an opera house. I couldn't see anyone. I thought Yassen must have got away.

"And then, without any warning, he stepped out in front of me.

"He'd waited! A whole town crowded with MI6 agents and he'd just stood there like he owned the place and none of us could touch him. I ran straight into him. I couldn't stop myself. His hand moved so fast that I didn't see it. I felt it smash into the nerve points in my wrist. I lost my gun. It went spinning away into the darkness. At the same time, his gun pressed against my neck.

"He was ten years younger than me. A Russian kid

who'd got sucked into all this because his parents had died in an accident. And he'd beaten me. He'd taken out half my team. I was going to be next.

"'Who are you?' he asked.

"'MI6,' I told him. There was no point in lying. We wanted Scorpia to know.

"'How did you know I would be here?'

"I didn't answer that. He pushed harder with the gun. It was hurting me. But that didn't matter. It would all be over soon anyway.

"'You should have stayed home,' he said.

"And then he turned and ran.

"To this day, I don't know why he didn't shoot me. Maybe his gun had jammed. Or maybe it was simpler than that. He'd killed Caxero, Travis, and three more of my men. Maybe he'd run out of ammunition. I watched him disappear down the next alleyway, and that was when I realized that he'd had a knife as well as a gun. The hilt was sticking out of my stomach. I didn't feel anything. But looking down . . . there was so much blood. It was pouring out of me. It was everywhere."

Ash stopped. The soft scream of the plane's engines rose in pitch for a moment. Alex wondered if they were coming into Jakarta.

"The pain came later," Ash said. "You have no idea how bad it was. I should have died that night. Maybe I would have. Only your dad had come after me. He'd feared the worst—and he'd put his own life at risk because if Yassen had seen him, he would have known that the whole thing was a setup. By then I was on the ground. I was slipping away fast. And I was cold. I've never felt so cold.

"Your father didn't take the knife out. He knew that would kill me right away. He put pressure on the wound and kept it there until the ambulance came. I was airlifted to Valetta, where I was in critical condition for a week. I'd lost five pints of blood. In the end, I came through, but . . . you've seen the scar. I'm missing about half my stomach. There wasn't anything they could do about that. There are about a hundred things I'm not allowed to eat because there's nowhere for them to go. And I have to take pills . . . a lot of pills. But I'm alive. I suppose I should be grateful for that."

There was a long silence.

"Scorpia got my dad in the end," Alex said.

"Yeah. A couple of months later. After you were born. I was there at the christening, Alex. It was almost the last time I saw your dad—and if it makes you feel any better, I never saw him happier than when he was holding you. He and your mother. It was like you made them real people again. You took them out of the shadows."

"You went with them to the airport. They were on their way to France. You said they were going to Marseille."

"They were looking for a new house. More than that. A new life."

"You were there when the bomb went off on their plane."

Ash looked away. "I said I wouldn't talk about that and I meant it. Somehow Scorpia found out they'd been tricked and they took revenge. That's all I know."

"What happened to you, Ash? Why did you leave MI6?"

"I'll tell you that, Alex, but that's the end of it. I think I've lived up to my side of the bargain."

Ash crumpled his plastic glass and shoved the broken pieces into the compartment in front of him.

"I didn't come out of it too well, if you want the truth," he said. "I was on sick leave for six weeks, and the day I got back to Liverpool Street, Alan Blunt called me into his office. He then chewed me out for everything that had gone wrong.

"First of all, there was the thing with the time. The wrong clock. But it turned out that the most stupid mistake I'd made was to stand up after Yassen had shot me. You see, that had told him we were all wearing body armor and that was the reason he'd shot Travis and the others in the head. It was all my fault . . . at least, according to Blunt."

"That wasn't fair," Alex muttered.

"You know what, mate? I thought more or less the same thing. And finally, chasing after Yassen when the whole point was to let him get away. That was the final nail in my coffin. Blunt didn't fire me. But I was demoted. He made it clear that I wouldn't be heading up any more operations for some time to come. It didn't matter that I'd almost been killed. In a way, that just made it worse."

Ash shook his head.

"It was a little while later that your parents died together on that plane, and after that my heart sort of went out of it. I told you when we were in Bangkok. It was your dad who was the patriot, serving his country. For me it was always just a job. And I'd had enough of it. I did a few more months' desk duty, but then I handed in my resignation and headed down under. ASIS were keen to have me. And I wanted to start again.

"I saw you a few times, Alex. I looked in on you to see that you were okay. After all, I was your godfather. But by then Ian Rider had started adoption proceedings. I had a drink with him the night before I left England, and he told me he was going to look after you and it was obvious you didn't need me. In fact, if truth be told, you were probably better off without me. I hadn't been much help, had I!"

"You shouldn't blame yourself," Alex said. "I don't."

"Anyway, I saw you again one more time. I was in London, working with the Australian embassy. You were still in elementary school—and Jack was looking after you."

"You went out with her."

"A couple of times. We had a laugh together."

Ash glanced briefly at Alex as if searching for something. "I couldn't believe it when I heard that MI6 had recruited you," he muttered. "Alan Blunt doesn't miss a trick. And then, when you wound up in Australia! But I still wish you hadn't come on this mission, Alex. I don't want you to get hurt."

"A bit late now, Ash."

The lights in the cabin came back on. The stewardesses began to move up the aisle. At the same time, Alex felt his stomach lurch as they began to come down.

They had arrived in Jakarta, the next step on their way. The end of the pipeline was in sight.

13

UNWIN TOYS

SOMETIMES ALEX WONDERED IF all the airports in the world hadn't been designed by the same architect: someone with a love of shops and corridors, plate-glass windows and potted plants. Here he was at Soekarno-Hatta, the international airport of Jakarta, but it might just as well have been Perth or Bangkok. The floors might be more polished and the ceilings higher. And every other shop seemed to be selling rattan furniture or the colorful printed cloth known as batik. But otherwise he could have been right back where he started.

They came through passport control quickly. The official in his glass-fronted booth barely glanced at the forged documents before stamping them, and without a word being spoken, they were in. Nor did they have to wait at baggage claim. They had just one suitcase between them, and Ash had carried it on and off the plane.

Alex was tired. It was as if the events of the last five days in Bangkok had finally caught up with him, and all he wanted to do was sleep—although somehow he doubted he would spend what was left of the night in a comfortable bed. Most of all, he wanted time on his own to reflect over what Ash had told him. He had learned more about his past in the last hour than he had in his entire life, but there were still questions he wanted to ask. Had his father blamed Ash for the mistakes that had been made in Mdina? Why had his parents decided to go to France, and why had Ash been with them at the airport? What had he seen that he was so unwilling to talk about?

They passed into the arrivals area, and once again they were surrounded by a crowd of touts and taxi drivers. This time there were two men waiting for them, both Indonesian, slim and slightly effeminate in jeans and short-sleeved shirts. One of them was holding a placard that read: Karim Hassan. Alex stared at it for a few seconds before the name registered, and he was annoyed with himself. He had completely forgotten that it was the name under which Ash was traveling. Ash was Karim. He was Abdul. It didn't matter how tired he was. A mistake like that could get them both killed.

Ash went over to them and introduced himself using a mixture of Dari and sign language. The two men didn't even try to be friendly. They simply turned and walked away, expecting Ash and Alex to follow.

It was ten o'clock, and outside, away from the artificial climate of the air-conditioning, the heat was thick and unwelcoming. Nobody spoke as they crossed the main concourse to the curbside where a dirty white van was parked with a third man in the driving seat. The van had sliding doors and, at the back, no windows. Alex glanced nervously at Ash. He felt as if he was about to be swallowed up, and he remembered the last time he had gotten into a car with members of the snakehead. But Ash didn't look worried. Alex followed him in.

The door slammed shut. The two men got in front with the driver, and they moved off. Alex and Ash sat on a metal bench that had been welded to the floor. Their only view was out the front window, and that was so filthy, Alex wondered how even the driver could see where they were going. The van was at least ten years old and had no suspension at all. Alex felt every bump, every pothole. And there was plenty of both.

The airport was about twelve miles from the city, connected by a highway that was clogged with traffic even at this time of the night. Squinting over the driver's shoulder, Alex barely saw anything until, at last, Jakarta came into sight. It reminded him at first of Bangkok, but as they drew closer, he saw that it was uglier and somehow less sure of itself, still struggling to escape from the sprawling shantytown it had once been.

The traffic was horrible. They were carried into Jakarta on a concrete overpass, and suddenly there were cars and motorcycles above them and below them as well as on both sides. Skyscrapers—bulky rather than beautiful—rose up ahead, a thousand lightbulbs burning uselessly in offices that must surely be empty, coloring the night sky yellow and gray. There were brightly colored food stalls—*warungs*—along the sidewalks. But nobody seemed to be eating. The crowds were drifting home like sleepwalkers, pushing their way through the noise and

the dirt and the heat as the storm clouds closed in overhead.

They turned off the overpass and seemed to leave the
main sprawl of the city as quickly as they had entered it.
Suddenly the van was rumbling over a dirt track, splashing through puddles, and weaving around loose bricks
and rubble. There were no streetlamps, no signs, no illu-
mination from a moon that had been blocked out by
cloud. Alex saw only what the headlights showed him.
This was some sort of suburb, a slum area with narrow
streets, houses with tin roofs and corrugated iron patches,
walls held up by wooden scaffolding. Strange, spiky
shrubs and stunted palm trees grew out of the side of the
road. There was no pavement. Somewhere a dog barked.
But nowhere was there any sign of life.

They came to a gate that seemed to have been bolted
together from pieces of driftwood. Two words—in Indonesian letters—had been scrawled across it in red
paint. As they approached, the driver pressed a remote
control in the van and the gate opened, allowing them
into a large, square compound with warehouses and offices, lit by a couple of arc lamps and fenced in on all
sides. The van stopped. They had arrived.

No one else seemed to be there. The doors of the van
were pulled back, and the two men led Alex and Ash into
one of the warehouses. Alex saw crates piled high, some
of them open, spilling out straw and plastic toys. There
was a pile of scooters, tangled together, a Barbie house

lying on its side. A furry monkey was slumped with its legs apart, foam hanging out of a gash in its stomach, staring at them with empty glass eyes. Alex hoped it wasn't an omen. He had never seen a collection of toys that looked less fun. From the look of them—dusty and dilapidated—they could have been here for years.

Two thin mattresses spread out on the floor told him the worst. This was where they were supposed to sleep. There was no sign of any toilet or anywhere to wash. Ash turned to the men and signaled, cupping his hand against his mouth. He was thirsty. The men shrugged and walked out.

It was to be the longest nine hours of Alex's life. He had no sheets or blankets, and the mattress did almost nothing to protect him from the stone floor underneath. He was sweating. His clothes were digging into him. The whole of Jakarta was in the grip of a storm that refused to break, and the air seemed to be nine parts water. Worst of all were the mosquitoes. They found him almost immediately and refused to leave him alone. There was no point slapping at his face, and after a while Alex stopped bothering. The mosquitoes didn't seem to care. The only escape would be sleep, but sleep refused to come.

Ash couldn't talk to him. There was always a chance there might be microphones in the room. Anyway, he was used to this. To Alex's annoyance, his godfather was asleep almost at once, leaving him on his own to suffer through every minute of the night.

But at last the morning came. Alex must have drifted into some sort of half sleep because the next thing he knew, Ash was shaking him and gray daylight was seeping in through the windows and the open door. Someone had brought them two glasses of sweet tea and a basket of bread rolls. Alex would have preferred eggs and bacon but decided it was probably better not to complain. Squatting on his mattress, he began to eat.

What was going on? Alex realized that the false passports they had been given in Bangkok had been enough to get them into Indonesia but that Australia, with far stricter border controls, would prove more difficult. The island of Java was about as near as they could get to Australian soil, and the last part of the journey would have to be taken across the sea—a passage of just forty-eight hours, Ash had said. The place they were in now was connected to Unwin Toys . . . a storage depot and office complex from what Alex had seen the night before. They were going to have to wait here until their boat was ready. And what sort of boat would that be? He would find out in good time.

Shortly after nine o'clock, one of the two men who had met them in the airport came for them and led them out of the warehouse where they had slept. The morning light was thick and gloomy, but at least it allowed Alex to take better stock of his surroundings. Unwin Toys reminded him of an old-fashioned prisoner-of-war camp, something out of a movie from World War II. The buildings were made of wood and seemed to have been slapped together in a hurry, using whatever was at hand, with rickety staircases leading up to the first floor. The main square was cracked and uneven, with weeds sprouting out of the cement. It was hard to imagine an innocent toy wrapped up under a Christmas tree in England might have begun its life here.

By now there were a dozen or so men and women in the complex. Some of them were office staff, sitting behind windows, tapping away at computers. A truck had arrived and there were people unloading it, passing cardboard boxes from hand to hand. Two guards stood by the gate. They seemed to be unarmed but—with the wire fence surrounding them, the arc lamps, and the security cameras—Alex suspected they must be carrying guns. This was a secret world. It wanted to keep its distance from the city outside.

He looked up. The clouds were thick, an ugly shade of gray. He couldn't see the sun, but he could feel it, pressing down on them. Surely it would rain again soon. The entire atmosphere was like a balloon filled with water. At any time it would have to burst.

It was time to go. The white van was there with its engine running. The sliding door was open. Somebody called out to them. Ash took a step forward.

Alex would remember the moment later. It was like a flash photograph . . . a few seconds caught in time when everything is normal and everyone in the picture is still unaware of the approaching danger. He heard a car approaching the main gate. It occurred to him that the car was being driven far too fast, that it would surely have to slow down so that the gate could be opened. Then the realization came that the car wasn't going to slow down, that the driver didn't need an open gate to enter.

Without any further warning, the gates of the complex were smashed to pieces, one side flying open, the other hanging drunkenly off its hinges as first one, then a second huge Jeep Cherokee burst through. Each one carried five men who came tumbling out almost before the Jeep had stopped. They were all armed with CZ-Scorpion submachine guns or AK-47 assault rifles. Some also carried knives. They were dressed in combat outfits, and most of them wore red berets, but they didn't look like soldiers. Their hair was too long, and they hadn't shaved. Nobody seemed to be in charge. As they spread out across the yard, waving their weapons from side to side and screaming out orders, Alex was convinced that he had stepped into the middle of an armed robbery and that he was about to witness a shoot-out between different Jakarta gangs.

Everyone in the yard had scattered, trying to reach the safety of the buildings, but Ash had stopped dead. He turned to Alex and muttered a single word. "Kopassus." It meant nothing to Alex. So, making sure nobody could hear him, he added in English: "Indonesian SAS."

He was right.

Kopassus is an abbreviation of *Komando Pasukan Khusus,* and it's the name of one of the most ruthless fighting forces in the world. It is well known—indeed, it is expected—that at least one recruit will die during basic training. After all, they use live ammunition and any injury, even a broken arm or leg, is considered a sign of weakness and will lead to immediate dismissal. In addition to reaching a standard of fitness that is almost superhuman, Kopassus soldiers are expected to acquire a range of specialist skills, including diving, mountaineering, close-quarter combat (CQC), electronic warfare, and at least two foreign languages.

There are five different groups within Kopassus, specializing in sabotage, infiltration, direct action, intelligence, and counterterrorism. The men who had just broken into the compound came from Group 4, also called Sandhi Yudha, a counterintelligence group based in Cijantung in the south of Jakara with special responsibility for smuggling operations in and out of Jakarta. It might have been luck that had brought them here. Or it could have been the result of a tip-off. But Alex saw that as far as he and Ash were concerned, their work might be over. They'd eventually be able to talk their way out of prison . . . Ash would only have to prove that he worked for ASIS. But doing so would destroy his cover. They would never find out how the snakehead had planned to get them into Australia. And, Alex reflected bitterly, he would never catch up with the stolen weapon that Mrs. Jones was looking for—Royal Blue.

In other words, he would have failed twice.

But there was nothing he could do. The Kopassus soldiers had taken up positions across the square so that every angle was covered and nobody could move without being seen. They were still shouting in Indonesian. It didn't really matter what they were saying. Their aim was to confuse and intimidate the opposition. And they seemed to have succeeded. The civilians inside the compound were standing helplessly. Some of them had raised their arms. The Kopassus was in control.

They were made to line up. Alex found himself between Ash and one of the men who had first met them when they came from the airport. They were covered by at least half a dozen guns. At the same time, three of the soldiers were searching inside the offices and warehouses, making sure there was nobody hiding. One of the toy workers had decided to do exactly that. Alex heard a scream, then the smash of breaking glass as the unfortunate man was hurled, headfirst, through a window. He came crashing down in the courtyard, blood streaming from his face. Another of the soldiers lashed out with a foot and the man howled, then gathered himself to his feet and limped over to join the line.

One last man had climbed out of the jeep. This was presumably the commanding officer. He was unusually tall for an Indonesian, with a long, slender neck and black hair coming down to his shoulders. Alex heard one of the soldiers refer to him as *kolonel* and guessed that must be his rank. Slowly the colonel made his way along the line, shouting out instructions. He was asking for ID.

One after another the toy workers produced scraps of paper, driver's licenses or work permits. The man who had been thrown out of the window held his up with shaking hands. The colonel didn't seem interested in any of them. Then he reached Ash. Alex tried not to look as Ash took out the fake passport they had been given in Bangkok. He was afraid his eyes might give something away. He glanced down as the colonel opened the passport and held it up to the light. On the edge of his vision, he saw the colonel hesitate. Then suddenly the man struck out, hitting Ash on both sides of the face with the offending document and screaming at him in his own language. Two soldiers appeared from nowhere, pinning Ash's arms behind his back and forcing him down onto his knees. The barrel of a machine gun was pressed into his neck. The colonel handed the passport to one of his subordinates. For a moment he examined Ash's face, gazing into his eyes as if his true identity might be found there. Then he moved on.

He stopped in front of Alex.

Alex looked up. He was scared, and he didn't care if he looked it. Maybe the man would decide that he was just a kid and leave him alone. But the colonel didn't care how

old he was. He smelled blood. Something like a smile
spread over his face, and he rapped out a sentence in Indonesian, holding out a hand for Alex's ID. Alex froze. He
didn't have his own passport. That was in Ash's pocket.
But even if he was able to produce it, the colonel would
know it was fake. Should he tell the man who he was?
Just a few words in English would do the trick. End the
danger. End the mission too.

It began to rain.

No. It wasn't quite like that. In London, rain has a
beginning, a few drops that send people scattering for
cover and allow time for umbrellas to rise. In Jakarta,
there was no warning. The rain fell as if a skin had burst.
In an instant it was flooding down, warm and solid, an
ocean of rain that spluttered out of the drainpipes, hammered against the roofs, and turned the earth to mud.

And with the flood came a brief moment of confusion.
Up until then, the Kopassus had been in complete control
of the complex, working with a plan that allowed them to
cover every inch of ground. The sudden downpour
changed things. Alex didn't even see where the gunfire
began. But someone must have decided that they had too
much to lose and that the rain would give them enough
cover to risk shooting their way out of here. There were
half a dozen shots. The bullets came from somewhere
near the warehouse where Alex had slept, a single gun,
fired carefully, at exactly equal intervals. One of the
Kopassus men went down, clutching his arm. The rest re-

acted instantly, diving for cover, returning fire even as they went. The sound of their machine guns was deafening. They didn't seem to care where they were aiming. Alex saw an entire wall ripping itself apart, the wooden planks shredded. A man who had been standing near the door was blown off his feet by the first volley. Alex had seen him just two minutes before, sweeping out the yard.

But the Kopassus were taking casualties too. At least three guns were being fired at them. As Alex turned, searching for cover, the soldier whose gun had been pressed against Ash's neck fell back, a mushroom of blood erupting out of his shoulder. Immediately a second man stepped into his place, firing in the direction from which the bullets had come, the nozzle of his machine gun flashing white behind the rain.

The colonel had pulled out a pistol, a Swiss-made SIG-Sauer P226 and one of the ugliest nine-millimeter weapons on the market. Alex saw him take aim at Ash. His intention was clear. He had been about to arrest a man and that had provoked a firestorm . . . at least, that was what he thought. Well, whoever the man was, the colonel wasn't going to let him get away. Rough justice. He would execute him here and now and put an end to all this.

Alex couldn't let it happen. With a cry, he hurled himself sideways, his shoulder slamming into the colonel's stomach. The gun went off, the bullet firing into the air.

The two of them flew backward, carried by Alex's veloc-ity, and came crashing down in a puddle. The colonel tried to bring the gun around to aim at Alex. Alex caught hold of his wrist and slammed it down, smashing the back of his hand against a rock. The colonel cried out. Rain was driving into Alex's face, blinding him. He forced the hand up and down a second time. The fingers opened and the gun fell free.

Part of him knew that this was all wrong. He was on the same side as the Kopassus, both of them fighting the snakehead, who were the true enemy. But there was no time to explain. Alex saw a soldier throw something—a round, black object about the size of a baseball—through the deluge. He knew at once what it was, even before the explosion that tore open the side of the warehouse, smashed three windows, and blew a hole in the roof. A tongue of flame leapt up, only to be driven back by the rain.

More gunfire. The man who had thrown the grenade cried out and reeled backward, clutching his shoulder. The white van was moving. Alex heard the engine rev, then saw the van begin a clumsy three-point turn. At the same moment, Ash grabbed hold of his arm. His hair was matted. Water was streaming down his face.

"We have to go!" he shouted. With the noise of the rain and shooting there was no chance of his being over-heard.

The colonel lunged sideways and tried to reach the gun. Ash kicked it away, than brought a fist crashing down on the man's head.

"Ash . . . ," Alex began.

"Later!"

The van had completed its first turn. It was being brought around to face the shattered gate. Ash started forward, and Alex followed. They reached the van just as it began to pick up speed. Ash reached out and wrenched open the back door. The driver wasn't waiting for them. There was a burst of machine-gun fire, and Alex cried out as a line of bullet holes stitched themselves across the side of the van right in front of him.

"Go!" Ash shouted.

Alex threw himself forward, through the door, and into the back of the van. A second later, Ash followed, landing on top of him. The driver didn't even seem to have noticed they were there. All he cared about was getting away himself. One of the side mirrors exploded, the glass shattering, the metal casing tearing free. The engine screamed as the driver pressed his foot on the accelerator. They leapt forward. There was an explosion, so close that Alex felt the flames scorch the side of his face. But then they were away, shooting out through the gate and into the street beyond.

The van skidded all over the road. It slammed into a wall and one side crumpled, sparks flickering as metal and brick collided. Alex glanced back. One of the van's doors had been blown off, and he saw two soldiers—they looked like ghosts—kneeling in the gate, firing at them. Bullets, burning white, sliced through the rain. But they were already out of range. They hurtled up the track they had come down the night before . . . by now it was little more than a brown river of mud and debris. Alex looked back, expecting the Kopassus to follow. But the rain was falling so hard that the warehouse complex had already disappeared, and if the two Jeep Cherokees were after them, he wouldn't have been able to tell.

The driver was the same man who had brought them from the airport. He was clutching the steering wheel as if his life depended on it. He looked in the mirror and caught sight of his two unwanted passengers. At once, he let loose a torrent of Indonesian. But he didn't slow down or stop. Alex was relieved. It didn't matter where they were heading. All that mattered was they hadn't been left behind.

"What was that about?" he demanded. His mouth was right next to Ash's ear, and he was confident that the driver wouldn't be able to hear what he said or what language he was speaking.

"I don't know." For once, Ash had lost his composure. He was lying on his side, trying to catch his breath. "It was routine . . . bad luck. Or maybe someone hadn't paid. It happens all the time in Jakarta."

"Where are we going?"

Ash looked out the back. It was hard to see anything

in the half-light and swirling water of the storm, but he must have recognized something. "This is Kota. The old city. We're heading north."

"Is that good?"

"The port is in the north . . ."

They had joined the morning traffic, and now they were forced to slow down, falling in behind a line of cars and buses. All the food stalls had disappeared beneath a sea of plastic sheeting, and the people were crowded in doorways, squatting under umbrellas, waiting for the storm to pass.

The driver turned around and shouted something. Even if it had been in English, Alex doubted that he would have been able to hear.

"He's taking us to the boat," Ash explained. "He wants us out of here."

"You speak Indonesian?"

Ash nodded. "Enough to understand."

The van emerged from a side street and cut across a main road. Alex saw a taxi swerve to avoid them, its horn blaring. Behind them, an old house loomed out of the rain. It reminded him of something he might have seen in Amsterdam, but then the whole city had belonged to the Dutch once, a far outpost of the East India Company. They crossed a square. It was lined with cobblestones, and lying in the back of the van, Alex felt every one of them. A crowd of bicyclists swerved to avoid them, crashing into one another and tumbling over in a tangle of chains and obscenities. A man pushing a food stall threw himself out of the way with inches to spare.

Then they were on another highway. There was more traffic here—an endless procession of trucks, each one piled up with goods that were concealed beneath garish plastic tarps. The trucks looked overloaded, as if they might collapse at any time under the weight.

Finally, just ahead, the buildings parted and Alex saw fences, cranes, and ships looming high above them. There were warehouses, guard posts, and offices made of corrugated iron, huge gantries, and great stretches of empty concrete with more trucks and vans making their way back and forth. It was almost impossible to see anything through the endless rain, but this was the port. It had to be. There was a security barrier straight ahead of them and, beyond, a stack of containers behind a barbed wire fence. The van slowed down and stopped. The driver turned around and shouted something in a torrent of Indonesian before stepping out of the van. Then he was gone.

"Ash—" Alex began again.

"This is Tanjung Priok Docks," Ash cut in. "They must be taking us on a container ship." He pointed. "You see those fenced-off areas? They're EPZs. Export Processing Zones. Stuff comes into Jakarta. It gets assembled there, and then it's shipped out again. That's our way out of here. Once we're in an EPZ, we'll be safe."

"How do we get in there?" Alex had seen the barriers

ahead of them. There were guards on duty, even in the driving rain.

"We pay." Ash grimaced. "This is Indonesia! The docks are run by the military. But the military are in the pay of the *premens*. You want a translation? They're gangsters, Alex. The Indonesian mafia. Small beer compared to the snakeheads but still in control around here. You can do anything so long as you pay." Ash got to one knee and peered out of the window. There was nobody in sight. He glanced back at Alex. "Thank you for what you did back there," he said.

"I didn't do anything, Ash."

"The colonel was about to shoot me. You stopped him." Ash grimaced. "That's Kopassus for you. Kill the wrong guy and send flowers to the funeral. Really charming."

"What happens when we get to Australia?"

"Then it's over. I get a pat on the back from Ethan Brooke. You go home."

"Will we see each other again?"

Ash looked away. Like Alex, he was completely drenched, his clothes dripping and forming a pool around him in the back of the van. They both looked like shipwrecks. "Who knows?" he growled. "I haven't been much of a godfather, have I? Maybe I should have sent you a Bible or something."

But before Alex could respond, the driver came back,

and this time he wasn't alone. There were three men with him, their faces hidden beneath the hoods of their plastic anoraks. They were all talking at once, jabbing their fingers at Alex and Ash, gesticulating wildly. Slowly their meaning became clear, and Alex felt a chasm open up beneath him. They wanted Alex to come with them. But Ash was to stay behind. The two of them were being separated.

He wanted to cry out, to argue—but even one word would be fatal, and he forced himself to keep his mouth shut. He tried to resist, pulling away from the hands that grabbed at him. It was useless. As he was bundled roughly out of the van, he took one last look at Ash. His godfather was watching him almost sadly, as if he had guessed that something bad was going to happen and knew that he was powerless to stop it now that it had.

Alex was half dragged onto the road. Ahead of him, a gate had swung open, and he was marched through with a man on each side of him and one ahead. A security guard appeared briefly but the men shouted at him and he quickly turned away.

It was hard to see anything in the driving rain. There was a dock ahead of them and a ship, bigger than any Alex had ever seen, the equivalent of about three soccer fields in length. The ship had a central section where the crew must work and live. Alex could see the bridge, with four or five huge windows and giant windshield wipers swinging back and forth, fighting against the rain. The ship had a name, printed in English along the bow: the *Liberian Star.* It was being loaded with containers, the rectangular boxes dangling from the huge machine known as a spreader, which loomed over them like some sort of monster creature in a science-fiction film. A man in a cabin was controlling the cables and pulleys, lowering each box into place with incredible precision.

They entered the EPZ, where the next containers were waiting their turn, each one painted a different color, some carrying the names of the companies that owned them. Alex saw a yellow box, this one sitting on a truck, and knew that it was his destination. Again, the name was painted in English: Unwin Toys. He looked back, hoping against hope that Ash would be following him after all. But they were alone. Why had the two of them been separated like this? It made no sense. After all, they were supposed to be father and son. He just hoped that Ash would be in a second container and that somehow they would meet up again when they arrived in Darwin. He turned his hand toward himself. The telephone number that Ash had given him had almost vanished, reduced to an inky blur by the constant rain. Fortunately, Alex had committed it to memory, or at least he hoped so. He would know for sure soon enough . . . if he ever found a phone.

They reached the container, and Alex saw at once that

it was locked. More than that, there was a steel pin connected to the door. He was able to guess its purpose. All containers had to be checked by customs officials both going on and coming off a ship. Obviously they couldn't be opened halfway across on their journey or anything—guns, drugs, people—could be added. The steel pin would have a code number that would already have been checked. It would be checked a second time when they arrived in Australia. And if the pin had been tampered with or broken, the entire container would be impounded and examined.

So how was he expected to get in? Alex could see that this was how he was going to travel. Presumably it was too dangerous for him to have a cabin on board the ship, and anyway, as far as the snakehead was concerned, this was all he was: cargo, to be dumped along with all the other merchandise. The man who had been leading the way turned and put a hand on his shoulder, urging him to get down. Alex realized that he was expected to climb underneath the truck, between the wheels.

A moment later he saw why. The container had a secret entrance, a trapdoor that was open, hanging down. He could climb in without touching the main door or the pin that secured it, and once the container was in place, part of a tower with dozens more on top and underneath, there would be no way that anyone could examine it. The whole thing was simple and effective, and part of him

even admired the snakehead. It was certainly a huge business, operating in at least three countries. Ethan Brooke
had been right. These people were much more than simple criminals.

He crouched under the truck. Immediately he felt
claustrophobic. It wasn't just the weight of the container
pressing down on him. He could see that the trapdoor
would be locked from the outside. There was a single
solid bolt that slid across. Once that happened, he would
be trapped. If the ship sank or if they simply decided to
drop the whole thing overboard, he would drown in his
own oversized metal coffin. He hesitated, and at once the
man jabbed him between the shoulders, urging him
forward.

Alex turned, pretending to be scared, pleading with
his eyes to be reunited with Ash. But how could he make
himself understood when he couldn't utter a single word?
One of the other men thrust something into his hands: a
plastic bag with two bottles of water and a loaf of bread.
Supplies for the long journey ahead. The first man pushed
him again and shouted. Alex couldn't delay any longer.
He crawled under the truck and over to the trapdoor.
The men gestured and he pulled himself up. But as he
went, he stumbled. One of his hands caught hold of the
sliding bolt and he steadied himself.

That was his last sight of Indonesia. Mud, dripping
rain, and the undercarriage of a truck. He pulled himself
into the container, and seconds later the trapdoor

slammed shut behind him. He heard the bolt slide across with a loud clang. Now there was no way out.

It was only as he straightened up that he realized he could see. There was light inside the container. He looked around. Two dozen anxious faces stared at him.

It seemed he wasn't going to make this part of the journey alone.

14

THE *LIBERIAN STAR*

IN FACT, THERE WERE twenty people inside the container, huddled together in the half-light thrown by a single battery-operated light. Alex knew at once that they were refugees. He could tell from their faces: not just foreign but afraid, far removed from their own world. Most of them were men, but there were also women and children . . . a couple of them as young as seven or eight. Alex remembered what Ethan Brooke had told him about illegal immigrants when he was in Sydney. "Half of them are under the age of eighteen." Well, here was the proof of it. There were whole families locked together in this metal box, hoping and praying that they would arrive safely in Australia. But they were powerless, and they knew it, utterly dependent on the good will of the snakehead. No wonder they looked nervous.

A gaunt, gray-haired man, wearing a loose, dark yellow colored shirt and baggy pants, made his way forward. Alex guessed he must be in his sixties. He might once have been a farmer. His hands were coarse, and his face had been burned dry by the sun. He muttered a few words to Alex. He could have been speaking any language—Dari, Hazaragi, Kurdish, or Arabic—it would have made no difference. Alex knew that without Ash, he was exposed. He had no way of communicating and nobody to hide behind. What would these people do if they discovered that he was an imposter? He hoped he wouldn't have to find out.

The man realized that Alex hadn't understood him. He tapped his chest and spoke a single word. "Salem." That was presumably his name.

He waited for Alex to reply, and when none came, he turned to a woman, who came forward and tried a second language. Alex turned away and sat in a corner. Let them think he was shy or unfriendly. He didn't care. He wasn't here to make friends.

Alex drew his legs toward his chest and buried his face against his knees. He needed to think. Why had he been separated from Ash? Had the snakehead somehow found out that the two of them were working for ASIS? All in all, he doubted it. If the snakehead even suspected who they were, they would have dragged them out together and shot them. There had to be another reason for the last-minute decision at the harbor but try as he might, Alex couldn't work out what it was.

There was a sudden jolt. The whole container shook, and one of the children began to cry. The other refugees drew closer together and stared around them as if they could somehow see through the flat metal walls. Alex knew what had happened. One of the huge machines— the spreaders—had picked them up, lifting them off the truck and loading them onto the *Liberian Star.* Right now, they could be fifty yards above the dock, dangling on four thin wires. Nobody was moving, afraid of upsetting the balance. Alex thought he heard the hum of machinery somewhere above his head. There was a second jolt and the electric light flickered. And that was a horrible thought. Suppose it went out! Could they endure the entire journey in pitch darkness? The container was swaying very slightly. Somebody shouted, a long way away. They began the journey down.

Alex hadn't been able to see very much of the *Liberian Star* in the rain and the confusion of their arrival, but he had taken in the metal boxes piled up on great blocks, one on top of the other, separated by a space that couldn't have measured more than a couple of feet. Where would they end up? On top, in the middle, or buried somewhere deep in the hold? He had to fight back a growing sense of claustrophobia. There were no holes drilled in the walls. The only air would come in through the cracks around the door and the secret trapdoor. The container had already reminded Alex of a coffin. Now he felt as if he and the twenty other occupants were about to be buried alive.

They came to a halt. Something clanged against the outer wall. Two of the children whimpered, and Salem went over to them, putting his arms around their shoulders and holding them close. Alex took a deep breath. There could be no going back now—that much was certain. They were on board.

And what next? Ash had said it would take them forty-eight hours to reach northern Australia, and by the time they had waited to be unloaded, it could be as much as three or four days. Alex wasn't sure he could bear to sit in here all that time, locked up with these strangers. He had only the two bottles of water and the bread that he had been given at the last moment. He hoped the other refugees had brought their own supplies. There was a chemical toilet in the far corner, but Alex knew that conditions inside the container would soon become disgusting. For the first time, he understood how desperate these people must be even to dream of making such a journey.

For his own part, he knew he couldn't just sit here. He was worried about Ash—and he was going to learn nothing about the snakehead, locked up in the dark. Of course, there was always the watch that Smithers had given him. But despite everything, there was no real reason to send out a distress signal. There was still a chance that Ash was somewhere on board the *Liberian Star*. Alex was just going to have to find him.

He had made up his mind. There was nothing he could do until the ship had left Jakarta, but once they were at sea, there was every chance that the container would be unguarded. Why bother when there was no chance of escape? Alex closed his eyes and tried to sleep. He needed to gather his strength. He wasn't going to use the watch, but there was another gadget Smithers had given him. Alex had already slipped it into position. When the time was right, Alex would use it to break out.

• • •

He waited until they were halfway across before he made his move.

At least twenty-four hours had passed, night blending into day with no difference between the two inside this blank, airless box. The smell was getting worse and worse. At least no one had been seasick, but the chemical toilet was barely adequate for so many people. Nobody was talking. What was there to say? In a way, the crossing had become a sort of living death.

Alex had caught up on the sleep he'd missed at Jakarta, although he'd had bad dreams . . . Ash, Thai boxing, sardines! Now he'd had enough.

He dug into his pocket and took out the pack of chewing gum, then slid open the panel in the side. He had to hold it against the light to see properly, but there were the three numbers: 1, 5, and 10, each with its own switch.

The five-baht coin was already in position. When Alex had climbed into the container, he had pretended to stumble, and as he reached out to steady himself, he had slipped it behind the sliding bolt. As long as none of the snakehead members had seen it, it was still there, magnetically held in place underneath him. Now was the time to find out. He would just have to hope that the noise of the engines and the sea swell would cover any sound made by the explosion.

He went over to the trapdoor and knelt beside it. He couldn't hear anything outside, but that was hardly surprising. The other refugees were looking at him, wondering what he was doing. There was no point in waiting any longer. Alex pressed the switch marked 5.

There was a sharp crack underneath the trapdoor, and a wisp of acrid smoke rose up inside the container. One of the women began to gabble at Alex, but he ignored her. He pressed down with one hand, and to his relief, the trapdoor fell open, forming a small chute that angled into the darkness between the two blocks. The bolt had snapped in half. There was just enough room for Alex to slither out—but into what? It was always possible that he would find himself in the very depths of the hold, hemmed in on all sides, with nowhere else to go.

He had caused a minor panic inside the container. Everyone was talking at once, at least half a dozen languages fighting with one another all around him. Salem came over to him and tugged at his shirt, pleading with him not to do whatever it was he had planned. He looked bewildered. Who was this boy, traveling on his own, who had dared to antagonize the snakehead by attempting to leave without their permission? And how had he done it? They had heard the bolt shatter, but that was all. It seemed to have happened by magic.

Alex looked Salem in the eyes and pressed a finger against his lips. He was pleading with the old man to be silent and not to let the others give him away. It was the most he could hope for. These people were here to make a journey. He had nothing to do with them. With a bit of luck, none of them would try to follow him out or, worse still, tell the ship's crew what had happened. But if he waited any longer, one of them might try to stop him. It was time to go.

Still not sure what he was letting himself in for, Alex slid through the trapdoor headfirst, easing himself into the black square that had opened up below. It was much cooler outside. He had been sharing the same air with twenty people for an entire day and night, and he had been unaware how stifling it had become. It was noisier too. He could hear the hum of the ship's engines, the grinding of machinery in constant motion.

But at least there was a way out. Alex found himself in what was effectively a long, flat tunnel. The containers were piled up on top of him, and he could feel their huge weight pressing down. But there was a crawl space about half a yard high between the floor above him and the ceiling of the container below. He could see the daylight bleeding in—a narrow strip like a crack in a brick wall. Using his knees and elbows, he pushed himself toward it. It was a painful process, constantly scraping his legs and banging his shoulders on the rusty metal above and below him.

At last he reached the edge, only to find himself high above the deck, caught three stories up a tower of containers with no obvious way to climb down. Alex could see the ocean rushing past on the other side of the ship. There was no sign of land. For a moment he was tempted to crawl back inside. He had nowhere to run. Swimming was out of the question. He would be safer back with Salem and the others.

And was there really any chance of finding Ash? The *Liberian Star* was huge. It probably held a thousand containers. Ash could be stuck in any one of them, locked up with his own crowd of refugees. Alex had never felt so helpless. But going back would be admitting defeat. Ever since he had first encountered the snakehead in Bangkok, he had allowed them to push him around. He'd had enough. It was time to fight back.

He had come out at one of the long sides of the container, with a sheer drop to the deck below. There was no way down, so he crawled all the way along the edge and over to the front. He had more luck here. The container doors were fastened with long steel rods that formed a climbing frame, and there were the metal security pins and locks that would provide perfect footholds. Alex knew he had to move quickly. It was still light—he guessed it must be late afternoon—and he would be seen by anyone who happened to appear on deck. On the other hand, he would have to be careful. If he slipped, there was a long way to fall.

Holding on to one of the bars, he squeezed himself out and then began the journey down, trying to ignore the sea spray that whipped into his back and made every surface slippery. His worst fear was that a crew member would come out, and despite the danger, he forced himself to move faster, finally dropping the last few yards and crashing down onto the deck, anxious to get himself out of sight. Nobody had seen him. He looked back up, checking the position of the container just in case he needed to return. There was the name, Unwin Toys, in great white letters. Alex thought about the secret it concealed. He had to admit that he had never come across a criminal organization—or a crime—quite like this.

He looked around. It was only now, crouching in the open air, that he realized quite how enormous the *Liberian Star* actually was. It measured at least three hundred yards in length, and it must have been about fifty yards across. The containers were piled up like metal office blocks, surrounded by decks, gantries, and ladders that would allow the crew to scurry around in what little space was left. Alex was at the back of the ship, where the huge anchor chains disappeared into a cavity below. In front of him, the bridge rose up, the eyes and brain of the entire ship. Behind him, the water boiled, churned up by the propellers below. He guessed they must be traveling at about thirty-five knots, or thirty miles per hour.

He had already accepted the fact that he had no hope at all of finding Ash. But now that he was out, he decided to explore. They could only be about twenty-four hours from Darwin. If he could survive that long without being seen, he might be able to get off the ship and find a telephone. The number that Ash had given him had completely vanished from the back of his hand. He just hoped that he had remembered it correctly and that Ash would still be able to take his call.

In the next couple of hours, Alex explored a large part of the ship. He quickly realized that despite their great size, container ships are almost entirely made up of containers and that their layout is actually very simple, with two decks running all the way from fore to aft and only a limited area for the crew to live and work. And the crew is actually surprisingly small. Only once did he spot a couple of crewmen—Filipinos in blue overalls, leaning against a handrail, smoking cigarettes. Alex slipped behind a ventilation shaft and waited until they left. That was something else to his advantage in this strange, entirely metal world. There were a thousand places to hide.

It was more dangerous inside, where the clean, brightly lit passageways were lined with dozens of doors, any one of which could open at any time. Alex was looking for the food store—he was hungry—but just as he came upon it, another crewman appeared, and he had to duck down the nearest stairway to get out of sight. The stairs led to a cargo hold. As he waited for the man to disappear, Alex heard voices . . . two men talking. They were speaking in English. Intrigued, he continued down.

He came to a platform perched on the edge of an area

that was like an oversized metal cube, with sheer walls rising to the deck above. A single container had been stored here. It was also marked Unwin Toys and was locked with the same security pin as the others. Four men were standing in a semicircle, deep in conversation. One of them was obviously in charge. He was standing with his back to Alex, and from his position high above, all Alex could make out was a thin, rather frail-looking body and strange white hair. The man was leaning on a walking stick. He was wearing gray gloves.

Alex assumed they were going to unlock the container, but what happened next took him completely by surprise. One of the men lifted something that looked like a television remote control and pressed a button. Immediately one side of the container opened electronically, the sections separating like elevator doors. There was a click, and then the floor of the container slid forward, bringing the contents out where they could be examined. What a box of tricks! The security pin was still in place and wouldn't need to be touched.

Alex knew at once what he was looking at. There could be no mistaking it. Royal Blue. That was the name that Mrs. Jones had given it. She had told him it was the most powerful non-nuclear weapon on the planet. Alex's first impression was that the bomb was strangely old-fashioned, like something out of World War II. In the great emptiness of the hold, it looked small, but he guessed that it was about the size of a family car. He wondered what it was doing out here—and where were they taking it? Australia? Was the white-haired man planning to set it off there?

Right now, it was surrounded by a bank of machinery, and as soon as the container had clicked into position, two of the men set to work connecting it all up. There was some sort of scanner—it looked like an office photocopier—and a laptop computer. A third man was explaining something. He was black, with a pockmarked face, very white teeth, and cheap plastic glasses that were too heavy for his face. He was wearing a short-sleeved shirt with half a dozen pens in the breast pocket. Alex edged forward to hear what he was saying.

". . . We had to modify the bomb to change the method of detonation." The man had an accent that Alex couldn't quite place—French, perhaps. "It would normally explode one yard above the ground. But this one will be required to explode one-half mile below it. So we have made the necessary adaptations . . ."

"A radio signal?" the white-haired man asked.

"Yes, sir." The tall man indicated a piece of equipment. "This is how you communicate with the bomb. The timing is crucial. I estimate that Royal Blue will only be able to function at that depth for around twenty minutes. You must send the signal during that time."

"I want to be the one who sends the signal," the white-haired man said. He spoke perfect English, like an old-fashioned news broadcaster.

"Of course, sir. I received your e-mail from London. And as you can see, I've arranged a fairly simple device. It allows you to scan your fingerprints into the system. From that moment on, you will have complete control."

"That's absolutely first rate. Thank you, Mr. Varga."

The white-haired man pulled off one of his gloves, revealing a hand that was small and withered. It could have belonged to someone who was dead. Alex watched as he placed it against the scanner. Mr. Varga pressed a few buttons on the laptop. A green bar of light appeared underneath the hand, traveling across the palm. It only took a couple of seconds, and then it was over.

One of the other men was overweight, with thinning ginger hair. He was about fifty years old, dressed in a white shirt and pants with blue and gold bands on his shoulders. The white-haired man now turned to him.

"You can put Royal Blue back into the container, Captain De Wynter," he said. "It'll be unloaded the moment we arrive at East Arm."

"Yes, Major."

"And one other thing . . ."

But the white-haired man—the major—never finished the sentence. There was a scream from a siren, so loud that Alex was almost knocked off the platform and had to cover his ears to protect himself from the noise. It was an alarm signal. The fourth man, who had so far said nothing, swung around, revealing a machine gun—a lightweight Belgian M249—hanging at his waist. Captain De Wynter pulled out a cell phone and speed dialed.

The siren stopped. The captain listened for a few seconds, then reported what he had heard, speaking in a low voice. Half deafened, Alex couldn't hear a word he said.

The white-haired man shook his head angrily. "Who is he? Where did he come from?"

"They are holding him on the deck," De Wynter replied.

"I want to see him for myself," the white-haired man exclaimed. "Come with me!"

The four of them left together, making for a door set in the side of the hold. A moment later they were gone, and to his astonishment, Alex found himself alone with the bomb. It seemed to be a heaven-sent opportunity, and without even hesitating, he climbed down the staircase and went over to the container. And there it was right in front of him. MI6 was searching for Royal Blue all over Thailand, but he had found it in the middle of the South China Sea. He had found Winston Yu at the same time—for that was surely who the white-haired man must be. After all, he had just heard the captain refer to him as "Major." But why were they both here? What did the major want with the bomb? Alex wished he had heard more.

He ran his eyes over it. Close up, it struck him as one of the ugliest things he had ever seen—blunt and heavy, built only to kill and destroy. For a fleeting moment, he wondered if he could detonate it. That would put an end to Yu's plans, whatever they were. But Alex had no wish to die, and anyway, there were at least twenty refugees, some of them children, concealed in the ship. They'd be killed too.

Perhaps he could disarm it. But there was no point. Yu or the man called Varga would soon see what he had done and simply reverse it. Could he use another of the exploding coins? No—they might be able to penetrate the thick shell of Royal Blue, but what then? And anything he damaged, Yu could easily replace.

He had to do something. The four men might be back at any time. He glanced at the laptop, and that was when he saw the instruction, printed in capital letters on the screen.

> PLACE HAND ON SCREEN

The laptop was connected to the scanner. Alex could see the outline of a human hand, positioned exactly to read the user's fingertips. Acting on impulse, he placed his own hand on the glass surface. There was a click, and the green light rolled underneath his palm. On the laptop, the readout changed.

> FINGERPRINT PROFILE ACCEPTED
> Add further authorization Y/N?
> Delete previous authorization Y/N?

Alex reached out and pressed Y for the first instruction and N for the second. There was no point in advertising that he had been here. The screen returned to its first message.

> PLACE HAND ON SCREEN

So that was interesting. He had given himself the power to override the system if he ever happened to come across it again—and with a bit of luck, neither Major Yu nor Mr. Varga would notice.

There was nothing more to be done here. Alex made his way back to the staircase and went up, intending to find somewhere to hide. He would wait until he got to Darwin. Then he would contact Mrs. Jones and tell her about her precious bomb. If she asked him nicely, he could even defuse it for her.

He reached the deck. Major Yu had arrived there ahead of him—Alex could hear his voice although he couldn't make out any of the words. Quickly he climbed a ladder that led to a narrow passageway dividing two of the container towers. There was no chance of anyone spotting him here. Feeling bolder, he made his way to the end and found himself looking down on the foredeck, where a single mast rose up amid a tangle of winches and cables.

What he saw there chilled him.

He had thought the siren was a useful diversion, perhaps announcing some problem in the engine room. It had gotten Major Yu and his men out of the way at exactly the right moment. But now he realized that it hadn't been good news at all. In fact, it could hardly be worse.

The old man from the container—Salem—had decided to follow Alex out. He must have squeezed through the trapdoor and found his way onto the deck. But there his luck had run out. A couple of the crewmen had discovered him. They were holding him now with his hands pinned behind his back while Major Yu questioned him. Captain De Wynter and Mr. Varga were watching. Salem was having difficulty making himself understood. He had been beaten. One of his eyes was swollen half shut, and there was blood trickling from a cut on his cheek.

He finished speaking, a gabble of words that were swept away by the wind. It wasn't cold out on the deck, but Alex found himself shivering. Major Yu still had his back to him. Alex watched as he carefully removed one of his gloves and reached into his jacket pocket. He took out a small pistol. Without hesitating, without even pausing to aim, he shot the old man between the eyes. The single report of the bullet was like a crack of wood. Salem died on his feet, still held up by the two crewmen. Yu nodded and the men tilted him backward, tipping his lifeless body over the rails. Alex saw it fall into the water and disappear.

Then Major Yu spoke again, and somehow his words carried up as if amplified.

"There is a child on this ship," he exclaimed. "He has escaped from the container. I don't know how. He must be found immediately and killed. Bring the dead body to me."

15

HIDE-AND-SEEK

THE CAPTAIN OF THE *Liberian Star* was not normally a nervous man, but right now he was sweating. Standing in front of the stateroom door, he tried to compose himself, mopping his forehead and tucking his cap under his arm. He was aware that he might have only a few minutes to live.

Hermann de Wynter was Dutch, unmarried, out of shape, and saving money for a retirement somewhere in the sun. He had been working for the snakehead for eleven years, transporting containers all over the world. Never once had he asked what was inside. He knew that in this game, the wrong question could prove fatal. So could failure. And now it was his duty to tell Major Yu that he had failed.

He took a breath and knocked on the door of the stateroom that Yu occupied, on the same level as the main deck.

"Come!"

The single word sounded cheerful enough, but De Wynter had been present the day before. Yu had smiled as he killed the Afghan refugee.

He opened the door and went in. The room was well appointed, with a thick carpet, modern English furniture, and soft lighting. Yu was sitting at a table, drinking a cup of tea. There was also a plate of shortbread, which De Wynter knew was organic and came from Highgrove, the estate belonging to the Prince of Wales.

"Good morning, Captain." Yu motioned for him to come in. "What news do you have for me?"

De Wynter had to force the words into his mouth. "I am very sorry to have to report, Major Yu, that we have been unable to find the boy."

Yu looked surprised. "You've been working for eighteen hours."

"Yes, sir. None of the crew has slept. We spent the whole night searching the ship from top to bottom. Frankly, it's incredible that we have found no trace of him. We've used motion detectors and sonic intensifiers. Nothing! Some of the men think the child must have slipped overboard. Of course, we still haven't given up . . ."

His voice trailed off. There was nothing more to say, and he knew that making too many excuses would annoy Major Yu all the more. De Wynter stood there, waiting for whatever might come. He had once seen Yu shoot a man simply for being late with his tea. He just hoped his own end would be as quick.

But to his amazement, Major Yu smiled pleasantly. "The boy certainly is trouble," he admitted. "Frankly, I'm not at all surprised that he's managed to give you the slip. He's quite a character."

De Wynter blinked. "You know him?" he asked.

"Oh yes. Our paths have already crossed once before."

"But I thought . . ." De Wynter frowned. "He's just a refugee! A street urchin out of Afghanistan."

"Not at all, Captain. That's what he'd like us to believe. But the truth is that he's quite unique. His name is Alex Rider. He works for British intelligence. He's what you might call a teenage spy."

De Wynter sat down. This was in itself remarkable. After all, Major Yu hadn't offered him a seat.

"Forgive me, sir," he began. "But are you saying that the British managed to get a spy on board? A child . . . ?"

"Exactly."

"And you knew?"

"I know everything, Captain De Wynter."

"But . . . why?" De Wynter had completely forgotten his earlier fear. Somewhere in the back of his mind, it occurred to him that he had never spoken to Major Yu so familiarly or for such a length of time.

"It amused me," Yu replied. "This boy is rather full of himself. He travels to Bangkok disguised as a refugee. His mission is to infiltrate my snakehead. But all along, I know who he is and I am simply choosing the moment when I will bring his young life to a fitting end. I have friends who would like me to do it sooner rather than later. But the time is my choice."

Yu poured himself some more tea. He picked up a shortbread cookie, holding it between his gloved fingers, and dipped it into the cup.

"My intention was to allow him to travel as far as Darwin," he continued. "As it happens, I have a use for him, and he might as well travel with the other refugees as anywhere else. Unfortunately, the old man was unable to tell me how he managed to break out of the container, and it's certainly an unwelcome surprise. But I am still confident that you will be able to locate him eventually. After all, we have plenty of time."

The Dutchman felt his mouth go dry again. "I'm afraid not, sir," he muttered. "In fact, it may already be too late."

"Why is that?" Major Yu's eyebrows rose behind the round wire frames.

"Look out of the window, sir. We've arrived at Darwin. They've already sent out a couple of tugs to tow us in."

"Surely we can delay docking for a few more hours."

"No, sir. If we do that, we could be stuck here for a week." De Wynter ran a hand over his jaw. "The Australian ports run like clockwork," he explained. "Everything has to be very precise. We have an allocated time for arrival, and it's a small window. If we miss it, another ship will take our place."

Yu considered. Something very close to anxiety appeared in his shrunken schoolboy face. This was exactly what Zeljan Kurst had warned him about in London. Like it or not, Alex Rider had taken on Scorpia once before and beaten them. Yu had thought it impossible that such a thing could happen a second time. And yet the boy did seem to have the luck of the devil. How had he managed to get out of the container? It was a shame nobody had been able to understand the old man before he had died.

"Even if we dock, the boy cannot possibly leave the ship," De Wynter said. "There is only one exit—the main gangway, and that will be guarded at all times. He can jump into the sea, but I will have men on lookout. We can cover every angle with rifles. We'll pick him off in the water. A single shot. No one will hear anything. We'll only be in Darwin for a few hours. Our next port is Rio de Janeiro. We'll have three weeks to flush him out."

Major Yu nodded slowly. Even as De Wynter had been speaking, he had made up his mind. In truth, he had little choice. Royal Blue had to be unloaded immediately in order to continue its journey. He couldn't wait. On the other hand, there was something that Alex Rider didn't know. Whatever happened, all the cards were in Yu's hand.

"Very well, Captain," he muttered. "We'll tie up at Darwin. But if the boy does slip through your fingers a second time, I suggest you kill yourself." He snapped a cookie in half. "It will spare me the trouble, and it will, I assure you, cause you a great deal less pain."

Alex Rider had heard everything that Major Yu had said.

The man who sat on the executive board of Scorpia and who headed the most powerful snakehead in south-

east Asia would have been horrified to know that Alex
was hiding in perhaps the most obvious place in the
world. Under his own bed.

Alex had known what he was up against. The moment
he had seen the refugee killed on the deck and had heard
Yu give the order for the crew to hunt him down, he had
realized he needed to find somewhere on the ship that
nobody would even dream of looking. It was true there
were hundreds of hiding places—ventilation shafts, the
crawl spaces between the containers, cabins, cable hous-
ings, and storage units. But none of these would be good
enough, not with the entire crew searching for him non-
stop throughout the night.

No—it had to be somewhere completely unthink-
able . . . and the idea had come to him almost at once.
Where was the last place he would go? It had to be the captain's cabin or better still, Major Yu's own quarters on board
the *Liberian Star.* The crew almost certainly weren't allowed
in either. It wouldn't even occur to them to look inside.

He'd only been given a few minutes' start. As the crew
members organized themselves and the various listening
devices were handed out, Alex was racing. The layout of
the ship was fairly easy to understand. He had seen much
of it already. The engine rooms and the crew's cabins
were somewhere down below. Yu, the captain, and the
senior officers—anyone important—would surely be
housed above sea level, somewhere in the central block.

Breathless, imagining the crewmen fanning out behind him, Alex stumbled on a door that led to the spotlessly clean, brightly lit corridor that he had explored the day before. He was on the right track. The first door he came to opened into a conference room, full of charts and computers. Next came a living space with a bar and TV. He heard the clatter of saucepans and ducked back as a man wearing a chef's hat suddenly crossed the corridor and disappeared into a room opposite. A moment later, he emerged again and went back the way he had come, carrying a box of canned food.

Alex hurried forward. The chef had clearly entered some sort of larder, and Alex wasted a few seconds pulling out a bottle of water for himself. He was going to need it. Continuing down the corridor, he passed a laundry, a game room, and a miniature hospital. He came to an elevator and was tempted to take it. According to the display, there were six floors above him. But he didn't have time and dreaded waiting for it to arrive, only to find it packed with Yu's men.

He came upon Yu's stateroom at the very end of the corridor. It wasn't locked—but there wasn't a man on board the *Liberian Star* who would have dared enter even if the door had been open and Yu miles away. Alex slipped inside. He saw a table with a number of files and documents spread across the surface and wished he had time to examine them. What secrets they might reveal! But he didn't dare touch anything. Moving even one page a fraction of an inch might give him away.

He looked around him, taking in the pictures on the walls—scenes of the English countryside with, in one image, a traditional hunt setting out across what might be Salisbury Plain. A sophisticated stereo system and a plasma TV. A leather sofa. This was where Yu worked and relaxed when he was on board.

The bedroom was next door. Here was another bizarre touch. Yu slept in an antique four-poster bed. But Alex knew at once that it was perfect for his needs. There was a silk valance that trailed down to the floor, and lifting it up, Alex saw a space half a yard high that would conceal him perfectly. God—it reminded him of being six years old again, playing hide-and-seek with Jack Starbright on Christmas Eve. But this wasn't the same. This time he was on a container ship, in the middle of the Indian Ocean, surrounded by people who were determined to kill him.

Same game. Different rules.

Alex took a swig of the water he had stolen and slid underneath, easing the silk valance back into shape. Very little light bled through underneath. Alex prepared himself, trying to find a comfortable position. He knew that he wouldn't be able to move a muscle once Yu entered the room.

He was suddenly struck by the craziness of his plan.

Could he really stay here all night? How stupid would he look if Yu found him? He was briefly tempted to crawl out and find somewhere else. But it was already too late. The search would have begun, and he couldn't risk starting again.

In fact, it was several hours before Yu came in. Alex heard the outer door open and close again. Footsteps. Then music. Yu had turned on the stereo system. His taste was classical . . . Elgar's *Pomp and Circumstance*, the music they played at the Albert Hall in London every summer. He listened to the piece while he ate his dinner. Alex heard one of the stewards deliver it to him and caught a faint scent of roast meat. The smell made him hungry. He sipped a little more water, glumly reflecting that it was all he had to last the night.

Later Yu turned on the television. Somehow he had managed to tune in to the BBC, and Alex heard the late-night news.

"Pop singer Rob Goldman was in Australia this week, just five days before the conference taking place on Reef Island, which has come to be known as Reef Encounter and which has been timed to take place at exactly the same time as the G8 summit in Rome.

"Goldman played to a sold-out audience at the Sydney Opera House and told an enthusiastic crowd that peace and an end to world poverty were possible—but that they would have to be achieved by people, not politicians.

"Speaking from 10 Downing Street, the British prime minister said that he wished Sir Rob every success but insisted that the real work would be done in Rome. It's a view that not many people seem to share . . ."

Much later, Major Yu went to bed. Alex barely breathed as he came into the bedroom. Lying in the semidarkness with muscles that were already aching, he heard the major undress and wash in the adjoining bathroom. And then came the inevitable moment: the creak of wood and shifting metal springs as Yu climbed into bed, just inches above the boy he was so determined to find. Fortunately, he didn't read before he slept. Alex heard the click of the light switch, and the last glimmer of light was extinguished. Then everything was silent.

For Alex, the night was yet another long, dreary ordeal. He was fairly sure that Major Yu was asleep, but he couldn't be certain, and he didn't dare sleep himself in case the sound of his breathing or an accidental movement gave him away. All he could do was wait, listening to the hum of the engines and feeling the pitch of the ship as they drew ever closer to Australia. At least that was one consolation. Every second that he remained undiscovered brought him a little closer to safety.

But how was he to get off the *Liberian Star?* One exit—guarded. The decks watched. Alex didn't like the idea of diving overboard and swimming . . . even assuming he could manage it without being crushed or drowned. And there would be a dozen or more men waiting to take a potshot at him. Well, he would just have to worry about that when the time came.

The ship plowed on through the darkness. The minutes dragged slowly past. At last a glimmer of light crept across the floor, pushing away the shadows of the night.

Yu woke up, washed, dressed, and took his breakfast in the stateroom. That was the worst part for Alex. He had barely moved for ten hours, and all his bones were aching. Still Yu refused to leave. He was working at his desk. Alex heard the rustle of pages turning and, briefly, the rattle of computer keys. And then the steward brought a mid-morning snack, and a short while later De Wynter arrived with the news of his failure.

So Major Yu knew who he was—and had known from the start! Alex tucked that information away, hoping he would be able to make sense of it later. For now, all that mattered was that his plan had worked and the long hours of discomfort had been worth it. They were docking at Darwin. Surely any minute now, Yu would go out on deck to see dry land.

But it was another two hours before he left. Alex waited until he was quite sure that he was alone, then rolled out from underneath the bed. He glanced into the stateroom. Yu had gone, but he had left some of the cookies, and Alex wolfed them down. Yu might notice—but Alex was too hungry to care. At the same time, he tried to ease some feeling back into his muscles. He had to prepare himself. He knew that he had just one chance to get away. They would set off to sea again in just a few hours' time, and if he was still on board, he would be finished.

He went over to the window. The *Liberian Star* had already berthed at the section of the port of Darwin known as the East Arm Wharf. To his dismay, Alex realized that they were still a very long way from land. The East Arm was an artificial cement causeway stretching far out into the ocean, with the usual array of gantries, cranes, and spreaders waiting to receive the ships. It was a world apart from the docks at Jakarta. Quite apart from the blinding Australian sun, everything seemed very clean and ordered. There were two long rows of parked cars and beyond them, a neat, modern warehouse and some gas tanks— all of them painted white.

A van drove past, heading up the dock. Two men walked past in fluorescent jackets and hard hats. Even assuming Alex could get off the ship, he still wouldn't be safe. It was at least a mile to the mainland, and presumably there would be security barriers at the far end. At least Yu wouldn't dare gun him down in plain sight. That was one consolation. But however Alex looked at it, this wasn't going to be as easy as he had hoped.

Even so, he couldn't wait any longer.

Alex crept over to the door and opened it an inch at a time. The corridor was empty, lit by the same hard light that made it impossible to tell if it was night or day. He had already worked out a strategy based on what he had overheard in the cabin. Everyone was waiting for him to break out. That meant their attention would be fixed on the main gangplank and the decks. So the rest of the ship was his. Right now he needed a diversion. He set out to create one.

He hurried past the elevator and found a staircase leading down. He could hear a deep throbbing coming from below and guessed that he was heading the right way—to the engine room. He came upon it quite suddenly, a strangely old-fashioned tangle of brass valves and silver pipes and pistons, all connected to one another in a steel framework like an exhibition in an industrial museum. The air was hot down here. There was no natural light. The machinery seemed to stretch on for a mile, and Alex could imagine that a ship the size of the *Liberian Star* would need every inch of it.

The control room was raised slightly above the engines, separated from them by three thick glass observation windows and reached by a short flight of metal stairs. Alex crept up on his hands and feet and found himself looking at a much more modern room with rows of gauges and dials, TV screens, computers, and intricate switchboards. A single man sat in a high-backed chair, tapping at a keyboard. He looked half asleep. Certainly he wasn't expecting trouble down here.

Alex saw what he was looking for: a metal cabinet about fifteen yards high with thick pipes leading in and out and a warning sign.

AIR SUPPLY
DANGER: DO NOT CUT OFF

He didn't know what needed the air or what would happen if it didn't get it, but the bright red letters were irresistible. He was going to find out.

He reached into his pocket and took out the one-baht coin that Smithers had given him. Using it would mean he would only have the ten-baht coin left. With a bit of luck, he wouldn't be needing it. Alex watched the man in the chair for a minute, then slipped into the control room and placed the coin against the pipe just where it entered the cabinet. The man didn't look up. The coin clicked into place, activating the charge inside. Alex tiptoed out again.

He found the chewing gum pack, slid the side open, and pressed the switch marked 1. The bang was very loud and, to his surprise and delight, highly destructive. The explosion not only tore open the pipe, it wrecked the electrical circuits inside the cabinet too. There was a series of brilliant sparks. Something like white steam gushed out into the control room. The man leapt up. Another alarm had gone off, and red lights were flashing all around him. Alex didn't wait to see what would happen next. He was already on his way out.

Down the stairs, past the engines, and back up again. This time he took the elevator, guessing that in an emergency, the crew would be more likely to use the stairs. He pressed the button for the sixth floor, and the elevator slid smoothly up.

He knew where he was heading. He had seen the bridge when he was being loaded into the container at Jakarta and had noticed that it had its own deck, a sort of balcony with a railing and a view over the entire ship. This was going to be his way off the *Liberian Star.* For— once again—Yu's guns might be pointing everywhere, but surely they wouldn't be pointing here.

The elevator reached the sixth floor and the doors slid open. To Alex's dismay, he found himself facing a squat Chinese crewman who had been waiting to come down. The man was even more shocked than Alex and reacted clumsily, scrambling for the gun that was tucked into the waistband of his pants. That was a mistake. Alex didn't give him time to draw it, lashing out with the point of his foot, aiming straight between the man's legs. It wasn't so much a karate strike, more an old-fashioned kick in the balls, but it did the trick. The Chinaman gurgled and collapsed, dropping the gun. Alex scooped it up and continued on his way.

And now he was armed. Alarms were going off everywhere, and Alex wondered what damage he had done with the second coin. Good old Smithers! He was the one man in MI6 who had never let him down. The corridor led directly to the bridge. Alex passed through an archway, climbed three steps, and found himself in a narrow, curving room, surprisingly empty, with large windows looking over the decks, the containers, and, to one side, the port.

There were two men on duty, sitting in what could have been dentist's chairs in front of a bank of television screens. One was a second officer that Alex hadn't seen before. The other was Captain De Wynter. He was on the telephone, talking in a voice that sounded strained and hoarse with disbelief.

"It's the reefers," he was saying. "We're going to have to shut them all down. The whole ship could go up in flames . . ."

The reefers were refrigerated containers. There were three hundred of them on the *Liberian Star,* storing meat, vegetables, and chemicals that needed to be transported at low temperatures. The containers themselves needed constant cooling, and Alex had smashed the pipes that provided exactly that. At the very least, he was going to cause Major Yu tens of thousands of dollars' worth of losses as the contents deteriorated. If the chemicals became unstable in the heat, he might even set fire to the whole ship.

The other officer saw Alex first. He muttered something in Dutch, and De Wynter looked around, the phone still in his hand.

Alex raised the gun. "Put it down," he said.

De Wynter went pale. He lowered the phone.

What did he do now? Alex realized that he had made it this far without any real plan at all. "I want you to get me off this ship," he said.

"That's not possible." De Wynter shook his head. He was afraid of the gun, but he was even more afraid of Major Yu.

Alex glanced at the phone. Presumably it could be connected to Darwin. "Call the police," he said. "I want you to bring them here."

"I cannot do that either," De Wynter replied. He looked a little sad. "There is no way I will help you, child. And there is nowhere for you to go. You might as well give yourself up."

Alex looked briefly out the window. One of the containers bound for Australia was already being lifted off the ship, dangling on wires beneath a metal frame so huge that in comparison it seemed no bigger than a matchbox. The spreader was controlled by a man in a glass-fronted cabin, high up in the air. The container rose up. In a few seconds it would swing across and down to the piles that were already mounting on the dock.

He judged the distance and the timing. Yes—he could do it. He had arrived at the bridge at exactly the right moment. He pointed the gun directly at De Wynter. "Get out of here," he snapped.

The captain stayed where he was. He didn't believe Alex had the nerve to pull the trigger.

"I said—get out!" Alex swung his hand and fired at a

radar screen right next to the chair where De Wynter was sitting.

The sound of the gunshot was deafening inside the confined space. The screen shattered, fragments of glass scattering over the work surface. Alex smiled to himself. That was another piece of expensive equipment on the *Liberian Star* that was going to need replacing.

De Wynter didn't need telling again. He got up and slowly left the bridge, following the second officer, who was already clambering down the stairs. Alex waited until they had gone. He knew they would call for help and come back with half a dozen armed men, but he didn't care. He had seen his way out. With a bit of luck, he would be gone long before they arrived.

A glass door led onto the outer walkway. Alex opened it and found himself about twenty yards above the nearest container, far enough to break his neck if he fell. The sea was another thirty yards below that. Diving into the water was out of the question. He could see Yu's men on the main deck, waiting for him to try. But he was too high. They wouldn't need to shoot him. The impact would kill him first.

But the container he had seen was directly in front of him, moving closer all the time as it traveled over the deck. Alex climbed onto the railing in front of him and tensed himself. The container loomed over him.

He jumped—not down, but up, his arms stretching out. For a moment he was suspended in space, and he

wondered if he was going to make it. He grimaced, trying not to imagine the crushing pain, his legs smashing
into the deck if he fell. But then his hands caught hold of
the lashings beneath the container and he was being carried outward, his legs dangling in the air, his neck and
shoulder muscles screaming. The man operating the
spreader couldn't see him. He was like an insect, clinging
to the underbelly of the container. And Yu's men hadn't
noticed him either. They were following orders, their eyes
fixed on the deck and the sea below.

Alex had thought the container was moving quickly
when he was on the bridge. Now that he was desperately
holding on, it seemed to take forever to reach the dock,
and he was certain that at any moment, one of Yu's men
would glance up and see him. But he was already over the
side of the ship, and now he saw another danger. Drop
too early and he would break a leg. Leave it too late and
he risked being crushed as the container was set down.

And then someone saw him.

He heard a yell of alarm. It was a worker on the wharf,
wearing overalls, a fluorescent jacket, and a hard hat.
He probably wasn't working for Yu, but that didn't matter . . . as far as Alex was concerned, he was just as much
a threat. Alex couldn't wait any longer. He let go with
both hands and fell for what seemed an eternity through
the air. He had been hanging over a container with a tarp
cover. The tarp provided a soft landing—even if the wind
was knocked out of him as he hit it, shoulders first. He

didn't stop to recover his breath but rolled over and climbed down the sides.

As he ran down the dock, dodging behind the containers, Alex tried to work out a strategy. The next few minutes were going to be vital. If he was captured by the port authorities, there was always a chance that he might be handed back to Major Yu. Or if he was locked up, Yu would know where to find him. Either way, Alex knew what the result would be. He would end up dead. He had to stay out of sight until he had reached the mainland itself. So long as he was on the East Arm Wharf, he would never be safe.

But once again luck was on his side. As he came around the corner of the last container tower, a pickup truck drew up in front of him, the back filled with old cartons and empty gas cans. The driver rolled down the window and yelled something at another dockworker. The man replied and the two of them laughed. By the time the truck rumbled forward again, Alex was in the back, lying on his stomach, concealed among the cartons.

The truck followed a railroad line, curving around on the edge of the water, and stopped at a barrier, as Alex had expected. But the security guards knew the driver and waved him through. The truck picked up speed. Alex lay there, feeling the warm Australian breeze on his shoulders as they drove away.

He had done it! He had achieved everything that Ethan Brooke and ASIS had demanded. He had been smuggled illegally into Australia, and on the way he had uncovered much of Major Yu's network: the Chada Trading Agency in Bangkok, Unwin Toys, the *Liberian Star*. For that matter, he had also located Royal Blue for Mrs. Jones. If he could just get to Darwin in one piece and find Ash, his mission would be over and he could finally go home. All he had to do was find a phone.

Twenty minutes later, the truck stopped. The engine cut out and Alex heard the driver door open and shut again. Cautiously, he looked out. The port was out of sight. They had parked outside a café, a brightly colored wooden shack on an empty road. It was called Jake's, and it had a hand-painted sign reading: The Best Pies in Darwin. Alex was desperate for food. He had barely eaten anything for two days. But it was what he saw next to the café that mattered more to him right now. It was a public telephone.

He waited until the driver had disappeared into the building, then climbed out and ran over to the phone. Apart from the last coin that Smithers had given him, he had no money, but according to Ash, he wouldn't need any to make the call. Now, what was the number he had been given? For a horrible moment, the separate digits danced in his head, refusing to come together. He forced himself to concentrate. 795 . . . No, 759 . . . Somehow the full number took shape. He punched it in and waited.

He'd gotten it right. Somehow the numbers were able to override the system, and Alex heard the connection being made. The phone rang three times before it was answered.

"Yes?"

Alex felt a wave of relief. It was Ash's voice. "Ash . . . it's me. Alex."

"Alex . . . thank God! Where are you?"

"I'm in Darwin, I think. Or somewhere near it. There's a café called Jake's. About fifteen minutes from the port."

"Stay where you are. I'm coming to get you."

"Are you here too? How did you get here?"

A pause, then Ash replied, "I'll tell you when I see you. Just watch out for yourself." There was another silence. Alex listened for background noise, anything that might tell him where Ash was. But there was nothing. "I'll be with you as soon as I can," Ash said, and hung up.

Alex knew that something was wrong. It had definitely been Ash on the phone but he hadn't sounded like himself. His voice had been strained, and there had been something in that last pause. It was almost as if he had been waiting to be told what to say.

Alex made a decision. He had contacted Ash first as he had promised. But that might not be enough. He turned his wrist and looked at the watch that Smithers had given him, then deliberately moved the hands to eleven o'clock. According to Smithers, the watch would send out a signal every ten minutes. Ash might not be happy about it, but Alex didn't care. He wasn't going to take any more chances. He just wanted to know that MI6 were on their way.

After that, he waited for Ash to arrive. Alex couldn't think what else to do. He was exhausted after three nights with almost no sleep and weak from lack of food. He crept around the side of the café and sat in the shade, keeping himself out of sight. It was likely that Major Yu's men were still looking for him, and apart from the knife concealed in his belt, he had no way of defending himself. He had left the gun behind on the bridge. He wished he had it with him now.

Ten minutes later, the door of the café opened and the driver who had brought him here came out carrying a brown paper bag. He got into the pickup truck and drove off again, leaving a plume of dust behind him.

More time passed. There were flies buzzing around Alex's face, but he ignored them. The café seemed to be in the middle of nowhere, surrounded by scrubland and on the edge of a road with little traffic. Alex had to struggle not to doze off. But then he saw a car heading toward him, a black four-wheel drive with tinted windows. It pulled in outside the café. Ash got out.

But he wasn't alone. He hadn't been driving. His hands were chained in front of him. His black hair was in disarray, and his shirt was torn. A streak of blood ran down the side of his face. He hadn't seen Alex yet. He looked dazed.

Major Yu got out of the back of the car. He was wearing a white suit with a lavender shirt, buttoned at the neck. He moved slowly, supporting himself on a walking stick. As always, his hands were gloved. At the same time, the driver and another man got out. They were taking no chances. The three of them surrounded Ash. Yu took out the pistol he had used to kill the old man on the *Liberian Star*. He held it up against Ash's head.

"Alex Rider!" he called out in a thin voice, filled with hate. "You have three seconds to show yourself. Otherwise you will see your godfather's brains all over the highway. I am counting now!"

Alex realized he wasn't breathing. They had Ash! What was he to do? Give himself up and they would both be killed. But could he forgive himself if he turned and ran?

"One . . ."

He regretted now that he hadn't used the telephone to call ASIS, the police, anyone. He had known something was wrong. How could he have been so stupid?

"Two . . ."

He had no choice. Even if he tried to run, they would catch him. There were three of them. They had a car. He was in the middle of nowhere. Ash wasn't moving. His shoulders were slumped and he looked miserable, completely defeated.

He stood up, showing himself.

Major Yu lowered the gun and Alex began to walk forward, worn out and defeated. Ash must have been on the *Liberian Star* all the time, a prisoner like him. His eyes were full of pain.

"I'm sorry, Alex," he rasped.

"Well, here you are at last," Major Yu said. "I have to say, you've caused me a great deal of time and inconvenience."

"Go to hell," Alex snarled.

"Yes, my dear Alex," Yu replied. "That's exactly where I'm taking you."

Yu raised the hand with the walking stick, then swung it with all his strength. This was the last thing that Alex remembered—a silver scorpion glinting brilliantly as it swooped toward him out of an Australian sun. He didn't even feel it as it smashed into the side of his head.

"Pick him up!" Yu commanded.

He turned his back on the unconscious boy and climbed back into the car.

16

MADE IN BRITAIN

THERE WAS A VASE of roses on the table. Alex smelled them first . . . sweet and slightly cloying. Then he opened his eyes and allowed them to come into focus. They were bright pink, a dozen of them arranged in a porcelain vase with a lace mat underneath. Alex felt sick. The side of his head was throbbing, and he could feel the broken skin where the walking stick had hit him. There was a sour taste in his mouth. He wondered how long he had been lying here.

And where was he? Looking around at the antique furniture, the grandfather clock, the heavy curtains, and the stone fireplace with two sculpted lions, he would have said he was back home in Britain—although he knew that wasn't possible. He was lying on a bed in what could have been a country hotel. A door to one side opened into a bathroom. There were bottles of Molton Browne shampoo and bubble bath beside the sink.

Alex rolled off the bed and staggered into the bathroom. He splashed water on his face and examined himself in the mirror. He looked terrible. Quite apart from the dark hair and skin color and the two fake teeth, his eyes were bloodshot, there was a huge bruise next to his eye, and generally he could have been dumped here by a garbage truck. On an impulse, he reached into his mouth and pulled out the two plastic caps on his teeth. Major Yu knew perfectly well who—and what—he was. There was no need for any further pretense.

He ran himself a bath, and while the water was flowing, he went back into the bedroom. The main door was locked, of course. The window looked out onto a perfect lawn with—bizarrely—a set of croquet hoops arranged in neat lines. Beyond, he could see a rocky outcrop, a jetty, and the sea. He turned back. Someone had left him a snack: smoked salmon sandwiches, a glass of milk, a plate of McVitie's Jaffa Cakes. He ate it all greedily. Then he stripped off his clothes and got into the bath. He didn't know what was going to happen next, and he didn't like to think, but whatever it was, he might as well be clean.

He felt a lot better after half an hour in the hot scented water and although he hadn't been able to get off all the makeup Mrs. Webber had put on him, at least some of his own color had returned. There were fresh clothes in the wardrobe: a Vivienne Westwood shirt and Paul Smith jeans and underwear—both London-based designers. He was still wearing his old clothes, but the belt that Smithers had given him had been taken away. Alex wondered about that. Had Major Yu discovered the knife hidden in the buckle or the jungle supplies inside the leather itself? He was sorry that he hadn't gotten the chance to use it. Maybe there would have been something inside that could help him now.

On the other hand, nobody had searched the pockets of his jeans—or if they had, they had missed the ten-baht coin and the chewing gum pack with the secret detonators. The watch was also still in place, the hands fixed at eleven o'clock, and that gave Alex a sense of reassurance. The eleventh hour indeed. Major Yu might think he held all the cards, but the watch would still be transmitting, and even now MI6 Special Operations must be closing in.

Alex got dressed in the new clothes and sat down in a comfortable armchair. He had even been supplied with some books to read: *Biggles, The Famous Five,* and *Just William.* They weren't quite his taste, but he supposed he should appreciate the thought.

Just after midday, there was a rattle of a key turning in the lock and the door opened. A maid, wearing a black dress with a white apron, came in. She looked Indonesian.

"Major Yu would like to invite you for lunch," she said.

"That's very kind of him," Alex replied. He closed his copy of *Biggles Investigates.* "I don't suppose there's any chance of our eating out?"

"He's in the dining room," the maid replied.

Alex followed her out of the room and down a wood-paneled corridor with oil paintings on the walls. They all showed scenes of the English countryside. Briefly he thought of overpowering the maid and making another bid for freedom, but he decided against it. There was part of him that reacted against the idea of attacking a young woman, and anyway, he had no doubt that—following the events on the *Liberian Star*—Yu would be taking no chances. Security here would be tight.

They reached a grand staircase that swept down to a hall with a suit of armor standing beside a second, monumental fireplace. More classical paintings everywhere. Alex had to remind himself that he was still in Australia. The house didn't fit here. It felt as if it had been imported brick by brick, and he was reminded for a moment of Nikolei Drevin, who had transported his own fourteenth-century castle from Scotland to Oxfordshire. It was strange how very bad men felt a need to live somewhere not just spectacular but slightly insane.

The maid held back and gestured Alex through a door and into a long dining room with floor-to-ceiling windows looking out over the sea. The room was carpeted with a table and a dozen chairs, suitable for a medieval banquet. The paintings in this room were modern: a portrait by David Hockney and a wheel of color by Damian Hirst. Alex had seen similar works in galleries in London and knew that they must be worth millions. Only one end of the table had been laid. Major Yu was sitting there, waiting for him, the walking stick leaning against his chair.

"Ah, there you are, Alex," he said in a pleasant voice, as if they were old friends meeting up for the weekend. "Please come and sit down."

As he walked forward, Alex examined the snakehead

boss properly for the first time, taking in the round, shrunken head, the wire-frame glasses, the white hair sitting so oddly with the Chinese features. Yu was wearing a striped blazer with a white, open-necked shirt. There was a silk handkerchief poking out of his top pocket. His gloved hands were crossed in front of him.

"How are you feeling?" Yu asked.

"My head hurts," Alex replied.

"Yes. I'm afraid I must apologize. I really don't know what came over me, hitting you like that. But the truth is, I was angry. You did a lot of damage on the *Liberian Star* and made it necessary for me to murder Captain De Wynter, which I didn't really want to do."

Alex filed the information away. So De Wynter was dead. He had paid the price for failing a second time.

"Even so, it was unforgivable of me. My mother used to say that you can lose money, you can lose at cards, but you should never lose your temper. Can I offer you some apple juice? It comes from High House Farm in Suffolk, and it's quite delicious."

"Thank you," Alex said. He didn't know what was going on here but had decided he might as well play along with this madman. He held out his glass, and Yu poured. At the same time, the Indonesian maid came in with the lunch: cold roast beef and salad. Alex helped himself. He noticed that Yu ate very little and held his knife and fork as if they were surgical implements.

"I'm very glad to have had this opportunity to meet

you," Major Yu began. "Ever since you destroyed our operation Invisible Sword and caused the death of poor Mrs. Rothman, I've been wondering what sort of boy you were . . ."

So Mrs. Jones had been right. Major Yu was indeed part of Scorpia. Alex filed the information away, knowing with a sense of dread that it gave Yu another reason to want to kill him . . . to settle an old score.

"It's just a shame that we have so little time together," Yu went on.

Alex didn't like the sound of that. "I have a question," he said.

"Please go ahead."

"Where is Ash? What have you done with him?"

"Let's not talk about Ash." Yu gave him a thin smile. "You don't have to worry about him. You'll never see him again. How is the beef, by the way?"

"A little bloody for my taste."

Yu sighed. "It's organic. From Yorkshire."

"Where else?" Alex was getting a bit fed up with all this. He toyed with his knife, wondering if he had the speed and the determination to stick it into the man's heart. It might be five or ten minutes before the maid came back. Enough time to find a way out of here . . .

Yu must have seen the idea forming in Alex's eyes. "Please don't think of anything foolish," he remarked. "There is a pistol in my right-hand jacket pocket, and, as the Americans would say, I am very quick on the draw. I think I could shoot you dead before you had even left your chair—and that would spoil a perfectly pleasant lunch. So come now, Alex. I want to know all about you. Where were you born?"

Alex shrugged. "West London."

"Your parents were both English?"

"I don't want to talk about them." Alex looked around. Suddenly the paintings, the furniture, the clothes, even the food made sense. "You seem to like England, Major Yu," he remarked.

"I admire it greatly. If I may say so, Alex, I have enjoyed having you as my adversary because you are English. It is also one of the reasons I have invited you to eat with me now."

"But what about Invisible Sword? You tried to kill every child in London."

"That was business, and I really was very unhappy about it. You might also like to know, by the way, that I voted against sending a sniper to kill you. It seemed so crude. Some more apple juice?"

"No, thank you."

"So where do you go to school?"

Alex shook his head. He'd had enough of this game. "I don't want to talk about myself," he said. "And certainly not to you. I want to see Ash. And I want to go home."

"Neither of which is possible." Yu was drinking wine. Alex noticed that even that was English. He remembered Ian Rider once describing English wine as the sort of liquid that might have been extracted from a cat. But Yu sipped it with obvious enthusiasm.

"I love England, as a matter of fact," he said. "Since you won't talk about yourself, perhaps you will permit me to tell you a little about me. My life has been a remarkable one. Maybe one day someone will write a book about me . . ."

"I've never much cared for horror stories," Alex said.

Yu smiled again—but his eyes were cold. "I like to think of myself as a genius," he began. "Of course, you might remark that I have never invented anything or written a novel or painted a great painting, despite what I said just now, it is unlikely that I will become a household name. But different people are talented in different ways, and I think I have achieved a certain greatness in crime, Alex. And it's not surprising that my life story is a remarkable one. How could someone like me have anything else?"

He coughed, dabbed his lips and began again.

"I was born in Hong Kong. Although you wouldn't believe it to look at me now, I began with nothing. Even my cot was a cardboard box filled with straw. My mother was Chinese. She lived in a single room in a slum and worked as a chambermaid at the Hilton Hotel. Sometimes she would smuggle home soaps and shampoos for me. It was the only luxury I ever knew.

"My father was a guest there, a businessman from Tunbridge Wells, in Kent. She never told me his name.

The two of them began an affair, and I have to say that she fell hopelessly in love with him. He used to talk to her about the place where he lived, this country called Great Britain. He promised her that as soon as he had enough money, he would take her with him and he would turn her into a British lady with a thatched cottage with a garden and a bulldog. For my mother, who had nothing, it was like an impossible dream.

"As a young person, I'm sure you have no attachment to your country, but the truth is that it's a remarkable place. At one time, this tiny island had an empire that stretched all around the world. You have to remember that when I was born, you even owned Hong Kong. Think how many inventors and explorers, artists and writers, soldiers and statesmen have come out of Britain. William Shakespeare! Charles Dickens! The computer was a British invention—as was the Internet. It's sad that much of your country's greatness has been squandered by politicians in recent years. But I still have faith. One day, Britain will once again lead the world.

"Anyway, my mother's affair came to an unhappy end. I suppose it was inevitable. As soon as he found out that she was pregnant, the businessman abandoned her and she never saw him again. Nor did he ever pay a penny toward my upkeep. He simply disappeared.

"But my mother never lost sight of her dream. If anything, it became more intense. She determined that I should grow up with full recognition of my English blood.

She named me Winston, of course, after the great wartime leader Winston Churchill. The first clothes I wore were made in Britain. As the years went on, she became more and more fanatical. For example, one day she decided that I would be educated in a British public school—even though it was obviously quite impossible when she was earning only a few pounds an hour changing beds and cleaning toilets. But nonetheless, when I was six years old, she left her job and began to look for other ways to make money.

"It took her just two years—a tribute, I think, to her single-mindedness and courage. And that was how I found myself, first in a prep school in Tunbridge itself and later at Harrow School, dressed in their smart blue jacket with the marvelous straw hat. All the boys wore them. On Sundays we dressed in cutoff tailcoats . . . bum freezers we used to call them. It was actually Winston Churchill's old school, and I found it hard to believe I was there. I mean, I could actually imagine I might be sitting at his desk or reading a book that had once belonged to him. It was thrilling . . . and my mother was so proud of me! I did sometimes wonder how she could possibly afford it all, but it wasn't until my second year that I found out, and I must say, it came as a bit of a surprise.

"This is what happened . . ."

He poured himself some more wine, swirled it in the glass, and drank.

"You might imagine that I was bullied at Harrow," he

said. "After all, this was back in the fifties, and there weren't many half-Chinese boys there, particularly with a single parent. But by and large everyone was very kind to me. However, there was one boy . . . a chap by the name of Crispin Odey. The strange thing is that I rather liked him. He was a pleasant enough chap, very good with money. Anyway, I don't quite know what I did to upset him, but he made a whole lot of rather hurtful remarks, and for a couple of terms, thanks to him, life was very uncomfortable for me. But then my mother heard about it and I'm afraid she dealt with him very severely. A hit-and-run accident, and they never found the driver. But I knew who it was, and I was completely horrified. It was a side of my mother that I had never seen. And that was when I found out the truth.

"It turned out that when I was just six years old, she had managed to track down one of the main snakeheads operating in Hong Kong and had volunteered her services as a paid assassin. I know it sounds remarkable, but I suppose that being abandoned so cruelly had changed her. She no longer had any respect for life. And the fact was, she was extremely good at her new job. She was very small and Chinese, so nobody ever suspected her and she was utterly without mercy because mercy, of course, wouldn't pay the school fees. And that was how she was supporting me at Harrow! Every time a bill arrived at the start of a new term, she would have to go out and kill someone. It's strange to think that fifteen men died to make my education possible—sixteen, in fact, when I decided to take up horse riding.

"After she'd finished with Crispin Odey, I never had any more trouble. Even the teachers went out of their way to be pleasant to me. I was actually made head boy in my last term, although between you and me, I was the second choice."

"What happened to the first choice?"

"He fell off a roof. From Harrow, I went to London University, where I studied politics, and after that I joined the army. I was sent to Sandhurst, and I will never forget the day of my graduation parade, when I received a medal from the queen. I'm afraid it was all too much for my mother. A few weeks later she died quite suddenly. A massive heart attack, they said. I was shaken to the core because I loved her very much—and here's something you might like to know. I bribed one of the gardeners and had her remains scattered in the grounds of Buckingham Palace . . . in the roses. I knew it was something she would have appreciated."

Major Yu had finished eating and the maid suddenly appeared to clear the dishes. Alex wondered how she had known when to arrive. Dessert was a rhubarb pie served with cream. At the same time, the maid brought in a cheese plate: cheddar, Stilton, and Red Leicester. All English, of course.

"There is not much more to tell," Yu continued. "I served with distinction in the Falklands and the first Gulf

War and was given two letters of commendation. I was as happy in the army as I had been at Harrow . . . happier, in fact, as I had discovered that—taking after my mother, perhaps—I rather enjoyed killing people, particularly foreigners. I rose to the rank of major, and it was then that the great tragedy of my life occurred. I was diagnosed with a quite serious illness. It was a rare form of osteoporosis known as brittle bone disease. The name tells you everything you need to know. What it meant was that my bones had become very fragile. In recent years, the condition has gotten considerably worse. As you can see, I need a stick to walk. I am forced to wear gloves to protect my hands. It is as if my entire skeleton is made of glass, and the slightest blow could cause a terrible injury."

"You must be all broken up about that," Alex remarked.

"You remind me of that boy I mentioned—Crispin Odey," Yu replied. "He learned how unwise it was to annoy me and so, Alex, will you."

He poured himself another glass of wine.

"I was forced to leave active service, but that was not the end of my career. I still had an excellent mind, and I was recommended for a job in intelligence . . . in MI6. That's quite a coincidence, don't you think? In other circumstances, you and I could have been working together. Unfortunately, though, it didn't quite work out that way.

"You see, at first I thought that it was all going to be very exciting. I imagined myself as quite the young James

Bond. But I was never invited to be part of Special Operations like you, Alex. I never met anyone senior like Alan Blunt or Mrs. Jones. I was sent to the communications center at Cheltenham. It was a desk job! Can you imagine someone like me slaving away from nine to five in a boring little office, surrounded by secretaries and coffee machines? It was miserable. And all the time I knew that my disease was getting worse and that it was only a matter of time before I would be thrown out and put on the scrap heap.

"And so I decided to look out for myself. Despite everything, a lot of the information that passed my way at Cheltenham was highly sensitive and confidential. And of course there was a market for this sort of material. So, very carefully, I began to steal secrets from British intelligence—and guess where I took them! I went to the very snakehead that had employed my mother when she was in Hong Kong. They were delighted to have me, and quite soon I was being paid quite handsomely for my services.

"In the end I had to resign from MI6. The snakehead was paying me a fortune and they were offering me all sorts of career opportunities very quickly. I rose up the ladder until—by the early eighties—I had become number two in what was now the most powerful criminal organization in Southeast Asia."

"And I suppose number one fell off a roof," Alex said.

"As a matter of fact, he drowned . . . but you seem to have got the general idea." Yu smiled. "Anyway, it was about this time that I heard rumors of a new organization that was being formed by people who were, in their own way, quite similar to me. I decided to diversify and, using my snakehead connections, I managed to contact them and eventually we met up in Paris to finalize details. That, of course, was the birth of Scorpia and I was one of the founding members."

"So what are you doing now? Why do you need Royal Blue?"

Major Yu had been helping himself to cheese. He stopped with a piece of cheddar on the end of his knife. "You saw the bomb?" he asked.

Alex said nothing. There was no point in denying it.

"You really are a very capable young man, Alex. I see now that we were quite unwise to underestimate you last time." Major Yu dropped the cheese onto his plate and reached for a cookie. "I'm going to tell you what the bomb is for because it will amuse me," he went on. "But then I'm afraid you must be on your way." He looked at his watch. "The plane will be here any minute."

"Where am I going, Major Yu?"

"We'll get to that in a minute. Cheese?"

"Do you have any Brie?"

"Personally, I find French cheese disgusting." He ate silently for a moment. "There is an island in the Timor Sea, not very far from here, in fact. Its name is Reef Island. You may have heard of it."

Alex remembered the newscast he had heard on board

the *Liberian Star*. A conference was taking place there.
The alternative to the G8 summit. A meeting of famous
people who were trying to make the world a better place.

"Scorpia has been given the job of destroying the island and the eight so-called celebrities who will be on it,"
Yu went on. He was sounding pleased with himself. Alex
imagined that must be one of the problems of being a
criminal. You could never find anyone to tell about your
crimes. "But what makes the task particularly interesting
is that we have to make it look like an accident."

"So you're going to blow them up," Alex said.

"No, no, no, Alex. That wouldn't work at all. We have
to be much more subtle. Let me explain." He swallowed
a piece of cheese and dabbed his lips with his napkin. "As
it happens, Reef Island is located in what is known as a
subduction zone. Perhaps you've studied that in geography. What it means is that underneath the sea, a few
hundred miles north of the island, there are two tectonic
plates pushing against each other with a fault line between them.

"Among its many business interests, the Chada Trading Agency is involved in deep-sea oil exploration and
leases an oil platform in the Timor Sea. In the last couple
of months, I have arranged for a shaft to be driven into
the seabed, precisely over the fault line. This was quite a
feat of engineering, Alex. We used the same reverse cir-
culation system that was developed to build the ventilation
shafts for the Hong Kong subway. I'm delighted to say

that it was designed by Seacore, a British company . . . once again, one step ahead of the world.

"Normally, the pipe running down from the rig would be no more than five inches in diameter by the time it hit the oil field. However, our shaft will have ample room for Royal Blue. We will place the bomb half a mile below the surface of the seabed. I will then travel to the oil platform and personally detonate it . . ."

But what was the point? Alex went through what he had just been told, and suddenly he understood. He knew exactly what the result would be. Not just an explosion. Something much, much worse. He couldn't keep the horror out of his voice. "You're going to cause a wave," he said. "A huge wave . . ."

"Go on, Alex." Yu couldn't keep the glee out of his voice.

"A tsunami . . ." Alex whispered the word.

He could see it clearly. That was what had happened on December 26, 2004. An earthquake underneath the sea. A tsunami that had hit first Sumatra, then the coast of Somalia. More than two hundred thousand people had died.

"Exactly. The bomb will have the effect of lubricating the fault line." Yu rested one hand on top of the other. "This will force one of the plates to rise." He lifted the upper hand a few inches. "The result will be a deep water wave, just one yard high. You wouldn't think it could do much harm. But as it approaches the coastline, where the seabed begins to rise, the front will slow down and the rest of the water will pile up behind. By the time it hits Reef Island, a one-hundred-foot wall of water will have formed, traveling at about five hundred miles an hour . . . the speed of a jumbo jet. One cubic yard of water weighs about one ton, Alex. Imagine hundreds of cubic yards rushing in. There will be no warning. The island will be destroyed utterly. It is low-lying. There will be nowhere to hide. Every building will be smashed. Every single person on the island will be killed."

"But the tsunami won't stop there!" Alex exclaimed. "What will happen to it after that?"

"That's a very intelligent observation. No. The tsunami will unleash the same amount of energy as several thousand nuclear weapons. It will continue on its way until it hits the coast of Australia. We'll be all right up here in Darwin, but I'm afraid a very large section of the western coast will disappear. Everything from Derby to Carnavon. Fortunately, there's nowhere very important or even attractive in that part of the country. Broome, Port Headland . . . few people have even heard of these places. And they're not exactly overpopulated. I wouldn't expect more than about ten or twenty thousand people to die. A small price to pay for a job well done."

"But I don't understand . . ." Alex could feel his chest tightening. "You're going to do all this just to kill eight people?"

"Perhaps you didn't hear what I said. Their deaths

have to look accidental. Our job is to make the world forget that this stupid conference ever took place. And so we will provide a natural disaster on a massive scale. Who will care about the extinction of eight people when the number of deaths rises into the thousands? Who will remember a little island when an entire continent has been hit?"

"But they'll know it was you! They'll know it was all started with a bomb."

"That would be true if we used a nuclear bomb. There is an international network of seismographs. The *Poseidon* satellite in outer space. The Pacific Tsunami Warning Center. And so on. But the blast made by Royal Blue won't register. It will be lost as the tectonic plates shift and the devastation begins."

Alex tried to make sense of what he was hearing. He had been sent to uncover a smuggling operation, and somehow instead he had stumbled into this terrible nightmare . . . another attempt by Scorpia to change the world. He had to stop himself from glancing at his watch. Several hours had passed since he had set the hands to eleven o'clock. Surely MI6 were on their way. Why weren't they already here?

"I expect you're wondering whether such a relatively small bomb will really be able to cause such havoc," Major Yu continued. "Well, there is one other thing you need to know. As luck would have it, in three days' time, a rather special.event is taking place. I'm afraid I don't know the astronomical term for it, but what we're talking about is the alignment of three celestial bodies—the sun, the moon, and the earth. And the moon is going to be particularly close. At midnight, in fact, it will be as close as it ever is.

"As a result, there will be a particularly strong gravitational pull on the earth's surface. I'm sorry, Alex. I'm beginning to sound like a schoolteacher. Let me put it more simply. The sun will be pulling one way. The moon will be pulling the other. And for just one hour, from midnight, the tectonic plate will be at its most volatile. A single explosion will be more than enough to begin the process I have described. Royal Blue is the perfect weapon for our needs. Undetectable. Invisible. And above all, British."

Yu fell silent, and in that moment Alex heard the drone of a plane. He looked out the window and saw it circling. It was a seaplane, a tiny two-seater with floats instead of wheels. It could land on the sea right outside the house and tie up on the jetty that Alex had seen from his room. He knew it had come for him.

"Where are you taking me?" he demanded.

"Ah, yes. Now we come to the rub." Major Yu had finished eating. He sat back and suddenly the gun was in his hand, pointing at Alex. He had certainly moved quickly. Alex hadn't even seen him draw it. "The easiest and perhaps the most sensible thing would be to shoot you now," he said. "In half an hour you could be at the bottom of the ocean, and neither Mrs. Jones nor Mr. Ethan Brooke would ever know what had happened to you.

"But I'm not going to do that. Why? For two reasons. The first is that I really don't want to get blood on the carpet. You may have noticed that it's an Axminster—from the town of Axminster in Devonshire. The second is more personal. You owe me a great deal of money, Alex. You have to pay for the damage you did on the *Liberian Star*. There is still the rather more considerable debt that you owe to Scorpia following the collapse of Invisible Sword. And the truth is that although you may not realize it, right now you are worth a great deal to me alive.

"How much were you told about my snakehead? People smuggling, weapons, drugs . . . these are all part of my business. But I have another highly profitable activity based a couple of hundred miles from here in a facility hidden in the heart of the Australian jungle. This facility deals in the sale of human organs."

Alex said nothing. No words would come.

"Do you know how hard it is to find a kidney donor even if you are rich and live in the West?" Yu pointed the gun at Alex's stomach. "You are young and fit. I will be able to sell your kidney for a quarter of a million dollars. And the operation won't even kill you. You will live through it, and after that we'll be able to come back, perhaps, for your eyes." The gun rose up to the level of Alex's head. "Your eyes will sell for fifty thousand dollars each, leaving you blind but otherwise in good health." The gun dropped again. "You can live without your pancreas. It will make me a further one hundred thousand dollars. While you are recovering from each operation, I will drain off your blood cells and your plasma. They will be kept frozen and sold at five hundred dollars a pint. And finally, of course, there is your heart. The heart of a young healthy boy could fetch up to a million dollars more. Do you see, Alex? Shooting you does me no good at all. But keeping you alive is good for business, and you might even get some satisfaction in knowing, when you do finally die, that you have restored the health of quite a few people around the world."

Alex swore. He spat out every foul word he knew. But Major Yu was no longer listening. The door to the dining room had opened again, but this time it wasn't the maid who had come in. Two men. Indonesian, like the maid. Alex hadn't seen them before. One of them placed a hand on his shoulder but Alex shrugged it off and stood up on his own. He wasn't going to let them drag them out of here.

"Good-bye, Alex," Major Yu said. "I enjoyed meeting you."

"Go to Hell, Major Yu," Alex replied.

He turned around and, followed by the two men, walked out of the room.

17

SPARE PARTS

THE PLANE WAS A two-seater Piper Super Cub PA-18-150 with a top speed of just 130 miles per hour—but Alex had already been told that they wouldn't be traveling very far. He was sitting behind the pilot in the cramped cockpit with the buzz of the propellers wiping out any chance of conversation. Not that Alex had anything to talk about. His wrists and ankles were shackled. The seat belt had been fastened in such a way that he couldn't reach the release buckle.

He wondered briefly about the balding, red-necked man in front of him—paid to carry a boy to an unspeakable death. Was he married? Did he have children of his own? Alex had considered trying to bribe him. ASIS would pay twenty thousand dollars or more for his safe return. But he never even got a chance. The pilot only glanced at him once, revealing black sunglasses and a blank face, then put on headphones. Alex guessed that he would have been chosen carefully. Major Yu wasn't going to make any more mistakes.

But his worst mistake had already been made. He had left the watch on Alex's wrist . . . the same watch that was even now—surely—sending out a distress signal to MI6. It had to be. Inside Alex knew that without this one hope, if he didn't believe that despite everything he still had the advantage, he would have been paralyzed with fear. Major Yu's plan for him was the most evil thing he had ever heard . . . turning him from a human being into a bag of spare parts. Ash had certainly been right about the snake-head, and maybe Alex should have listened to his warn-ings. These people were death itself.

And yet . . .

Alex had been locked up at Yu's house throughout the night and for much of the morning. It was now almost midday. How long had it been since he had begun send-ing the signal? Fifteen hours at the very least. Maybe longer. MI6 would have received the signal in Bangkok. It would take them time to reach Australia. He had noth-ing to worry about. MI6 would be tracking him even now, watching him every inch of the way as he moved to the east.

But still Alex had to force himself to ignore the little voice in his ear. They should have been here already. They had decided not to bother. After all, he had called them once before when he was a prisoner in the academy in Point Blanc. That time, the panic button had been con-cealed in a CD player. He had pressed it, and they had done nothing. Was it happening a second time?

No. Don't go there. They would come.

He had no idea where they were heading, and the pilot's body was effectively blocking out the compass and any of the other controls that might have given him a clue. He had assumed at first that they would stick to the coast. After all, the plane had no wheels. It had to land on water. But for the last hour, they had been flying inland, and only the position of the sun gave him any sense of his direction. He looked out the window, past the blur of the propeller. The landscape was flat and rocky, covered in scrub. A brilliant blue river snaked down like a great crack in the surface of the world. Wherever this was, it was huge and empty. There was no sign of any roads. No houses. Nothing.

He tried to make out more of the pilot's features, but the man's eyes were fixed on the controls as if he were making a deliberate effort to ignore his passenger. He pulled on the joystick, and Alex leaned to one side as the plane dipped. Now he saw a canopy of green . . . a band of rain forest. Yu had spoken of the Australian jungle. Was this what he had meant?

The plane dipped down. Alex had been in rain forests before and recognized the extraordinary chaos of leaves and vines, a thousand different shades and sizes, each one of them endlessly fighting for a place in the sun. Surely there would be nowhere for them to land here? But then they flew over the edge of the canopy, and Alex saw a clearing and a river that swelled suddenly into a lake with a cluster of buildings around the edge and a jetty reaching out to welcome them.

"We're landing," the pilot said—for no obvious reason. It was the first time he had spoken throughout the flight.

Alex felt his stomach shrink and his ears popped as they circled and began their descent. The sound of the engines rose as they neared the surface of the water. They touched down, sending spray in two directions. An osprey, frightened by the sudden arrival, leapt out of the undergrowth in a panic of beating wings. The pilot brought the plane around and they headed smoothly toward the jetty.

Two men had come out. They were both muscular, black, unsmiling, dressed in dirty jeans and string vests. They were Aboriginal. One of them was carrying a rifle, slung over his bare shoulder. The pilot cut the engines and opened the door. He had unhooked a paddle from the side of the cockpit and used it to steer the plane the last few yards. The two men helped tie it to the jetty. One of them opened the door and released Alex from his seat. Nobody spoke. That was perhaps more unnerving than anything else.

Alex took a look around him. The compound was clean and well ordered, with lawns that had recently been mown and neat flower beds. All the buildings were made of wood, painted white, with low roofs stretching out over long verandas. There were four houses, square and compact with open shutters and fans turning behind. Each of them had a balcony on the second floor with views down to the lake. One of the buildings was an office and administration center connected to a metal radio tower with two satellite dishes. There was a water tower and an electrical generator with a fence running around it, topped with razor wire.

The last building was the hospital itself, long and narrow with a row of windows covered in mosquito net and a red cross painted on the front door. This was where Alex would be sent when the time came . . . not once but again and again until there was nothing left of him. The thought made him shiver despite the damp heat of the afternoon, and he turned his head away.

At first sight, there didn't seem to be too much security—but then Alex noticed a second fence, this one on the edge of the compound and about ten yards high. It was painted green to blend in with the forest beyond. There were no boats moored to the jetty and no sign of any boathouse, so an escape downriver would be impossible too—unless he swam. And at the end of the day, what would be the point of breaking out of here? He had seen from the plane. He was in the middle of the outback with nowhere to go.

The two Aboriginals had each clamped hold of one of his arms, and now they led him toward the administrative building. As they reached the door, a young woman appeared, dressed as a nurse. She was short, plump, and blond. She had put on bright red lipstick, which seemed strangely at odds with her starched white uniform. One of her stockings had runs.

"You must be Alex," she said. "I'm Nurse Hicks. But you can call me Charleen."

Alex had never heard such a broad Australian accent. And what the woman was saying was simply crazy. She was welcoming him as if he might actually be glad to be here.

"Come right in," she continued. Then she noticed the handcuffs. "Oh, for heaven's sake!" she exclaimed in a voice full of indignation. "You know we don't need those here, Jacko. Will you please remove them?"

One of the men produced a key and freed Alex's hands and feet. The nurse tut-tutted at them, then opened the door and led Alex down a corridor that was clean and simple, with rush matting and whitewashed walls. Fans were turning overhead, and there was music playing somewhere . . . a Mozart opera.

"The doc will see you now," the nurse said brightly, as if he had booked an appointment weeks ago.

There was another door at the far end, and they went through. Alex found himself in a sparsely furnished room—little more than a desk and two chairs. There was a screen to one side, a small fridge, and a cart with some bottles, a stethoscope, and a pair of scalpels. The window was open, with a view of the jetty from where they had just come.

A man was sitting behind the desk, dressed not in a white coat but a turquoise open-neck shirt with the sleeves rolled up and jeans. He was in his forties, with thick blond hair and a craggy, weather-beaten face. He didn't look like a doctor. He hadn't shaved for a couple of days, and his hands were grubby. There was a glass of beer on his desk and an ashtray with a pile of stubs.

"Good day, Alex." He also spoke with an Australian accent. "Take a seat!"

It wasn't an invitation. It was a command.

"I'm Bill Tanner. We're going to be seeing a lot of each other over the next few weeks, so I might as well get a few things clear from the start. Fancy a beer?"

"No," Alex replied.

"You'd better drink something anyway," the nurse said. "You don't want to get dehydrated." She went over to the fridge and produced a bottle of mineral water. Alex didn't touch it. He had already decided. He wasn't going to play these people's game.

"How was the flight?" Tanner asked.

Alex didn't answer.

The doctor shrugged. "You're angry. That's okay. I'd be pretty angry if I were in your shoes. But maybe you should have thought about the consequences before you took on the snakehead."

He leaned forward, and Alex knew, with a sense of revulsion, that he had had this conversation many times before. Alex wasn't the first person to be brought unwill-

ingly to this secret hospital. Others would have sat right
where he was sitting now.

"Let me tell you how this works," Dr. Tanner began.
"You're going to die. I'm sorry to have to tell you that, but
you might as well get used to it. We all have to die sometime, although for you it's probably a little sooner than
expected. But you have to look on the bright side. You're
going to be well looked after. We have a really qualified
team here, and it's in our interests to keep you going as
long as possible. You're going to have a lot of surgery,
Alex. There are some bad days ahead. But you'll come
through . . . I know you will. We'll help you to the finish line."

Alex glanced briefly at the cart, measuring the distance
between himself and the scalpel. He thought about making a grab for it, using it as a weapon. But that wouldn't
help him. Better to take it with him, to find a use for it
later. He realized that the doctor was waiting for him to
reply. He answered with a single, ugly swearword. Tanner
just smiled.

"Your language is a little ripe, son," he said. "But that's
all right. I've heard it all before." He gestured out the
window. "Now, you're probably wondering how you can
escape from here," he went on. "You've seen the fence,
and you're thinking you can climb over it. Or maybe
you've looked at the river and decided you can try swimming. It all looks pretty easy, doesn't it? No TV cameras.

Just the seven of us in the compound. Me, four nurses, Jacko, and Quombi. Not much security . . . that's what you're thinking.

"Well, I'm sorry to tell you, mate. But you're wrong. You go out at night and you're going to have to reckon with Jacko's dog. It's a pit bull. His name is Spike, and he's a nasty piece of work. He'll rip you apart as soon as look at you. As for the fence, it's electrified. Touch it and it'll take you a week to wake up. And you're not getting anywhere near the generator—not unless you know how to bite your way through razor wire—so you can forget about tampering with the current.

"And even if you did manage to get out, it wouldn't do you much good. We're on the edge of the Kakadu National Park . . . two billion years old and as bad as the world was when it began. The start of Arnhem Land is about a mile from here, but that's a mile of tropical rain forest, and you'd never find your way through. Assuming a death adder or a king brown didn't get you, there are spiders, wasps, stinging nettles, biting ants, and—waiting for you on the other side—saltwater crocodiles." He jerked a thumb. "There are a hundred ways to die out there, and all of them are more painful than anything we've got lined up for you here.

"That leaves the river. Looks pretty tempting, doesn't it? Well, there are no boats here. No canoes or kayaks or rafts or anything else you can get your hands on. We even keep the coffins locked up after one guy tried to bust out in one of those. You remember that, Charleen?"

The nurse laughed. "He was using the lid as a paddle."

"But he didn't get very far, Alex, and neither would you. Because this is the start of the storm season . . . what the Aboriginals call Gunumeleng. The water's swollen and fast-moving. About ten minutes downriver you'll hit the first rapids, and after that it just gets worse and worse. You try to swim, you'll be cut to pieces on the rocks. You'll almost certainly drown first. And waiting for you a mile downstream is the Bora Falls. A fifty-yard drop with a ton of water crashing down every minute. So do you get what I'm saying? You're stuck here, mate, and that's that."

Alex said nothing, but he was storing away everything Tanner was telling him. It was just possible that the doctor was giving away more than he realized. Outside the window, he heard a sudden whirring. The engine of the Piper had started again. He glanced out and saw the seaplane moving away from the jetty, preparing to take off.

"We're not going to lock you up, Alex," Tanner went on. "The grub's good, and if you want a beer, just help yourself. There's no TV, but you can listen to the radio, and I think we've got a few books. The point I'm trying to make is—right now, you're here as our guest. Soon you'll be here as our patient, And after we've begun work, you won't be going anywhere. But until then, I want to you take it easy."

"We have to watch your blood pressure," the nurse muttered.

"That's right. And now, if you don't mind, I'd like you to roll up a sleeve so I can take a blood sample. It doesn't matter which arm. I also want a urine sample. It looks to me like you're pretty fit, but I need to get it all down on the computer."

Alex didn't move.

"It's your choice, son," Tanner said. "You cooperate or you don't cooperate. But if you want to play hardball, I'll have to call Jacko and Quombi in. They'll rough you up a little and then they'll tie you down and I'll get what I want anyway. You don't want that, do you? Make it easy on yourself . . ."

Alex knew there was no point refusing. Although it made him sick, he allowed Tanner and the nurse to give him a thorough examination. They checked his reflexes, probed his eyes, ears, and mouth, weighed and measured him, and took the various samples. At last they let him go.

"You've looked after yourself, Alex," Tanner said. "For an English immigrant, you're in great shape." He was obviously pleased. "Your blood type is A positive," he added. "That's going to be an easy match."

It was as he was putting his clothes back on that he did it. Tanner was typing something into his computer. The nurse was looking over his shoulder. Alex was pulling on his shoes, leaning against the cart as if to support himself.

He allowed one hand to cover the scalpel, then slid it sideways and dropped it into his pants pocket. He would have to walk very carefully for the next few minutes or he'd give himself a nasty cut. He just hoped nobody would notice what he had done.

The nurse looked up and saw that he was dressed. "I'll take you to your room," she volunteered. "You should have a rest. We'll bring you supper in about an hour."

The sun had already set. The sky was a deep gray with a streak of red like a fresh wound above the horizon. It had begun to rain, fat drops of water bursting one at a time along the ground.

"There's going to be another storm," the nurse said. "I'd get tucked up and have an early night if I were you. And remember . . . stay indoors. The dog's trained not to come into the buildings. I mean, this *is* a medical facility. But remember—take one step outside and he'll go for you . . . and we don't want you losing too much of that blood of yours, do we? Not at five hundred dollars a pint!"

She left Alex alone in a small room on the ground floor with a bed, a table, and a single fan rotating in the center of the ceiling. In one corner, there was a heavy silver filing cabinet. Alex opened it, but there was nothing inside. A second door led into a small shower room, which also contained a toilet and a sink. Alex slid the scalpel out of his pocket and hid it inside the hanging roll of toilet paper.

He didn't know if he would have any use for it, but at least it made him feel better having taken it. Maybe these people weren't quite as clever as they thought.

He went back into the bedroom. A single window looked down to the lake. The Piper Super Cub had gone. Alex had watched it become nothing more than a speck in the sky at the same time as he was being examined.

He sat down on the bed and tried to collect his thoughts. Only the day before he had been in Darwin, congratulating himself on what he had achieved, thinking that his mission was over. And now this! How could he have been so stupid? He wondered what was happening to Ash. He still didn't understand why the two of them had been separated. If Yu knew that Ash was working for ASIS, why hadn't he sent him here too? Alex was filled with a longing to see his godfather again. It made everything even worse being here alone.

About an hour later, the door opened and a second nurse came in carrying a tray. She was dark-haired and slim and would have been pretty except that she had a broken nose that had set badly. She was younger than Charleen but equally welcoming.

"I'm Isabel," she said. "I'm going to be looking after you. I've got a room just past the stairs, halfway down the corridor, so if you need anything, just yell."

She set the tray down. Alex's dinner consisted of steak and chips, fruit salad, and a glass of milk, but the sight of the food sickened him. He knew they were only building him up for what lay ahead.

He noticed two pills in a plastic cup. "What are these?" he asked.

"Just something to help you sleep," Isabel replied. "Some of our patients have difficulty nodding off, especially the first couple of nights. And it's important you get your rest." She paused at the door. "You're the youngest we've ever had," she said, as if Alex wanted to know. "Leave the tray outside the door. I'll pick it up later."

Alex picked at the food. He wasn't hungry, but he knew he had to keep up his strength. Outside, the rain fell more heavily. It was the same tropical rain that he had experienced in Jakarta. He could hear it hammering against the roof and splashing into ever-widening puddles. There was a flicker of lightning, and for a couple of seconds he saw the rain forest, black and impenetrable. It seemed to have moved closer, as if it was trying to swallow him up.

Later, somehow, he slept. He didn't take off any of his clothes. He couldn't bear to. He simply lay down on the bed and closed his eyes.

When he opened them again, the first light of the morning was already slanting in. His clothes felt damp. His muscles ached. He lifted his wrist and examined the watch. The two hands were still set at eleven o'clock.

Almost twenty-four hours had passed since he had called for help. He listened to the world outside. The harsh cry of some sort of bird. The rustle of the grasshoppers. The last drip of the water as it fell from the branches. There was nobody out there. MI6 hadn't arrived yet, and Alex couldn't fool himself any longer. Something had gone wrong. The watch wasn't working. They never were going to come.

18

DEAD OF NIGHT

TWO DAYS LATER, IN the afternoon, the Piper Super Cub returned.

By now, Alex had fallen into a strange mood and one that he could barely understand. It was almost as if he had accepted his fate and could no longer find the strength or even the desire to escape it. He had met the two other women working at the hospital: Nurse Swaine and Nurse Wilcox, who had proudly told him that she would be his anesthetist. Nobody had been unkind to him. In a way, that was what made it all so nightmarish. They were always checking that he had food and water. Would he like something to read? Would he like to listen to some music? Soon, the very sound of their voices made his skin crawl, but he couldn't break free of the feeling that they owned him and always would.

But he hadn't given up completely. He was still searching for a way out of this hideous trap. The river was impossible. There were no boats; nothing that would pass as a boat. He had followed the fence all the way around. There were no gaps, no convenient overhanging branches. He had considered blowing a hole in it. He still had the one coin that Smithers had given him. But the fence was connected to an electrical circuit. The guards would know instantly what he had done, and without a map, a compass, or a machete, Alex doubted he would be able to find a way through the rain forest.

He thought about sending a radio message. He had seen the radio room in the administration building . . . it was neither locked nor guarded. He soon realized why. The radio transmitter was connected to a numeric keypad. You had to punch in a code to activate it. Major Yu really had thought of everything.

Alex watched as the plane hit the surface of the lake and began a slow, lazy turn toward the jetty. He had been expecting it. Dr. Tanner had told him it would be coming the night before.

"It's your first customer, Alex," he had said cheerfully. "A man called R. V. Weinberg. You may have heard of him."

As usual, Alex said nothing.

"He's a reality TV producer from Miami. Very successful. But he's contracted a serious eye disease, and he needs two transplants. So it looks as if we'll be starting with your corneas. We'll operate first thing tomorrow morning."

Alex examined the American from a distance as he was helped out of the plane. Dr. Tanner had warned him not to approach or try to speak to the "customer." It was one of the house rules. But looking at him, Alex found himself filled with more hatred than he had ever felt for any human being.

Weinberg was overweight in a soft, flabby way. He had curling gray hair and a face that could have been made of putty, with sagging cheeks and jowls. He was a million-aire, but he dressed shabbily, his gut pressing against his Lacoste shirt. But it wasn't just his appearance that disgusted Alex. It was his selfishness, his complete lack of heart. Tomorrow Alex would be blind. This man would take his sight without thinking about it simply because it was what he wanted and he had the money to pay for it. Major Yu, Dr. Tanner, and the nurses were evil in their own way. But Weinberg, the successful businessman from Miami, made him physically sick.

He waited until the man had disappeared into the house that had been prepared for him, then walked down to the edge of the lake. So this was it. He had just one night to make his escape. After that it really would be impossible.

But the anger that Alex had felt had broken through his sense of helplessness. It had come like a slap in the face, and suddenly he was ready to fight back. These people thought he was helpless. They thought they'd covered everything. But they hadn't noticed the missing scalpel. And there was something even more important that they'd overlooked—despite the fact that it was sitting there right in front of them.

The plane.

The pilot had climbed out, dragging a kit bag with him. It looked as if he was going to stay until Weinberg was ready to leave. Alex had no doubt that the Piper would be incapacitated, the engine closed down and the keys locked away. And Dr. Tanner would be fairly certain that no fourteen-year-old boy knew how to fly.

But that was his mistake—to leave the plane, and everything inside it, moored to the jetty.

Alex examined it, working out the angles, thinking about what lay ahead.

They sent Alex to bed at eight thirty, and Nurse Isabel came into the room once he was tucked in. She was carrying two sleeping pills and a little cardboard cup of water.

"I don't want to sleep," Alex said.

"I know, dear," Isabel replied. "But Dr. Tanner says you've got to get your rest." She held out the pills. "It's going to be a big day for you tomorrow," she went on. "You're going to need your rest."

Alex hesitated, then took the pills. He threw them into his mouth and swallowed the water.

The nurse smiled at him. "It won't be too bad," she said. "You'll see." She put a hand to her mouth. "Or rather, you won't . . ."

They checked Alex's room an hour later and again at eleven. Both times they saw him lying, utterly still, in bed. In a way, Dr. Tanner was surprised. He had been expecting Alex to try something. After all, Major Yu had warned him to take extreme care with this particular boy, and the fact was that tonight was his last chance. But it sometimes happened that way. It seemed that—despite his reputation—Alex had accepted the hopelessness of his situation and had chosen to find a brief escape in sleep.

Even so, Dr. Tanner was a cautious man. Before he went to bed himself, he called the two guards, Quombi and Jacko, into his office.

"I want the two of you outside the room all night," he ordered.

The two men looked at each other in dismay. "That's crazy, boss," Jacko said. "The kid's asleep. He's been asleep for hours."

"He can still wake up."

"So he wakes up! Where's he going to go?"

Tanner rubbed his eyes. He liked to get a good night's sleep before he operated, and he was in no mood for a lengthy debate. "I've got my orders from Major Yu," he snapped. "You want to argue with *him*?" He thought for a moment, then nodded. "All right. Let's do it this way. Jacko—you take the first shift until four o'clock. Quombi—you take over then. And make sure that dog of yours stays outside the whole time. I just want to be sure that no one goes anywhere tonight. Okay?"

The two men nodded.

"Good. I'll see you tomorrow . . ."

At three thirty that night, Jacko was sitting on the porch of Alex's building, reading a magazine he had read fifty

times before. He was in a bad mood. He had passed
Alex's window at least a dozen times, listening for the
faintest sound. There'd been nothing. It seemed to Jacko
that everyone had got themselves into a complete panic
about this kid. What was so special about him? He was
just one of the many who had passed through the hospital. Some had screamed and cried. Some had tried to buy
their way out. All of them had ended the same way.

The last thirty minutes of his watch ticked away. He
stood up and stretched. A few yards away, lying on the
grass, Spike cocked an ear and growled.

"It's all right, dog," Jacko said. "I'm going to bed.
Quombi will be here soon."

He belched, stretched a second time, and walked off
into the darkness.

Ten minutes later, Quombi took his place. The other
man was the younger of the two and had spent almost a
third of his life in jail until Dr. Tanner had found him and
brought him here. He liked his work at the hospital, especially taunting the patients as they got weaker and
weaker. But he was in a bad mood right now. He needed
his sleep. And he didn't get paid overtime for working
through the night.

As he reached the building, his eye was caught by
something glinting in the grass just in front of the door.
It was some sort of foreign coin. Quombi didn't even
wonder how it had gotten there. Money was money. He
walked right over and reached down to pick it up.

He was faintly aware of something falling out of the sky, but he didn't look up quickly enough to see it. The silver filing cabinet could have crushed him, but he was lucky. One corner struck him, a glancing blow on the side of the head. Even so, it was enough to knock him out instantly. Fortunately, it made little sound as it thudded into the soft grass. Quombi fell like an axed tree. The dog got up and whined. It knew that something was wrong, but it had never been trained for this. It went over and sniffed at the motionless figure, then sat on its hind legs and scratched.

On the first-floor balcony, Alex Rider looked down at his handiwork with grim satisfaction.

He had never been asleep. He had palmed the pills and swallowed only water and had been waiting quietly ever since. He had gotten up several times in the night, waiting for Jacko to leave, and had heard the words he had spoken to the dog. That was when he had gotten dressed and set to work.

Carrying the heavy filing cabinet up one flight of stairs had almost been beyond him, and it was probably only desperation that had lent him strength as he clutched it in both arms and balanced it on his knee. The worst part had been making sure the metal frame never banged against the walls or the wooden steps. Nurse Swaine had a room on the ground floor, halfway down the corridor, and the slightest sound might awaken her.

He had dragged it into the bedroom over the front

door and, with one last effort, had somehow managed to heave it up onto the balcony rail, balancing it there while he fumbled in his pocket. He had only just been in time. Quombi had made his appearance a few seconds after he had dropped the ten-baht coin that Smithers had given him onto the lawn as bait. From that moment, the trap had been set.

And it had worked. Jacko was in bed. From the sound of it, Nurse Swaine hadn't woken up. Quombi was unconscious. With a bit of luck, he might even have fractured his skull. And the dog hadn't spoiled it all by barking.

The dog was next.

Alex crept back downstairs and went over to the main door. As he appeared, Spike began to growl, its hackles rising and its ugly brown eyes glaring out of the darkness. But—like Dr. Tanner—Nurse Hicks had told him more than she should have. She had said that the dog was trained not to come into the building. The animal was clearly lethal. Even for a pit bull, it was ugly. But it wouldn't harm him so long as he didn't step outside.

"Nice dog," Alex muttered.

He stretched out his hand. He was holding a piece of steak that he had been given on the first night. It had been kind of Dr. Tanner to warn him that there was a dog. Cut into the meat were the six sleeping pills that he had been given over the last three days. The question was—would the dog take the bait? It didn't move, so Alex threw the meat onto the grass, close to the sprawled-out body of the guard. Spike ran over to it, his stubby tail wagging. He looked down, sniffed, and scooped up the meat greedily, swallowing it without even chewing.

Just as Alex had hoped.

It took ten minutes for the pills to take effect. Alex watched as the dog grew more and more drowsy until finally he collapsed onto one side and lay still, apart from the rise and fall of his stomach. At last things seemed to be going Alex's way. But even so, he stepped outside cautiously, expecting either the dog or his master to wake up at any time. He had no need to worry. He scooped up the coin—it was lying a few inches from the edge of the filing cabinet—and hurried into the night.

There was a soft echo of thunder that trembled through the air like a drum rolling down a hill. It wasn't raining yet, but there was going to be another storm. Good. That was exactly what Alex wanted. He checked left and right. The compound was kept permanently lit by a series of arc lamps. The rest of the hospital staff, the pilot, and the American television producer would all be fast asleep. Alex hesitated for just a few seconds, thinking how wonderful it would be if MI6—perhaps Ben Daniels and a platoon of SAS men—chose this moment to make their appearance. But he knew what wasn't going to happen. It was all up to him.

He hurried toward the jetty. If only he had learned how to fly! He might have been able to get the Piper started up and in minutes he would have been out of here, on his way to freedom. But at fourteen, and despite all the other skills his uncle had taught him, he had been too young for flying lessons. Never mind. The plane was still going to be useful to him—for that was Dr. Tanner's big mistake. The security at the hospital had been thoroughly checked—*but only when the Piper was away*. Right now it was back, and even though he couldn't fly it, the seaplane was still going to help him escape.

He reached the jetty without being seen and crouched in the shadow of the plane, which was sitting on its two floats, rocking gently in the water. There was another rumble of thunder, louder this time, and a few drops of water splashed against Alex's shoulders. The storm was going to break very soon. Alex examined the Piper Super Cub. There were two metal struts on each side, supporting the weight of the cockpit and fuselage. They tapered to a point, where they were bolted into the long, fiberglass floats. Just as he remembered.

Alex reached into his pocket and took out the ten-baht coin again. It was the last one that Smithers had given him, and it occurred to him that all three would have saved his life. He placed it against the larger of the metal struts. He looked up at the sky. There were few stars tonight, the clouds swirling overhead. Behind them, the lightning flickered, white and mauve. Alex had the chewing gum pack in his hand. He waited for the thunder and pressed the switch at exactly the right moment.

There was a flash and a small explosion. Even without the storm, it might not have been heard. But the coin had done its job. One of the struts had been ripped apart. The other had come free. The Piper sagged in the water. Alex lay down on the jetty and pressed his feet against the float, pushing with all his strength. Slowly the float moved away from the main body of the plane. Alex pushed harder. The float came free. The rest of the plane sagged uselessly in the water. Moving more quickly now, Alex grabbed hold of the float and dragged it to the shore.

What he had was something almost exactly the same shape and size as a kayak or a canoe. He had even managed to blow a hole in the top, which would allow his legs to fit inside. Admittedly, the float had no foot braces, no thigh hooks, and no support for his lower back. The hull was too flat. That would make it stable in the water, but with such a wide footprint it would be hard to control. It was also much too heavy. Most modern kayaks are made of Kevlar or graphite cloth, glued together and strengthened with resin. The float from the Piper would be as nimble as a London bus. But at least it would carry him. It would just have to do.

Alex had gone kayaking three times in his life. Twice with his uncle, Ian Rider, in Norway and Canada. Once in Wales with the Brookland School when he was doing his Duke of Edinburgh award. He'd had some experience with rapids—the pillows and eddies, the holes and the pour-overs that made the journey such a white-knuckle ride. But the truth was, he was no expert. Far from it. All he could remember of his last trip was speed, screams, and exploding water. He had been twelve at the time and had thought himself lucky to reach thirteen.

The scalpel was back in his pocket, wrapped in toilet paper to prevent the blade from jabbing into him. Now he took it out and unwrapped it, glad that he'd decided to take it from Dr. Tanner's office in the first place. Being careful not to slip and slice open the palm of his own hand, he cut away the jagged edges where the strut had been torn away, trying to make a smooth line. He knew that the journey ahead of him was going to be tough. He didn't want his stomach and hips to be cut to pieces on the way. The blade was small but very sharp. Soon the float was ready. He left it on the shoreline.

Now he needed a paddle.

That was the easy part. For all his smug jokes about coffin lids, Dr. Tanner had overlooked the obvious. The Piper Sea Cub itself carried a paddle as part of its safety equipment. Alex had noticed it when he had flown in, clipped to the side wall of the cockpit. The pilot had used it to steer the plane ashore.

Alex went back to the edge of the lake, where the plane seemed to have tilted even farther below the surface of the water. Eventually, it would sink. He found a piece of the broken strut and twisted it free. Now he had a makeshift crowbar. He waited for another roll of thunder, then used it to smash a window, then opened the passenger door from the inside. The paddle was there. He reached in and took it.

Alex was tempted to get under way at once, but he made himself wait. If the rapids were as bad as Tanner had described, he couldn't possibly risk hitting them in the dark. He needed the first light of dawn. It was raining harder now. Alex was soaked through. But in a way he was glad. The rain would provide him with cover if anyone chanced to look outside. While he was on the wide section of the lake, he would be exposed. It would take him about five minutes of hard paddling to reach the cover of the rain forest.

He needed a diversion, and it suddenly occurred to him that the Piper could provide it. Once again, he worked out the various possibilities. Could he do it? Yes—he had at least another hour until he would have enough light to take on the river. He might as well put the time to good use. And he wanted to leave his mark on Dr. Tanner, R. V. Weinberg, and this entire setup.

Alex smiled grimly. These people were poison, but they'd been in control for too long.

Now it was time to bite back.

19

WHITE WATER

ALEX WENT BACK TO the plane and soon found what he was looking for, rummaging around in the hold: two big empty cans that might have been used to carry water or fuel. He needed a length of rubber tubing and tore it out of the engine itself. It didn't matter. This plane wasn't going anywhere. He opened the nozzle under the wing and put one end into the fuel tank and the other into his mouth and sucked, reeling back, gagging as the acrid taste of aviation fuel cut into his throat. Nothing happened. He forced himself to try again, and this time it worked. He had created a vacuum, and the liquid was flowing out. He dragged over the cans and filled them both.

By the time he had finished, the cans were almost too heavy to lift. Gritting his teeth, he set off across the lawn, heading back to the hospital. He knew he was taking a risk, but he didn't care. He wondered how many other people had been brought here, poor refugees who had set out in hope of a better life but who had never arrived. He wanted to wipe this place off the face of the earth. Someone should have done it years ago.

The biggest risk of all was creeping into Dr. Tanner's office. The first thin cracks of light were appearing in the sky, and one of the nurses could wake up at any time. But he found what he was looking for in a drawer of the doctor's desk. A cigarette lighter. Tanner should have known that smoking could be harmful to his health. It was certainly going to prove expensive.

Moving faster but still being careful not to make any sound, Alex emptied both cans over the side of the building, the veranda, the roof. The fuel sat on top of the rainwater, not mixing with it as it was carried down the drainpipes and along the gutters. He saw it in the puddles, a strange mauve color that almost seemed to glow. When he had just half a can left, he went back to the lake, leaving a trail of fuel behind. The can was empty. He threw it into the water, then climbed into his makeshift kayak, resting the paddle across his legs.

He was almost ready.

The paddle was too short, and the kayak was hopelessly unbalanced. It should have been trimmed out—with the bow and the stem holding the same position in the water. Unfortunately, the hole he had made wasn't central. He tried to shift his weight. At once he found himself wavering helplessly and thought he was going to capsize, but at the last minute he managed to right himself. He tried again more cautiously, and this time he got it right. The float sat evenly on the surface. He dropped a shoulder. The fiberglass dug into his back, but the kayak tilted slightly. He had it under control.

He took a deep breath and pushed off.

At the last minute, he flicked the lighter on. The tiny flame leapt up, battling against the falling rain. Alex touched it against the grass, and at once the fire took hold, rushing up toward the hospital, which was now clearly visible in the rapidly breaking day. Alex didn't wait for it to arrive. He was already paddling, leaning forward and driving with his shoulders to give each stroke more power. He wobbled a couple of times as he got used to the weight, but the float was living up to its name. It was carrying him away.

Behind him, the line of flame reached the hospital.

The result was more spectacular than Alex could have hoped for. The rainwater had spread the aviation fuel everywhere, and although the wood was wet on the surface, years of Australian sunshine had baked it dry inside. Alex heard the soft explosion as the fire caught hold and felt the heat on his shoulders. He glanced back to see that the entire building had become a fireball. The rain was actually steaming as it hit the roof, and there was an epic struggle going on between the falling water and the rising flame. Nobody had come outside yet, but suddenly the American, R. V. Weinberg, appeared, dressed ridiculously in striped pajamas, his pant legs on fire. Alex smiled grimly as he hopped about, screaming, in the rain. It wasn't just his eyes that were going to need medical treatment.

Jacko was next, shocked out of his sleep and unable to take in what had happened. He was followed by Dr. Tanner. By now, it wasn't just the hospital that was on fire. On the other side of the rain, the administrative building and one of the houses was also alight. The whole compound was being torn apart.

Tanner looked around him and saw Quombi lying stretched out on the grass, the great bulk of the filing cabinet still resting on his head and neck. He understood at once. "The boy!" he shouted. "Find the boy!"

Weinberg had thrown himself into a puddle and lay there whimpering. The rest of them ignored him, scattering around the complex looking for Alex. But even if they had thought of looking on the lake, they were already too late. Alex was already out of sight, behind the curtain of rain. There was a deafening crack and the generator shuddered to a halt with a series of sparks and a plume of black smoke. Unable to contend with the joint attack of water and fire, the electricity had failed. Tanner howled.

"Sir—the plane!" Jacko had noticed the Piper resting lopsidedly on its single float.

With the rain streaming down his face, Tanner gazed at it and pieced together what had happened. Now he knew where Alex had gone. He scanned the river, searching for him, but the smoke, the rain, and the half-light had blotted out the world. But he couldn't have gone far. It wasn't over yet.

Dr. Tanner dragged his cell phone out of his pocket and began to dial.

• • •

Alex heard the first rapids before he saw them. The lake wasn't a lake at all . . . it was simply a widening of the river. There was probably a word for it, but it had been far too long since he had sat in a geography lesson. At the far end, it became narrower again, the banks closing in like a letter *V*, and Alex could feel the current driving him on. He hardly had any need to paddle. At the same time, the rain forest closed in on both sides, the trees towering above him, the foliage squeezing out the very air. And there was a sound that he remembered well. It was distant and elemental and immediately filled him with dread. Rushing water, somewhere around the corner, daring him to come on.

He dipped the paddle into the water, testing his makeshift kayak, knowing that he would have to be able to twist and turn, reacting to whatever the river threw at him with split-second timing. He could see already that he wasn't going to be able to stop. The current was too strong and the banks too steep. The nearest trees simply disappeared into the water, the roots trailing down with ugly-looking rocks behind. But at least he was putting distance between himself and the compound . . . or what was left of it. And Dr. Tanner had already told him that there were no boats. The Piper was a wreck. Smoke was still rising from the hospital—he could see it over the line of the trees. There was no way that anyone would be able to follow him.

He turned the corner and came to the first section of rapids. The sight reminded him that he wasn't safe yet, that the worst still lay ahead of him and that he might only have exchanged one death for another.

Ahead of him, the river dipped steeply downward, hemmed in by massive boulders and tree trunks on both sides. A series of jagged ledges had created a sort of natural staircase. If he landed where the water was too shallow, the kayak would be snapped in half—and Alex with it. White water was frothing and foaming, thousands of gallons thundering down from one level to the next. To make matters worse, the whole stretch was dotted with boils, areas where the water were rushing to the surface as if it was being heated in a saucepan. Hit one of those and he would lose all control, and then he'd be completely at the mercy of the river.

"The thing is, Alex, you're never really in control, whatever you may think. Just keep paddling and never fight the current because the current will always win."

The words of his uncle, spoken a lifetime ago, came to his mind. Alex wished he could grasp some comfort from them. He felt like a loose button in a washing machine. His fate was out of his hands. Gritting his teeth, he tightened his hold on the paddle and charged forward.

Nothing quite made sense after that. He was struggling, thrown left and right, blind. Water shot past him, smashed into his face, pulverized him from above. He dug down, using a forward sweep to turn the boat, missing a black boulder with vicious, razor-sharp edges by a matter of inches. The green canopy spun around him. The trees had all blurred into one another. He couldn't hear. His ears were full of water, and when he opened his mouth, gasping for air, water rushed into the back of his throat. Two more sweep strokes, dodging the rocks, then a terrible crash as the kayak slammed into one of the shelves. Mercifully, it stayed in one piece. A huge blanket of water fell on him. He was drowning. He had gone under.

But then suddenly, somehow, he was through. He felt battered and exhausted as if he had just been in hand-to-hand combat with the river, which, in a sense, he had. His stomach and back were on fire where the broken edges had cut into him. Alex slid a hand under the sodden rag that was his shirt and felt the damage. When he took it out, his fingers were bloody. Behind him, the white water leapt and hurled itself against the rocks, displaying its fury that the kayak had gotten through.

Alex knew that he wouldn't be able to take much more. It was only desperation—and pure luck—that had brought him this far. From the moment he had entered the white water, he had lost all sense of his center of gravity, which really meant that he had lost everything. He might as well have been a piece of driftwood, being swept no matter where. It wasn't just that the kayak was the wrong shape. It wasn't a kayak at all. It was a float ripped off a seaplane, and if Alex had decided, after all, to steal a coffin for the journey, he doubted he would have had any less control.

He tried to remember what Dr. Tanner had told him about the river. After the first rapids, it got worse. And then, a mile downstream, came something called the Bora Falls. Alex didn't like the sound of that. He would have to find somewhere to come ashore and take his chances in the rain forest. He had already covered a certain amount of ground. With a bit of luck he might even have reached the edge of the floodplain on the other side. There had to be some civilization somewhere in the area; a ranger, a flying doctor, somebody! Somehow he would find them.

But there was still nowhere to land. The banks climbed steeply, with rocks forming an almost-permanent barrier. When Alex looked up, the tops of the trees seemed a long way away. As wet as he was, Alex wasn't cold. The rain forest throbbed with its own muddy heat. He was moving swiftly, still being swept along by the current. He was listening for the next stretch of rapids—but that wasn't what he heard. Instead, it was the last thing he had expected.

A helicopter.

If he had still been in the rapids, he wouldn't even have been able to hear the chatter of the blades, but right now he was in one of the straits, where the water was fast-moving but silent. Even so, he had to look up to make sure he wasn't imagining it. Somehow it seemed unlikely, early in the morning, in the middle of an Australian rain forest. But there it was. It was still a small speck, some distance behind, but drawing nearer with every second.

Alex's first thought was that MI6 had finally arrived, almost when it was too late. He looked back a second time and felt his hopes shrivel and die. There was something mean and sinister about the helicopter, the way it was zeroing in on him like an insect about to sting. If MI6 were coming, they would have been here days ago. No. This was something else. And it wasn't on his side.

The helicopter was a Bell UH-1D, also known as a "Huey," one of the most famous flying machines in the world ever since the Americans had sent hundreds of them to Vietnam back in the sixties. Alex recognized the long, slim fuselage with the extended tail. The cargo door was open and there was a man sitting with his legs hanging out and some sort of weapon on his lap. It had to be nothing more than bad luck. Dr. Tanner couldn't have called up support in the few minutes that Alex had been gone. The helicopter must have been on its way anyway, perhaps dropping off supplies, and Tanner had simply redirected it after him.

Alex had nowhere to hide. He was in the middle of the river, and he wasn't moving fast enough to get away. At least the helicopter didn't seem to be equipped with door guns, rocket launchers, or antitank missiles. And the man only had a rifle. That was good too. If it had been a machine gun, Alex would have had no chance at all. But even so, a half-decent marksman would be able to pick him off with no trouble. Suddenly Alex's back and shoulders felt horribly exposed. He could almost feel the first bullet slamming into them.

He lowered his head toward the water, changing his center of gravity and tilting the float onto its side. His left shoulder was touching the water now as he lanced forward, pounding down with the paddle, heading for the nearest bank. It was a technique known as the low brace, and Alex hoped that as well as giving him extra momentum through the water, it would also present less of a target to the sniper above.

Something snapped against the surface inches from his head, and a microsecond later, he heard the discharge of the rifle. The bullet had reached him faster than its sound. Alex jerked upright again. Water dripped off the side of his face. But he had reached his destination, a clump of trees hanging over the river, forming a green tunnel for him to go through. At least he would be out of sight for the next few seconds.

The next stretch of white water was about fifty yards in front of him, directly ahead. The rapids had been his enemy, but now, in a strange way, they had become his friend. The churning water, the current spinning him, and the waves tossing him from side to side would make him more difficult to hit. But could he reach them? The helicopter was directly above. The leaves and branches were thrashing around madly, tearing themselves apart.

The downdraft was beating at the river, and the howl of the Huey's engine was shattering the very air.

Alex emerged from the tunnel and dug down, using all the strength of his upper body and shoulders, propelling himself forward. There were two more shots. One of them hit the kayak, and Alex found himself staring at a hole, right in front of him. It had been fired at an angle, boring through the fiberglass and exiting just above the waterline. It must have missed his leg with barely an inch to spare.

Left and then right, two more power strokes and he was into the rapids. He hadn't had time to pick a line— or to form any strategy for surviving the next section. And this stretch was even worse than the first one had been, with faster water, a bigger slope, rocks that seemed purposely built to impale him or tear him in half.

Even the sniper seemed to hesitate, letting the river do its work for him. *"When in doubt, keep paddling."* That was another of Ian Rider's instructions, and Alex did just that, swinging the paddle automatically, first on one side, then the other, battling his way through. The helicopter had gone from sight. The spray had wiped it out. Surely that meant they couldn't see him. There was an earsplitting bang, but it wasn't the rifle. The nose of the kayak had slammed into a rock, jerking Alex around in a crazy circle, so that for the next few seconds he found himself traveling down the river backward. He jammed the paddle in, using the current to turn him. His arms were almost torn off by the strain, but the boat came around, then shot forward. All the water in the world fell on him. But then, like before, it was over. He was through.

Ahead of him, the river was wider, and this time the vegetation was set farther back, providing no cover. The kayak was being carried rapidly. In fact, the river seemed to be moving faster and faster. Why? Alex had no time to find an answer. He heard the thudding of the rotors, glanced up, and saw the sniper taking aim. He was so close that Alex could make out the stubble on his chin, the finger closing on the trigger.

There was only one thing he could do, one last trick he could play. It might easily kill him, but Alex was fighting back. He wasn't just going to sit there and let this man gun him down.

The sniper fired. Alex felt the bullet crease the side of his neck, just above his shoulder. He wanted to scream. It was as if someone had purposefully drawn a kitchen knife across his flesh. But at the same exact moment, he took a deep breath, threw himself sideways, jerked up a knee, and turned the kayak upside down.

He wanted the sniper and the helicopter pilot to think that they had gotten him. From the air, all they would be able to see was the upturned hull of the kayak. Alex was dangling beneath, his face and shoulders buffeted by the current, the paddle gripped tightly in his hands. He was still traveling very fast. If he hit a rock, he would be killed.

It was as simple as that. But it was either that or a bullet from above.

For Alex, the next minute was the longest of his life. He could feel himself moving, but he could see nothing. When he tried to look, everything was a swirl of dark gray, and the water beat against his eyes. He could hear strange echoes of the river and, far away, the helicopter hovering in the air. His legs were trapped, locked above his head inside the kayak. His heart was pounding. His lungs were beginning to demand fresh air.

But he had to stay underwater. How long would the helicopter follow him before the pilot decided that his work was done? His chest was getting tighter. There were bubbles escaping from his mouth and ears, precious oxygen leaking out of him. He had no idea how long he had been submerged. He felt the kayak hit something, sending a shudder down his spine. This was madness. He was drowning. If he waited much longer, he wouldn't have the strength to flip himself back up.

At last, at the very end of his endurance, on the edge of a blackout, he acted. The move was called the hip snap. Alex curled his face into his body and pushed with the paddle. At the same time, he rolled his hips, forcing the kayak to turn. Everything happened at once. His head and shoulders cleared the surface, water streaming down his face. Daylight burst all around him. The kayak swayed, then righted itself. Gasping, dazed, Alex found himself in the middle of the river, moving faster than ever.

And he was alone. The helicopter had gone. He could hear it fading into the distance behind him. So it had worked. They thought he was dead.

Alex looked ahead of him. And saw that he was.

Now he understood why they had left him. It wouldn't have mattered if he was still alive underneath the kayak because what lay in front of him would kill him anyway. He had reached the Bora Falls.

A straight line that marked the end of the world. The river was rushing over it . . . hundreds, thousands of gallons. There was a white cloud, a mist hanging over the abyss. And beyond that nothing. He could hear the water thundering down endlessly and knew that there could be no going back. There was no power on earth that could stop him now.

Alex Rider opened his mouth and yelled as the kayak was swept helplessly over the edge.

20

BATTERIES NOT INCLUDED

FOR A LONG, DRAWN-OUT second, he hung in space with the roar of the Bora Falls in his ears, the spray in his eyes, and the certain knowledge in his mind that he couldn't possibly survive. The water was like some huge living thing—rushing and exploding over the side of the rock face. And there would be no safe landing. Looking down, Alex saw a boiling cauldron, fifty yards below, waiting to receive him.

There was no time to think, no time to do anything but react instinctively, half remembering lessons taught long ago. Somehow he had to lessen the impact when he hit the surface below. Be aggressive! Don't let the waterfall just take you. At the very last moment, as he began to fall, Alex tensed himself, took a deep breath, and then paddled hard with a single, powerful stroke.

The world tilted.

The roar in his ears was deafening. He was blind. His head was being hammered. He was only aware of his hands, gripping the paddle, the wrists locked, his muscles seizing up.

Lean forward. You don't want to fight the water—you have to go with it. The higher the drop, the more angle you'll need when you hit the bottom. And—he remembered when it was almost to late—turn your head to one side or the impact will smash every bone in your face.

Falling. Half in the water, half in the air. Faster and faster.

Try to aim for the white. That's where there's the most air in the water, and the air will cushion your fall. Don't shout. You have to hold that breath.

How much farther could it be? And how deep was the basin? God—he would be smashed to pieces if he hit a rock. Too late to worry about that now. He closed his eyes. Why watch his own death?

The kayak hit the cauldron nose first and was instantly sucked inside. Alex's legs and stomach took the full force of the impact before the water overwhelmed him. It pounded down on his shoulders, crushing him. His head was thrown back, and he felt the whiplash twist his neck. The paddle was torn free. And then he was floundering, scrabbling desperately with his hands, trying to free himself from the kayak, which was now dragging him into the depths below. His elbow struck a rock, almost breaking the bone. The shock made him release his breath, and he knew he had only seconds to reach the surface. But his legs were trapped. He couldn't pull them free. The kayak was sinking, taking him with it. Using all his strength, he twisted his lower body, and somehow his hips cleared the edge of the kayak. He pulled. First one leg, then the other. He was swallowing water. He no longer knew which way was up and which was down. His feet were free. He lashed out once and then again. The water spun him, throwing him violently from side to side. He couldn't take any more. One last try . . .

His head and shoulders burst up into the air. He was already far downstream. The Bora Falls were behind him, impossibly high. There was no sign of the kayak. It had surely been smashed to pieces. But as Alex sucked in fresh air, he knew that he had done everything right and that by a miracle he had survived. He had taken on the falls and he had beaten them.

The current had slowed down. Alex's arms and legs were completely limp. All his strength had gone, and the best he could manage was to keep himself afloat, tilting his head back so that his mouth stayed in the air. He felt as if he had swallowed a gallon of water and vaguely wondered about cholera, yellow fever, or whatever else this tropical river might contain. ASIS hadn't bothered giving him any injections before he flew to Bangkok.

How far had he traveled? Dr. Tanner had said that the falls were a mile from the camp but he felt he had gone twice that distance. No sign of the helicopter, though. That was a good thing. They thought he was dead. So they'd leave him alone. He had never felt so weary. The water was now a cushion, and he wanted to lie back and sleep.

Some time later, he found himself lying on a riverbank made up of gravel and sand. He had been washed up without even noticing it and must have nodded off since the sun was now high in the sky. He allowed the warmth to creep into him. As far as he could tell, none of his limbs were broken. His neck and back were bruised and hurting—his spine had taken the full force of the impact—and there were cuts and scratches all over his waist, his hips, and his legs. But he knew he had gotten off lightly. The chances of his surviving the waterfall must have been about fifty to one . . . but to have done so without a major injury would have been considerably less. He remembered what Ash had told him about his father. The luck of the devil. Well, that was something Alex seemed to have inherited.

Ash.

Reef Island.

The tsunami heading for Western Australia.

For the last few days, Alex had been so worried about himself that he had lost sight of the bigger picture. How long did he have left before Major Yu set off the bomb that was going to have such a devastating effect on the earth's tectonic plates? Was he already too late? Alex forced himself into a sitting position, warming himself in the sun and trying to get life back into his battered frame. At the same time, he worked it out. Yu had spoken of three days. At midnight the earth was going to be in the grip of some sort of gravitational pull and the fault line deep down in the seabed would be at its most vulnerable.

Three days. Alex had spent two of them as a prisoner in the hospital compound. So it was going to happen

today! Right now it couldn't be much later than ten or
eleven o'clock in the morning. So Alex had only twelve
hours to prevent a terrible catastrophe, the murder of
eight people on Reef Island and the deaths of thousands
more in Australia.

And that was when the complete hopelessness of his
situation hit him. It was true that he had managed to escape from the horrific death Major Yu had planned for
him. But where was he? Looking around him, Alex saw
that he had left the rain forest behind him. He was on the
edge of a floodplain with mountains in the far distance,
perhaps thirty miles away. He was surrounded by stubby,
dwarflike trees that he couldn't name, a few boulders,
and some termite mounds. There was a sweet smell—
something like moldering wood—in the air. And that was
all. If nowhere had a middle, this was it.

There was nothing he could do. Nobody was going to
operate on him, but he would die anyway—either from
starvation or disease. Assuming, of course, that a saltwater crocodile or a snake didn't get him first. Alex wiped
a grimy hand across his face. It seemed to him that from
the moment this mission had begun, nothing had gone
right. He had never been in control. He cast his mind
back to the office in Sydney and Ethan Brooke outlining
what he would have to do. He was there to provide cover,
that was all. It was going to be easy. Instead of which, he
had been thrown into the worst two weeks of his life.
God! He should have listened to Jack Starbright!

He looked again at the mountains. It would take him forty-eight hours to reach them at the very least. Too long. And why should he assume anyone lived there? He hadn't seen any roads or houses from the plane. If only he could get in touch with MI6. He glanced at his wrist. Miraculously, despite the battering it had taken, the watch was still in place. The question was—why hadn't it worked? Smithers had built it for him personally. The watch *must* be sending out a signal. So what possible reason could MI6 have to ignore it? Alex remembered his meeting with Mrs. Jones and Ben Daniels—Fox, as he had once been known. Alex couldn't believe that the SAS man would let him down. So what had gone wrong?

He took the watch off and examined it. Although it looked cheap and tacky, like something he might have gotten in a street market in Afghanistan, the watch would have been built to last. The strap must have been strong to survive the journey over the Bora Falls, and Alex guessed the case would be waterproof. The hands were still showing eleven o'clock. Alex turned it over. There was a groove going all the way around the underside. He realized that the back must screw off. He pressed his thumb against it and twisted. The case opened with surprising ease.

The watch contained some complicated microcircuitry that Smithers must have designed and installed. It was completely dry. There was no evidence of any water seeping in. The whole thing was powered by a battery, which should have been sitting in a circular compartment, right in the middle.

But there was no battery. The compartment was empty.

So that was the answer, the reason why his signal hadn't been heard. There had been no signal. But how could it have happened? Smithers had always been on his side. It was completely unlike him to forget something so basic. Alex had to fight back a wave of fury. His whole life snatched away from him simply because of a missing battery!

For a moment, Alex was tempted to fling the watch into the river. He never wanted to see the wretched thing again.

For a long time he didn't move. He let the sun beat down on him, drying out his clothes. A few flies buzzed around his face, but he ignored them. He found himself playing back everything that had happened to him . . . the waterfall, the flight through the rapids, the moment he had set the hospital ablaze. Had it really all been for nothing? And before that, his dinner with Major Yu, the chase on the *Liberian Star*, the discovery of Royal Blue, the toy warehouse in Jakarta, and the arrival of Kopassus.

No battery!

He remembered his time in Bangkok with Ash and the story he had been told about his father in Malta. That was the only reason he had agreed to all this, to learn something about himself. Had it been worth it? Probably not. The truth was that Ash had disappointed him. His godfather. Alex had hoped he would have been more of a friend, but despite all the time they had spent together, he had never really gotten to know him. Ash was too much of a mystery—and from the very start he had set out to trick Alex. That business on the beach in Perth.

He remembered his first sight of Ash, dressed as a soldier and carrying an assault rifle, looming out of the darkness as Alex stood on a fake mine in the middle of a fake barrage. How could they have done that to him? It had all been a test.

"You weren't in any real danger. We knew exactly where you were all the time."

That was what Ash had told him that first night at the Peninsula Hotel, sitting out at the swimming pool. Alex remembered it now.

And how had they known?

"There was a beacon inside the heel of one of your sneakers."

His sneakers.

Alex looked down at them. All the color had faded, and they were ragged, full of holes. Was it possible, what he was thinking? Could it possibly be true? Alex had been given the sneakers when he was on the aircraft carrier that had picked him up when he first landed in Australia. The beacon had been added by Colonel Abbott when he was staying with the SAS in Swanbourne.

He was wearing the same sneakers now.

He had been given a complete change of clothes by Cloudy Webber when she had dressed him as an Afghan—but the shoes hadn't fit him, so she had allowed him to keep his own. He hadn't changed again until his dinner with Major Yu. He had worn the English designer shirt and jeans until he had arrived at the hospital. There had been fresh clothes in his room. But neither Major Yu nor Dr. Tanner had provided him with new footwear. So the beacon that he had been given in Swanbourne must still be on him. It wouldn't be working. It had been designed for short-range use.

But it might be battery-operated.

Alex fought back the surge of excitement. He was too afraid of being disappointed. He leaned down and pulled the sneakers off so that he could examine them. If there was a tracking device, it would have to be buried in one of the heels. There was nowhere else to hide it. Alex turned the shoes over. The soles were made of rubber, and he couldn't see any openings or anything that looked like a secret compartment. He pulled out the insoles. And that was when he found it. It was in the left shoe, directly over the heel: a flap that had been cut into the fabric and then sealed.

It took Alex ten minutes to get it open, using his fingers, his teeth, and a sharp stone from the riverbank. As he worked, he knew that this might all be for nothing. The battery had been there for two weeks. It might be dead. It surely wouldn't fit the transmitter in the watch anyway. But the chances of finding a second battery in the Australian outback had been zero to begin with. Alex found it hard to believe that he had been carrying it all the time.

He pulled open the flap and there it was—the little pack of circuitry that had been designed to save his life during the bombardment in Swanbourne. And there was the power source too, a straightforward lithium battery, about twice the size of the one that should have been fitted into the watch. Alex eased it out and held it in the palm of his hand as if it were a nugget of pure gold. All he had to do was connect it. He had no screwdriver, no conductor, no metal contacts, nothing. Easy!

In the end, he broke two spikes off a nearby shrub and used them as miniature tweezers to pry out some of the wires from inside the heel of the shoe. It seemed to take forever, and as the sun climbed higher, he felt the sweat trickling down his forehead, but he didn't stop to rest. Painstakingly, he unstitched the inside of the radio beacon until he had two lengths of wire, each one barely more than an inch long. Did the battery still have any life? He rubbed the wires against it, and to his delight, he was rewarded by a tiny spark. So now all he had to do was connect the battery to the watch, using a couple of pebbles to keep everything in place. There really was nothing more he could do. He set the battery next to the watch with the wires trailing inside, the two of them feeding precious electricity into the transmitter, and balanced the entire thing on a rock. After that, he went and lay down in the shadow of a tree. Either the transmitter was working now or it wasn't. He would find out soon enough.

A few minutes later he was sound asleep.

21

ATTACK FORCE

ALEX WAS WOKEN BY the sound of a helicopter. For a moment he was filled with dread, fearing that the Bell UH-1D had returned. If that were the case, he would let them take him. He simply didn't have in him to fight anymore. There was nothing left with which to fight back. But squinting into the sun, he saw at once that this was a bigger helicopter with two sets of rotors: a Chinook. And there was a figure already leaning out of the front door.

Blue eyes. Short black hair. A handsome, slightly boyish face. It was Ben Daniels.

Alex clambered to his feet as the Chinook landed on a patch of scrubland a short distance away. He went over to it, taking care where he put his bare feet. It would be just his luck to step on a death adder now! Ben stepped out and stared at him.

"So here you are!" he exclaimed, shouting over the noise of the helicopter rotors. "We were getting worried about you!" He shook his head in disbelief. "What on earth are you doing out here? Where have you been?"

"It's a long story," Alex said.

"Has it got anything to do with the smoke coming from upriver?" Ben jerked a thumb. "We saw it as we flew in."

"That used to be a hospital." Alex couldn't hide his delight that things were finally going his way. "I'm really glad to see you . . ."

"Mrs. Jones has been frantic. We knew you'd flown to Jakarta, but we lost you after that. She's got people all over Indonesia, but she sent me to Darwin in case you made it across. I've been waiting there for three days, hoping you'd get in touch. You look terrible! Like something the cat dragged in . . ."

"That's how I feel." Alex stopped. "What time is it, Ben?" he asked.

Ben was obviously surprised by the question. He looked at his watch. "It's ten past one. Why do you ask?"

"We have to get moving. We've got less than twelve hours."

"Until what?"

"I'll tell you on the way . . ."

Alex was feeling a lot better than he had in a long time. He was warm and dry and well fed, and all the dangers of the last few days had slipped away behind him. He was lying on a comfortable bunk in a military compound just outside Darwin, which was where Ben Daniels had brought him earlier that day. He was wearing combat fatigues, the only clothes Ben had been able to find for him. For the last few hours he had been left on his own.

He could see a certain amount of activity outside the window. Soldiers crossing the parade ground, jeeps speeding in and out of the main gate. The helicopter was still sitting where it landed. Half an hour ago, a gas truck had pulled up and Alex had watched as refueling began. He wondered if it was significant. Maybe something was happening at last.

Despite everything, he couldn't relax completely. It was six thirty, and very soon the sun would be setting, at the same time moving into the alignment with the earth and the moon that Major Yu had been waiting for. At midnight, Royal Blue would be lowered to the seabed and detonated. The devastation would begin.

And what were MI6 or ASIS doing to prevent it?

Alex had explained everything . . . not just to Ben but to a whole posse of Australian army officers. His story was incredible, almost beyond belief, but the strange thing was that not one person in the room had doubted him. This was, after all, the boy who had dropped in from outer space. Alex supposed that where he was concerned, anything was now considered possible. One of the men was a technical adviser, and he had quickly confirmed what Major Yu had said. It would be possible to manufacture an artificial tsunami. From midnight onward, the fault line would be in the grip of enormous gravitational pressure. Even a relatively small explosion would be enough to trigger a global catastrophe, and Yu had all the power of Royal Blue at his command.

Of course, in one sense Scorpia's mission had already failed. Thanks to Alex, the intelligence agencies knew what Scorpia were planning, and even if everyone on Reef Island were killed in a freak wave, nobody would now think it was an accident. Alex assumed that the island would be evacuated anyway, just to be on the safe side. There was no longer any need for Major Yu to press the button. If he was sensible, he'd already be looking for somewhere to hide.

There was a knock on the door. Alex straightened up as Ben Daniels entered. He was looking grim.

"They want you," he said.

"Who?"

"The cavalry's just arrived. They're in the mess hall . . ."

Alex walked across the compound with Daniels, wondering what had gone wrong. But at least he was grateful he was still being included. MI6 had always treated him as a spy one minute, a schoolboy the next, dumping him out of the way whenever it suited them.

The mess hall was a low wooden building running the full length of the square. With Daniels right behind him, Alex opened the door and went in.

Most of the officers he had spoken to earlier that day were still there, poring over maps and sea charts that had been spread out over the dining tables. They had been joined by two men that Alex recognized at once. This was the cavalry that Ben had referred to. Ethan Brooke was sitting at a table, with Marc Damon standing just behind him. Presumably they had been flown up from Sydney.

Garth—the guide dog—saw Alex come in and thumped his tail. At least someone was pleased to see him.

"Alex!" The blind man had become aware of his presence. "How are you doing?"

"I'm okay." Alex wasn't sure he was too happy to see the head of ASIS—Covert Action. Ethan Brooke had manipulated him as cold-bloodedly as Alan Blunt would have in London. It seemed to him that all these people were of a type.

"I know what you've been through. I can't believe the way things played out. But you did a fantastic job."

"Major Yu knew about me all the time," Alex said. Even as he spoke the words, he knew they were true. The fight in Bangkok had been designed to cripple him. And on the *Liberian Star,* Alex had overheard Yu boasting to the captain. He had known Alex's identity before he entered the container. He has simply been playing with him, for his own amusement.

"Yes. We have a security leak, and it's worse than we thought." Brooke glanced in the direction of his deputy, who looked away, as if he didn't want to make any comment.

"What's happened to Ash?" Alex asked.

"We don't know. We only know what you told us." Brooke fell silent, and Alex could see he was preparing himself for what he had to say.

"So what are you going to do?" Alex asked.

"We have a problem, Alex," Brooke explained. "Here's the situation . . . I'll give it to you straight. The first thing is, the Reef Island conference is still going ahead."

"Why?" Alex was shocked.

"We told them they were in danger. Obviously, we couldn't give them all the details, but we suggested they pack their bags and get out of there in the strongest-possible terms. They refused. They said that if they left, they'd look like cowards. Tomorrow's their main press conference, and how's it going to look if they've all skulked away overnight? We're still arguing with them, but in a way, I suppose they've got a point. Scorpia wanted them out of the picture. If they simply disappeared, they'd be doing the job for them."

Alex took this in. It was bad news—but Reef Encounter was only part of the picture. After the tsunami hit the island, it would continue on its way toward Western Australia.

"Have you found Major Yu?" he asked.

"Yes." Brooke smiled briefly. "He told you he was on an oil platform in the Timor Sea, and we've gone through all the records, including the latest satellite images. There's an oil rig licensed to the Chada Trading Agency in Bangkok. It's a semi-submersible platform moored in four thousand feet of water a hundred miles north of Reef Island."

"Right in the subduction zone," Damon muttered. It

was the first time he had spoken since Alex came into the room. "It's called Dragon Nine."

"So that's it," Alex said. It seemed obvious to him. "You bomb it. Blow it out of the water. Kill Major Yu and everyone who works for him."

"I'd love to do just that," Brooke replied. "But first of all, Dragon Nine is just outside Australian waters. It's in Indonesian territory. If I send a strike against it, I might accidentally start a war. It seems I can't even send one man in a boat without written authority, and that could take days. Officially, we're stuck . . ."

"Why can't you ask the Indonesians for help?"

"They don't trust us. By the time we've persuaded them we're telling the truth, it'll be too late."

"So you're just going to sit back and let him get on with it?" Alex couldn't believe what he was hearing.

"Obviously not. Why do you think we're here?"

Ben Daniels took a step forward. "Why don't you tell Scorpia that you know what they're up to?" he asked. "You said it just now. The plan only worked if we all thought the tsunami was caused naturally. If we tell them they've failed, maybe they'll back off."

"We've already tried," Damon replied. "But Dragon Nine has shut down. It's observing radio silence. And even if we did find a way to contact Major Yu, he might go ahead anyway. Why not? He's obviously mad. And if the bomb's already in place . . ."

"So what is the answer, Mr. Brooke?" one of the other officers asked.

"A small British-Australian task force. Unauthorized and illegal." Brooke turned to Alex. "I've already spoken to your Mrs. Jones and she's agreed. We have very little time, but I've assembled some of our best people. They're getting equipped right now. You and Daniels go with them. We parachute you onto the oil rig. You find Royal Blue and deactivate it. Meanwhile, my people kill Major Yu. If you can locate the whereabouts of Ash, so much the better—but he's not a priority. What do you say?"

Alex was too shocked to say anything, but next to him, Ben Daniels shook his head. "I'm happy to go," he said. "But you can't be serious, asking Alex. He's only a kid, if you hadn't noticed. And I'd have said he's already done enough."

Some of the Australian officers nodded in agreement, but Brooke wasn't having any of it. "We can't do it without Alex," he said simply.

And Alex knew he was right. He had already told them what he had done on board the *Liberian Star:* the bomb and the scanning equipment. "I scanned my fingerprints into Royal Blue," he said. "I'm the only one who can deactivate it." He sighed. It had seemed like a good idea at the time.

"I'll expect you to look after him, Mr. Daniels," Brooke continued. "But we don't have a lot of time to

argue about this. It's already seven o'clock, and it's a
two-hour trip." He turned to Alex. "So, Alex. What do
you say?"

Two men and a woman were watching the sun set on
Reef Island.

The island was only a quarter of a mile long, but it was
strikingly beautiful with white beaches, deep green palm
trees, and a turquoise sea . . . all the colors somehow too
vivid to be quite real. The north side of the island rose up,
with limestone cliffs covered in vegetation and mangroves
below. Here sea eagles circled and monkeys chattered in
the trees. But on the southern side, everything was calm
and flat. There was a wooden table and a bench on the
sand. But no deck chairs, no sun umbrellas, no Coke
bottles or anything that might suggest that, just over
the horizon, the twenty-first century was ticking on.

There was only one building on Reef Island, a long
wooden house with a thatched roof, partly on stilts. Normally, there were no generators. The only electricity was
supplied by wind or water power. A large organic garden
provided all the food. The owner of the house ate fish but
not meat. A few cows, grazing in a field, were milked
twice a day. There were chickens to lay eggs. An elderly
goat, wandering free, was no use at all, but it had been
there so long that nobody had the heart to ask it to leave.

In the last few days, the island had been invaded by a
press corps, which had established itself in a series of

tentlike structures behind the house. The journalists had brought their own generators. And meat. And alcohol. And everything else they would need for the press conference the next day. They were enjoying themselves. It was nice to be able to report a story that people actually wanted to hear. And the weather during the last week had been perfect.

The woman on the beach was the actress—Eve Taylor—who owned the island. She had made quite a lot of bad films and one or two good ones, and she didn't really care which was which. They all paid the same. One of the men was an American multimillionaire . . . a billionaire, in fact, although in recent years he had given much of his wealth away. The other man was the pop singer Rob Goldman, who had just returned from his tour of Australia.

"ASIS are still insisting we should leave," Goldman was saying. "They say we could all be killed."

"Have they explained the nature of the threat?" the millionaire asked.

"No. But they sounded serious."

"Of course they did." The actress let sand run through her fingers. "They want us to go. This is a trick. They're just trying to scare us."

"I don't think so, Eve," Goldman said.

Eve Taylor gazed at the horizon. "We're safe," she said. "Look how beautiful it is. Look at the sea! That's part of the reason we're here. To protect all this for the next generation. I don't care if there's danger. I'm not going to run away." She turned to the billionaire. "Jason?"

The man shook his head. "I'm with you," he said. "I never ran away from anything in my life and I'm not starting now."

Three hundred miles farther south, in the cities of Derby, Broome, and Port Headland, thousands of people were watching the same sunset. Some of them were on their way home from work. Some were tucking children into bed. In pubs, in cars, on the beaches, wherever . . . they were simply edging toward the end of another day.

And none of them knew that inch by inch, the bomb known as Royal Blue was already making its way down the pipe that would carry it to the seabed and below. That the sun and the moon were moving, inexorably, into an alignment that wouldn't happen again for another century. And that a madman was waiting to press the button that would unleash chaos on the world.

Five hours until midnight.

And in an army camp south of Darwin, Alex Rider gave his answer and the final preparations began.

22

DRAGON NINE

ETHAN BROOKE HAD HANDPICKED ten soldiers from the Australian SAS for his assault team, and at least some of them needed no introduction. As Alex joined them in the hanger that was going to be used as a briefing room, he saw Scooter, Texas, X-Ray, and Sparks waiting for him, and suddenly he was back where this had all begun, on the beach near Swanbourne. He wasn't sure if he should be glad or annoyed to meet up with them again.

Scooter was equally uncomfortable. "I'm really sorry about that trick we pulled on you, Alex," he said. "We all felt bad about it. But we had our orders . . ."

"Colonel Abbott asked us to pass on a message," Texas added. "No hard feelings. And if you ever come back to Swanbourne, we'll throw a proper Aussie barbecue."

"With no hand grenades," Alex muttered.

"You got it."

Alex looked at the other soldiers. None of them seemed to be older than twenty-four or twenty-five, meaning there was an age gap of just ten years between him and them. Maybe that was why all of them had accepted him. Like Alex, they had changed into night combat gear. A couple of them carried balaclavas. The rest had painted their hands and faces black.

The hanger was vast and empty. A blackboard had been placed in the middle with a row of metal benches. Alex sat down next to Ben. The others took their places with Scooter facing them in front of the board. Once again, he seemed to be in charge. Scooter was looking tired. He seemed to have grown a lot older since Swanbourne—or maybe it was just that he knew how much was at stake. "We haven't got a lot of time," he began. "Nor do we have much of a plan . . . so this won't take long.

"We're parachuting in from about eight thousand feet. I know a boat would have been easier and less conspicuous, but by the time we got there it would all be over. Anyway, it's always possible our friend Major Yu has radar."

He turned to the blackboard. Someone had taped up what could have been an engineer's drawing of two oil rigs—one square, the other triangular, joined by a narrow bridge. Each of the rigs had three cranes and one of them had a helicopter pad, represented by a square in a circle. Scooter picked up a stick, which he used as a pointer.

"All right—listen up!" He tapped the picture. "This is what we *think* Dragon Nine looks like. We don't *know* because we don't have any pictures and we haven't had enough time to take any. All I can tell you for certain is that it's a semi-submersible platform, which means that basically the whole thing floats on the surface of the water, connected to the seabed by a dozen steel tendrils.

In case you're wondering, each one of them is about a mile long."

"What happens if they break?" someone asked.

"Nothing much. The whole thing will float away, like a ship without an anchor. At least that's something we don't have to worry about." He pointed again. "The processing platform is on the left. Dragon Nine isn't in production, so the whole area will be quiet—and that's where we're going to start. We'll land on the helicopter pad. You'll recognize it because it's got this big letter H . . ."

Scooter turned his attention to the square-shaped rig.

"This is the drilling platform," he continued. "Once we've assembled and checked everyone's there, we'll make our way across the bridge, heading for the main derrick . . . that's the metal tower over the well hole. And that's where we're going to find Royal Blue. Our friend Major Yu will be using some sort of system—maybe guide wires—to lower it down to the seabed."

"So let's blow it up," X-Ray growled.

"It's our first target," Scooter agreed. "The power unit will be our second. But we can't take anything for granted. Yu could just as easily be using a submarine to take the bomb down. That's why Alex is here. Our job is to find the control room and get him there. He can deactivate Royal Blue—but no one else can, so if he gets shot we might as well pack up and go home. You hear what I'm saying? I want you to watch his back. And his front and his sides."

Alex glanced down. He understood what Scooter was saying and why he had to say it, but he still didn't like being picked out in this way.

"I'm afraid this mission isn't as easy as it seems," Scooter continued, although Alex wouldn't have said it looked simple to begin with. "We've got no idea where the control room is. There are five different levels, two separate platforms. Yu could be on either. You've got to think of Dragon Nine as two metal cities. They've got their own storage depots, dormitories, mess halls, and recreation rooms as well as fuel tanks, desalination units, pump rooms, engineering blocks, and all the rest of it. Somehow we have to find our way through all that until we find what we're looking for. Then we have to deal with Royal Blue. And when we start, it's possible that we're going to be spread out all over the place. We're lucky that there's not too much breeze, but there's no moon. Just try not to fall into the sea."

He paused. Eleven silent faces watched him from the two rows of benches. Alex could feel the clock already ticking. He wanted to be out and away.

"So what do we have on our side?" Scooter asked. "Well, first there's the element of surprise. Major Yu thinks he killed Alex, so he'll have no idea we're on our way. And also, there's the question of timing." He looked at his watch. "Yu can't detonate the bomb whenever he likes. He's tied into the one hour starting at midnight.

That's when the earth, sun, and moon are going to be in the right position. It's nine o'clock now, and we're only two hours from drop-off. That means we'll have one hour plus to find Royal Blue before he can throw the switch. And there's something else we know, thanks to Alex. The bomb can only remain at depth for twenty minutes. So it's not there yet. And if all goes well, it never will be."

He looked around.

"Any questions?"

There were none.

"We've got to move quickly and quietly," he concluded. "Take out as many of Yu's people as we can before they know we're there. Leave the guns and grenades for as long as possible. Use your knives. And find the control room! That's what this is all about."

He set down the pointer.

"Let's go."

Everyone stood up. Ben had Alex's parachute—black silk, for a night drop. He'd packed it himself before the briefing, and now he helped Alex put it on, pulling the straps tight across his chest and around his thighs.

"It's probably a bit too late to ask you this," he muttered. "But have you ever parachuted before?"

"Only once," Alex admitted. That had been eight months ago. Alex had landed on the roof of the Science Museum in London. But he decided not to go into all that right now.

"Well, don't worry if you miss the target," Ben said. "The sea's warm. Conditions are perfect. And with a bit of luck, there won't be too many sharks."

The Australian SAS men were already moving. Ben strapped on his own parachute, and the two of them followed the others out of the hangar. There was a helicopter waiting for them on the tarmac—the same one that had picked Alex up in the jungle. The Chinook CH-47 was the ideal machine for this night's work. Often used to ferry troops or supplies, its wide rear exit was also perfect for parachute drops. It would fly them to the target at 190 miles per hour and at an altitude no higher than 8,500 feet. That wouldn't leave long to deploy the chute.

Ben must have been reading his thoughts. "We're using static line," he said. The static-line deployment system meant that they wouldn't have to pull a rip cord. The parachutes would open automatically.

Alex nodded. His mouth was suddenly too dry to speak.

They climbed in the back. In the jungle, Alex had used a door just behind the cockpit, but this time the whole rear section of the Chinook had been opened, forming a ramp big enough to take a jeep. Alex looked in. The pilot and the co-pilot were already in their seats. There was a third man, a flight engineer, cradling a 7.62-millimeter M60 general-purpose machine gun, which must have been bolted on at some time during the day. Alex hoped it wouldn't be needed.

The twelve of them took their places. There was a long row of seats facing each other on either side of the fuselage. Although they were made of canvas stretched over metal, they reminded Alex a little of dining room chairs. Normally, the Chinook carries thirty-three men, so at least there was plenty of room. Alex sat next to Ben. It was clear that everyone expected them to stick together—although how they would manage that, parachuting out into the night, was something they hadn't discussed. Scooter leaned over and clipped Alex's rip cord to a silver rail running all the way to the cockpit. The pilot pressed a switch and slowly the rear door closed. A red light flashed on, the helicopter lurched off the ground, and moments later, they were on their way.

It was already dark, and there was nothing to see out of the windows, which were too small anyway to provide much of a view. Alex could only tell their height from the feeling in his stomach and the pressure in his ears. The SAS men were sitting silently, some of them checking their weapons—machine guns, pistols with silencers attached, and a wide variety of vicious-looking combat knives. Next to him, Ben Daniels had nodded off to sleep. Alex guessed he'd be well practiced at taking a catnap whenever he needed it, conserving his strength.

But Alex couldn't sleep. He was in a Chinook heli-

copter with the Australian SAS, on his way to attack an oil
rig and defuse a bomb before it caused a tsunami. And as
usual, he was the only one who hadn't been given a gun.
How had he managed to get himself into this? For a moment, he remembered walking with Jack Starbright on
the Rocks in Sydney. It seemed a long, long time ago.

Below them the Timor Sea was black and still. They
were rapidly approaching Indonesian airspace. The helicopter droned on through the night.

The light turned orange.

Smoothly, one inch at a time, the great door at the
back of the helicopter dropped open, revealing the black
rush of the night behind. Although it was true there was
no moon, the sea seemed to be shining, as if with some
natural phosphorescence—Alex could see it glinting
far below.

He hadn't even thought about the parachute jump
until now, but as the reality hit him, his stomach lurched.
The simple truth was that he wasn't some sort of daredevil
who enjoyed the prospect of hurling himself from eight
thousand feet in the dark. Right now he would give anything to be back in London with Jack.

Well, all he had to do was survive the next hour. One
way or another, in just sixty minutes this would all
be over.

The door had gone down as far as it could and clicked
into position. It was jutting out of the back of the heli-

copter. A short walk into nothing. "I'll be watching you," Ben shouted. With the roar of the wind, only Alex heard. "Don't worry! I'll stick close . . ."

"Thanks!" Alex shouted back the single word.

Then the light went green.

No time to think. Because of his position, Alex was going to be the first out. Maybe they had planned it that way. He didn't even hesitate. If he stopped to think what he was doing, he might lose the resolve. Three steps, trailing the cord from his parachute behind him. Suddenly the blades were right over his head, thrashing the air. He felt a hand on his shoulder. Ben. He jumped.

There was a moment of complete disorientation—he remembered it from the last time—when he couldn't quite believe what he'd done and had no idea what would happen next. He was falling so fast that he couldn't breathe. He was completely out of control. Then the parachute opened automatically in the slipstream. He felt the jolt as his descent slowed. And then the peace. He was floating, dangling underneath an invisible silk canopy, black against the black night sky.

He looked down and saw the oil rig. He could only make out its vague shape—two geometric islands with a narrow corridor in between. There were about twenty lights, flickering and still tiny on the twin platforms. By joining them in his imagination, Alex was able to draw a mental image of Dragon Nine.

He twisted around and saw the helicopter, already far

away, and beneath it the eleven black flowers that were the other parachutes. It seemed to him that the Chinook was surprisingly quiet. If he could barely hear it at this altitude, perhaps Major Yu would have heard nothing below. Just as Scooter had promised, there was no wind. The sea was utterly flat. Alex didn't need to steer himself. He seemed to be heading in exactly the right direction. He could make out the white *H* in the middle of the heliport. *H* for happy landing . . . at least, that was what he hoped.

There are three stages to a parachute descent. The raw fear of the jump itself. The sense of calm once the chute has opened. And the first panic as the ground rushes up. Alex reached the third stage all too soon, and that was when he realized that he had drifted off course after all. Maybe he had been overconfident. Maybe some sea breeze had caught him unawares. But suddenly he found himself with nothing but water below him. He was drifting away from the triangular processing platform. Urgently, Alex tugged the two cords at his shoulders, trying to change direction. He was plunging toward the sea. He couldn't let that happen. The splash might give the others away. Worse than that, he might drown.

Alex jerked and writhed helplessly but at the last minute another breeze caught him and carried him over the lip of the drilling platform and onto one of the decks. He had been doubly lucky. The deck was wide enough to allow him to land safely, dropping to one knee and folding in his parachute in a single movement. And the area he had chosen was like a metallic courtyard, enclosed on all sides. With a bit of luck, he would be completely out of sight. What about the noise of landing? No worries there. He had landed on a bumpy, uneven surface, close to some sort of electrical generator. The noise of the machinery would have covered the crash of his feet as they made contact with the metal surface.

Five seconds later, a figure dropped out of the sky and landed just a few yards away. It was Ben Daniels. Unlike Alex, he must have chosen the deck with pin-point accuracy. He gathered in his chute and gave Alex the thumbs-up. Alex twisted around. As far as he could see, all the other SAS men had landed on the processing platform. He looked up. The helicopter had already gone, but presumably it would be nearby in case it was needed.

Alex realized that his own inexperience had spoiled Scooter's plan. The whole idea had been to stick together. It was vital that Alex should be protected at all times. In fact, he and Ben were cut off on the drilling platform. The SAS men would have to make their way across the bridge to find him. And if Yu's control room was on the other side, they would have to take Alex all the way back again.

Not good.

He looked around him. He realized now that he was standing on a row of pipes. The whole deck was covered with them, cut into lengths of about ten feet. A huge metal trough rose up out of the ground, slanting toward the metal tower that housed the wellhead. Presumably, the pipes would be dragged up and somehow assembled in a straight line before they were lowered all the way to the seabed and beyond. On the other side, a metal wall rose up, like the side of a fortress. There were windows on the third or fourth floor, but they were so covered in dirt and grease that surely nobody would be able to see through them. One of the cranes stretched out over the water, its arm silhouetted against the stars and the night sky.

Ben Daniels had taken off his parachute. He scuttled over to Alex, keeping low. He must have already come to the same conclusion—but he had decided what to do. "We won't wait for them," he whispered. "We'll start looking over here. We don't have a lot of time."

Alex didn't have a watch. He looked at Ben's. It was 11:10. He wondered how so much time could have passed so quickly.

The two of them set off together, making their way across the pipes, trying to find the way into the wellhead. Dragon Nine was bigger than Alex had expected, but at the same time every inch was crammed with pipes and cables, cog wheels, chains, dials, and valves. The oil rig was also a living thing, throbbing and humming as different machines carried power or coolant to the various outlets. It was a hard, unpleasant environment. Every surface had a permanent coating of mud, oil, grease, and puddles of salt water. Alex could feel his sneakers sticking to the floor as he walked.

But Yu didn't seem to have posted any guards. Scooter had been right about that. With Alex supposedly dead, why should he have been expecting any trouble, miles from anywhere, in the middle of the Timor Sea? Together, they eased their way around corners and between ventilation towers, immediately lost in the great tangle that had been designed to pump oil from the seabed, thousands of feet below. Ben was carrying a miniature flashlight, which he kept cupped in his left hand, allowing only a trickle of light to escape. His right hand held an automatic pistol, a Walther PPK with a Brausch silencer attached.

Scooter and the other SAS men had dropped out of sight. Alex could imagine them moving toward him on the other side of the water. In the far distance he thought he heard a sound: a soft thud, the clatter of metal against metal, a stifled cry cut off very quickly. Maybe there were guards after all. If so, one of them might be wishing that he had been a little more alert.

Ben was opening doors, peering in through windows. There was still no sign of life on the drilling platform. They climbed a flight of steps that brought them to a metal walkway on the very edge, high over the sea. Alex looked down, and that was when he saw it. The oil rig was actually balancing on four huge legs, like an oversized metal table. One of the legs had a ladder that ran all the way down to the surface, actually disappearing beneath it. Next to the ladder and tucked away almost underneath the platform was an executive yacht, the sort of thing that would have looked more at home in a private marina—perhaps in the south of France. The boat was about sixty feet in length, sleek and white, with several sundecks and a bow that was clearly designed for speed. Alex tapped Ben on the shoulder and pointed. Ben nodded.

It had to belong to Major Yu. It was surely there to provide him with a fast escape, meaning that he must be on the processing platform, just as Scooter had suspected. If Alex had known the make of the yacht, there would have been no doubt in his mind at all. It was a Sealine F42/5 flybridge motorboat with a unique extending cockpit system. It had been designed and manufactured in Britain.

Ben signaled the way forward. More than ever, Alex wished that Scooter and the others were with them. They were following a narrow gantry that led to a door set in a circular building, jutting out over the corner of the rig with curving windows that provided views in three directions.

The control room. It had to be.

They crept toward it. Alex didn't know what Ben had in mind. Maybe he was going to wait for the rest of the squadron to catch up. That would have been the sensible thing to do.

But in the end, he was never given a choice. Without warning, a spotlight swept through the air, searing its way across the drilling platform. A second later, a machine gun began firing, bullets ricocheting crazily off the railings, slamming into the walls and sparking as they flew off the metal walkways. A siren began to wail, and at the same time Alex heard answering fire from the other side of the bridge. The silence of the night had been shattered. There was an explosion, a ball of flame erupting into the night like a brilliant flower. More shooting. Ben twisted and fired twice. Alex didn't even see his target, but there was a cry and a man fell out of the sky, slammed into a gantry, and bounced off it into the sea.

"This way!" Ben shouted. He had already started forward, and Alex went after him, knowing that Yu would be expecting them now but that there could be no going back. Yu's men would be taking positions all over the oil rig. They had the advantage. There were a dozen ladders they could climb and platforms high above from where they could pick off the invaders one by one. He and Ben would be safer inside. The door was ahead of them, leading into the circular room. Ben reached it and crouched down. "Stay back!" he commanded.

Alex saw him count to three.

He slammed the door open and went in firing. Despite what he had been told and even though he wasn't carrying a weapon himself, Alex followed. And that was how he saw what happened in the next few seconds, even though it would be a lot longer before he took it all in.

There had been two men in the control room, surrounded by computer screens, a radio transmitter, and

the equipment that Alex had seen on the *Liberian Star.*
One of them was Major Winston Yu. He was holding the
pistol that he had just used to gun down Ben Daniels.
Ben was lying on the floor in a spreading pool of his own
blood. The Walther PPK had dropped out of his hand and
lay pointing toward Alex. There was another man lying
facedown a short distance away, and Alex realized that
Ben must have shot him as he came in. Major Yu himself
was unhurt. He was staring at Alex in astonishment
and disbelief.

Somehow he managed to recover. "Well, this is a surprise," he said.

Alex didn't move. He was less than three yards away
from Yu. He had nowhere to go. Yu could shoot him
down at any time.

"Come in and close the door," Yu said.

Alex did as he was told. Outside, the battle was still
going on—but it was happening on the other platform.
Too far away. The heavy door clicked shut.

"I knew you hadn't drowned in the river," Yu said.
"Something told me. And when we couldn't find your
body . . ." He shook his head. "I have to say, Alex, you're
very hard to kill."

Alex didn't reply. Out of the corner of his eye, he could
see Ben's pistol lying on the floor, and part of him wondered if he could dive down and grab it. But he would
never be able to bring it around and fire it in time. He was
too easy a target.

"You're finished, Major Yu," Alex said. "And you've failed. ASIS knows what you're trying to do. Reef Island has been evacuated. There's no point in setting off a tsunami. Everyone will know it was you."

Yu considered Alex's words carefully. Part of what he had said had been a lie—the Reef Island conference was still taking place—but there was no way Yu could know that. Alex was here. He had brought the SAS with him. The facts spoke for themselves.

Eventually, Yu sighed. "You're probably right," he said. "But I think we'll go ahead anyway. After all, it's been months of planning, and I'd like to make my mark on the world."

"But you'll kill thousands of people—for no reason."

"What reason can you give me to spare them?" Yu shook his head. "World chaos does have its uses, Alex. This was never just about Reef Island. The reconstruction of the Australian coast will cost billions of dollars, and I have commercial interests all over Southeast Asia. The Chada Trading Agency has shares in many building companies that will be first in line for the new contracts. Unwin Toys will offer gifts to the many hundreds of new orphans—paid for, of course, by the Australian government. There are all sorts of other interests too. A snakehead thrives on misfortune and unhappiness. For us it just means new business."

He glanced at one of the television screens. Alex saw a white line running straight from the top to the bottom.

There was a blinking red square attached to it, moving slowly downward.

"Royal Blue," Yu said. "In six or seven minutes it will reach the seabed and enter the shaft that I told you about. The shaft continues a further half mile down. At midnight exactly the bomb will detonate, and my work will be done. By then, I will be a long way away and you will be no more than a fading memory."

He raised the gun. The single black eye searched for him.

"Good-bye, Alex."

And that was when Alex heard a groan. It came from the floor. The man who had been shot by Ben Daniels was struggling to drag himself into a sitting position. Major Yu was delighted. "How very fortunate!" he exclaimed, lowering the weapon. "Before you die, I can introduce you to one of my most trusted and effective colleagues. Although on second thought, I believe you've already met."

The man looked up.

It was Ash.

He had been shot twice in the chest and the life was seeping out of him. Alex could see it in the dark eyes, which were filled with pain and remorse and something that was less definable but that might have been shame.

"I'm sorry, Alex," Ash gasped. He had to stop himself to catch his breath. "I didn't want you to know."

"I'm not sure that Alex is surprised," Yu remarked.

Alex shook his head. "I guessed."

"May I ask how?"

This time there was no point in ignoring the question. Yu had been about to shoot him anyway. The longer Alex could keep him talking, the more chance there was that the SAS might finally arrive. Alex could hear the alarm, but there was less shooting and it seemed to be farther away. Had the SAS been overpowered, or were they already in command and on their way? He glanced at the television screen. The little red square was continuing its journey down.

"Everything went wrong from the start," he said, talking directly to Major Yu. "Ethan Brooke had already lost two agents. Somehow the snakehead knew everything he planned. They knew about me too. Why else was I chosen for that fight in Bangkok? It didn't make any sense. But then, when I was in the arena, Mr. Sukit said something to me. He said he'd kill me if I didn't take part, and he said it first in French, then in English. Why? If he really believed I was an Afghan boy, he'd have known I wouldn't speak either.

"I wondered about that. But it got worse. Ash gave me an emergency telephone number. I called it and it led me straight to you."

Ash opened his mouth to speak, but Alex cut in.

"I know," he said. He looked briefly at the dying man. "You made it look good with the fake blood, as if you'd been taken prisoner like me. But then I lost two of the gadgets Smithers had given me, and that was when I knew it had to be you.

"I told you about the watch and the belt. Somehow the battery disappeared out of the watch. I suppose you must have done that when I was asleep that night in Jakarta. As for the belt, Major Yu took that when I was in his house. But I'd never told you about the coins. Smithers had also given me coins with an explosive charge and those stayed in my pocket. If I'd told you, I guess those would have gone too."

He stopped.

"When did you start working for Scorpia, Ash?" he asked.

Ash glanced at Major Yu.

"Tell him—but be quick," Yu snapped. "I don't think we have very much time."

"It was after Mdina." Ash's voice was weak. His face was gray, and he could no longer move from the chest down. One hand was on his chest. The other lay palm upward on the floor. "You can't understand, Alex. I was so badly hurt. Yassen . . ." He coughed, and blood speckled his lip. "I had given everything to the service. My life. My health. I wasn't even thirty, and I was crippled. I was never going to sleep properly, never eat properly. From that day on it was just pills and pain.

"And what was my reward? Blunt humiliated me. I

was demoted, taken out of the field. He told me . . ." Ash
swallowed hard. With every word he was finding it hard
to go on. "He told me what I already knew," he rasped.
"I was second rate. Never as good . . . as your dad."

He had almost come to the end of his strength. His
shoulders slumped, and for a moment Alex thought he
had gone. The blood was all around him now. There was
a steady flow of it from his mouth.

Major Yu was enjoying himself. "Why don't you tell
him the rest of it, Ash?" he crowed.

"No!" Ash straightened his head. "Please . . ."

"I already know," Alex said. He turned to Ash one last
time. He could hardly bear to look at him. "You killed my
parents, didn't you? The bomb in the airplane. You put
it there."

Ash couldn't answer. His hand tightened on his chest.
He had only seconds left.

"We had to test him," Major Yu explained. "When he
came over to us, we had to make sure he was telling us the
truth. After all, we had just been tricked by one British
intelligence agent—John Rider. So we set him a very simple task, one that would prove to us with no doubt that he
was ready to switch sides."

"I didn't want to . . ." It wasn't Ash's voice. It was just
a whisper.

"He didn't want to, but he did. For the money. He put
the bomb on the plane and he detonated it with his own

hand. Rather more successful than his mission in Mdina. And the start of a long association with us."

"Alex . . ."

Ash tried to look up. But his head fell forward. He was dead.

Major Yu prodded him with his foot. "Well, as they say, Ash to ashes and dust to dust," he remarked. "I'm glad you heard that from him, Alex. You can take it with you to the grave."

He raised the gun once again and pointed it at Alex.

There was an explosion, loud and near. But it wasn't the gun. The entire room shook, and dust and metal filings came showering down from the roof. Alex heard a shearing of metal as the crane overhead broke in half and came crashing down. The shock sent Major Yu reeling back. His arm banged against one of the work surfaces and the gun went off, the bullet smashing uselessly into a wall. Major Yu was shouting in agony, and Alex realized that the impact of the blow had shattered the brittle bone in Yu's arm. The gun now lay useless on the ground.

Deafened, half dazed, Alex threw himself onto the gun, snatched it in both hands, desperate to protect himself from further attack. But he was already too late. Yu had already decided to leave. The room was full of smoke. The SAS were here. Alex Rider would have to wait until another day.

There was a trapdoor set in the floor, with the ladder leading down underneath. Somehow, using his one good arm, he pulled it open and climbed down, dropping into the boat below. But the fall had been too far for his bones. The impact broke both his ankles. Howling with agony, barely able to stand, he groped his way over to the controls. He used a knife to cut through the mooring rope. A second later, he was speeding away.

Meanwhile, Alex had staggered over to the controls. On the TV, the little square representing Royal Blue was about two inches above the seabed but edging closer all the time. There was the scanner, wired into the computer. Alex slammed his palm onto the glass panel and let out a sigh of relief as a line of text appeared on the computer screen.

> AUTHORIZATION ACCEPTED

There was a pause, then a second line scrolled across.

> Override master commands? Y/N

Alex tapped on the *Y* key just as the door crashed open and about half a dozen SAS men somehow managed to burst in, covering every angle with their weapons. Scooter was at the front of them with Texas and X-Ray right behind him. It looked as if Sparks, the young soldier who had once played a guitar on an Australian beach, hadn't made it.

Scooter saw Alex. "Where's Yu?" he demanded.

"Gone." Alex had his eyes fixed on the screen. A menu had come up. He ran his eye down the list of options, looking for the one that said DISARM or DEACTIVATE. But it wasn't there. Instead, his eyes settled on the last command.

> DETONATE

"Over here!" It was Texas. He had found Ben Daniels and was already kneeling beside him, tearing open his shirt to examine his wound. One of the other soldiers rushed over with a medical kit.

Alex slid the mouse, highlighting the last command. He looked at the television screen. Royal Blue was still above the seabed but almost touching it. He remembered what he had heard. The bomb still had another half mile to travel, far down into the Earth's crust. A timeline read 23:47:05:00, the microseconds flickering and changing too fast for his eye to follow. But the bomb still had thirteen more minutes until it would be in position. The moon and the sun were not quite ready yet.

Could Alex destroy the bomb without accidentally setting off the tsunami?

In desperation he turned to the SAS leader, who seemed to understand the stakes almost at once.

"Do it," he said.

Alex double-clicked on the command.

Three thousand, five hundred feet below Dragon Nine

but five hundred feet above the seabed, the bomb exploded. Alex felt the entire oil rig shudder violently, and the floor veered crazily beneath his feet as five of the steel tethers along with the drill pipe itself were torn apart.

And half a mile away, speeding through the water in his Sealine yacht, Major Yu heard the explosion and knew, with an overwhelming sense of bitterness and defeat, that even his last hopes had been destroyed. Somehow Royal Blue had been detonated too early. There would be no tsunami. He sat, hunched up in front of the steering wheel, moaning quietly to himself. He had comprehensively failed.

He didn't even feel the shock wave from the explosion until it hit him, but this of course was the main purpose of Royal Blue, to flatten anything for miles around. The pulse smashed into the yacht, destroying the electric system, snuffing out the lights, ripping every fitting apart. Major Yu's bone structure wasn't strong enough to withstand it. Every single bone in his body fractured at the same time. For about two seconds, he remained vaguely human. Then his body, with no frame to support it, crumpled in on itself, a bag of skin full of broken pieces. The boat veered around, a hundred thousand dollars' worth of British engineering with no one to steer it. Zigzagging crazily, it disappeared into the night.

Back on Dragon Nine, Yu's remaining men were being rounded up. The SAS had lost two men, with three more injured. Ben Daniels was still alive. He'd been given a shot of morphine, and there was an oxygen mask strapped to his face.

Scooter had finally noticed the other body lying in the control room.

"Who was that?" he asked.

Alex took one last look at his godfather.

"It was nobody," he said.

23

DINNER FOR THREE

"IT'S VERY GOOD TO see you, Alex. How are you getting on at school?"

It seemed a very long time since Alex had last found himself back in this room, the office on the fifteenth floor of the building on Liverpool Street that called itself the Royal and General Bank but that in fact housed the Special Operations division of MI6. Alan Blunt, its chief executive, was sitting opposite him, his desk as neat and as empty as ever: a couple of folders, some papers awaiting signature, a single pen, solid silver, resting at an angle. Everything in its place. Alex knew that Blunt liked it that way.

Blunt didn't seem to have changed at all. Even the suit was the same, and if there was a little more gray in his hair, who would notice when the man had been entirely gray to begin with? But Blunt was not the sort of person to grow old and wrinkled, to wear baggy sweaters, play golf, and spend more time with his grandchildren. His job, the world he inhabited, had somehow pinned him down. He was, Alex decided, a twenty-first-century fossil.

It was the first week of December, and suddenly the temperature had dropped, as if in response to the Christmas decorations, which were going up all around. There had even been a few scatterings of snow. There wasn't enough to stick, but it had added a certain chill to the air. Walking to the office, Alex had passed a Salvation Army band playing "Good King Wenceslas." The players had been huddling together as if for comfort, and even their music had been cold and mournful . . . as well as slightly out of tune.

He couldn't hear the music in the office. The windows would doubtless have been double or triple glazed to stop any sound from coming in or—more importantly—leaking out. He focused his attention on the man sitting opposite him and wondered how he should answer the question. Blunt would know already, of course. He would probably have access to Alex's school reports before they were even printed.

Alex had just completed his first week back at Brook-land School. Blunt would know that too. Alex had no doubt that he had been under twenty-four-hour surveil-lance from the moment his Qantas flight had touched down at Heathrow Airport and he had been hurried out through the VIP channel to the waiting car outside. The last time he had taken on Scorpia, he had been shot, and MI6 certainly weren't going to let that happen again. He thought he had seen his tail once: a youngish man stand-ing on a street corner, seemingly waiting for a taxi. When he had looked for him a second later, the man had disap-peared. Maybe it was, maybe it wasn't. Blunt's field agents knew how to live in the shadows.

And so, finally, he was back at school.

For most kids of his age, it meant coursework and homework, lessons that dragged on too long, and terrible food. For Alex it was all that and something more. He had been nervous, walking back into Brookland on a chilly Monday morning. It had seemed a long time since he had seen the familiar buildings: the bright red brickwork and the stretches of plate glass. Miss Bedfordshire, the school secretary, who had always had a soft spot for him, had been waiting in the reception area.

"Alex Rider!" she had exclaimed. "What has it been this time?"

"Glandular fever, Miss Bedfordshire."

Alex's illnesses had become almost legendary in the past year. Part of him wondered if Miss Bedfordshire really believed in them or if she was just playing along.

"You're going to have to drop a whole year if you're not careful," she remarked.

"I'm very careful, Miss Bedfordshire."

"I'm sure you are."

In Sydney, Alex had been worried that he wouldn't fit in, but from the very first moment he arrived, it was almost as if he hadn't been away. Everyone was pleased to see him, and he wasn't as far behind as he had feared. He would have extra tutoring over the Christmas vacation, and with a bit of luck he would be at the same level as everyone else by the time he began the next semester. Surrounded by his friends and swept along by the day's routine—the ringing bells, the slamming doors, and desks—Alex realized that he wasn't just back at school. He was back in normal life.

But he had been expecting Alan Blunt to make contact, and sure enough, he had got the call on his cell. Blunt had asked Alex to come to a meeting on Friday afternoon. Alex had noticed the one small difference. Blunt had asked. He hadn't demanded.

So here he was with his backpack still full of books for the weekend: a particularly vicious math paper and *Animal Farm,* by George Orwell. Another British writer, he reflected. Major Yu would surely have loved it. Alex was wearing his school uniform—a dark blue jacket, gray trousers, and a purposefully crooked tie. Jack had bought him a scarf when she was on vacation in Washington and it was hanging loosely around his neck. He felt relieved to look the same as everyone else. He just wanted to get back to normal.

"There are a few things you might like to know," Blunt said. "Starting with a message from Ethan Brooke. He asked me to pass on his thanks and his good wishes. He said that if you ever decide to emigrate to Australia, he'll be happy to arrange a permanent visa."

"That's very kind of him."

"Well, you did a remarkable job, Alex. Quite apart from tracking down our missing weapon, you've more or less destroyed the snakehead. The Chada Trading Agency has gone out of business, as has Unwin Toys."

"Did you realize it was an anagram?" Mrs. Jones asked. She was sitting in a chair next to the desk, one leg crossed over the other, looking very relaxed. Alex got the sense that she was glad to see him. "Unwin Toys. Winston Yu. That was the vanity of the man . . . he named it after himself."

"Have you found him?" Alex asked. He had last seen Yu climbing into the motorboat and didn't know if he'd gotten away.

"Oh yes. We found what was left of him. Not a pleasant sight." Blunt folded his hands in front of him. "Yu dealt with quite a lot of his own people before ASIS could reach them," he went on. "I think you know that he killed the captain of the *Liberian Star* . . . De Wynter. After your escape from the hospital, Dr. Tanner committed suicide, possibly following orders from Yu. ASIS did manage to pick up the rest of the staff, though. Two guards—one of them with a fractured skull—and a handful of nurses. They also arrested a man called Varga . . ."

The name meant nothing to Alex.

"He was a technician," Mrs. Jones explained. "He helped adapt Royal Blue to work underwater. He also set up the detonation procedure."

Now Alex recalled the man he had glimpsed on the *Liberian Star,* setting up the scanner for Major Yu.

"He was a fairly low-level Scorpia operative," Blunt added. "Out of Haiti, I understand. He's being questioned and may provide some useful information."

"How is Ben?"

"He's still in the hospital in Darwin," Mrs. Jones said. "He was lucky. The bullets didn't do any serious damage, and the doctors say he'll be out by Christmas."

"We'll look after him," Blunt added.

"Better than you looked after Ash." Alex looked Blunt straight in the eyes.

"Yes." Blunt shifted uncomfortably. "I wanted you to know, Alex, that we had no idea about Ash's involvement with Scorpia. Even now I find it hard to believe that he had any involvement with . . . what happened to your parents."

"I'm so sorry, Alex," Mrs. Jones cut in. "I understand how you must be feeling."

"Do you think Ethan Brooke knew?" Alex asked. It was something he had been thinking about on the long flight home. "He knew someone was a traitor. Someone had been feeding the snakehead with information all along. He put me together with Ash. Was that what he really wanted? To flush him out?"

"It's quite possible," Blunt said, and Alex was surprised. The head of MI6 wasn't normally so honest. "Brooke is a very devious man."

"It's what makes him so good at his job," Mrs. Jones remarked.

It was five o'clock. Outside, it was getting dark. Alan Blunt went over to the window and shooed away a couple of pigeons. Then he lowered the blind.

"There are only a couple of things to add," he said as he took his place again. "Most important of all, we want you to know that you're safe. Scorpia aren't going to have another crack at you." He blinked twice. "Not like last time."

"We've been in contact with them," Mrs. Jones explained. "We made it clear that if anything happened to you, we would let the whole world know that they had been beaten—for a second time—by a fourteen-year-old boy. It would make them a laughingstock and would destroy what little reputation they have left."

"Scorpia may be finished anyway," Blunt said. "But they got the message. We'll keep an eye on you just to be on the safe side, but I don't think you need to worry."

"And what was the other thing?" Alex asked.

"Only that we hope you found what you were looking for, Alex." It was Mrs. Jones who had answered.

"I found some of it," Alex said.

"Your father was a very good man," Blunt muttered. "I've told you that before. You obviously take after him, Alex. And maybe, when you leave school, you'll think again about intelligence work. We still need people like you, and it's not a bad career."

Alex stood up. "I'll show myself out," he said.

He took the subway back to Sloane Square and then a bus along King's Road to his house. He had told Jack he would be late home from school. The two of them would have supper together when he arrived, and then he would start his homework. He was seeing his friend Tom Harris on Saturday. The Chelsea soccer team were playing at home against Arsenal, and somehow Tom had managed to scrounge two tickets. Otherwise, Alex had no plans for the weekend.

Jack Starbright was waiting for him in the kitchen, putting the final touches to a salad. Alex helped himself to a glass of apple juice and hoisted himself onto one of the bar stools by the counter. He liked to talk to Jack while she cooked.

"How did you make out?" she asked.

"It was fine," Alex said. He reached out and stole a piece of tomato. "Alan Blunt offered me a job."

"I'll kill you if you take it."

"Don't worry. I let him know I wasn't interested."

Jack knew everything that had happened to Alex since she had left him in Sydney, including Ash's final moments on Dragon Nine. He had told her his story the moment he got home, and when he had finished, she had turned away and sat for a long minute in silence. When she had finally turned back again, there had been tears in her eyes.

"I'm sorry," Alex had said. "I know you liked him."

"That's not what's upsetting me, Alex," she had replied.

"Then what?"

"It's this world. MI6. What it did to him, to your parents. I suppose I'm scared about what it'll do to you."

"I think I've finished with it, Jack."

"That's what you said last time, Alex. But the question is—has it finished with you?"

Now Alex glanced at the table. He noticed that it was set for three. "Who's coming for supper?" he asked.

"I forgot to tell you." Jack smiled. "We have a surprise guest."

"Who?"

"You'll find out when they get here." She had barely spoken the words when the front doorbell rang. "That's good timing," she went on. "Why don't you answer it?"

Alex noticed something strange in her eyes. It wasn't like Jack to have secrets from him. He was still holding the piece of tomato. He tossed it back into the salad, swung himself down, and went out to the hall.

He could just make out a figure shimmering behind the mottled glass of the front door. Whoever it was had activated the automatic light on the porch. Alex threw open the door and stopped in complete surprise.

A young, dark-haired, and very attractive girl was standing there. The car that had dropped her off was just moving away. Alex was so stunned that it took him a minute to recognize her. Even then, he didn't believe who it was.

"Sabina!" he exclaimed. The last time he had seen Sabina Pleasure, the two of them had been on Richmond Bridge on the river Thames when she had told him she was leaving for America. He had been convinced that he would never see her again.

That had been only a few months ago, but she looked completely different. She must be almost sixteen now. Her hair had grown longer, and her shape had changed. She looked wonderful in tight-fitting DKNY jeans and a soft cashmere jersey.

"Hi, Alex." She stood where she was as if she were a little wary of him.

"What are you doing here?"

"Aren't you glad to see me?"

"Of course I am. But . . ." Alex's voice trailed off.

Sabina smiled. "That was my dad in the car. We're visiting for Christmas. He's over here writing a story for the paper. Something about some sort of weird church or something. He got me out of school early, and we're going to stay over here until the new year."

"In London?"

"Where else?"

"Is your mom here?"

"Yeah. We're renting an apartment in Notting Hill."

The two of them stared at each other. There were all sorts of things Alex wanted to say. He didn't know where to begin.

"Are you two going to come in?" Jack called from the kitchen. "Or would you like me to serve dinner in the street?"

There was a moment of awkwardness. Alex realized that he hadn't even invited Sabina into the house. Worse than that, he was actually blocking the way. He stepped to one side to let her pass. She smiled a little nervously and stepped inside. But the doorway was narrow, and as she came in, he felt her briefly against him. Her hair brushed his cheek, and he smelled the perfume she was wearing. At that moment, he realized how glad he was to see her. It was as if everything was beginning all over again.

Now she was in the hall and he was the one outside.

"Sabina . . . ," he began.

"Alex," she said, "I'm freezing. Why don't you shut the door?"

Alex smiled and closed the door, and the two of them went in.

ACKNOWLEDGMENTS

AS WITH ALL THE Alex Rider books, I've tried to make *Snakehead* as accurate as possible—and I wouldn't have been able to do this without the generous help of people all around the world. So it seems only polite to mention them here.

Dr. Michael Foale at NASA spoke to me at length for a second time, and the opening chapter is largely based on his own experiences returning from outer space. The mechanism by which Major Yu brings chaos to the world was suggested to me by Professor Bill McGuire at University College London . . . he also came up with the planetary alignment that makes it feasible.

Panos Avramopoulos at CMA-CGM Shipping (UK) Ltd. kindly arranged for me to visit a container ship, and Captain Jenkinson allowed me on board. A few weeks later, Andy Simpson of Global SantaFe and Rupert Hunt from Shell gave up a whole day of their time to show me around an oil rig near Aberdeen. Neither of these visits would have been possible without Jill Hughes, to whom I am eternally grateful.

I spent a week in Bangkok, where I was looked after by the author Stephen Leather, who took me to all sorts of locations, many of which I wasn't allowed to mention in the book! He also accompanied me to the Thai kick-boxing fight that is the basis of Chapter Eight. I also want to thank Justin Ractliffe, who showed me around Perth and Sydney during a lengthy book tour.

Joshua King, Alfie Faber, Max Packman-Walder and Emma Charatan all read the manuscript and gave me great notes and advice. Not for the first time, my son Cassian suggested some major changes.

Finally, my assistant Cat Taylor organized everything and then organized it again when I changed my mind. Justin Somper continues to be the guiding light behind much of Alex's success. And my very lovely editor, Jane Winterbotham, spent hours trawling through some of the most painful notes ever to come out of a publishing house to ensure that all the dates and times make sense.

AH